Dora's Dream

BY THE SAME AUTHOR

Birmingham Rose
Birmingham Friends
Birmingham Blitz
Orphan of Angel Street
Poppy Day
The Narrowboat Girl
Chocolate Girls
Water Gypsies
Miss Purdy's Class
Family of Women
Where Earth Meets Sky
The Bells of Bournville Green
A Hopscotch Summer
Soldier Girl
All the Days of Our Lives
My Daughter, My Mother
The Women of Lilac Street
Meet Me Under the Clock
War Babies
Now the War is Over
The Doorstep Child
Sisters of Gold
The Silversmith's Daughter
Mother and Child
Girls in Tin Hats
Black Country Orphan
Secrets of the Chocolate Girls
Wartime for the Chocolate Girls
Homecoming for the Chocolate Girls
The Pearl Button Girl

ANNIE MURRAY
Dora's Dream

MACMILLAN

First published 2026 by Macmillan
an imprint of Pan Macmillan
The Smithson, 6 Briset Street, London EC1M 5NR
EU representative: Macmillan Publishers Ireland Ltd, 1st Floor,
The Liffey Trust Centre, 117–126 Sheriff Street Upper,
Dublin 1 D01 YC43
Associated companies throughout the world

ISBN 978-1-0350-7364-1

Copyright © Annie Murray 2026

The right of Annie Murray to be identified as the
author of this work has been asserted in accordance with
the Copyright, Designs and Patents Act 1988.

All rights reserved. No part of this publication may be reproduced, stored in
a retrieval system, or transmitted, in any form, or by any means (including,
without limitation, electronic, mechanical, photocopying, recording or
otherwise) without the prior written permission of the publisher.

Pan Macmillan does not have any control over, or any responsibility for,
any author or third-party websites (including, without limitation, URLS,
emails and QR codes) referred to in or on this book.

1 3 5 7 9 8 6 4 2

A CIP catalogue record for this book is available from the British Library.

Typeset in Stempel Garamond by Six Red Marbles UK, Thetford, Norfolk
Printed and bound in the UK using 100% Renewable Electricity by CPI Group (UK) Ltd

This book is sold subject to the condition that it shall not, by way of
trade or otherwise, be lent, hired out, or otherwise circulated without
the publisher's prior consent in any form of binding or cover other than
that in which it is published and without a similar condition including this
condition being imposed on the subsequent purchaser. The publisher does not
authorize the use or reproduction of any part of this book in any manner
for the purpose of training artificial intelligence technologies or systems.
The publisher expressly reserves this book from the Text and Data Mining
exception in accordance with Article 4(3) of the European Union
Digital Single Market Directive 2019/790.

Visit **www.panmacmillan.com** to read more about
all our booksand to buy them.

For Martin, with all my love

Birmingham
1854

The little girl they called Annie Lunn sat on the bare floorboards amid the other workhouse girls, dressed, like them, in a scratchy, shapeless frock worn over a calico chemise. The child was just eight years old and had flaming red hair and stone-grey eyes that seemed to look deeply into a person, when she troubled herself to look at anyone at all. But now, she was doing what she did much of the time: sitting cross-legged and staring across the restless young heads around her, out through the window, to her imaginary lands. Despite the dull routine, her days narrow as the inside of a thimble, this was a child whose mind must travel up and beyond.

Through the window she floated, her gaze directed out through the veil of filth on the glass, past the smut-coated brick of a chimney, its sharp edges cutting into the sky and beyond the great, smoking, clanging city out there to a kingdom hidden in the towers of grey-white clouds.

Her mind travelled far out of this small life into the few stories they had read to them in the schoolroom. Princesses locked in towers, fairy godmothers, heroic princes and wicked goblins. And from these crumbs of other people's fancies, she created stories of her own. She flew over the clouds on a swan to a land where anything was possible, to where the earthbound children – and above all adults – around her, could not follow. She had her dreams, and in her dreaming, she was free.

I

One

Summer 1858

'Well, these won't do, will they?'

The Matron, Mrs Hodges, deposited a pitifully small bundle on to the desk in her office. For the first time since the day she entered the workhouse, Annie Lunn was looking at the few possessions she had brought with her. A faded blue frock with frayed smocking across the chest and of a size to fit the child of just six-years old she had been then, was wrapped round a tiny, yellowed chemise, a pair of brown shoes whose soles and uppers had by now almost parted company and a hair clip fashioned out of horn.

'We'll provide you with a set of clothes,' Mrs Hodges was saying. 'Start you off right. Dr Gordon is a distinguished gentleman and the family are very respectable – you're a lucky girl going to work for them, Annie.'

As usual, the girl was barely listening. Drifting off was her way, dreaming of adventures beyond the tiny confines of this life. A life of high walls, of bells commanding her to wake or go here or there, of a rumbling belly and smells of thin porridge, of hunger and despair. But in her daydreams she could fly out over the rooftops. The only time she paid attention was in the workhouse classroom when it came to reading and writing, at which she was outstandingly quick and able. Arithmetic meant nothing. It was a language she barely spoke. Reading and writing – that was where she excelled.

But now for a different reason she was not listening. She had picked up the hair slide, a gently curved thing with three prongs extending out of a strip of fan-shaped, tortoiseshell-coloured horn. Holding the thing, a memory jolted through her. The feel of it – the prongs pushing into her hair. Somewhere else – not here. There was John and . . . Other sisters. Mary – Mary? Elsie! Not Mary as she had been called in this place. Her mind spun in turmoil. Someone else standing behind her, slipping the slide into her hair.

'*There – that looks pretty . . .*'

That voice. It came rushing back to her – a voice she had not heard in years. Mother. She had had a mother. Mom . . . Mom!

'The Gordons are expecting you tomorrow,' Mrs Hodges was saying. 'Will you *pay attention*, Annie?'

She snapped back to the present. 'Where's my sister?' she asked. 'Where's Mary? Elsie – that's her name. Where has she gone? Am I Annie? What's my name?'

'What're you chattering about, child?' Mrs Hodges said irritably. 'You've always been Annie Lunn since you came here. So that must be your name.'

'But . . .' she tried to say.

There was something wrong – terribly wrong with the name Annie Lunn. It didn't belong to her. It was someone else's name. She could not hear Mrs Hodges because suddenly everything going on in her head was so loud.

'*That looks pretty, Dorrie . . .*'

'*Why's Dora got one and not me?*' Another voice – whose was it? Who *was* that talking to her?

Dora. *Dora.* That's my name. My real name!

'*Listen*, girl . . .' Mrs Hodges leaned over and slapped her on the wrist. The girl yanked her hand back without another word, trembling at the memories lifting like dust in her mind. 'You can't go about with your head in the clouds now you're starting work. I'm trying to tell you about your new employer so pay attention for once, you ungrateful girl!'

Mrs Hodges softened then, as people so often did. This girl standing in front of her, twelve years old, a solid child even on workhouse rations, with her fiery hair and soulful grey eyes, had no idea how lovely she was to look at. In fact, she had no idea about anything much after more than six years of workhouse life. Years which had all but wiped out her memory of having a life before – until today.

'I'll be taking you,' Mrs Hodges said. 'They want a young maid of all work but they've said the work won't be too heavy. And you'll be a good girl, do as you're told, won't you, Annie?'

Still nursing her stinging hand, the child nodded. Except she wasn't Annie. She was Dora. That's who she was! The knowledge was sparking and burning inside her.

'Dora? You start on the brasses this morning.'

'Yes, Miss Pyman,' she responded to the Gordons' housekeeper with a smile as the woman stood over her that morning. Doing the brasses was all right. She could be out in the sunshine polishing up the plate on the front door with salt and vinegar until 'Dr Sidney Gordon' glinted in the bright light. Then inside, all the hearth tools: poker handle, the brass-backed brush and shovel and the coal scuttles, a warming pan or two. And best of all she could think her own thoughts – as well as keeping away from the day maid, Agnes the Misery as she called her in her head.

She had been in the house a week by now and had finally got everyone's names straight. First of all, she had got them to do the same with hers.

When she and Mrs Hodges arrived they had been admitted at the back of the house by a woman in her fifties, dressed in a stiff grey dress and modest bustle, all of which rustled as she walked. Her hair was parted severely in the middle and fastened back from her face in an austere style and her grey eyes wore a closed, wary look.

'You've come from the workhouse?'

'Yes, Mrs . . .' To Dora's confusion Mrs Hodges gave what seemed like a curtsey and Dora wondered if she was supposed to do the same but by then it was too late. 'This is the maid – Annie Lunn.'

As soon as Mrs Hodges had departed – with no sentimental farewells – and the door was closed, the woman started instructing her.

'I'm Miss Pyman, the Gordons' housekeeper,' she said, leading Dora into the kitchen. 'I live in, as will you.' To a girl who Dora would learn was the kitchen maid, 'Agnes, pour her a glass of milk. This is—'

'Dora,' she interrupted.

Miss Pyman looked put out. Agnes looked miserable.

'But she said—' Miss Pyman protested.

'She got it wrong. My name is Dora Lunn.'

'Very well.' Miss Pyman seemed a prim lady who Dora would learn was deeply religious and of the same Unitarian persuasion as her mistress, Mrs Eliza Gordon. The air of quiet rage which accompanied her at all times stemmed from Mrs Gordon having rescued her from penury by giving her a position in her own home. For which she was – necessarily, but resentfully – truly thankful.

'This is Agnes,' she said, nodding towards the kitchen maid as Dora gulped down the milk. 'She comes in every day.'

Agnes, a thin, beaten-down sort of girl of about fourteen with a spotty face, looked neither delighted nor dismayed at meeting a new face. She just said, 'Oh,' and stared. Dora wondered if she was a bit simple.

At that moment a woman stepped into the kitchen from the garden beyond and Dora saw a small, plump, energetic-looking person in a mob cap and apron, with pale blue eyes, watery as pools, and a cheerful smile.

'Oh, hello – who's this then – the new maid, is it?'

She had a sing-song accent that Dora had never heard before and she looked kind.

'This is Dora,' Miss Pyman said. She nodded at the woman. 'This is Cook, Mrs Morgan.'

Dora stared at her and remembered to give a polite nod though she was not sure what to say.

'Now – I see they have at least clothed you,' Miss Pyman went on. 'Come upstairs and I'll tell you about your uniform. You will be provided with two sets of clothing at your own expense – it will be deducted from your earnings.'

Dora only vaguely took this in as she stared around her. The journey here to this place on the edge of Birmingham that Mrs Hodges called 'Edgbaston' had been astonishing enough. Houses of a size she had never set eyes on before, set back along wide roads with trees and gardens and flowers . . . And now inside the house, glimpses of walls decorated in lovely colours – crimson here, soft blue or cream there – not like the endless drabness of the workhouse. Whether or not she had to pay for her uniform made no impact on her at all. She had never earned money in her life so it meant nothing. In fact, she was too speechless with amazement that first day to say anything else at all.

Dora came to realize, gradually, that this house of the Gordons, which seemed like a palace to her, was modest compared to some of the other grand Edgbaston houses. It was a long, spacious house but with only two floors. Dr

Gordon and his wife had a room at one end of the house and beside them, each of their children – Alicia who was sixteen and Robert, thirteen – had a bedroom. Dora was allocated a small room at the other end of the upstairs corridor, opposite which was Miss Pyman's room. They were the only staff who lived in, apart from Billy, the lad who lived over the coach house; he looked after the horse and carriage and drove Dr Gordon around. Apart from meals, which he polished off silently and at cheek-bulging speed, they hardly saw him.

The main staircase – the servants' one being a dark, low-ceilinged tunnel at the back of the house – with its ornate banister and pink runner of carpet, was washed in light which poured in from a window at the far end and was reflected in mirrors on each side. The hall carpet glowed in rich, bright colours and along it, at intervals, there were small tables on which stood decorative lamps, vases of flowers and a Chinese pot decorated with curling dragons from which a plant trailed down, its curling tendrils reaching almost to the floor.

The kitchen and store rooms were of course at the back of the house. To one side of the front door was a large, beautiful reception room with pale blue walls behind which extended an elegant dining room. To the other side, in front of the kitchen, were Dr Gordon's study and at the front, a room called the Library.

At first Dora felt as if she hardly dared walk about the house even while doing her work, it was so lovely. The drapes and furniture in silky, pale shades of blue, the gorgeous rugs and yes, the gleaming brass which she was already getting to know. The big, homely kitchen, the long garden stretching between sun-warmed walls, and the way the light fell through the long windows – all of it seemed heavenly.

And the food! Her diet in the workhouse had been a grey mix of gruel, of bread and potatoes and scrag-end stews and never enough of any of it. The Gordons, as she discovered, were keen to develop the social good of their servants. This included making sure their staff were fed well to fuel sufficient energy to carry out their jobs. Dora was introduced to meals she could never have dreamt of! Meat – delicious beef and even chicken – with plentiful potatoes and green vegetables and fruit, many of them grown in the garden behind. And puddings – fruit tarts and pies, junket and suet puddings studded with raisins or soaked in syrup . . . She could hardly believe her luck in being sent to this house just for the food, if nothing else.

Two

Dora was sitting at the kitchen table, hurriedly downing a bowl of porridge. She had been up at six, before anyone else, had stoked the range and put on the washing water to heat, and carried up pails to each of the bedchambers, very carefully so as not to spill it all down the stairs. She laid the breakfast table before clearing away the washing things and bringing down the slop buckets. At least with the summer coming there was only one fire to lay in the main sitting room, which would be lit in the evenings. By the time she had done all that she was ravenous and Mrs Morgan gave her a wink and ladled plenty into her bowl.

'There you are, *cariad* – you get that down you.'

Dora had heard Mrs Morgan use that word before and she thought she kept saying 'chariot'.

'Why did you say that?' she dared ask, scraping out her bowl. 'You keep saying "chariot"?'

Mrs Morgan found this very amusing. '*Cariad*, dear,' she said, chuckling. 'It means love or darling. It's Welsh – like me.'

Dora felt tears rush into her eyes and suddenly the lump in her throat was aching so that she could not swallow the last mouthful. No one in her life that she could remember had called her darling and she felt as if she might burst inside.

'Don't take on.' Mrs Morgan came and patted her on the shoulder, seeming moved by what she had caused. 'It's just what we say, that's all.'

Miss Pyman came bustling in then, like a chill wind.

'Dora, hurry up now – Friday's the day for dusting the library.'

'Is that . . . Dr Gordon's room?' Dora asked fearfully.

Since she had arrived she had only a couple of times set eyes on the sharp-featured whirlwind of a man who was master of this house, but from what she had seen as he went striding along the hall and took the stairs two at a time, he seemed absolutely terrifying. And just now his voice with his clipped accent, which she had learned was Scottish, had come ringing through from the hall, crying, 'Good morning to you, Miss Pyman!'

'No, stupid,' Aggie sneered, suddenly springing into life as she did when there was something nasty to say. She was carrying a pile of the family's breakfast plates for washing. 'That's next door.'

'That's enough from you, Aggie,' Miss Pyman snapped. Dora noticed she seemed flustered, even pink in the face after being greeted by Dr Gordon. 'When we need any direction from you I'll ask for it. Dora, you will be thorough. Mrs Gordon sets great store by the books. You are to dust the sills and fireplace and table, of course – but also all the books. There is a stepladder to reach the higher shelves.'

'Yes, Miss Pyman,' Dora said, scrambling to her feet. 'Shall I start now?'

'Of course start now! Why else would I have asked you? Knock on the door first and only go in if there's no answer.'

Dora quickly fetched cloths and a long-handled feather duster from the cupboard and left the room to Agnes's smirking. Silly bint, she thought. She had met Agnes's type in the workhouse and she wasn't about to give her any ground here.

*

The day she had first arrived, alone in a bedroom for the first time in her life, she had put on the uniform that she found laid out on the bed. Set on the chest of drawers was a three-part looking glass, each section in a wooden frame, the two side-mirrors folded in at an angle. The glass was spotted and distorted but also for the first time she could ever remember, Dora could see her own image and from three different angles. There had been no looking glasses in the workhouse.

Gazing back at her was a thin, yet still sturdy figure in a serviceable – but new! – black dress, the white apron she had just tied on carefully standing out fresh and clean against it. Holding the white, frill-edged cap ready to cover her hair, Dora stared at herself in astonishment. A softly rounded face looked back at her, the eyes seeming full of an intense curiosity, the thick, autumn red hair straight and sleek in a cascade over her shoulders. All in all the girl looking back at her had an intense, interested look to her.

'Is that me?' she said out loud. Her blood thumped faster in surprise.

In the few stories she had ever heard, fairy tales which for a treat the teacher in the workhouse might read to them, the princesses had tresses of long, golden hair. Never red like hers. And in the stories she made up in her head the heroines were pale as lilies, their hair a yellow gold. Dora had never heard that someone with hair like hers could be pretty.

She pulled her hair back, twisting it up so that she could pin it on top of her head, then fixed the white cap over it. There, she was a proper maid in her new clothes and black shoes. It made her feel rather important.

Carrying the dusters she crept along the hall, quite unaware of the fact that two things were about to happen which would affect the whole course of her life.

She was a little afraid to move in this house, as if she might disturb someone. Mrs Eliza Gordon, she heard from the other servants, was a religious, studious woman. She wore clothes in sober hues – though sometimes with a stylish touch of colour, a grey dress with perhaps a rich rust- or crimson-coloured belt and cuffs. She had a pale, oval face and serious expression which Dora found intimidating, but the others said she was a good woman, kind and fair.

Now though, she was afraid of running into Mrs Gordon in the library. However, there was no reply when she knocked on the dark wood door. Cautiously, Dora pushed it open and stepped in, gasping at the sight that met her.

For some minutes she just stood on the thick rug in the middle of the floor, completely dazzled by its rich reds, greens and golds, which in its turn covered a shiny floor made up of strips of wood, all arranged in a pattern. A thick beam of sunlight from the window facing the street lit the dust motes dancing in the disturbed air and fell on the few visible strips of wall which were of a muted gold, making them glow. But little of the walls could be seen because they were covered from floor to ceiling by shelves crammed full of books, their spines of deep green, red or brown leather; others cloth-bound in red or blue, cream or black, many of them faded by the light. Lower on the shelves were two well-worn Bibles and squeezed in piles beside them, a great many newspapers and periodicals.

Dora's eyes moved greedily round the room. Books – and more books! She had only ever seen a scant number of books. Their schooling on slates, their pencilled work rubbed out to begin again, were all she had known for years except for the occasional, usually black-covered, book in the teacher's hands. As older children they had learned to use a dipping nib on paper – an activity she loved more than almost anything else in life, however scratchy the pen and cheap the paper.

The dusting forgotten, she moved round the shelves, eyes feasting on the titles, her lips moving to pronounce them. Her fingers reached hungrily for the little booklets, discovering their titles: '*Household Words, The Christian Teacher, Eliza Cooke's Journal* . . .' Her lips moved, her feet taking her along the shelves to find more and more books. '*The Pilgrim's Progress* by John Bunyan; *Notes on Nursing* by Florence Nightingale . . .'

She pulled out one volume, holding it like something holy. Turning it round, she examined the spine. '*Household Education* by Harriet Martineau . . .' She flicked through the pages, all those lines of close print. Imagine writing a *whole book*. She bent and sniffed the old paper smell of the pages then closed it with reverence.

One day, she thought, I'm going to write a whole book. Placing it back on the shelf, she superimposed her wild dream on to the spine. '*By Dora Lunn* . . .'

But her whole body jarred and jumped then, as everything went black, strong hands pressed over her eyes and someone close to her, laughing. Dora could not help herself. She let out a scream.

'Shush!' a voice urged. 'You'll get me in trouble!'

Light was allowed back into her eyes again as the hands were removed and Dora found herself looking into a face topped with dark brown curls, the deep blue eyes dancing with life and a mischievous grin all over his face. She had only glimpsed Robert Gordon, younger of the two Gordon children, when she took in his morning washing water. But all she had ever seen of him was the curl of his hair as he still lay fast asleep under the covers. And she had caught sight of him a couple of times from a distance as he ran about in the garden.

'He's a handful, that one,' Miss Pyman had remarked disapprovingly as he went tearing out through the kitchen one afternoon, sweeping up a huge slice of cake with him as he went.

Dora stared at him now. She had no idea what to do.

'Who're you?' Robert asked. 'Have I seen you before?'

She shrugged.

'Well – what's your name? You're the new maid?'

'Dora,' she said.

Robert put his head on one side. 'How old are you? I'm thirteen.'

'Twelve,' Dora said, adding, 'I think.'

'I've escaped,' he said, starting to move restlessly round the room. 'I'm supposed to be ill in bed but really it's just that I didn't want to go to school. I *loathe* school with all my might and main.' The way he said it was so dramatic that Dora laughed.

'You're lucky – I wish I could go,' she said.

'You can go instead of me,' he said, so woefully that she started to feel truly sorry for him. 'But I suppose you're a servant so you can't.'

There came the sound of hurried footsteps along the hall and an exasperated voice called, 'Robert? Where are you?'

A moment later Mrs Gordon appeared at the door.

'There you are! You really are the end, Robert. Get back to bed at once.' She glanced at Dora, taking in that she was there. 'Stop bothering the servants. If you're unwell you must stay upstairs. *Are* you unwell – truly?' A lovely scent of lavender had floated into the room with her and Dora breathed it in. 'Because your father is losing patience with you – if he thought you were telling untruths he would be terribly angry.'

Dora watched Robert struggle with his conscience for a

few seconds before he nodded, appearing to wilt before her eyes into a decline.

'He's always angry with me whatever I do,' he said, and the words were so full of a genuine upset that Dora felt her heart melt towards him.

'That's not true, dear,' Eliza Gordon protested, her voice gentler now. 'But you do provoke him – you know he has such strong opinions . . .' She rested a hand on her son's shoulder.

'I felt better for a moment,' Robert added faintly. 'But I think I'd better go and lie down again.'

'Come along then.' His mother steered him with one hand, her voice loving now, which filled Dora with longing. How would it be to have a mother like that, someone to care for you? 'I'll come and see you into bed again.'

As they turned to go back into the hall, Robert suddenly inclined his head towards Dora and gave such an exaggerated wink that she had to stop herself bursting out laughing, before he slunk back to his sickbed.

She watched him go, this lad who moments ago was bouncing and energetic. She remembered his laughing eyes, the full pink lips and mischievous grin and smiled to herself as she picked up her duster.

Three

'Give that back – it ain't yours,' Dora snapped, enraged to find Agnes not only nosing about in her room but also holding her horn hair slide. 'What d'you think you're doing in here?'

'I was just looking,' Agnes said, her white face puckering up as she threw the thing back across the bed. 'Ain't no charge for looking.'

'Keep your thieving mitts to yourself!' Dora grabbed the slide, clutching it tight in her hand. She was trembling with rage and all she wanted was to go up and slap that mean, sly face with all her strength. She certainly wasn't going to explain to Agnes what it meant, that little slide – something her mother had touched. The one thing that connected her to Before. To all she had lost.

'Fancy getting all het up over that bit of tat,' Agnes sneered, backing away from the fearsome glint in Dora's eye. Once she was safely on the other side of the bed she spat out, 'Little workhouse rat.'

Dora rounded on her. 'I dunno what kind of family you come from – but at least someone taught *me* right from wrong.' She went up close to Agnes, hissing at her. 'Now get out – and don't come in here again.'

Still holding the slide, she watched Agnes who stuck her tongue out rudely before leaving the room. Dora shut the door, clinging to the doorknob for a moment, trembling with anger.

If I catch her in here again, I'll *throttle* her, she said to herself.

Apart from Miserable Agnes, she was content enough, working for the Gordons. Her job was as maid of all work – to do whatever jobs needed doing. Up and down the stairs cleaning and laying fires, in and out to the garden with messages for the gardeners, or waste for the compost heap, or bringing in herbs and other produce.

On Mondays Mrs Slater the laundry woman came and toiled out in the brewhouse, a brick building out at the back. She was a chatty, relentless person in her forties who often asked Dora to 'Come and lend us a hand, wench, will yer?'

Dora would go out to find her wreathed in steam from the copper of boiling water, which she stirred with a wooden paddle, her plump face and arms running with damp. As often as not she tucked the ends of her skirt up into her waistband to keep it out of the wet and out of her way, displaying ragged flannel bloomers underneath.

'Help me get these into the tub, will yer?' she'd say and they would haul the tangle of bedding or clothing out in a steaming mass to be fed into the maiding tub and pounded with the dolly. 'Fetch up a couple more pails of water . . . Give us a hand mangling this lot . . .' And so on.

Mrs Slater never stopped work herself, barely even for a moment – just long enough to down gulps from the bottle of beer she always brought with her which stood just inside the door. She told Dora she worked like this six days a week.

'No good waiting for my old man to bring in the wages,' she said, with matter-of-fact cheerfulness. ''E were a shunter up the station – but 'e went and got 'isself mangled by a locomotive.'

Dora was never sure if she would have preferred more

or less detail about this terrible event. Mrs Slater never told her any more and she never liked to ask, but the stark facts played on her mind.

Fridays were the only day she dared venture into the library. In the morning, she had to dust and sweep Dr Gordon's study. He seemed always to be out then which was a great relief to Dora. She definitely did not fancy running into her master who, she had found out, was a surgeon at the General Hospital. Quite what this meant he was doing all day was another thing she was not sure she wanted to know more about.

But in the early afternoon, the library was her job. During her first month at the Gordons' she did as instructed, knocked on the door and hearing no answer, went in and dusted the room. She lingered over the task, reading the titles on the spines of the lovely books, longing to take something away to read. But there were so many and she had no idea if she was even allowed to touch them.

That summer afternoon, carrying her dusters, she knocked as usual and hearing no reply, walked in. She was shocked to see the young lady of the house, Miss Alicia Gordon – who Dora knew, from chats with Cook, to be sixteen – sitting at the table.

The young woman's thick, blonde hair was fastened low at the back of her neck and she wore a dress in dusty pink cotton with lace at the neck. She turned as Dora entered, her oval face much like her mother's, but firmer and pinker with youth, lit with a smile.

'Sorry, miss,' Dora said. 'I didn't hear you. I'll come back later.'

'No – it's all right.' Alicia was seated in front of a newspaper at the table. 'You can carry on. You didn't hear anything because I didn't say anything!'

Though Dora had encountered the girl most mornings

when she took up her washing water and received a sleepy 'Thank you', and had seen her in passing in the house, they had never properly met.

'You're the one who brings up my washing water, aren't you?' she said. 'So what's your name?'

'Dora,' she said, 'Dora Lunn.' She stood uncertainly with a duster in each hand, but the girl seemed friendly and not someone to be afraid of.

'Please – do your work.' She gestured round the room and Dora went to the window to begin cleaning the sill. 'I was just reading about Her Majesty coming to open Aston Hall and the big Park. I wish we could have gone to see – Mother had one of her meetings – but I would love to have gone to see the Queen.'

'I've seen her.' The words rushed from Dora's lips before she had even thought.

She stopped, the cloth resting on the sill, as her mind churned again, just the way it had done when Mrs Hodges showed her her belongings before she left the workhouse. Blushes burned in her cheeks. Why on earth did she say that and to this young mistress of hers, of all people? And yet somehow, she knew that what she had said was true.

'Have you?' Alicia said. She sounded intrigued, but doubtful.

She thinks I'm lying, Dora thought. And she knew she was not lying but at this moment she could not explain why she could remember looking over a sea of heads at the little royal figure processing along. A tight feeling across her body, someone holding her up off the ground. And light, so much light . . .

The next thing she knew, she was lying looking up at the ceiling rose at the centre of the room, feeling very peculiar. A face loomed into view, oval, blue-eyed, with blonde hair smooth backed, and an expression of genuine concern.

'Dora? Are you all right? Whatever happened?'

Dora tried to sit up. She felt a bit sick.

'Have you eaten properly today?'

Dora nodded. Oh yes – she always ate something at any opportunity!

'Sorry, miss,' she said. 'I don't know what . . . I just . . .'

The door opened then and a voice said, 'Alicia?'

'I'm here, Mother,' the girl said. 'With the maid. She fainted.'

Mrs Gordon came and looked down at Dora and to her utter astonishment said, 'Oh dear – some water.' She left again for a moment and they heard her asking Miss Pyman to bring a cup of water.

Alicia laughed at the astonished expression on Dora's face. 'Well, she can't ask you to fetch it, can she?'

Mrs Gordon came back in and the two of them helped Dora carefully on to a chair. Having expected a telling-off, she was overwhelmed by their kindness. She could smell Mrs Gordon's lavender scent.

'I was talking to her about the Queen coming to Aston Park and . . .' Alicia gestured to the floor. 'She went down like a ninepin.'

Dora heard Miss Pyman's footsteps and she was handed a cup of water. She sat sipping it, as the two women stood each side of her, mortified and not knowing what to do, the confusion still raging in her mind.

'She said *she* had seen the Queen,' Alicia went on, baffled. 'And then – bang . . .'

Dora felt, rather than saw, the two women exchange looks above her head. They don't believe me, she thought. They think I'm a fibber – or a loony. They'll have me put away.

'I did,' she said managed to say. 'She went walking past – she was in a pink dress . . . And there were people, lots and lots of them all together, clapping. And glass – everywhere. It was so hot, and bright . . .'

There was a puzzled silence and then Mrs Gordon leaned down, her expression somewhere between stern and intrigued.

'Are you talking about the Great Exhibition?'

Dora nodded slowly, images, sensations, flitting through her. The arm holding her up – Pa, and on the other arm was . . . Who was that? Elsie?

'Did you see a picture?'

'No. I went with Pa.' It came crashing in then. 'And Mom – and . . . and . . .' She was gulping, sobs overtaking her even though she desperately did not want them to. 'And my sisters . . . and my brother, John his name was . . .'

'Didn't she come from the workhouse?' she heard Alicia say in a puzzled voice as she wept.

'She did, the poor child,' Eliza Gordon said as she stood upright again. 'But there are not many *begin* life as an orphan. Heaven knows what tragedy landed them in there.'

To Dora's confusion, she found her mistress kneeling at her side, her face full of concern.

'Drink your water, that's right. You may rest a little here before you continue your work.'

Alicia knelt down the other side of the chair and Dora felt overcome by this concentration of concern for her welfare.

'Can you read, Dora?' she asked.

Dora wiped her face; her body was still heaving with sobs but she tried to control herself. She nodded.

'Here . . .' Alicia got up and went to the shelves. She showed her mother a little magazine.

'My goodness – I had no idea we still had any of those old penny dreadfuls. I'd hardly call that educational.'

'But she might enjoy it,' Alicia said, and Dora could hear that she really did want to cheer her up. 'I used to love them! Would you like to take this – you may have it if you like?'

She held out the little booklet which had a brightly coloured picture on the front of a black horse galloping along. Dora reached for it, thrilled.

'Thank you!' She looked up at both of them in astonishment. 'I love stories.'

'Well, there are plenty of stories in here,' Alicia said, laughing. She looked at her mother. 'You can move on to something more improving later.'

After a few moments, both women left the room and Dora was left to continue her work, the little magazine in her hands. She was full of astonishment.

Four

The next morning, when Dora carried up the washing water and knocked on Robert Gordon's door, for once he was awake.

'Come in!'

The boy, rumpled from sleep with his dark curls falling over his forehead, looked at her with sleepy interest.

'Oh,' he said. 'It's you again.'

Dora watched him, fascinated, out of the corner of her eye as he pushed himself further up in bed, the sheets and blankets in disarray. He wore a very creased, pale blue nightshirt.

'You look as if you've been fighting dragons all night like St George,' Dora said, pouring water from the pail into the flowery china jug. For a split second she imagined a huge spiny beast with a flailing tail pushing its way in through the window and it made her smile.

Robert laughed in surprise.

'What a queer thing to say.' He pushed back the bedclothes and the nightshirt fell down past his knees. 'Alicia said you swooned yesterday – in the library.' He seemed to find this funny. 'One moment she was talking to you and the next, wham! You were flat out on the floor!'

Dora, arranging the soap and washcloths, did not reply.

'Are you all right now?' Robert asked, seeming to feel he had not been very kind.

'Yes, thanks,' Dora said.

She looked up at him at last and his good-looking face

with its infectious grin was too much to resist. She found a smile curving her own lips up.

'If there's nothing else you need?'

'You're Dora, aren't you?' As she nodded he said, 'If you could get me off school that would really be something.'

'But you're lucky going to school,' she retorted before she could help herself. 'Why don't you like it?'

'Oh, don't you start.' He flumped back on the bed with as much drama as a woman with the vapours. 'Father never stops telling me: "King Edward's is the top school in the country – you're being given the best chance life could possibly afford you."' Robert imitated his father's clipped Scots accent so perfectly that Dora could hardly stop herself laughing.

He sat up suddenly, his face falling into lines of real distress.

'I can't *do* it. I try and try and everything just . . .' He made a helpless gesture. 'When I read, the words all end up crushing together – like a train crash. And it all goes in one ear and out the other. I'm just very stupid and Father doesn't understand. I've tried talking to Mother about it but all she says is that I just need to *concentrate* and *try harder*. But I *can't* . . .'

By the end of this outburst the lad was almost in tears. Dora could feel all his desperation coming to her in waves but it was very hard to know what to say. Reading came to her so easily, was so enjoyable – and writing too, if she ever had the chance. It was hard to imagine finding it so difficult.

'Oh dear,' she said. 'I suppose you've got to go to school today?'

'Yes.' Robert said tragically. 'I need to get a move on as well – the carriage will be outside.' He sat up again, looking so sad and upset. 'The other boys rag me all the time – "Your father's so clever, why're you such a blockhead?"' He punched both hands down on the mattress so that dust rose and shimmered in the air.

'I *hate* it. I wish I was you!'

That was Dora's afternoon off and it was a lovely summer day. Up until now when she had a little spare time she had just stayed around the house, up in her room. But it was so warm that the outside beckoned her and once she had eaten bread and cheese and some tangy pickled onions, she dared to take herself off for a little walk around the neighbourhood.

A horse and carriage was passing as she stepped out through the side gate, but once the sound of its hooves and lumbering wheels had faded away, for a moment it was quiet enough to hear bees buzzing in the flower heads.

She stood there for a moment, disorientated by suddenly having a choice of her own. It was the first time she could remember that she had ever had the freedom to roam out by herself. It felt strange, even frightening. For want of any other clothes, she still had on her maid's uniform, minus apron, and her little black straw hat. Surely someone would see her and tell her to get back inside?

Her heart beating hard, she turned left and started to walk along the elegant street. A hammering started from further along. Moving slowly past, self-conscious and still expecting someone to ask her what she thought she was doing there, she watched for a moment as workmen hammered long nails into the beams of a half-built house. One of them raised his cap to her with a smirk on his face and she went on to where the end of the street met the junction that she knew was called Five Ways. She did not dare go further and strolled back, enjoying the scents of flowers in the front gardens and the afternoon's sleepy warmth.

She passed the Gordons' place again and walked to the other end of the street, where the houses ended and it petered out to a scrubby path. Feeling adventurous, she followed it along a strip of land, pushing aside stinging nettles and cow parsley until the path opened on to another, cutting sideways across it, and beyond that her way was blocked by the ribbon of water that was the cut.

Footsteps were approaching and she heard the chink of a horse's bit. A man in a billycock hat, trousers tucked into sturdy leather boots, was leading a horse along the towpath, the big strong animal's eyes blinkered. The harness glinted in the sun and the horse was pulling on tow ropes which in their turn hauled a long, colourful boat behind it. Dora stared, fascinated.

'How do.' The man raised his hat. He was sunburnt, his face lined and weather-beaten.

'Good day,' Dora said shyly, standing back out of the way.

As they passed she caught the smell of hot horse and the man's sweat. Then her eyes fixed on the boat. Its paint was chipped but the colours were bright and she saw the hold was heaped with sharp lumps of shiny, blue-black coal. Planks ran over the cargo and above was strung a washing line with a few cloths flapping in the breeze.

Standing at the long tiller at the back was a swarthy woman, her head covered by a black hat which had drapes fastened to it, extending down her back. Close to her were three small children, two of them with a scarf over their head and tied under their chin, the third and youngest wearing a black cap. The woman had the tiller tucked under one arm, but at the same time she was busy sewing something on the roof of the tiny, painted cabin.

For a moment Dora felt afraid of these strange people, but the woman was so busy she did not even notice the girl watching them from the bank, though the children stared back at her in fascination.

And then they were gone, the horse, the gliding boat, leaving Dora wondering how it would be to live the way they did, forever on the move, the water opening out in front of them. She imagined herself, the one in charge of a boat like that, steering her way to new places, new adventures ... She sat for a while near the water, then turned for home again.

When she got back the house was quiet. Cook was half-snoozing on a chair in the kitchen and Agnes was sloshing water in the scullery. Dora downed a glass of water and asked Cook if it was all right for her to sit in the garden.

'Miss Pyman says it's all right so long as none of the family are out there to be disturbed,' Cook said sleepily. 'If they were to come out you could go down to the vegetable garden and sit there, I suppose.'

Dora ran up to the attic and fetched the booklet that Miss Alicia had given her. She had carefully hidden it among her bedclothes so that sneaking Agnes would not find it. She still did not trust Agnes not to go nosing around. Then she went out of the back door.

'Snooty cow,' she heard Agnes say as she went out.

'There's no call for that,' Cook said.

It was a long garden enclosed by brick walls with plants trailing up and over them in profusion. To the left of the house, from the garden point of view, was the brewhouse, a modest building separate from the house. To the other, as an extension of the building, was a long conservatory of low brick walls, the top of the walls and ceiling all glass. It was a lovely building and Dora always enjoyed looking at it, often seeing one of the gardeners inside tending the tomatoes and the fruit trees espaliered along the back wall – apricots and vines – and outside against the wall, a large, spreading tree with odd, bulbous fruits hanging from it that Cook told her was a fig tree.

Looking carefully round she saw that no one was out there, but she walked down the lawn, with lavender and roses on each side, until she was close to the vegetable garden. She tucked herself behind a bush, excited to read more of the little booklet.

It was called *Black Bess, Knight of the Road* and was all about a highwayman. Dora sat, completely taken up in the story. Some of the words were difficult and she stumbled over them but she was determined and reading came easily to her. Soon she was miles away in her head, galloping along the highways on Black Bess. Her pulse was racing so fast as the horse galloped up behind a coach, pistols at the ready and gaining on the coach to terrify the passengers into handing over their riches — when someone crashed down next to her, behind the bush.

Dora almost left the ground. She gasped loudly, seeing Robert Gordon's skinny legs, still in his school trousers, splayed out in front of him, his scuffed black shoes, his face looking into hers.

'Oh my – you frightened me!' She laid her hand over her thumping heart.

'What're you doing here?' he asked, though his tone was amiable. 'You've pinched *my* hiding place.'

'Have I?' she said. 'Sorry.'

'Are you *reading*?' he asked, astonished. 'What's that?' He took the booklet from her hand and stared at the dog-eared cover.

'Miss Alicia gave it to me,' Dora explained. 'Said I could borrow it to read, I mean.'

'So you can read?' He handed the booklet back, seeming chastened by realizing this.

'Yes,' she said confidently.

'Can you write as well?'

'Yes. We had a school room in the—' She could not bring herself to say the word 'workhouse'. It felt shameful. 'We did some lessons.'

Robert stared ahead of him at the raspberry canes, suddenly miserable.

'What do you do at school?' she asked.

'Oh, you know. Arithmetic and geometry. Latin. Greek. All that stuff. I hate the classics. It's bad enough trying to read in English.'

Once again, Dora felt sorry for him. He seemed so cast down by it all.

'But we play rugby and cricket and that's marvellous! So it's all right some of the time, but . . . Everyone's so . . .' He couldn't seem to think of the word. Turning to Dora he said earnestly, 'I can talk to you more easily than them. Except for Freddie – he's a good sort.'

He lay back on the grass and put his hands behind his head.

'Read to me a bit then, if you're so good at it.'

Dora obediently turned back to the beginning of the booklet. Having read it before she was now fluent and she started to read. Robert lay quite still beside her. When she paused after a while and turned to look at him, he was fast asleep, his long lashes a dark curve above his cheeks. And he had caught the edge of her skirt between his fingers, was clutching on to it, as if for comfort.

Five

It was a sultry Saturday afternoon in July. Miss Pyman had stopped lurking about and retired to her room. Dora was in the kitchen sweeping the floor as Cook prepared the last of the vegetables for the evening meal, bossing Agnes as she did so.

'If I've told you once I've told you a hundred times, that's no good. Get it out and do it properly.'

She glared accusingly at the peeled potato that Agnes had thrown sulkily into a pan. The potato peered back with the numerous eyes that Agnes had failed to gouge out of it. The gardeners had not long brought in this fresh box of potatoes and the table was dusted with a light silt of earth.

'Don't,' Agnes snapped at Dora as she swept around her feet. 'You're getting on my nerves.'

'Cook told me to . . .' Dora was arguing, only just defeating the urge to bash Agnes's ankles with the broom, when there came a tap at the door. To their surprise, Miss Alicia appeared.

'Dora – could you please come into the library a moment – my mother wants you?'

She left again immediately, certain of being obeyed. Dora righted herself, holding the broom handle. Mrs Gordon asking for *her*? She wondered if they wanted the little book back, but if so why not just ask her there and then?

'Don't just stand there, get your apron off and go,' Cook instructed.

Dora saw Agnes's eyes go narrow and mean.

'Trust *her*,' she said, ramming her knife viciously into the potato. 'Currying favour.'

'I'm not!' Dora protested. 'I don't know what she wants!'

As she left she wished she hadn't bothered – it was no good saying anything to Agnes.

Dora was standing outside the library door, quickly brushing her skirt and tucking a couple of strands of hair under her cap, when the front door opened. Dr Gordon came billowing in, banging the door shut and only pausing to pick up letters from the hall table before sweeping towards the back of the house. To Dora's relief, he did not even notice her as he passed. He disappeared into his study, leaving behind him a waft of the odd chemical smells that she knew were the smells of the hospital.

Dora listened at the library door. All seemed quiet inside.

She had been with the Gordons just over a month and once or twice had been asked to carry a tray of refreshments to this room of an afternoon when Mrs Gordon was having one of her meetings. She had learned in that time that Eliza Gordon was something called a Unitarian, which Miss Pyman, who was apparently one also, explained stiffly:

'Unlike other Christians we do not believe that God is three persons – only one. And we believe that all souls can be saved.'

This left Dora none the wiser – three persons? But what she did pick up from Mrs Gordon and the other earnest ladies seated round the table on those afternoons, was that they were interested in helping other people and spent a good deal of their energy working out how to do so. They even took an interest in her and asked her questions – especially about the workhouse.

Now, heart thumping, she knocked on the door.

'Do come in!' She heard Eliza Gordon's calm voice.

Dora entered to find her mistress seated at one side of the library table and Alicia at the other, seemingly absorbed in reading a newspaper.

'Ah – Dora.' Mrs Gordon pulled out the chair beside her. 'Do sit.'

'Me?' Dora couldn't help saying.

Alicia glanced up with a smile. 'I don't think there's anyone behind you.'

But Dora still could not get her legs to move and take up a chair right beside the rather awe-inspiring Mrs Gordon in her plain blue-grey dress, her tobacco-brown hair visible round the edges of her lace cap, smoothed back from a middle parting, and her pale blue, rather penetrating eyes.

'Alicia tells me that you enjoy reading and writing?' Eliza Gordon coaxed. 'Would you like to read with me?'

'Oh yes – please!' Dora said. But she was trembling as she perched on the edge of the chair.

'Do sit back or it will tip,' Mrs Gordon said, tucking her chair further in. 'And I promise I shan't bite.'

'I've finished reading your booklet,' Dora dared say to Alicia. 'Shall I fetch it?'

'Oh no – keep it. I'm sure no one else wants to read it,' Alicia said.

Mrs Gordon had a book in front of her. Dora silently read the lettering on the cover: *The Peasant and the Prince*. It looked exciting. Beside it, neatly laid out, were a dipping pen, a small glass inkwell with a brass top and some sheets of paper.

'Firstly, take up the pen, my dear,' Mrs Gordon instructed. 'Are you able to write your own name?'

Dora, nervous, held the pen, a lovely thing compared to the rough ones she had used before. It had a polished, dark wood handle and the nib was pointed and elegant instead of the cheapest, most scratchy of things.

Alicia took the top from the inkwell and Dora dipped, carefully, then set to write 'Dora Lunn' in her careful copperplate.

'I know all my letters and I can write,' she said, sitting up. She was good at writing and she wanted Mrs Gordon to know it.

'So, can you write . . .' Mrs Gordon thought for a moment. 'All things bright and beautiful, all creatures great and small?'

Dora dutifully and speedily obeyed.

'Very good!' Mrs Gordon seemed genuinely impressed, as if she had not expected it of her. 'You are quite the little scribe.'

Dora glowed at this praise. If there was anything she hungered for in the way of praise, it was this.

'I like writing,' she said timidly. 'And stories.'

'Well, I have a story for you here,' Mrs Gordon said, pulling the book towards her. 'It is written by a lady who I admire greatly. Her name is Harriet Martineau. Her brother was, until recently, the Mayor of our city.'

Dora gave a polite little nod. She was not certain what being the Mayor meant, but she was burning with curiosity about the story, especially when Mrs Gordon opened the first page to reveal a coloured picture. She peered at it.

'Let us see how well you can read,' Mrs Gordon said.

And Dora, bathed in the lavender smell of her mistress and with the prospect of a story opening out in front of her like an inviting and unknown path, leaned over the book.

'"One fine afternoon in April 1770, there was a good deal of bustle in the neighbourhood of the village of Saint Menehould . . .?"' She stumbled over the last word and looked up.

Mrs Gordon told her the word. 'It's in France,' she said.

'This story is written about the time before the Revolution in France.'

And to Dora's frustration she closed the cover again and started talking about the revolution by the poor in France and then again about Harriet Martineau who had written the story, and how she was a passionate abolitionist and supporter of the right for women to have the vote – not to mention an education – and the improvement of her servants—

'Mother,' Alicia interrupted, when it seemed as if Mrs Gordon was settling in to talk for the rest of the afternoon. She could see Dora's head was spinning. 'I think she'd like to read the story.'

Dora gave Alicia a grateful smile.

'Harriet Martineau is Mother's hero,' Alicia said. 'Once she gets started . . .'

'Well, she is a woman much worth talking about,' Eliza Gordon said, her face lifting into a smile. 'Forgive me. Let's go on – your reading is surprisingly good as well.'

'Yes and I want to hear it too,' Alicia said, though also reaching for another newspaper.

Dora had just begun on the next sentence when there came the sound of a door opening next door and Dr Gordon's voice thundered through the hall.

'Robert! Come down here – immediately! *Now* – do you hear?'

He sounded furious, his voice brutal.

There was a pause as all of them listened, frozen, to the footsteps coming closer down the stairs. Dora glanced at Mrs Gordon and saw a look of awful dread on her face before she managed to control her features.

'Yes, Father?' they heard.

'What is this?' Dr Gordon bellowed, his temper lost to the point where anyone overhearing was no consideration.

'Dunderhead of a boy! I come home, to find this waiting for me. Not only a card with the lowest possible marks in almost every subject – oh, except for cricket. Apparently you can throw a ball . . . But the headmaster has seen fit to write to me of his abject disappointment . . . "No application . . . Discipline poor . . . Absolutely no scholarly aptitude and niggardly effort . . . Very disappointing."' His voice rose to a roar. 'What do you have to say for yourself?'

Eliza Gordon suddenly shot to her feet looking distraught.

'Mother . . .' Alicia warned. 'He's in a terrible temper.'

'All the same,' Mrs Gordon said, gliding calmly to the door. She turned to Dora, beckoning her out of the room. 'I think we shall have to leave it there for the day.'

Dora followed her mistress out and scooted past the three of them as Dr Gordon continued to rant at his son and Mrs Gordon to protest. As Dora went to the kitchen, she caught a glimpse of Robert at the foot of the stairs, head down and as helpless as if a giant wave was breaking over him.

'Whatever's going on out there?' Cook said as Dora scuttled into the kitchen.

The rage of Dr Gordon directed at his son did not last long, but afterwards, Dora could not stop thinking about it and her stomach turned with dread. Dr Gordon was so clever and so frightening. She felt terribly sorry for Robert who just could not seem to keep up.

When things had gone quiet she crept into the hall. Voices came from the library and she could hear Dr and Mrs Gordon having a heated conversation. Dora hurried upstairs, to the Gordons' side of the house. She stood at Robert's bedroom door and straight away, from inside, she heard his sobs. The boy sounded so wretched that she longed to knock on the door and go to him. But she did not dare. She sensed that he found comfort in being with her and she wanted to try and cheer him up. But after all, who was she, a servant? She could not just go willy-nilly into his room.

She stood for a few moments, listening to the anguished sounds from inside, her fists clenched at her sides. Then she made herself turn away and go back downstairs.

Dr Gordon was not a religious man but Eliza Gordon made sure her two children attended the Unitarian Church of the Messiah on Broad Street every Sunday.

The next morning, as they prepared to set off, Dora passed through the hall. It was only then that she saw Robert properly that morning. When she had taken up his washing water he had been so soundly asleep that he looked as if he would never wake, and by the time she went back for the slop bucket he had already gone downstairs.

'Come along.' Mrs Gordon laid a hand on her son's shoulder, steering him towards the door. Dora saw the kindness in it, that Mrs Gordon was feeling tender towards him as well, in the face of his father's rage and disappointment.

As Robert Gordon followed his mother and Alicia to the front door, he turned and saw Dora standing at the bottom of the stairs. She hesitated, then smiled, wanting to send him all the sympathy she could through her eyes which she fixed fully on his. For a second, Robert, so downcast-looking, was startled. Then, seeming cheered, he smiled back, his lovely face lighting up. And just for those few seconds, the two of them were caught, as if as equals, in each other's gaze.

Six

Edgbaston
Summer 1862

Dora held the door of her room open a few inches and peered out into the corridor. Having made sure no one was around – especially nosey Agnes – she closed the door again and hurried across to her bed.

It was a Wednesday, her afternoon off, and by rights no one else should come up here. Reaching deep under the mattress, her fingers met her most prized possessions which she pulled out, almost leaping in her eagerness to get on the bed.

Sitting cross-legged, excitement bubbling inside her, she caressed the cheap cover of her little notebook, its beige card almost furry now from all her handling. In her most ornate writing she had inscribed on it: 'DORA LUNN, HER STORIES'. In front of her on the bedcover, she laid her two pencils and sharpening knife like a surgeon preparing for an operation.

She was so proud of these possessions of hers, all bought from her wages. During her weekly lessons with Mrs Gordon, her employer gave her writing exercises with the smooth dipping pen, but it was no use trying to use ink in her bedroom. Imagine if she spilled it all over the sheets! So she had bought pencils.

She leafed through the book – page after page of her neat, closely written handwriting. Just the sight of it on the page made her happy. If she could keep writing maybe one day she could make it into a whole book!

Dora sat dreaming for a moment. One afternoon in the library she had picked from the shelves a copy of *Nicholas Nickleby* by Charles Dickens. She was deep into reading it when Mrs Gordon came in. Seeing Dora bent, absorbed, over the table, she had asked what she was reading.

'Ah – Mr Dickens!' She smiled. 'A marvellous writer – so entertaining, but always with a social conscience. I saw him when he came to read at the Town Hall. It was packed! Everyone loved him.'

Dora gazed at her in astonishment. 'Charles Dickens – here in Birmingham?'

'He was here to read his books – but it would be more accurate to say he performed them.' Mrs Gordon let out a peal of laughter, which only added to Dora's astonishment. 'A quite extraordinary man.'

So, she thought now, Mrs Gordon had been in the very same room as Charles Dickens and she herself had been in the same room as Mrs Gordon . . . This seemed astonishing and important. She shook herself and got to work.

The story she was in the middle of writing on her afternoons off, or in snatched private moments, already covered a dozen pages and it was not the first in the notebook. 'The Mistress's Revenge' was the title of the first, and it was a tale drenched in blood.

But now, the story unfurling from her mind was the shocking tale of a highway*woman*, dressed as a swaggering man armed with pistols. So far, she had held up a carriage in the depths of the countryside, on a bleak moor and on a night thick with fog. On the course of this fateful journey, the passenger, William Fellows, a haunted, passionate widower, subdues the female heroine despite her guns. Wrestling with her in the swaying coach he sees her radiant beauty, the golden hair and ice-blue eyes, and he falls headlong in love with this extraordinary female, especially when she tells him she grew up as an orphan and has no one in the world.

> *'You see, kind sir – I should never live this desperate life if I had other means, but I am reduced –'* her voice sank to a shameful whisper – *'to the lowest of the low. I have no one and nothing in the world . . .'*
>
> *And Fellows's heart swelled with pity, and with passion at the feel of this lovely creature filling his empty and desolate arms.*
>
> *'My dearest, I can see that you are indeed an angel,'* he cried, yearning to kiss her rose petal lips. *'You need never fear again. I am a man and everything in my power I will give you – if you can only feel it in your heart to love me, to give yourself to me in return . . .'*

Dora sat, twiddling her pencil between her fingers. The thought of such passion and longing filled her with excitement. Imagine if a man said things like that to her and promised to look after her for ever!

For a moment she imagined the wedding between the highwaywoman, Desdemona Harkness (though she was not entirely satisfied with that name) and the grieving but now newly joyful widower. She saw a froth of a dress, garlands of flowers, the couple walking down the petal-strewn aisle of a church . . .

Holding the pencil poised to write, she changed her mind. No. It would be much better if she murdered him before the end of the journey. That way she could take off with all his money and there could be another story.

'Desdemona Fellows', angelic wife after her exciting life on the highway, didn't sound quite right – and he was really pretty annoying.

Just as she was settling to write she heard footsteps outside. She just managed to shove all her writing materials under the pillow when the door opened after a quick rap.

'Dora?'

Robert Gordon's face broke into a smile at the sight of her. He was seventeen now, to her sixteen. He may have been the despair of his father in terms of his schooling but he had grown from boyish sweetness into a handsome and athletic young man, still with wayward dark curls of hair and a ready grin.

'It's your afternoon off, isn't it?'

Dora looked back.

'Well, what're you doing sitting in here for goodness' sake? The sun's out – it's lovely outside. Come on – let's go somewhere.'

'All right.' She started to get off the bed.

'You're looking shifty,' Robert teased. 'Oh – I know. Another story in the making?'

Dora blushed. Robert was the only person in the world who knew her secret, that she wrote stories. That she adored writing and that one day she was going to be a writer with her name on everyone's lips, people riveted to her stories. Because she knew so many of Robert's secrets and they protected secrets for each other, she knew he would not tell. No one would much care anyway, but still, she wanted to keep her passion to herself.

'Can you tear yourself away?' he teased.

'I suppose so.' She smiled, slipping her shoes back on.

If there was one thing almost as good as writing it was going out on a secret jaunt with Robert. No one had found out, not even Miss Pyman, who tended to run out of steam for creeping about by the afternoon. Now Agnes was gone, sacked for stealing from Miss Alicia's bedroom, and there was another maid, Lucy, stodgy and harmless. There was no one else who would want to sneak on them anyway.

'You go first,' Robert said. 'Meet in the usual place, all right?'

She waited just round the corner on Islington Row and after not many minutes saw him hurrying along.

'Mother and Father are both out and old Saggy's gone as well,' Robert announced cheerfully.

Dr Gordon was desperately clinging to the notion that his son might improve at his studies and follow in his footsteps as a surgeon or at least as a physician. He still thought Robert's failure was out of laziness and when he reached sixteen, took him away from King Edward's school, to Robert's huge relief, and employed a private tutor.

Christopher Sargent, a droopy, academic character in his late thirties, was doing his best. But he had told Robert, quite sympathetically, that there must be something wrong with him, some block in his brain that stopped him reading properly. Even Dora had tried to help over the years and she could see Robert just could not do it.

'Poor old Saggy,' Robert said, almost fondly. 'I'm surprised he's held out this long with me.'

'He seems quite nice really,' Dora said. She had often seen him, this thin, nervous-looking fellow with his mournful features, when he came to the house to tutor Robert.

'He's all right – and at least if I try and learn, he earns,' Robert said. He touched her shoulder. 'Come on – let's go to town.'

Over the last year, Robert had introduced Dora to the city in which she lived. The two of them had become friends in a way which both knew was to be kept quiet.

What would his parents think if they knew he was jangling off with one of the maids? It just wasn't done, however much Mrs Gordon was giving Dora improving lessons.

Dora had settled into the Gordons' household and no one had reason to find fault with her. She was also being given some education, thanks to Mrs Gordon's belief that servants and the lower classes were to be worked on and improved. Dora – unlike Aggie – was happy to be improved, to read stories and learn to write better. Over the years Mrs Gordon had taught her the outlines of British and Overseas history, some basic geography and had led her into literature, which Dora lapped up. They were reading *Othello* together this week. And all the while, Mrs Gordon's own son could hardly read at all and was certainly not up to following in his father's footsteps.

The friendship had grown gradually. Each morning Dora carried the pail of water up to Robert's room and later, went back to take out the slops. And when he was awake and she was working, they talked. In such an intimate situation, he sitting in his bed or on the side of it, she washing out the bowl and drying the pitcher with a cloth, it was easy to become relaxed. More and more they talked as equals.

'Wakey-wakey, sleepyhead,' she said sometimes, after knocking on the door.

He would sit up and chat to her, groaning if it was a school day. And he confided his difficulties, what a dunce he felt even when he was trying his hardest, and how much he wanted his father's approval and never seemed to be able to win it.

She felt for him. Dr Gordon was a tyrant in her eyes.

'The thing is, Dor,' Robert said one morning, 'I just can't seem to fit in the way they want me to. The person I feel most at home with is you.'

Feelings jolted inside her as he said this. She felt at home with him and felt *for* him, for all his struggles, with a tenderness which often took her by surprise. But in her situation she could not expect anything. She gave him her mysterious, dark-eyed smile and their eyes fixed on each other's. That day, something changed.

Soon afterwards she confided in him about her stories.

'Really?' Robert said. 'Actual stories? That's very clever. You'll have to read them to me – I'm so hopeless I doubt I could read them myself.'

Once or twice she did and he listened. She used him to judge whether the stories were exciting enough by whether his attention started to wander or whether, if she paused, he would say, 'Go on – I want to know what's behind that locked door!' And then she knew she had him captive.

There was only a few months difference in their ages, and for a while he felt like a friend, or like the brother she had lost.

It had been a few months ago that they began sneaking out together, on Dora's afternoon off. Robert played sports on most other afternoons but she noticed he started to save Wednesdays to be with her. And when they were away from the house, it felt as if they were just two people together, friends who liked each other rather than master and servant, and they could move and talk freely.

'We'll be all right so long as we don't bump into any of Ma and Pa's pals,' Robert said. He kept a careful lookout and so far, there had been no danger.

Robert had shown her all he could think of to see. They saw the Town Hall and Bull Ring, the grand building of King Edward's school in New Street, the bustling railway station and all the pubs and shops and teeming roads and alleys.

'D'you mean you've never been here before?' he asked, the first time they walked into town. 'What, *never?*'

Dora shook her head, looking round her in fascination as they walked along amid the racket and pungent smells of Digbeth – effluent from all the packed-in little houses in streets along Digbeth, the stenches of boiling cows' guts from the leather tanneries, of smoke and vegetable waste in the gutters. She gazed at the Old Crown pub with its ancient timbers, the tripe shop, all the carts and carriages coming and going, the beggars and shoe-shine boys, the hawkers of ballads and pies and trinkets, the scurrying people moving to and from the Bull Ring. Every single person seemed to be in a hurry and she laughed sometimes, catching the energy she could see all around her.

She loved going into town, just to be part of it all, to see the chimneys, the busy workshops, to hear the thump and hammer of so many factories, the shops and stalls, organ grinders with a monkey posing on top, the knife grinders making sparks, the little lad who danced for a farthing or two, the cut with the boats loading and unloading coal or nails or metal pipes. All the smells – smoke and grime, acid and metal, the foul stench of meat skins – and in the Bull Ring, lemons and cabbages mingled with the delicious scents of roasting joints of meat.

'But we've seen it all already,' Robert said that day. 'I can't think what else to show you. How about we go to where you grew up?' He looked down at her, his face kindly, but she stopped abruptly in the street, her heart hammering.

'No! I mean – I don't know where it was. We had a house . . . And then another house – I mean, where my mother and father were . . .'

'But you were in the workhouse?' he said amiably, as if this was nothing much. 'Why don't we go there?'

'Oh.' She felt queasy suddenly, and full of shame. A workhouse girl, that was what she was, even if the son of the big house was being nice to her. Why would she want to remember that? 'I don't want to go there. I don't know where it is, anyway.'

'I'm not trying to do you down,' Robert said earnestly. 'I've never seen it, that's all. I know where it is, roughly, anyway. Mother told me.'

Dora nodded reluctantly. All right.

So they walked. A tall, good-looking lad and this small, lovely woman with her vivid hair and eyes, just like any other couple who might walk in the afternoon if they were free. A handsome pair. Except that they were not a couple and never could be.

They stood in Dudley Road looking up at the imposing brick building with its entrance arch and forbidding, soot darkened, institutional walls.

'I remember the morning I left to come to your house,' Dora said shakily. Immediately she could feel it, what it was like in there, those walls, the smells. 'I can hardly believe it now. It feels like another life.'

'Was it bad in there?' he asked.

Dora shrugged. 'You get used to it. The food's bad. But you get used to that too. We played, sometimes. And I had my brother and sisters.'

'Did you?' Robert turned in amazement. 'You never said.'

He was so kind and interested that as they walked home she told him what she could remember. Her chest ached as she talked, with all the feelings it brought back.

'Our youngest sister was given away soon after we got there. I don't know where she went. And our eldest sister – she wasn't there. But the rest of us . . . John left about the same time as me. But my other sister, Mary – I think her real name was Elsie – they sent her somewhere, a few years back.'

Robert was listening. Often when they were together he was the one who talked – about his father, his lessons, his worries about all that was expected of him – after all he had more to say, unlike Dora with her kitchen gossip. Usually she was the one trying to comfort him. But today he was quiet as she talked, pouring out all she could remember. That they had had a mother and a father, that their mother died . . .

'How sad,' he said, genuinely shocked. 'How very sad.'

And somehow his reaction brought her to tears, something that almost never happened, as if his sympathy allowed her feelings that she did not allow to herself.

'Oh, Dora,' he said, seeming unsure what to do. 'Don't take on.'

They stopped, quite close to home now in Frederick Street, at the front of a site where one of the new houses was being built. In the daytime there was hammering and sawing all over the neighbourhood with all the new houses going up. But now, the workmen had gone home and Robert took her hand and drew her in to the side of this shell of a new building.

'Here.' He rummaged in his pocket and brought out a crumpled handkerchief, looking so ruefully at it that Dora managed to laugh through her tears. 'Sorry . . .'

As she wiped her eyes Dora felt Robert's arms wrap round her, pulling her into an embrace so tight that she could hardly move. She raised her head to look at him, shocked, and in his face she saw a great tenderness, although he was bashful and unsure how to express it.

'Loose me a bit,' she said. As he relaxed his arms she threaded her own round him, her heart thumping hard at what she felt. Under her hands, for the first time, was that powerful young body. And the feeling of holding someone and being held. She could not remember when anyone had last put their arms round her and it almost made her cry again. She ran a finger along the dip of his spine, feeling the warmth, the strength of him. And she kept her eyes fixed on his. She had written about such moments – Desdemona and William Fellows – so that now it felt almost that she had conjured this up. But this was different – she could feel him, smell his salty boy smell, which filled her with affection and longing.

Cautious, as if daring himself, his face came closer to hers.

'You're ever so beautiful, d'you know that?' he said quietly. 'You're the most beautiful thing ever.'

His lips touched hers just for a second, then he drew back and his eyes searched hers, more tender and vulnerable than she had ever seen him. It shook her to the core. His words overwhelmed her. They were friends, she knew this – in a secret way. And she already loved him, this kind, confused boy, as her friend. But now – and her legs felt weak, unsteady suddenly – he felt for her as she felt for him, even if she was a maid and not of his family's class. In those moments none of that seemed to matter at all.

Seeing the powerful answer in her eyes he moved close again so that their lips were joined, each of them answering the other in the first kiss that either of them had ever given or received.

Seven

As they walked along the street back to the house, safely apart, even though each was wrapped in the wonder of the other, Dora moved in a haze of astonishment. To have someone who wanted her, felt things for her! . . . Her mind drifted to her story. She would let Desdemona marry William Fellows. They would fall in love, have a beautiful church wedding . . .

'What if someone sees you with me?' Dora said, suddenly realizing how close they were to the house. It wasn't the first time she had said this but now things felt different. 'Your mother's friends? You need to be careful.'

Robert sighed, looking round to check in an exaggerated way as if his mother's spies might be peeping over walls everywhere.

'I'm already in the doghouse all the time as it is.'

He gave her a rueful look and they both laughed.

'Walking out with the maid,' Dora said, shaking her head.

'Mother thinks you're marvellous. One of her more successful little projects. She likes to "improve" people – but not everyone wants to learn even if you give it to them on a plate.'

'She's been very kind to me,' Dora said. She knew the Gordons treated their staff well and she did not want to offend Mrs Gordon in any way. 'She helps me.'

'Helped you write your stories?'

'Oh no,' Dora defended herself quickly. 'I write those all on my own. She doesn't know about them. But she has let me read books and your sister gave me some papers to read – with stories in.'

'Perhaps one day you'll be a famous writer like Miss Austen or Wilkie Collins.'

He was teasing, but Dora flashed back, 'Yes – p'raps I shall. I can tell stories – I *can*!'

Perhaps, she thought, annoyed, she would have Desdemona murder William Fellows after all.

As they turned down the narrow path along the house to the back door, out of sight of the street, Robert stopped her and they fell into each other's arms again. They stood there kissing for some minutes before a sound in the garden made them leap apart.

'You go in,' Robert whispered. 'I'll go back round the front.'

Dora stepped into the kitchen feeling as if everything that had happened – love and kisses! The whole world changed! – must be written all over her face.

But Cook looked up sleepily from her chair, not seeming to notice the radiance of this miracle.

'Nice walk? Put the kettle on, will you?'

'Yes, ta,' Dora said, pouring water into the kettle. 'It's a nice day.'

The next morning, when she carried up Robert's washing water, he bounced up in bed.

'Dora! Come here and give me a kiss!'

'You're a very naughty man, Mr Gordon,' she said to cover her blushes.

'I know.' He pretended to hang his head, dark curls falling over his face, and she laughed. He looked up and grinned at her. 'And you're rather a naughty girl, too. Come on . . .' he wheedled.

'No – I've got work to do,' she said tartly. She tipped the

water into the jug and laid the soap beside it. 'I'll have Miss Pyman after me if I'm too long up here.'

All she really wanted was to go and put her arms round him, but they had to be so careful. And she had to be sure he was not just playing with her. Dora prised herself away and went to the door.

'You'd best get going. Saggy will be on the warpath otherwise.'

Robert rolled his eyes. 'At least if I was actually at school we'd have holidays. Who else does lessons in August? Father still can't admit I'm a lost cause.'

Dora loosed the door and ran back suddenly. She planted a kiss on Robert's cheek and ran off even as he tried to grab her.

'To your studies,' she instructed. 'Be a good boy.'

In the mornings Dora was busy with household tasks and the martyred Christopher Sargent tried his best with Robert's book learning. He passed Dora in the hall as he arrived, smelling of mothballs and looking as if someone might have died.

Time in the afternoon was looser. There were often extra things to do in the kitchen – helping prepare vegetables with Lucy, the new kitchen maid – or on days when Mrs Slater was at the house doing the laundry, Dora might help her with carrying water, turning the mangle or pegging out in the garden. On summer days like these, this was even a pleasure, unfurling sheets in the warm garden together, pegging them to the line and feeling the sun on her face.

But Robert was also free by afternoon and now he appeared at any opportunity. He would come into the garden if she had gone outside for a breather, or he might say, 'Don't you need to dust such-and-such a room?' if he was sure there was to be no one in there. And they would meet and kiss, and their kisses were becoming more passionate.

In the library, with the blinds closed one sultry afternoon, when both Dr and Mrs Gordon were out, they lingered, fondling and kissing. Robert's hand moved to Dora's chest and she felt him stroke her rounded breasts. The feel of it, over her dress and shift, made her gasp, half with pleasure and half at his daring.

'Oh,' he whispered. 'You feel lovely.'

And he kept touching, pulling her closer, and she both wanted and did not want him to stop.

The next time it was, 'Let me see you? Can I see?'

'What?' she said, shocked. She had never removed her clothes in front of anyone. 'No! I can't get undressed in here! Anyway, what if Miss Pyman comes in!'

'Imagine her face.' They both got the giggles then and had to stifle their laughter so that Miss Pyman did *not* come in to enquire what on *earth* was going on.

'Come to my room – tomorrow afternoon,' he said. It was her afternoon off again. 'We can just be us. No one else will be around and they wouldn't come in there anyway.' Closer to her ear, even more quietly, he whispered, 'I want you so much, my love.'

That night Dora lay in bed thinking of him as she did every night now. Tomorrow they would be together, alone and safe. And all she knew was that this was what she wanted. Him. To be desired. Though she had only the haziest notion of what that might mean.

They lay together, naked, in the shadowy light of the room. It was sunny and hot outside and the room was a refuge. But they did not even need a sheet over them as it was so warm – and they were warm. Now, their shared nakedness felt natural.

It had all been clumsy and new. Neither of them had any experience but they learned together like young animals. They laughed and were awkward. But from the moment she saw that look on Robert's face, when naked to the waist she turned to him and he beheld her, all she felt was desire – and the love of being desired, despite the strangeness of the whole thing.

'I've never done this,' he admitted.

Dora shook her head, hoping it was obvious she hadn't either.

She unbuttoned his shirt, saw how beautiful his young body was. He was athletic, the strong shoulders and arms emphasized by the shadows of the room. The sight of him fully naked was a shock – she had only ever seen little boys before. Even catching sight of her own curving body was a shock as she so seldom saw herself either. Her bright hair fell over her skin making it look even whiter. It was all so strange. But they overcame it, wanting each other so much and lying warm and content afterwards, hearing the distant sound of the gardeners outside and an insistent metallic clanging from one of the builders somewhere.

'Oh, Dora, Dora,' Robert said, running his hand along her side, from her waist, along the curve of her hip. 'Like a guitar – a cello,' he said.

She looked into his eyes. 'Is this wrong?' she said. 'Can it be wrong?'

'No.' He moved his hand, caressed her face instead. 'You save me, Dora. Every day. You're the only person I can talk to – really talk to, I mean.' He closed his eyes for a moment and kissed her lips.

'Do you love me?' she said.

'I love you.'

'And I love you.'

They lay quiet, Dora stroking the gentle curves of his

chest. It was all impossible. She was shrinking inside. *Why would you bother with me?* she felt like saying. *I'm a servant, a workhouse girl. I'm not of your class. I'm nobody.*

Yet inside her something rebelled. I am *not* nobody. I had a family once – not a high-class one maybe, but we could do things. *I* can do things. Why do I have to think you are better than me?

'What are we going to do?' she said in a low voice.

'What d'you mean?'

In her mind, *this* – what they had just done, was equivalent to marriage. But how could that be possible?

'I just mean . . .' She couldn't put it into words. That they belonged together now, after this act that was somehow serious and sacred. They were flesh of each other's flesh. She was *not nobody*. For a moment she imagined them eloping, not caring what anyone else might say, climbing out of windows, a coach to Gretna Green . . .

'I think what we're going to do, my Dora, my lovely –' Robert moved against her, vigorous and aroused – 'is do it again!'

Eight

Three months later

'My dear,' Mrs Gordon was saying in a sharp tone as Dora walked into the library that rainy autumn afternoon, 'how you do exaggerate.'

She was seated under the hissing gas light, her slender figure strictly upright as usual, across the table from Alicia, who was a magnificent woman of twenty now, her fair hair fastened back in an elaborate style, and frowning like a storm.

'Well, if you don't wish me to have ideas for myself –' Alicia pushed her chair back, equally stormily, and stood up – 'why introduce me to all your feminist ideas? If you think women should have the vote, then we should have rights in other areas of life – and marriage, so far as I can see, is simply to turn oneself into some man's vassal!'

Mrs Gordon's eyes seemed to harden and her face tightened in a way that made Dora realize this self-controlled woman was very much on the verge of losing her temper.

'Alicia, you are being absurd. Am I a mere vassal in your eyes?'

'Yes – in so far as this house is concerned.' Alicia swept past Dora who was trying hard to pretend she wasn't there. Alicia's gown gave off a sweet whiff of lily-of-the-valley. 'The only will that ever counts is Father's – you are just lucky that he "allows you" to follow some of your own interests. If he didn't –' she gave an exaggerated shrug – 'you would be quite scuppered. And I –' she hurried on as Mrs Gordon opened her mouth to protest – 'do not wish simply to be kept – fed and watered like a horse – so long as I do exactly as I am told. Oh no – that's not for me, so please stop trying to pair me off. I'm not going to marry Richard Taylor however well connected he is – or anyone else for that matter. And that is that.'

And off she went.

Dora kept her face blank as she walked towards Mrs Gordon, who carefully took in a deep breath and arranged her own countenance in an expression of calm welcome. Somehow she managed instantly to gather her thoughts.

'Ah, Dora. Shall we look a little further at the Romans in Britain?' she began as Dora sat down. 'Of course, where we live here, in the Midlands, was at the very edge of the Roman incursion at that time . . .'

As Mrs Gordon bent over the book, pointing out a line here and there with her finger, Dora snatched glances at her, at this good woman with her high morals who was doing her best to help her. What if she found out about her and Robert? About her son's behaviour, his feelings for a maid?

Dora sat burning with guilt and shame. Nothing about what she did with Robert – had been doing for some weeks now – felt wrong at the time. She loved him, she knew that, and she thought he loved her. The way he looked at her, touched her. But in the eyes of anyone else – especially of this upright, religious woman . . .

'Child, are you listening?' Mrs Gordon's voice broke through to her suddenly and blushes spread all over her face. 'You seem distracted today.'

Dora almost wanted to break down and confess everything – to ease the load on her own conscience. But that would be madness. Mrs Gordon would dismiss her instantly. She could not bear the thought of how her employer would see her if she knew the truth – the look that would come into those pale blue eyes.

'Yes, sorry, Mrs Gordon,' she said humbly. 'I am listening.'

She could not keep away from him – and he could not keep away from her. Any possible moment was a chance to hold each other, to talk and kiss – and occasionally more – as lovers do.

And in those brief times when they were together, her early-morning tasks carrying his water, a snatched moment in the garden or, when possible, her afternoon off, then there could be just the two of them. No one else's rules or opinions of the unfitness of her class mattered. And it was like heaven. He was truly with her, his eyes fixed on hers, their talk and love as natural and free-flowing as ever. He was hers – her love.

But towards the end of October was Robert's birthday. He was to be eighteen. This seemed to have caused a disagreement between Dr Gordon and his wife, because as he went sweeping out of the house one morning in his long black overcoat – like a bat, Dora thought – Dr Gordon threw angry words over his shoulder.

'Do as you please then! If you must indulge the boy – though heaven knows he's been indulged quite enough.'

He rushed out so fast that he did not wait to fasten the door properly and Dora hurried to shut it to keep out the chill. It was a cold autumn day, leaves crisp on the ground.

'Mrs Gordon is to hold an evening party for Master Robert's birthday,' Miss Pyman told the servants as they gathered in the kitchen. 'There will not be more than a dozen at most and they are to have cold meats and cakes and Master Robert has asked for there to be jellies.'

Cook laughed, her chins wobbling. 'He's still a boy, isn't he? Jellies always were his favourite. Well, we've plenty of apples and I might add a touch of blackcurrant . . . We'll need to buy lemons . . .'

'In our last house Cook made Silver Jelly,' Lucy announced, in a tone of hopeful awe. 'It were ever so pretty. And it *is* his birthday . . .'

Cook sniffed, unassailable. 'Mrs Gordon wouldn't be having that,' she said. 'Plain living she is – using isinglass is one thing, but silver leaf in food! And,' she added scandalized, 'that has *gin* in it! Ooh no, apple jelly it is, for him and his lads.'

The days before the party were more exhausting than usual. As well as all the fires to lay, the cleaning and serving and toing and froing, there was the special meal to prepare. Cook toiled over pans of apples, boiling and straining. There were cakes to bake and joints to roast. Lucy scuttled round the kitchen like a clumsy insect.

When Dora went up to Robert in the morning she teased him.

'Everyone's working full tilt for your party,' she said. She joked about it, but in part she felt chilled by it and shut out. There was no way in which she could ever be invited to his party – she would be the outsider, waiting on them all as if she was nothing to him.

As she spoke, Robert slipped out of bed and padded over to her in his pale blue nightshirt. He slipped his arms round her and looked down into her eyes.

'I wish you could come and be there – at my side. It would make it all so much nicer.'

'Nicer?' she teased. 'Don't you like your friends?'

'Of course, but . . . all my friends are boys.'

Dora smiled, feeling better. 'Well, I will be there, I s'pose. Waiting on you all hand, foot and finger.'

Robert grinned. 'Just as I like it.'

She gave him a playful punch but suddenly there was a lump in her throat. 'As befits my station.'

Robert looked serious suddenly. 'I wish you wouldn't say things like that.'

'Well, it's true.' She swallowed her feelings.

He nodded, sadly. What else could he say?

The food was laid out in the dining room beforehand and there was not in fact a great deal of need to wait on the crowd of young men whose deep, raucous voices Dora could hear carrying along the corridor before she had even entered the room. The sounds made her feel shy and she shrank inside as she carried two large jugs of ale – Mrs Gordon had generously allowed this as she was teetotal – into the room and put them down on the sideboard. The room rang with men, was full of their odours – sweat, hair cream – and their confidence. They were all muscles and fresh air and seemed to own the world.

Among the heads of hair of various colours and the dark clothes, she saw Robert talking to a fair-haired lad, sharing a joke. Robert leaned into his laughter, head tilted back, mouth open. Chilled, she watched for a second, suddenly feeling he was a stranger she did not know at all. A handsome, upper-class young man who was nothing to do with her.

A second later, as he turned, his eyes passed over her and there was not a flicker of recognition. The moment pierced Dora with such pain that she hurried from the room. I *am* nobody. That's who I am, really.

What in heaven was she doing loving this boy – acting as if he could be hers?

In the hall she had to fight with her rising sobs. She wanted to run to her room, throw herself down on the bed and cry out all the hurt and grief she felt. In this moment everything became clear. She could never truly matter to Robert Gordon. Seeing him with other people instead of alone, just the two of them, made this very clear. She was not of his class and she could never fit in with these young men with their air of command and their braying voices. Men who would always, always look down on her as a woman and a servant.

'What's up with you?' Cook asked as Dora went into the kitchen. Cook had finally sunk into a chair after several days of exertion. The meal was out there, served and being eaten, and now at last there was not much more she could do.

'Nothing,' Dora said, her voice thick as she turned away.

'Let's have a glass of that ale, eh? We've earned it,' Cook said as Lucy came hurrying back into the room as well.

'Loud, ain't they?' she said, grinning. She had enjoyed seeing all those young men, Dora could see. Whereas she felt destroyed by it.

They were all washing and clearing up and putting the rooms to rights until late into the night and it wasn't until gone one o'clock that Dora finally got into bed. By then she was almost beyond emotion, she was so exhausted. She slipped her hand under the mattress, feeling for her story notebook, and stroked it with the tips of her fingers for comfort. Now she could finally allow the tears to run down her face. Quietly, so quietly, she cried out her grief, until sleep came down on her like a heavy black blanket.

Rising at six the next morning as usual, she felt headachy and worn out as she set to on all the morning tasks. It felt a great effort carrying the pails of water upstairs on her tired legs, one for Miss Alicia and one for Robert. And with her feelings so close to the surface, she did not want to face Robert at that moment. She hoped he would still be asleep after all the revels of the night before.

To her surprise he sat up the moment she entered the room.

'Dor!' he said gladly. 'At last I can talk to you properly. Last night was horrible – having to pretend I hardly know you.' He patted the bed. 'Come here?'

He saw the hurt reluctance in her face, the tears shimmering close to the surface. Dragging her feet she went over.

'You do understand, don't you?' he said, looking very straight at her as she sat down.

Dora nodded. Oh yes. She did. All too well.

She was about to start on the things they needed to say. What was the point of going on with this if everything about their love was forbidden and impossible? In that moment, she saw clearly what she had to do. She must leave the Gordons' house and look for another position. That was the only way she could bear this – not constantly seeing him, loving him – and knowing they could never marry or allow anyone else to see this love.

She must speak – she must tell him . . . But she could not get the words to come out of her mouth.

'Look, I've got something for you.' Robert leaned over to the bedside table. 'A present from my Aunt Gwen – which just goes to show how little she knows me.'

He laid the notebook in her lap, a lovely thing with a dark green leather cover, embossed with gold patterns. Dora took it in wonder, stroking her hand over it. Inside, the paper was thick and creamy. There were no lines, just this lovely buttery space to be written on.

'Oh,' she gasped, enchanted. 'It's beautiful. For me – you really mean it?'

Robert beamed at her pleasure. 'What would I do with

it? You can write your stories in it. And then one day you can send them all off to a magazine so that someone puts them in print – how about that? Look, there's a fountain pen as well.'

He laid an elegant black pen into her hand. 'It's a man's one really, but never mind. Not a dip pen, see – you can put ink inside? Do you have ink? I'll get you some ink.'

He seemed so eager to please her. Dora's eyes filled with tears.

'Oh, Robert, they're so lovely – are you really giving them to me?'

'Course. I said so, didn't I? Don't take on – I can't imagine why the old girl thought of them as a present for me!'

She hugged the notebook to her. 'It's the best thing I've ever had. But you keep the pen – I like writing in pencil and then I can't spill ink anywhere.'

He nodded, taking the pen back. 'But you like the notebook?'

She hugged it to her. It was the best thing she had ever had.

'Give us a kiss then.'

Dora moved closer and they held each other. And at that moment she knew she could not bring herself to say anything else, even if her happiness was resting on such a deep well of sadness.

Nine

A few days after Robert's party, a terrible row broke out in the house. The servants could hardly help overhearing and Dora, clearing the breakfast table, was hurrying along towards the kitchen when the loud argument spilled into the hall, despite the door to the drawing room being shut.

Even Mrs Gordon's voice was raised to a shrill pitch and there was a tremor in it. Dora dawdled, listening, because whenever there was trouble it was nearly always about Robert.

'Am I to understand that you have arranged this without a word of consultation?'

'I shan't go . . .' Robert sounded completely distraught. 'I could end up anywhere . . . across the Empire! I might never come home again . . .'

'Don't be so dramatic.' Dr Gordon's voice was tetchy and weary. 'This is for your own good, boy. You've been hanging about all the summer. That tutor, whatever his name was, seems not to have been able to shoehorn any more knowledge or ability into your head than your schooling. My hopes of your following in my footsteps were dashed a long time ago – but you've got to do *something*. A career fit for a man. I have arranged a commission for you – which you should regard as an honour. Athletic chap like you should do well in the army. It's all arranged – no point in arguing.'

'You're cruel, Father . . . I can't go. I shan't . . .!'

The door opened then and Robert erupted out into the

hall, sobs choking out of him as he rushed to the stairs. He caught sight of Dora hovering at the side of the staircase and stopped for a moment, their eyes meeting.

'Did you hear?'

She nodded. She was still trying to take in what this could mean as Robert fled up the stairs. A moment later Mrs Gordon came rushing out of the drawing room and, all rustling skirts, hurried up after him.

Dora could think of nothing else. They were sending Robert away! The words thudded through her blood all day. Sending him away and he was in despair. Her belly felt heavy as if it was full of stones and she was queasy. It got so bad that she had to hurry to the outside privy and retch.

After she had emptied her stomach of what remained of her breakfast of bread and milk she leaned limply against the cobwebby bricks, tears running down her face. She had to go to him – *had* to.

It was only by the afternoon that there was enough of a lull in the work that she could quietly slip up to his room. Tapping on the door she rushed in, finding him lying on his back on the bed. Seeing her, he leaned up on one elbow.

'Dor, am I glad to see you. Come here.'

She rushed to him, flung herself into his arms and they lay together, desperately holding and kissing until she broke away.

'What's happening? Where are they sending you? I don't understand.'

'Father's bought me a commission in the army,' he said, lying back. She cuddled up close, gazing at him, bewildered. She had no idea about the army – to her knowledge she had never seen a soldier. Trying to put aside her own feelings about him going away, she said, 'Is that bad? You might like it?'

'I don't want it,' Robert said, his voice breaking close to tears again. 'I don't know what I want – but not that. I'm sure I could have found something else to do – build houses or make, I don't know, railway carriages. I'm a practical sort. But now . . .'

He knew all was already lost. He had no choice. His father had gone over his head and his future was settled for him. He would be a soldier in Her Majesty's army.

'You're leaving,' she said bleakly.

Suddenly he turned to her, pulled her tightly against him and held her as if he would never let go.

Pressed against his chest Dora thought, of course, one day he was always going to leave. She had known it all along. But it was now, and far too soon. It was a calamity that she did not know if she could bear. It felt like her mother dying all over again, like being dragged from her home by those tall strangers, like the workhouse in those first days when everything she knew had been snatched away. No one there ever asked anything about how you were or what you wanted.

'I don't want to go. I want a different life, not like Father's. I'm not clever like him . . . And I want to be with you, Dor – I want to marry you and be here and us have a life, just an ordinary life.' He looked directly into her eyes and everything at that moment was centred on them, on their look, that bed, that room. 'I love you, Dora. I don't care if you're a servant or a queen. I know who I am when I'm with you.'

'I love you too.' She stroked his lovely face. 'I love you so much – I don't want you to go. I want to come with you!'

They were silent then, knowing this was impossible. That he had no choice. He was heading off into an unknown that she was never going to be able to understand.

'I can't . . .' she began. But couldn't find words for *I can't bear it. How can I live if you're not here?* 'When have you got to go?'

'In a few days,' he said bitterly. 'Father's got it all sewn up. I've got to be a soldier and I can't get out of it – not for twenty-one years. Not if I want a pension and father says if I leave with no money I'll be unfit for anything else'

Dora gasped. Neither she nor Robert had even lived for twenty-one years yet. It was like a sentence of death. She had no idea if what Dr Gordon had said was true. But what she did know was that it felt that any hope was gone.

For those four nights before Robert left, Dora sneaked out of her room once the house had settled and lay with him. By the time he had to leave it was as if they were imprinted on each other, after lying so close, making love and holding each other during those dwindling night hours in a desperate bid to stop time.

'I'll never forget you, Dor,' Robert whispered into her hair as he held her that last night.

'You're my love,' she whispered back. 'Whatever else happens – you'll always be my love . . .'

'What if I'm bad at soldiering as well?' he said one night as they lay together. 'I'll die in some foreign place and never come home again.'

Dora stroked his chest, trying to comfort him when she could not find words to do so.

All week she was sick and distraught, and it was hard to hide it from the other servants. Miss Pyman kept giving her ominous looks and Cook said, 'You look peaky, wench. I hope you're not coming down with summat?'

I'm all right,' she said. *Only that my heart is breaking.* The next heroine she wrote about was going to have her heart broken in a tragic way, she decided. She clung to this. Her stories. Her secret. They were all she had left.

The day Robert had to leave she slipped out of his room soon after five in the morning to return to her own, feeling as if she was being torn apart. They had wept their goodbyes and it was only from a distance that she heard Dr Gordon and Robert leave the house. Hugging herself in tight as a second corset, she watched from the landing window as they climbed into a carriage, the horse's breath steaming on the air. She saw Robert's hunched shoulders, a glimpse of his pale face. But he did not look up. The carriage rolled away, the sound of the hooves receded and however long Dora stood at the window straining to hear these last traces of him, he was gone, for ever.

And life went on, even though to her it felt like a stopped clock. Everything had come to an end, all joy, all hope. But what did not stop was that every day now, she woke feeling sick, and the feeling lasted for much of the morning.

Ten

Steam wafted out of the brick wash house at the back of the house, vanishing into the crisp winter air. Mrs Slater was hard at work, thumping clothes on to the washboard and mashing them back and forth, her brawny arms pink and wet.

Dora staggered out from the kitchen with two more buckets of hot water, shivering as the cold air hit her damp clothes after the warmth inside. She had been told to help Mrs Slater this morning and a very moist experience it was, and very varied in temperature. She plunged into the warmer fug of the brewhouse, where the fire was crackling under the copper, to tip the water into the tub in which Mrs Slater was rinsing the clothes.

As usual Mrs Slater stank of beer and never stopped talking, despite the exertions of the work.

'Right, bab – that's it, tip that lot in there and help me get this lot moved over . . . As I were saying, I said to Arthur . . .' A long complaint would follow about her husband who, oh yes, he had suffered a work injury hit by a train in the shunting yard and had never been right since not least in losing a leg above the knee. But he'd got himself a peg leg and these days it never stopped him getting to the pub and if only he'd get off his idle backside and do something she wouldn't be chained to the washtub every day of her life . . .' And on it went.

Dora felt for Mrs Slater and thought Mr Slater sounded as if he needed a ticking-off, something he already received on a regular basis by the sound of things. But today she was too caught up in her own worries and the sick feeling in her belly to listen. Until Mrs Slater paused for a moment, ambled over to the door to pick up the brown bottle she always tucked just inside, and took a good swig of ale. She put the bottle down, wiped an arm across her warty face and suddenly looked at Dora, eyes narrowed.

'Well, you look groggy this morning, wench – bad as our Liza . . .'

To Dora's relief, as a hot panic rose in her, Mrs Slater bent over the stone tub again.

'Sick as a dog 'er is, every morning . . . I'd lay money on 'er being in the family way and I said to her, "I'd lay money you're in the family way, our Liza – and you and that lad of yours not even tied the knot yet," but 'er won't hear of it even when I know all the signs. And 'er's only seventeen – mind you, that's what I were when I had her.'

Dora snapped to attention, ears straining for any grain of information. Keeping her head down and busying herself with the pails, she said, 'How d'you know when you're, you know, in the family way?'

'Ah well . . .' Mrs Slater seemed energized by her dose of beer and started thumping the whites in the rinsing tub as if they had done her a personal injury.

'Bless you for an innocent child – tell-tale signs are missing your monthly and having a puke of a morning. I used to puke summat terrible, green as pond slime, but it'd pass in a few weeks. Back in those days I weren't doing washing, I worked for a dairyman and the smells used to upset me summat rotten. I'd have to go outside and puke up round the back . . . Not nice, that wasn't.'

Dora glanced up at her, breathing deeply as she tried to suppress the need to do exactly the same herself.

'Mind you, wench –' Mrs Slater gave a cackle and cast

a teasing look at Dora – 'to 'ave a bun in the oven, there has to be someone put it there in the first place, but I don't s'pose a simple young wench like you'd know anything about that, would you now?'

It was no good. Dora dashed outside and bent over, heaving, in the shadow of the brewhouse. After chucking up she leaned groggily against the wall, Mrs Slater's words slamming round in her head, her heart pounding as the panic mounted inside her.

The next day Dora was due to have her afternoon session in the library with Mrs Gordon. It would have been the first time since Robert left and every time Dora had seen her mistress she seemed paler and more drawn in the face herself.

She's missing him, Dora thought, her own heart a constant ache in her chest. She's worrying about him because she didn't want him to go. She had no say in any of it. At that moment she longed to be able to confide in this very upright, reserved woman. *I miss him too. I love him as well and I didn't want him to go!* But of course that was impossible. Each of them had to bear their pain and grief on their own.

The one thing Dora could not do now, however, was to sit beside Mrs Gordon at the library table as if nothing had happened. As if nothing *was* happening. She asked Lucy to pass the truthful message to Mrs Gordon that she was feeling ill and went upstairs to lie down.

As soon as she was alone that afternoon, lying limp and exhausted on the bed, she curled up and let her tears come. Her body shook with sobs and she grasped the pillow in her arms, remembering the feel of Robert beside her – his strong, lean body, his lips on hers – and she yearned for him to be there. For everything to be different.

But when she had cried herself out and turned on her back, still with the pillow clasped in her arms as if for safety, the panic took her over. She knew – and every day she became more sure – that something even more catastrophic was happening to her.

Mrs Slater was right. She didn't know anything about it. How it happened. That what she and Robert had done, which felt so strange at first but which felt so right, so joyful, would leave her with a baby.

As she lay there the full horror of realization washed over her. If only there was someone she could confide in, ask properly what was happening to her. Even in those early days in the workhouse, or her first arrival here, she had never felt so alone and so frightened.

'Why aren't you here?' she whispered to Robert's face as she conjured him up in her mind. 'I need you. I want to talk to you. To tell you what we've done.'

But only silence came back to her. There would never be an answer now. He would not write to her, she knew that. He was not a letter-writing sort and it would only drag out the inevitable fact that they were apart, for ever. But they had committed this act. The two of them, barely more than children themselves, had done something more adult than they really understood. Even now, though she was beginning to understand, Dora could barely piece this together – that it meant a baby, a person. None of that felt real.

As she lay there, the image of another face appeared in her mind. Mrs Gordon. Kindly, virtuous Mrs Gordon. Whatever else Dora felt she respected the woman. She had given her a great deal during her years here. On top of the absolute basics which Dora had lapped up in the workhouse, faster than anyone else, Mrs Gordon had given her an education, had given her access to books and writing and learning, and she knew she would owe her that for the rest of her life.

But she could not face her, not with the truth. Sooner or later she must leave this comfortable house in Frederick Street. Her questions to Mrs Slater had given her the knowledge that babies did not show – not straight away. But, terrifying as the thought was, sooner or later she was going to have to go out into the city that Robert had shown her and somehow find a new way for herself.

Eleven

January 1863

It was late afternoon, the light already dying and the night frost beginning to harden. Dora, frozen and exhausted, tramped the streets of a close-packed neighbourhood of small brick terraces and narrow entries. Her feet were sore, her back aching. The only emotion she had left in her for now was the longing to lie down.

The thought of saying goodbye to the rest of the Gordon staff had been unbearable. She had left the house after the midday meal, tucking chunks of bread into her bundle while Mrs Morgan was in the pantry and slipping out like a shadow down the side of the house and into the street.

Mrs Gordon had been quite unable to understand why she wanted to leave and tried to talk her out of it.

'I brought you here from the workhouse to give you a chance in life,' she said. She did not speak angrily, she just seemed bewildered and disappointed. 'I know the working world out there might seem more alluring. You might be paid a fraction more. But is factory work truly what you want, Dora?'

Factory work was not in the slightest what she wanted – *One day I'll be a writer, you'll see. I'll write a whole book and be someone of renown . . .!* – but she pretended to Mrs Gordon that she wanted other experience than being in service. Perhaps working up to a job in an office?

'You've been very kind to me, Mrs Gordon,' she said, tears pricking in her eyes because she could not tell Mrs Gordon the truth. She was going to miss the woman's cool kindness and her lessons. She had a lot to be grateful for. Her reading and writing had come on apace in this house.

She walked out of the gate for the last time, weighed down with sadness and especially because she was being torn away from all the sights and sounds that she associated with Robert. So many of those times and places they had shared. But she could not stay and bring this disgrace upon both of them. She imagined Dr Gordon's reaction if the truth came out.

With a last look, drinking in her memory of the house with its climbing wisteria at the front, she turned away and headed towards Five Ways and into Birmingham.

'D'you know of anyone needs a lodger? I can pay?'

After hours of walking she had long ago lost track of where she was. Smells of cooking food along the street reminded her that she was famished – the bread was long gone. But she must find somewhere first. Two men had offered her a room but neither of them were blokes she would go anywhere near however desperate she was.

At last, a kindly elderly lady, standing at her door, said she thought Mrs Lacey in court twelve, behind her, might be looking for someone.

As soon as Dora passed along the entry into the back yard, buried memories rushed at her with such force that she paused, in shock. She had lived in a place like this before. The walls black with smuts, the shared privies at the end next to the stinking pile of ash and refuse, the poor little houses – it was all powerfully familiar. She gasped: Mom. Dear God, Mom! A shadowy, reassuring figure seated at a table – she could not picture her face, not really – and them, as children, their little hands sorting bristles for brushes in the half-dark, round the table with her . . .

Number two's door was already wide open. When she knocked, her heart pounding, a moment's wait brought a black-clad figure shuffling painfully out of the shadows to lean on the door frame.

'Yer what?' she bawled, cupping a hand round one ear when Dora asked timidly if there was a room to rent.

Mrs Lacey was a plain-faced woman of heaven only knew what age, but immediately Dora could see there was a goodness to her. No sign of viciousness, a quality she could sniff out immediately after years in the workhouse. She looked Dora up and down and then, so loudly that the rest of the yard must surely have heard every word, she announced:

'I like yer face, bab – and you're on yer beam ends by the look. You can pay me one and six a week for the room if you'll cook and keep 'ouse – and I don't mind what you do to earn your keep. I can't move about so good these days so I need someone to cook me tea – soft, mind, I can't have gristle. I do best with soup or a bit of mince and I'll be happy to see a dish of faggots now and again. You keep the house up for me and we'll get along . . .'

Having broadcast this proposal to all and sundry and taken in that Dora was nodding, she was about to turn away as if everything was settled, when she added a further deafening utterance:

'I ain't going to tek against a babby – I can't hear a thing in any case.'

Dora was stunned. With her compact figure and a swathing shawl she thought she had hidden her swelling belly, but Mrs Lacey either had second sight or actual sight that was a great deal better than her hearing. Whatever the case, close to tears of gratitude, she followed her new landlady into the mouldy-smelling house.

Once Mrs Lacey had pointed her to the small room upstairs beside her own with just enough space to squeeze a double brass bedstead into it, all she wanted was to lie on it and go to sleep. But she was famished.

'I'll go and get us some fried fish,' she said. 'I could smell it along the road.'

Mrs Lacey readily agreed and handed her tuppence. As Dora left the yard and headed to the street, following the tempting cooking smells wafting from the fried fish shop, she fingered the wages she had from Mrs Gordon, tucked into a rag at her waist – four pounds owed her for the last three months. She thought about her mistress with deep regret.

She brought back a newspaper-wrapped bundle of fish, her mouth watering all the way, and Mrs Lacey carefully made space amid the dull gleam of the hooks and eyes – her outwork for a nearby factory – for them to sit down. She ate with relish, lips slapping in a satisfied way which turned Dora's stomach a little but Mrs Lacey was so deaf she could not hear herself whatever she was doing.

'So,' she enquired loudly, 'where's yer 'usband then? 'E run off and left yer, has 'e?'

'Oh no,' Dora said, making sure her face took on a look of deep sadness. Which was not difficult because she was grieving. 'He's passed on – he was killed in the shunting yard.' She still had only the vaguest idea what a shunting yard was – only that it could involve being hit by trains – and prayed that no one would ask for particulars.

'Oh, my word,' Mrs Lacey said, prising a sliver of fish from somewhere deep in her gums. 'Dangerous places them yards.'

'I know,' Dora said, recalling Mrs Slater's stories. 'They

said he didn't even see the train. It came up behind and he was killed instantly.'

As she spoke she could see the scene in her mind. The young man looking intently across the tracks, the train sliding along, his crushed body. She felt even sadder thinking about it.

'I didn't even know I was expecting then,' she said tearfully. 'I got such a shock – and my Robbie never knowing...'

'You poor wench,' Mrs Lacey said, loudly and matter-of-factly. 'You don't look old enough to be wed let alone a widow. I'll tell the neighbours – stop them canting.'

Dora suspected that the neighbours could likely already hear, given the volume of the conversation.

'How old are you, then?'

'Nineteen,' Dora fibbed. 'I've always been small.'

'What're you gunna do to bring in a wage? Factory work?'

Dora put the last remains of fish into her mouth and chewed, pretending to think.

'Might be better if I was to do something else. Take in washing? I've got some wages from my last job – I was in service, a house in Edgbaston. So I can set myself up.'

Mrs Lacey thought, her unsupported lips folding in on themselves.

'With a babby coming you won't last long in a factory. So I s'pose... My old man was a cooper, so I've got a couple of the best maiding tubs you could find. You'll have to take your turn in the brew'us if you want to use the copper. But you could do some here and in the yard. Boil up on the fire and that.'

'Would you mind?' Dora brightened. At least working for the Gordons she had learned a lot about cooking and laundering clothes.

'I don't mind, bab. It's nice to have some help – and some life about the place. You won't find many round 'ere with the money to pay for their washing – you'll have to look further out. And I'd get yer own mangle if I were you – or you'll be daggers drawn with 'er at number three before you know where you are.'

She paused and looked at Dora thoughtfully. 'You look strong enough – but you're going to be worn out.'

I don't care, Dora thought. I want to work for me, not for anyone else. And so long as I can earn enough and still have time to write, that's all that matters.

That first day she invested in her new working life. She bought an old mangle for a pound and wheeled it, with difficulty as its iron wheels stuck and squeaked, along the street and up the entry. She bought a washboard, a wooden dolly, a scrubbing brush, some soap and Reckitt's Blue and two new pails.

She also asked in the yard when she could use the copper for boiling up clothes. Wednesday, she was told – unless you want to work at night. Everyone else was using it until then.

'You can use my iron,' Mrs Lacey told her. 'But I need the table. And unless it's wet out, you can do most of your scrubbing in the yard – this house'll be wet through else.'

The sickness had worn off some weeks ago and Dora was feeling quite energetic now. She was ready for it – carrying pails of water from the pump out in the street, boiling water in the house if it was not her turn in the brewhouse and soaking, pounding and rinsing all the clothing, as well as mangling it and hanging it out. The one problem she had to sort out was ironing. There was nothing for it – she'd have to lay a cover on the brick floor and do it there.

I only need enough to get by, she reminded herself. And

she started walking the streets, heading for parts of town where there were bigger houses and towards Edgbaston because she knew the area. The way she was going she'd need stronger boots as well.

'We've already got someone coming in,' she was told by several big houses. Or once, 'You could come and work here, we need someone.' But she refused. She was going to work for herself. Even if it meant boiling up a copper when everyone else had gone to bed.

'I'm going to have to get myself a system,' she said to Mrs Lacey. 'Or everyone's going to end up with the wrong clothes.'

By the time she had bought spools of dark thread, needles and scissors and a second-hand pair of boots, on top of all her other expenses and fuel to light the fire under the copper, she only had a few shillings left. Now it was time to start earning.

Bit by bit she found a few customers, carrying bundles from several houses to be returned, washed, starched if necessary, dried and ironed. And that was as much as she could manage.

And she and Mrs Lacey managed to work around each other. Dora felt great gratitude towards her landlady. She was a poor old thing who kept body and soul together by sewing the hooks and eyes on to cards to be sold in the shops. Day in, day out, she sat with the table pushed close to the window, squinting in the dim light, her gnarled hands stitching the tiny metal items.

Mrs Lacey could sit and work, but she was not a well woman and really did need help. Her legs were swollen as bladders and climbing the stairs was an endless penance. Coming down she would thump her way, step by step, on her backside. A widow for some nine years, she was once married to George Lacey, a cooper, so they had the best washtubs on the yard. She spoke as loudly as a foghorn at all times and along with her hearing she had lost most of her teeth. She was rough and ready but, as Dora had sensed, a kindly soul, and the two of them had soon come to an arrangement that suited them both. Dora, frightened and grieving as she was, felt as if – even living in this cramped, rough place – she had fallen on her feet.

Some days later, when she had not been able to find a turn in the brewhouse, Dora worked late into the night. She heard a church clock chime two as she carried her pails out along the entry to fetch water from the pump. It was a chill, misty night, the light a dim blur from the gas lamps and a sickly glow round the moon. As she reached the street she heard the scuttle of rats and somewhere nearby, footsteps moving swiftly away. She was already shivering, her vest and drawers clinging, dank and cold after leaving the steamy atmosphere of the brewhouse.

She pumped the water vigorously, to keep warm as much as anything, looking around her fearfully as she did so. The streets filled her with disquiet – who, or what, might come out of the shadows? The hairs stood up on the back of her neck. Once the pails were full she lugged them back to the yard as fast as she could, the muscles in her belly pulling painfully.

Hauling the load of white linens and flannel into the maiding tub she pummelled it with the dolly, turning and bashing the remaining dirt out of it and hauling it again into the other tub for rinsing. She would leave it there and mangle and hang it in the morning. All that was needed now was to empty the copper into the outside drain – which everyone called the 'suff'.

Dora stood for a moment, the candle which had been lighting her toil almost burnt down, and felt a certain satisfaction. The work was exhausting but she was driven on by her will to succeed and so far she had found the energy to work fast and efficiently.

Her workhouse clothes had had marks sewn into them and she sewed similar tiny reminders into the corners of clothing from her customers. Now that a number of them had entrusted their frowsty bundles of clothing to her again, they were already marked up.

And while she was working, her mind raced along the paths of her stories. The characters, the passions and battles, the horrifying ghostly apparitions and awful mysterious noises. Sometimes she muttered to herself, playing out the parts – 'No! I will never marry you. You are a wicked sinner!' – of all the scenes which had been coming to life in her mind as she toiled through the dark hours, with no one to interrupt.

Her work finished, she went into the house, cut a slice of bread and poured half a cup of milk, devouring both of them impatiently, then went up to her room. She could sleep while the clothes were drying but for now she had things to do.

She drew her precious notebook out from under the mattress – the book Robert had given her. Not that Mrs Lacey would ever come in, but it was her long habit, her secret. She placed the candle on a narrow shelf at the side of the bed and opened the book, half the pages already densely covered in her tiny writing. Tired as she was, her pencil was soon scratching across the page . . .

The street was quiet, but for the solemn chime of a church clock and the frenzied scuttle of the rats along the gutters. Quiet, that is, until the sound of running footsteps broke into the sleeping calm. Out of the darkness appeared a sight to strike horror into the soul of any living creature abroad in the night . . .

Dora chewed her pencil for a moment. Best not to show what it was coming out of the darkness just yet . . .

She lay back, feeling a sudden lurch of movement inside her.

'Shhhh,' she murmured, 'go to sleep!' A thrill went through her, a surge of love. However frightened she was, her whole life overturned, there was this love. Stroking her hand gently over the growing globe of her belly she lulled both herself and the child – his child, a part of her beloved Robert – into slumber.

Twelve

May 1863

'Going up the shops are you, Dora?' Mabel Pickles, their kindly next-door neighbour came out of her house as Dora headed for the entry.

Apart from number three, Mrs Horne, a miserable old battleaxe who would pick a fight with her own shadow, the other neighbours in the yard had been kind to Dora. The poor young thing, left on her own at such a young age and left expecting a child. And she worked so hard to make a living . . .

The first time she ran into Mrs Horne, a bony, bitter woman always dressed in limp widow's weeds, she looked Dora up and down with obvious hostility.

'You're not a widow, are you?' she announced as if she thought she was the only person on the yard entitled to claim this status.

Dora stared back straight into her eyes.

'And how exactly would you like me to prove it?' she retorted. Though the woman's words made her feel as if a cold hand was clamping round her heart, Mrs Horne's nastiness roused her temper. 'Want me to dig him up, do you?'

Mrs Horne went off, muttering darkly to herself.

Now, Dora looked round wearily. It was Saturday, still a day of work but this included fetching the bulk of their week's food. And she was worn out, her feet and back aching, and she had strained a muscle in her side. The energy she had had four months back was fast running down the heavier she grew carrying the child. She felt sick more these days, from sheer exhaustion which for a couple of weeks now had left her only able to fall into bed at night with no energy to write. This was what got her down more than anything and she felt trapped and colourless.

'Yes,' she said to Mabel. 'I'd get to the Bull Ring if I had the energy but I haven't.'

'You poor wench.' Mabel was in her late twenties with three little children. She was very thin and looked constantly harassed, but at least she had a husband bringing in a wage. 'I'm going over there. Want me to bring anything back?'

Dora smiled. 'That's nice of you but you don't need to fetch and carry for me. There's only the two of us.'

'Three, you mean.' She nodded at Dora's belly and Dora raised a laugh.

'Yes, I s'pose so.'

'And old Ma Lacey's got you running round doing everything for her.'

'She's all right,' Dora said. 'Funny old thing, but she gave me a roof over my head and there's many wouldn't.'

'She's not a bad old soul,' Mabel agreed. Her face turned sour suddenly and she rubbed a hand over her belly. 'Ooh – I feel nasty today. Hope I've not caught for another – not this soon.'

'Your little one's barely a year!'

'Me and Eddie only have to look at each other.' Mabel shook her head, half bitter, half fond. 'And there's no stopping him, any road.'

They reached the corner and Mabel went off towards town. Dora watched her shabby, brown-clad figure striding away along the shabby street. *We only have to look at each other . . .* Suddenly she was full of anguish, a deep physical ache, faced by a surge of all the things she tried so hard not to think about because there was nothing she could do about any of them. Robert – where was he now?

She forced herself to walk on, out to the main road and the shops, her feet dragging. She felt so tired and low. She was earning – seven and six a week or thereabouts. She and Mrs Lacey were getting by – sometimes she cooked up bacon or eggs, at others went out for a jug of faggots to mop up with bread. And Mrs Lacey, placid as ever, did her outwork and put up with all the carry-on of Dora's work, the wet and steam, the washing strewn across her downstairs room. Dora only dared hang coloured laundry outside. The filthy air stained all the whites with smuts or turned them a weird yellow. But yes, they were getting by, just, by the skin of their teeth.

But the price of it on Dora's young frame, now heavily pregnant, was beginning to tell. Things kept going wrong and she had no energy to cope with it. Her hands were rubbed red raw and her fingers cracked open and stinging horribly.

'You want to get some oat paste on them,' Mrs Lacey remarked, seeing Dora wince every time she touched anything. 'I'd make you some if I could remember how.'

The pain became so bad that Dora resorted to buying a paste from the druggist which soothed them, at least at night.

But yesterday a line had snapped, dropping her clean wash into the dirt. And every so often the yard suff blocked, turning the place into a cesspool. On top of that she had had a stomach upset and been stuck in her bed for three days in a row. She still felt weak and off her food.

'How long can I go on?' she muttered, turning into Suffolk Street.

But she had to go on, somehow – there was no choice.

She went first to the sweet-smelling bakery, trying not to look at the buns and pastries. She bought a loaf, then to the butcher for bacon and chitterlings and a lump of lard. All she needed now was a couple of ounces of tea.

The street was Saturday-morning busy, women passing in and out of the shops with cloth bags, or standing in gaggles canting the latest neighbourhood gossip.

Dora bought her supplies from the grocer's and had turned back towards home, when she caught sight of a little figure sitting in a doorway, who stood out because she was so completely still. Her straw hat was pushed askew by her head leaning against the wall. Dora stepped closer to look. The child was painfully thin and her eyes were closed. A lank, mouse-brown plait dangled over her shoulder. She had a sweet face, but her skin was ashen, with blue rings under her eyes. For a terrible moment Dora wondered if she had passed on from this life in that lonely spot amid the crowds.

Moving closer, she managed to squat down beside the girl, widening her legs to accommodate her belly.

'Hey – you all right?' she asked softly.

There was no response and Dora's heart beat faster with dread. She dared to touch the girl's arm. She was warm, at least. She gave the arm a little shake and the girl stirred and opened her eyes. For a moment she looked frightened to death, but seeing Dora her face calmed. She gave a moan and leaned forward, resting her head in her hands.

Dora was about to go, not sure there was anything she could do, when the girl looked pleadingly up at her.

'I can't,' she said, her eyes welling with tears. 'I can't do it any more. And I can't go back – she'll kill me.'

'Who?' Dora asked, shaken by her desperation. 'Your mother?'

'No – I ain't got a mother. I mean *her*, the one I work for.' She grabbed Dora's arm suddenly. 'I can't go back there. I just can't!'

Dora stood up, starting to wish she had never got herself into this. This person was not as young as she had assumed at first and she had enough problems of her own. But there was something about the girl that she immediately liked.

'Well, I don't know,' she said. 'I was just seeing if you were all right.'

'You got anything to eat?' the girl pleaded. 'I've been up all night and I got it done. I *did* get it done. But I ain't eaten in . . . Since yesterday morning. I can't do it any more.'

She started crying then. Dora's bewilderment increased, but something about the girl had hooked into her. She couldn't just leave her here.

'Come back with me then,' she said. 'We'll give you a drink and a bite to eat and p'raps you'll feel better then.'

And that was how Dora came to meet Minnie Moon.

Dora and Mrs Lacey listened, drinking cups of tea, and Minnie, after a slice of bread and a rasher of bacon Dora had fried up for her, revived markedly. Though thin and waif-like, she had big, square, widely spaced teeth which gave her a humorous look, and Dora could see that the girl had a good deal of life in her. She liked her even more as Minnie sat and poured out her story.

Minnie had been working for a milliner, a Miss Best, who she described as being like one of the wickedest witches in any fairy story.

'Miss Worst?' Dora suggested, and Minnie cackled with laughter.

'She were that all right!'

Minnie was paid a paltry wage and expected to work endless hours if an order needed fulfilling. All night if necessary without a break, as she had done the night before.

On top of that, she was the only remaining child of a mother who had died when she was nine and her father was a harsh man without an ounce of sympathy.

'All he wants is my wages and he don't care about me – not a fig,' Minnie said passionately. 'If I come in a minute after he says he knocks me across the room. He sent me to work with *that woman*, Miss Best, and she's a cruel beast as well. I *hate* her – even if it is wicked to say so! There's just me and her and she never treats me nice, even if I do everything right. And our dad takes all my wages and I work hours and hours – all the time.' Her eyes filled again. 'I can't keep it up – not with my stomach growling empty for hours on end. It's a torment, that's what it is!'

With growing energy after her piece and bacon, she was ranting, even had a touch of colour in her cheeks. 'I hate *him* an' all. And I hate making stupid *hats*. And *she* won't touch 'em hardly, she just orders me about – do this, do that, that's not good enough. 'Cause she don't want the hatter's shakes – but she don't care if *I* end up like that, with all my senses gone!'

Mrs Lacey, who had sat with one hand cupped round her ear, casting questioning looks at Dora when she needed something – in fact, almost all of Minnie's account – repeated, sat up and came startlingly to life.

'That father of yours sounds just like mine,' she said. 'A right brute, wanted nothing off me but my wages, collaring all those hours and not a farthing for myself. I got to thinking, bugger him, 'scuse my language. He could go and roast in hell as far as I was concerned. I got out of home when I was fourteen and never went back and you want to do the same.'

'But I've got no one else – there's only me and him,' Minnie wailed.

Dora's mind was racing.

'D'you really want to leave all that behind?' she asked.

'Oh, I'd give anything. I would, truly.'

'I could do with some help.' Dora spoke loudly, looking at Mrs Lacey as she did so. 'What if she was to come and work with me?'

Mrs Lacey pursed her lips for a moment, but Dora could see she was already half persuaded.

'You up to doing laundry work?' Dora asked quickly. 'And helping out in the house?'

'Course.' Minnie looked back and forth between them. 'Oh! Can I come and live here with you? I'd help you, I would – I'd work like mad, *all the time*!'

Thirteen

After a couple of decent meals and a bit of kindness, Minnie Moon quickly recovered and was full of a sparky energy – far more so than Dora. The two girls were not far apart in age, but Minnie was not carrying a child. She was a wiry little thing and a survivor, and she threw herself into the work. Minnie's one overriding enthusiasm was for food and if she was well fed she seemed capable of almost anything.

'I know how to cook,' she told Dora that first day as they all sat at the table. 'I've been cooking for my father since Mom passed on. 'Cept he always got to eat the lion's share.' An expression of loathing passed across her little face. 'He's gunna have to shift for himself now. Serves him right, the old varmint.'

'Her father.' Dora passed this on to Mrs Lacey at high volume. 'Got to fend for himself now – Minnie won't be cooking for him.'

Mrs Lacey took this in with a nod which wobbled her chins.

'Were 'e never good to you, wench?'

Minnie shook her head. 'Only if he wanted summat,' she blared at Mrs Lacey. 'He thought about himself and that was that – even when our mom was alive.'

Dora showed Minnie all that needed to be done though she was already well acquainted with washing. She threw herself into it and to Dora's huge relief her load lightened.

'If you could do the ironing, it'd be a godsend,' she told Minnie. 'It's doing me in having to get down there like that.'

Minnie put her head on one side, looking down at Dora's ironing arrangements.

'We need another table,' she said. 'We'll get one – when we've got a bit of money going. But I'll do it for now – and carry the water in.'

Minnie was stronger than she looked.

'It's better here than being shut up in that shop with *her* breathing down my neck and that filthy stinking stuff,' she said.

'We can get more customers with you here,' Dora said. 'Make more money. I know where we could go to ask.'

Though it was quite a walk, they went out as far as Edgbaston, knocking on doors and gathering a few more customers from people who had just moved into the area and had not already made laundry arrangements. Dora bought a wooden barrow to carry the bundles instead of the two of them staggering home with them in their arms.

'You want to soak that in lye overnight,' Minnie observed, looking at a shirt heavily stained with grease. 'That'll shift it.'

She was full of handy hints that Dora had not known. And she would go to the shops for them, loved being out and about. Until one day.

Dora was in the yard, pounding sheets in the maiding tub, when Minnie came charging along the entry and dashed into the house.

'Someone's got 'er bloomers on fire,' Mabel commented, pegging out a couple of bits of handwashing on the line.

Something was wrong, Dora could see. Wiping strands of damp hair from her face with the back of her arm, she followed Minnie inside. She found her panting with alarm and trying to make Mrs Lacey understand what was up with her.

'He saw me! I was just going into the Bull Ring and there

he was – and he saw me!' Minnie was shaking. 'There 'e was all of a sudden with his red puffy face. He shouted my name and . . . I just ran for it. People were staring but I just ran and I never stopped, all the way home!'

She sank on to the chair opposite Mrs Lacey who was busy with her needle and thread.

Dora felt a clutch of absolute dread round her innards.

'Did he follow you? Does he know where you are?'

Minnie shook her head, still trying to get her breath. Her eyes were bulging. 'Don't think so. No – the old bugger couldn't run if he tried. But I thought he was behind me all the way here. I ran like the wind!'

They all looked out into the yard as if expecting Mr Moon to come steaming in any moment but there was no sign.

'You're all right,' Dora reassured her. 'He can't know where you've gone, can he?'

Minnie sank back, limp. 'Phew. That was close.' She looked at Dora and Mrs Lacey and said loudly, 'Thanks for taking me in. It's better here. Much, much better.'

Dora had Minnie sharing her bed now so it was impossible to keep her writing secret from her for long. Soon after Minnie arrived, Dora had waited until she was asleep, then sat up, moving very cautiously, with Robert's notebook, her most precious possession, clasped to her. She leaned over and lit the candle again and started writing.

Minnie's lashes were dark little crescents against her pale skin. She twitched and muttered in her sleep. After a while she stirred and opened her eyes. She pushed up, startled, on to one elbow.

'Dor? What're you doing?'

Dora instinctively closed the notebook and pressed it to her breast.

'You writing something?' Minnie sat up, seeming really intrigued.

Dora was growing fond of Minnie. Brave, hard-working Minnie. And suddenly it felt like a relief and a happy thing to share her dream with her.

'I like writing stories,' she said. It felt like a big thing to admit, as if she had just revealed her soul. A terrible pang passed through her. Robert. Before this, she had only told *him*. But Minnie was genuinely fascinated.

'You write *stories*? Whole stories – and books? What about? Will you read them to me?'

'Can't you read?' Dora asked.

'I can, a bit. And write. But it's nice to have someone read you a story. Mom tried to, when I was little. Only she couldn't read much. Go on – read me summat?'

'What, now?'

Dora, flattered, frightened that Minnie would say the story was stupid or dull, turned to her story of William Fellows and his murder (she had decided on the goriest end possible) by the elusive and powerful highwaywoman, Desdemona Harkness.

'I'm not sure I've got her name right,' Dora said when she had started reading. Minnie lay quiet, listening with absolute attention, even though they both heard a clock striking two o'clock in the distance.

'You should call her . . .' Minnie paused dramatically. 'Augusta Flit.'

Dora pondered this in surprise. Augusta Flit. Yes – that was just the right name!

'Go on,' Minnie urged. 'It's exciting.' She rolled over on to her belly and looked earnestly at Dora. 'This ought to be in a magazine. Why don't you send it to one and they can print it?'

'I don't know if it's good enough,' Dora said.

'Well, I think it is,' Minnie said firmly, lying back down again. 'Go on – I want to find out what happens. Is she going to finish him off? I hope so – I want her to!'

Dora felt her heart start to pound on hearing this crumb of encouragement. She had kept writing and writing and she knew her dream was to come up with stories that people loved and wanted to read. But she did not know how any of that worked. And did she really think she could put her little stories out into the world and actually call herself a writer? In reality she was a washerwoman! Suddenly she loved Minnie with a passion for her words, for her faith in her.

With a smile tugging at her lips, she kept reading.

II

Fourteen

June 1863

'Ada – come away from there. You can't do any good like that.'

Gert, Ada's old friend and employee, tugged on Ada's arm as she stood, shoulders hunched, her nails digging into the sill of the cobwebby window of her pearl button workshop.

'You can't see out there anyway, it's that grimy.'

The window overlooked Galton Passage, the narrow alley running between high factory walls which linked Livery Street and Snow Hill. Opposite was the workshop of the Drake family and in the rooms above the Drakes' gem cutting business, Ada's sister Elsie was labouring to bring her first child into the world.

'Did you hear that?' Ada turned to Gert, frantic. 'That was her. I heard a scream. Oh Lord, I can't bear this.'

Gert, blonde, plump and already a mother of four herself, looked into Ada's anguished young face. At twenty-two years of age, after many struggles and now running her own company, Fletcher's Pearl Button Manufacturers, she still looked young as a girl and at this moment as scared and vulnerable as a girl could be.

'Don't you fret.' Gert pushed her arm firmly through Ada's to ease her further away from the window. 'Come on – come away.'

'Babbies always get themselves born one way or another – that's what my mam says.' Biddy, the youngest of Ada's workers, a waif who had just turned eleven, looked up earnestly at her with her young, old face. From a large Irish family, Biddy ought to know. Ada smiled faintly at her.

'Elsie'll be all right.' Margaret, a solid, sensible woman, looked up from her lathe. She was in her forties and like Gert, had children of her own.

These three were her old, loyal employees, had been ever since Ada had started the company. Even though Ada was self-contained and always tried to keep her feelings to herself, too much had happened over these few years. Gradually she had had to open up to these women who worked beside her day after day. They knew Ada well enough by now to understand the horror that haunted her – the death of her own mother in childbirth when Ada and Elsie were young children and the splitting up of their family.

And now it was Elsie, fighting to bring forth a young life herself.

Just as Gert managed to prise Ada away from her vigil at the window there came a shriek that none of them could deny and everyone froze for a moment.

'Oh my Lord.' Jess, another of the workers close in age to Ada, with buck-teeth and usually a joker, was stopped in her tracks.

'That was her . . . I've got to go to her.' Ada broke away from Gert and seemed to half-fly across the room to the stairs.

They heard her feet crashing down the wooden steps to the store room below and out into the yard.

'I've never seen her like that before,' Jess said. 'The poor thing.'

'You can understand it.' Margaret paused to twist her long brown hair, thick with the dust they spent their days grinding off the shells, back from her face. 'But there's nothing we can do. Let's get on.'

Ada, beside herself, tore out of the yard, down the entry and across Galton Passage. The thought of Elsie, her fragile, emotional little sister, going through what seemed to her the butchery of childbirth, was almost too much for her.

The Drakes' lapidary business and home were on the upper floors and Ada took the steps two at a time. As she started up the attic stairs she heard a sound which made her stop, gasping. A cracked, unearthly little cry. A baby. Lord God, the baby, it was here! . . . And Elsie . . .?

Though her legs felt as if they were full of water she staggered upstairs. And came upon a scene that made her burst into tears of relief and gratitude.

Mrs Mills, the calm, dignified lady who helped women birth their babies in the neighbourhood, stood beside Elsie, massaging her belly. Beside the bed, large and pink-faced on a chair, sat Matty Drake, Elsie's mother-in-law, in a joyful and vaporous condition. Her eyes were fixed on the little bundle in Elsie's arms.

And Elsie, looking as Ada had never seen her before, luminous as if with a special, heavenly light shining on her face, was gazing in adoration at the little scrap of life that had just broken out of her. Ada felt awed. Even with Elsie's scarred face, hair slicked damp to her head from the efforts of the birth and her clothing in disarray, she had never seen her little sister look so beautiful.

'You want to put her to the breast, Elsie,' Matty Drake instructed. ''Er's rootling.'

'It'll bring on the afterbirth,' Mrs Mills added, with the air of someone who had seen it all a thousand times before.

'Ada.' Elsie pushed herself up. 'Come and see. She's a little girl.'

Ada forced her legs to move and went up close. She leaned over and kissed Elsie, tears running down her face, emotional words pouring out of her.

'Oh, Else, darlin' – you've done it. You're all right. Are you all right? Oh, bless you – she's lovely – oh, my dear sister . . .'

'Victoria's her name,' Elsie said. 'After the Queen. And May, for Mom.'

Ada took in the sight of the tiny new person who had arrived, snuffling, her little mouth searching for the nipple with which Elsie quickly supplied her. This scrap with a royal name. She smiled, sinking on to the edge of the bed, suddenly quite exhausted. As the baby sucked, Elsie's face creased in pain.

'That's it,' Mrs Mills said, reaching under the sheet that covered Elsie's knees. 'That's a girl.'

A moment later the afterbirth arrived. Ada kept her eyes fixed on the baby, not wanting to know about the blood and gore.

'She's beautiful,' she said to Elsie, even though all she had seen was a scrap of flesh.

Elsie cradled the little one close as she sucked. 'She's family,' she said, her eyes filling suddenly. She looked up at Ada. 'New family. This is what our mom did – for us.' Her tears spilled over and she was raw with emotion. 'We were a family once, weren't we? We've got to find the others, Ada. Somehow we've got to find out where they've gone.'

'I need to clean her up a bit,' Mrs Mills interrupted. 'All's well, Miss Fletcher. Why don't you come back later on?'

Ada walked back across Galton Passage, along the entry and up the stairs. She kept going until she was in her rooms above the shop, closed the door and sank, weak with emotion, on the side of her bed.

She could hear the routine sounds from the shop below, the thump and whirr of the lathes, voices. For those moments the life of every day felt distant. She was thrown back into memory. Her family. This was the very bed where she and Elsie had nursed their dying father, only a year and a half ago. Richie Fletcher, the father she had dreamt of seeing again all her life since he disappeared when Ada was ten. The bitter disillusion he brought with him when he did resurface at last. And Mom – the final day of her life, labouring to bring forth the child of a man who had already deserted her, which resulted in both her death and the baby's. Elsie and the other three – Dora, John and baby Mabs – all dragged away, in the absence of any other family, by a Relieving Officer from the workhouse.

All of it came back now in a stream of horror and upset. Ada herself had been rescued by Sarah Connell, their neighbour, who pretended she was her daughter and prevented her being taken away as well.

She hardly ever dwelled on these memories. They were so filled with grief and most of the time she had many other things to think about, running the business, fighting to make a success of it, looking forward, not back.

But now it all washed through her and she curled on the bed and wept and wept, as quietly as she could, all her grief and joy and relief. And mingled in with it was her guilt that although she and Elsie had been reunited – and that by chance – her brother and other two sisters were out there somewhere and she still barely knew how to begin trying to find them.

As her sobs calmed she rolled on to her back and looked at the ceiling, wiping her eyes. Family, that web of blood connecting them all, had just enlarged with the birth of this little girl. Family was more than blood – she knew that. Tom Connell, who she had lived with for years and who now worked for her, felt more like a brother than the one she had lost. But still, blood counted. Memories – a few at least – and the parents who, once upon a time, they had shared.

She went back to see Elsie in the evening, finding her sitting up with the baby still clutched to her and George, her husband, a pale, brown-haired, kindly man, sitting by the bed, gazing at them both in absolute wonder.

'A girl,' George said, seeming lost in astonishment. 'I can't believe it.'

Ada had recovered herself now. 'How is Her Majesty?' she asked, beaming down at Elsie.

'Asleep.' Elsie leaned forward to show her the little crumpled face.

'Our Princess,' George said.

'The girls all send their love and say congrats,' Ada said. Everyone at the works had been so pleased and excited for them.

'Ta.' Elsie smiled.

'I'll leave you a minute,' George said, prising himself away from his wife's side. 'Our mom's made some soup – I'll bring you some, Else.'

Ada took his place on the chair for a moment.

'You all right, Elsie?'

She was sitting to Elsie's right, the side of her face scarred by acid, thrown by a vicious jealous woman. It was a relief when Elsie turned to face her and she could see the pretty side of her face which was alight with joy.

'I am,' she said. 'Sore underneath, of course – but I'm all right.'

'Jonas hasn't seen her yet?'

Jonas Parry, an older man who worked in the box company along the Passage, had become like a grandfather to them all, especially Elsie.

'Not yet.' Elsie smiled fondly. 'He would never come up here. Far too much of a gent.'

'You were right, what you said.' Ada spoke quickly, while they were alone. She didn't know why their family matters seemed like something they should only discuss between the two of them. It still all felt shameful, everything that had happened, even though none of it was their fault. 'We've got to find them – Dora and the others. Somehow.'

'She could be anywhere.' Elsie frowned, running a finger gently over baby Victoria's tiny nose. 'But our John – that woman in the workhouse said he was at a firm somewhere over Smethwick way.'

Ada gazed down at her new niece, feeling hopeless. She barely knew where Smethwick was and how many firms must there be? But she nodded slowly. That was all they had to go on. And it would have to do.

Fifteen

A few days later

The violent pain had woken Dora, her belly clenching tight as a drum.

She curled up, gasping, under the threadbare cover, the pain building until she could hardly keep from crying out. Then, just as she thought she could stand no more, it shrank back and faded away.

'Lord God, help me . . .' She sat up, panting, hands moving in terror over the mound of her belly.

This must be it. The thing she had tried to hide from herself, to believe it was not really ever going to be born, even when she could feel it moving inside her. This was what happened when a baby started coming.

The rusty bedsprings screeched as she swung her legs over the side. Even her own breathing sounded deafening to her. But Minnie in the bed beside her did not stir. Dora pushed her feet into her old shoes in the dark, then thrust her hand under the mattress, her fingers reaching for her most precious possession, the one thing that would give her comfort, before groping her way to the stairs.

As she passed Mrs Lacey's bedroom, Dora thought how lucky it was that her landlady was deaf as a post.

In the pitch dark, Dora felt her way downstairs to the one living room. It was a stifling night and you could almost touch the air, fetid with seeping stinks from the yard and heavy with damp from all the washing hanging there.

She lit a candle, the tiny light turning the room into a place of shrouds and drapes, all sweating out their moisture. To one side was the table, half-covered by Mrs Lacey's outwork. Above and around it, strings ran from wall to wall draped in laundry which also festooned the backs of the three rickety chairs and dangled from the mantle, weighed down by a clock, a Bible with damp, curving pages and an earthenware jug.

Without thinking, Dora automatically reached out and felt some of the items of clothing that she and Minnie had pounded and dollied the filth out of that day, in the brewhouse at the end of the yard. They were drying well. So much easier in summer . . . Then another pain seized her and she grabbed the edges of the table, leaning over it, unable to stifle her whimpers of distress.

As it passed, she sank down at the table with the notebook and stroked her hand over the lovely thing, the dark green leather, the curling patterns in gold. It was her charm, her comfort, precious to her as her own heart because *he* had given it to her.

As she had gazed at it that day, stroking the thick, creamy pages in wonder, he had planted a kiss on the side of her neck. 'You can tell all your stories in there.'

Thinking of it now, her fingers reached to touch the spot just beneath her hairline, remembering the press of his lips. Tears fell on the polished green leather as she was washed in the hurt and sorrow of it all.

'No,' she said out loud to herself and fiercely wiped her eyes. 'No. Stop it.'

She picked up her pencil, turned to a new page, smoothing it with her palm, and then, in the flickering candlelight, she started to write.

Gwendoline tripped across the grass in her silken slippers to the rose bower, where she concealed herself, in all her tragic woe, scalding tears dropping from her eyes to run in rivulets down the chalky pallor of her cheeks . . .

'Dora? Oh, my stars!'

Minnie appeared at the bottom of the stairs as Dora writhed and groaned.

'I'll go and fetch the lady—'

'No,' Dora managed to gasp. 'I don't want her – not yet.'

The notebook, with her grand unfolding story which had kept her mind occupied for some of the night, was now hidden in the drawer. The pain had become too much. Nothing would do to distract her.

'But I dunno what to do.' Minnie stood gaping, helpless and hopeless. 'Tell me what to do.'

'Chuck some slack on the fire . . . Put some water on,' Dora managed as another pain seized her. 'And get that cover off the bed. I want to lie down.'

Minnie did as she was ordered, but at the sight of Dora writhing on the floor on her hands and knees, she fled out of the door.

'The lady lives down Old Inkleys – I'm gunna fetch 'er!'

The sound of Minnie's footsteps faded as she ran out of the yard and in the silence Dora whispered, 'Help me, someone . . . Lord above – just help me.'

'There you are, wench – a bonny-looking little girl for you.'

Dora was shaking, her teeth chattering at the suddenness of it all. Hardly had Minnie arrived back with this lardy, snub-nosed person, than the stranger was holding up a bloody, yowling scrap of life between her legs. Dora lay back in shock, broken open. The woman, whose name she did not even know, was cutting something, tying it.

'Got summat to wrap her in?' She looked round with seeming contempt. 'Ain't you got anything ready? What, nothing at all? I hope you've got the money to pay me.'

In desperation Minnie grabbed one of the shirts hanging off the mantle.

'Here – use that.' She looked at Dora. 'We can wash it again after.'

'I hope you can get the blood out. Soak it in cold—'

'We know, ta,' Minnie said, a bit tart. They were washerwomen after all.

The woman shrugged and handed the new little person to Dora, wrapped tight in some man's yellowed shirt. In the dawn light filtering through the grimy window, Dora saw a sweet little face, the mouth working, needing.

'Put her to your tit – that's what 'er wants.'

Dora felt the questing little mouth fumble, then latch on. It was a shock, how determined she was. The baby's cap of damp hair was dark. Like his. Her eyes filled. The father this little girl would never know. The way she could barely remember her own father – even his name. Her mother's face was a ghostly image in her mind. But she could remember her, just.

Once it was all finished, their helper held out her hand and Minnie dropped coins into it before she left.

Minnie, seeming excited now, stoked the fire, made tea and handed Dora a cup, black and strong, as she sat with the baby sucking hard. It made her belly contract and she winced.

'So,' Minnie said, smiling, though her eyes were puffy with tiredness. 'What you gunna call her?'

Dora took a sip, then looked down at the tiny mite. All of a sudden the tears were pouring from her eyes. It was so rare for her, all this weeping. Normally she buried her feelings in her stories.

'She's mine,' she said, overcome. 'She's lovely – and she's my family.' She started to sob then. 'I had a family – I did. Before they put us in the workhouse . . . And now she's all I've got.'

Dora looked into her friend's sad face. Minnie didn't have to say anything. Family? The best thing she had been able to do was escape hers. Dora reached out and touched her hand.

'She can be your family too,' she said. 'We'll stick together us three, won't we?'

Minnie looked back at her and then down at the baby and she nodded.

'I'm gunna call her Rose,' Dora said. 'That's the prettiest name there is. And Elizabeth – I like that name too. Rose Elizabeth Lunn.'

As she spoke they heard the heavy thumps of Mrs Lacey relying on the aid of gravity to get down the stairs for the day.

'The night I can't get up to my own bed,' they heard broadcast from the staircase, 'is the day you can throw me in a coffin.'

The idea of being able to throw Mrs Lacey anywhere made the girls exchange a smile.

Their landlady arrived on the lower steps in the frowsty dress she wore day and night, her steel-grey hair fuzzy round her head, a snaky plait falling forward over one shoulder. She took in the scene with eyes still much sharper than her ears. Her mouth dropped open.

'You've gone and had the baby!' she announced, as if perhaps Dora hadn't noticed. 'Lord have mercy – what've I missed, being a bit hard of hearing!'

She plumped down the last two steps, eased herself into an upright position and came shuffling over, accompanied by her usual pungent odours of sweat and camphor.

Leaning down, she peered at the tiny child, busy with her first meal as a person in the world.

'Well, I'll be blowed.' As Dora looked up she saw the old lady's face soften with pleasure. 'Look at her. A little beauty.'

She patted Dora's shoulder in a way which brought tears to her eyes yet again. For a moment, as Dora sat looking at the miracle of her own little daughter, dear old childless Mrs Lacey felt almost like a mother.

Sixteen

'Come over and have your dinner with us, Ada.'

Elsie had popped over to visit and was standing in the doorway of Ada's rooms above the works with baby Vicky asleep in her arms. Although it was a Sunday morning with bells ringing out all across town, Ada was sitting at the table, a shawl round her shoulders, totting up the account books.

'Matty wants you to come – she's been at it all morning, making plum duff,' Elsie wheedled, in the face of her sister's stubborn expression.

Elsie's mother-in-law, plump, talkative countrywoman Matty Drake, was a legendary maker of puddings so filling that one could barely stand up after eating them.

Ada looked up at her sister with mixed feelings – some of which she was deeply ashamed of. Elsie, even in spite of the deep scarring to the side of her face inflicted by a jealous rival who had drenched her in vitriol, was looking pale and tired, but beautiful. The other side of her face was unscathed and as pretty as ever. And Elsie was safe and happy, married to George, with her new daughter and living just across the way at the heart of the Drake family.

Ada was truly delighted. She had spent so many years worrying about Elsie – about where she and the others had gone when they had left the workhouse, whether she would ever see any of them again. And when she found Elsie, her sister had seemed so emotional, unbalanced even, at times, that for a while she had worried for her sanity. Now, Elsie had what she needed: security, a loving husband in George and a family. She was blossoming. And it made Ada's heart sing with joy and relief. But . . .

Even so, Elsie was gone, to live another life. Before she married George the sisters had shared a bed, the two of them against the world, cuddled together on cold nights, building up their little business.

The only other person Ada lived with now was Tom Connell. Ada considered him a brother even though they shared no blood. Ada had been taken in by the Connell family after Elsie and the others were dragged away to the workhouse. When Ada finally moved on from the sad and chaotic Connell household, she had vowed to go back for Tom as soon as she could. At last, as they started up their pearl button business, she had been able to fetch him from his neglectful family to come and work for her. It was a comfort to have him still living here – especially now Elsie was gone.

But Tom was seventeen now. A man. And he spent most of his time with his girl, Dinah Matthews, and her mother and father and brothers. Even though they were not married it was as if he had found another family already as well.

Ada did not like herself for it, but she was jealous. Her nose put out of joint. She had been used to being the one always in charge, looking after them all and deciding how things were going to be. And now they didn't need her – either of them. Even before she had married George, Elsie had started to build new family in the shape of a kindly, eccentric old man, Jonas Parry, who also worked in Galton Passage and had become like a father to her.

Elsie seemed to have everything now. And even if what she had was not necessarily what Ada would have wanted for herself, she sometimes felt lost and put out. She dragged her head up to look at her sister.

'Not sure I can spare the time,' she said, trying not to sound disagreeable but not entirely succeeding. 'I've got a business to run.'

'Oh, Ade.' Elsie came over. 'Why're you working on a Sunday? That's not right – come on, we miss you.'

She bent over, presenting baby Vicky like a peace offering, and Ada could smell the warm, curdy scent of the pair of them. Little pink-cheeked Vicky snuffled, then sneezed in her sleep, and Ada couldn't help laughing.

'See, someone else wants to see you,' Elsie begged. 'We all want you to come, Ade.'

'All right.' Ada caved in. 'I'll be over in half an hour, all right?'

Ada had time to pull herself together and change into her dark blue Sunday dress – with no bustle or any fripperies. She had no time for such things and in her choice of attire she cut a plain, businesslike figure. Looking in the glass she brushed back her long hair, brown with touches of honey-blonde in it, and parted it in the middle. In her business life she dealt with men and she had no intention of being treated like a 'little woman' when she had always been the bread-winner of the household.

The sight of her austere reflection gave her a pang. She had always favoured her father, Richard Fletcher, with his slight build, the same hair colour and brown eyes. As she grew older and her face settled into finer lines, she could see him in herself all the more. Pa, her hero – the hero who had betrayed her so badly she could hardly ever bear to think of it.

Her face stared back at her and she forced her lips into a smile. That was better. Surely once upon a time she could have been called pretty? Or at least, nice-looking and lively. Now she looked . . . old. She had just turned twenty-two, heading for the age where she would sail past love or marriage. Not that she wanted any of that, she reminded herself. Not a man, commanding her life. Even so, getting past it, having no choice or possibility . . .

She stood looking for as long as she could bear to before turning abruptly away.

'Family,' she lectured herself. 'You've got a nice new family.'

But as she crossed Galton Passage, hearing a train getting up steam out of Snow Hill station close by, her conscience was heavy. She might have found a part of her family, but in all the busyness of life, she still had not done anything about trying to find their brother, John.

The Drakes lived above their business – as lapidaries, cutting and polishing beautiful gemstones – but today the workroom was shut up and Ada could hear the buzz of family life as she climbed the stairs. She walked into the usual fug and chatter of the Drake family, crowded together in their first-floor living room.

Everyone was there. The Drakes had four children and Elsie's husband, George, came second in the family. He was standing behind Elsie now, looking down adoringly over her shoulder at his new daughter, Victoria May Drake.

Next to Elsie on the settle sat George's elder sister, Nancy, with her own little boy on her lap, eleven-month-old Charlie, who was staring in blue-eyed fascination at little Vicky. Squeezed in beside Nancy was her husband, Walt.

The younger two Drakes – Ernie, a plump lad of sixteen and Lizzie, who was thirteen – were helping their mother. Edwin Drake, George's father, whom he closely resembled, was shovelling coal on to the fire. He was a mild, strategically quiet man in a household of chatterboxes.

''Ello, Ada!' Matty Drake, Elsie's mother-in-law, greeted

her, foghorn loud, from her post by the cookpots on the fire. Matty wore her hair in coiled braids over each ear and her round face was pink, her forehead dewed with perspiration. She beamed fondly. 'Fancy seeing you!'

Ada forced a smile, though she could hear the slight reproach in Matty's tone.

'Thanks for inviting me, Mrs Drake,' she said.

But inside she was shrinking with the small, jealous feelings that she did not want to own. There were Elsie and lovely, blue-eyed, blonde-haired Nancy sitting with their little ones, sisters-in-law now, canting away together. And Nancy was supposed to be *her* friend – the first real friend Ada felt she had ever had. She had loved getting to know Nancy, popping round the corner to her and Walt's rooms to sit and chat. Being of some comfort to her when their first little boy, Billy, had died of a fever.

Now though, it felt as if she was being pushed out. The spinster older sister, the business-britches who had no time for love or children.

'Ada!' Nancy caught sight of her and beckoned her over happily. 'Come on, Walt, shove off and let Ada sit down. Here yer go – sit here with us!'

Ada obeyed, warmed, her feelings softening. Nancy *did* want to be her friend. It was just that now, she and Elsie had so much more in common. She squeezed in next to Nancy who bumped shoulders with her fondly.

'Elsie was telling me you've got a new lot of business,' Nancy said.

Ada nodded, her insecure mood vanishing. 'William Nichols. Their shop's along from you – other end of Edmund Street.'

Up until recently all her business – delivering the first stages of production of mother-of-pearl buttons – had gone to a bigger firm called Beardsmore's. Their works at the other end of Galton Passage would carry out the final processes to create the finished items. Ada wanted to build up her business so that they could do all of it from start to finish. In the meantime, though, they were to start supplying this other, smaller firm.

'Nichols?' Nancy's brow furrowed. 'No, I don't know them.'

'It's good work for us,' Elsie said. 'I'm going in again soon.'

Nancy smiled. 'Vicky'll be a pearly babe, all right. She going with you?'

'Just while I'm feeding her,' Elsie said. 'I'm ready for it – I miss the girls, Gert and Jess and the others. I can bring her with me to start with and then George's mom'll have her.'

'Oh yes, I will,' Matty said, coming up and bending over the two children. 'These two little terrors.'

'I'm gunna look after her some of the time.' Thirteen-year-old Lizzie came over and swooped down on Vicky, kissing her cheek.

Ada could see that Elsie's mother-in-law and young Lizzie could hardly wait to get their hands on the child – something she found utterly baffling. Had Matty not had enough, bringing up four of her own? Well, she told herself, we're all different – although, she thought bitterly, she seemed to be the one who was different, and no one else.

'Right,' Matty commanded, patting her puce cheeks with a rag. 'Get round the table, all of yer.'

It was always enjoyable being in the Drakes' crowded room, Ada had to admit. And she could see it was doing Elsie the power of good to be part of a family, with new brothers and sisters, Ernie slouching about and Lizzie's chatter. She was a bright spark, young Lizzie, Ada thought, chewing a mouthful of beef and watching the girl across the table as she tweaked baby Charlie's nose and burst into giggles when he chuckled at her. Lizzie was fair like Nancy, less beautiful but with a homely, cheeky face that was on the brink of shaping itself into that of a woman. Ada would have liked Lizzie to come and work for her, but she could hardly drag her across the Passage from the Drakes' business.

All the Drakes were pleasant – Edwin the father quiet and wryly patient, Matty bustling about, and the four children. Elsie could not have married better, she thought.

But all through the happy meal – the groans of pleasure as Matty paraded the enormous plum duff pudding to the table, its suet sides dotted with juicy fruits, and Ada joined in the cheers – she ached inside.

Because somewhere – who knew where? – she and Elsie had a brother and sisters, the remnant of their own, broken, once happy family. Or so it had seemed to her then. Before Pa took off to heaven knew where and Mom died in a pool of blood, birthing his final child. Before, when all had been good...

And in all this time she had still got no further with finding the others – Dora and John and baby Mabs. Not a baby now. She realized with a jolt of shock that Mabs was almost the same age as Lizzie Drake. A child on the verge of becoming a woman.

Now was the time, she thought helplessly. Somehow, they had to find a way to begin.

Seventeen

'I'll go, if you want,' Tom said.

He and Ada were sitting at the table that same night, Ada sleepy and half-immobilized by the weight of Matty's dinner, and Tom happy after a day with Dinah and her family. He had come through the door whistling, then laughed when he caught site of Ada prostrate on the chair.

'Plum duff,' she explained.

Still grinning, Tom came and sat opposite her.

'Dinah all right – and the family?'

'Yeah,' Tom said. 'They're all right.'

Tom was not generally a mine of information about anything so Ada didn't ask any more. It was still warm enough to have the window open a crack and the usual foul stenches drifted in from the boneyard of the glue factory at the back, but they were so used to it now that it took an especially hot day and prevailing breeze for them even to comment.

They spoke for a while about this and that but it was not long before Ada found herself talking to Tom about what, this evening, was most on her mind.

'I keep telling Elsie I'll go and see if I can find them,' she said, turning her finger round and round on the brass lid of the inkwell beside her on the table, so that she did not have to look Tom in the face. She had lived through so many years of the Connells, Tom's troubled family, but now her own family's past felt just as shameful. 'But I don't know how to begin – and I've got so much else to do.'

She could feel tears coming and quickly looked down, swallowing hard. She felt so alone when she allowed herself to think about it, even though she was surrounded by people. As if lonely in her very soul. When she was calmer and her eyes met his again, Tom was watching her, his face full of concern. Tom had been a wild lad at times but now she was moved to see that he was growing up, starting to have an eye for what others might need. And that was when he made his offer.

'You let me off early one afternoon, and I'll go over there, see what I can do?'

'Would you, Tom?' Ada sat up straighter, brightening. It never occurred to her that she could get help from anyone. She looked up at her 'brother' with his waves of dark hair and swarthy, handsome face and felt a surge of love for him.

'Course. You've done a lot for me, Ada. I'd like to help, if I can. I can ask around, see what I can find out. John, isn't it?'

Ada nodded. 'I suppose he might call himself John Lunn – Elsie said they all seemed to end up with that name. I don't think that was normal – someone made a mistake somewhere.'

'John Lunn.' Tom seemed to record the name carefully to himself. 'All right, Ada – let me go over there and see.'

Ada began her week with the relief she sometimes felt that the weekend was over. Much as she needed to rest, she was often not sure what to do with her Sunday. Time to herself or spent being sociable with others was still strange to her and she felt more comfortable being back in harness at the works.

She strode into the shop that Monday morning, into the haze of white dust which accompanied their work.

Everyone was hard at it. Tom was greasing his saw with mutton fat before he set to again, cutting sections of the shells into flat pieces. He was also responsible for collecting up the sections of shell not fine enough for buttons – they sent them to a firm in Sheffield for making into cutlery handles.

The women were bent over their treadle lathes, cutting and facing the blanks, backing and edging them, all the processes they carried out before the final stages of drilling and polishing the buttons which, Ada was sure, they would also be able to do very soon, once she could purchase the new machines.

'Right,' she told Gert and Margaret, the two women she considered her senior workers. 'I'm just going to check that delivery in and then I'll get over to Nichols's place and find out what exactly he wants. Shouldn't take too long.'

'All right, Ada,' Gert said, bending her matronly body over the lathe again.

Margaret nodded. 'All right – we'll keep an eye.'

'W. Nichols Pearl Button Makers' read the brass plate by the door.

Ada was surprised when she reached the place. She had imagined it would be a more imposing works, but it was no bigger than her own business. She frowned as she climbed the stairs, which like their own glimmered with minute fragments of shell. Why did Nichols need them to supply half-made buttons when they surely had been doing the manufacturing themselves?

When she walked into the shop her puzzlement deepened. At the far end, three women stood working, boxes of blanks beside them at what stage of finishing Ada could not make out from where she was standing. But the machines closest to her were all empty. No one was there working at the first stages of producing the buttons. What on earth could be going on?

One of the women came over to her, thin, ginger-headed and disgruntled-looking.

'You looking for Mr Nichols?' she said with a jerk of her head. "E'll be down in the yard if 'e's not in the house.'

'Thanks,' Ada said. She hesitated for a moment, tempted to ask questions, but she didn't like the look of the woman and also felt that it would not be good to pry. Whatever she needed to know, she could ask Nichols in person.

But the redhead saw her glancing about and threw words over her shoulder as she went back to work. 'All gone, the others. They'd had enough. And if he don't get sorted out soon we'll be off as well.'

The lathes had gone quiet and Ada felt the women watching her as she went back to the staircase.

Stepping into the back yard, she immediately saw a man in the doorway opposite. He had paused, adjusting his cap and seeming lost in his own thoughts. He was a slender, bearded, dark-eyed man, she guessed midway between thirty and forty, and in his serious expression she saw a weight of sadness so great that she almost retreated back inside so as not to intrude. The feel of it came from him almost like a smell.

But her slight movement caught the man's eye and he came to himself and strode over to her.

'Morning,' he said, his dark eyes looking uncertain. 'Can I help you?'

'I'm Ada Fletcher,' she said, holding out a hand. 'I hear you want work for finishing?'

'Oh – I spoke to your lad?' He seemed startled to find he was talking to a woman.

'That would be Tom Connell, one of my workers,' she

said, pulling her shoulders back as she instinctively did when any man showed a hint of talking down to her.

William Nichols looked at her for a moment as if taking all this in, then his thoughts seemed to wander, as if he'd shrunk back into himself. This man, Ada recognized, was not in a good state.

'We send most of our work to Beardsmore's,' she said. He would know the works, on the corner of Galton Passage and Snow Hill – it was one of the biggest amid a great many tiny shops. 'But since you asked, we can likely supply what you need.' If we crack on, she thought to herself. It would be a stretch but she was sure they could do it.

'Right,' William Nichols said, seeming to snap back to attention. 'Finishing's all we're doing at the moment, so that would be . . .' He seemed to drift off.

'But your shop's tooled up to do all of it?' Ada pushed him. 'Some of your workers're not happy.'

'Oh, Vi's been talking to you, has she?' William Nichols gave a sharp sigh. 'We were doing all of it. But it's true, I've let things slide.' He looked into her eyes then and his own seemed almost to contort with pain. 'My wife is sick – has been for a while now. I haven't been able to keep the work coming in. When I couldn't pay the wages they started leaving for other shops. Can't blame them really. I'm trying to get things picked up now . . . At least keep one end of it all going.'

Ada actually thought he was about to weep. And there was something fine and heartbreaking about him which moved her unexpectedly. But at the same time she couldn't help thinking, fancy letting his business sink into this state!

'I'm sorry to hear that,' she said and was continuing, 'Fletcher's should be able to supply you—' when a muffled cry came from inside the house. The sound chilled her. It was the cry of a woman in agony and Ada saw that this immediately seized William Nichols's full attention.

'Is there anyone with her?' she asked gently.

'Her sister . . .' He answered her vaguely, still listening, then turned that anguished gaze on her again. 'They say it can't be long now.'

Ada nodded, still shaken by that haunting sound.

'You will be paid,' he said, suddenly becoming a man of business again, as if he had sensed her misgivings. 'Have no fear.'

Ada walked back to Galton Passage, the feel of William Nichols's surprisingly strong handshake like an imprint on her hand. She found herself feeling stirred up, out of sorts in some way she could not make sense of. When a voice shrilled at her on a street corner, she actually jumped.

'Spare us a farthing, missus?' Her heart pounding, she found herself looking at a skinny, barefoot boy and she was brought back as if from another world.

'Here.' Ada reached into her pocket, dropped a halfpenny into the boy's grubby hand and he ran off.

As she walked on, her mind started to play over the visit again – the man emerging into the yard, that face, a rather beautiful face so dragged down by sadness that she felt her own innards respond with a pang of grief.

Whatever had come over her? But her mind kept working on William Nichols's problems, the way his business had sunk and dwindled almost to nothing. She made herself do sums in her head – how much she would charge for their half-made buttons, how many they could manage to produce? They were going to have to work fast to add this to the orders they already had.

Pulling her shoulders back she strode into Galton Passage, ticking herself off. Pounds, shillings and pence – income for her own firm, that was what she needed to be thinking about. Not mooning over the plight of some poor man she scarcely knew.

But as she climbed the stairs up to the shop, William Nichols's expression, his sad eyes, floated through her mind again.

'For goodness' sake,' she muttered, and before going in to face her workers, she gave herself a good shake.

Eighteen

'Is this the way to Smethwick?'

Tom would have preferred to ask the way of a man but there seemed none around. The women who approached along this busy highway of clattering hooves and creaking wagons looked strange and most intimidating. He took courage and asked a burly matron in a man's coat and felt hat, who was driving a string of donkeys, great bundles loaded on to them from which poked the ends of thin iron rods.

'Ar.' The woman, leathery-skinned and buck-toothed, pulled her hat further back on her head and gave this young, muscular fellow a slow, blatant, head-to-toe examination. Even though she appeared old enough to be his mother, he could tell she was a big-breasted wench under the linsey-woolsey jacket she wore, and the look in her eyes – despite him thinking himself a man of the world – brought flames to his cheeks. Without adding any further instruction she goaded the donkeys on with ripe curses that deepened Tom's blushes even more.

Tom took his cap off and wiped his sleeve along his forehead. He had walked for an hour and a half in daylight gloomy as twilight and his face was rough with grit. Two hours' walk, Jonas Parry had predicted, but he was not sure of being anywhere close to the right place.

'Wait!' He trotted after her. This time the woman did not stop moving.

'I've been sent to look for someone. Works at one of the

firms over here.' This had seemed straightforward when he started out but now, out in this wider world, he was bewildered and had no idea how to begin.

She said something in reply but he could not make it out. 'What's that?'

She seemed to be asking what work the person did.

'I dunno.' He felt foolish. 'He would've gone young, apprenticed, like.'

She reeled off various sentences which he found impossible to decipher except that mingled with her strange words were what seemed to be the names of firms. 'The Foundry at Soho . . . Fox, Henderson—' She stopped suddenly. 'Start with a big'un.' Tom almost cheered. He understood!

'Chance, the glass-makers on Spon Lane.'

Feeling more purposeful, Tom hurried on. He was enjoying himself, being out of the shop, out of town and walking fast in the open air. Heading west this morning he had left Birmingham behind and passed through snatches of countryside, feeling suddenly happy and heroic. He was a man, striding across the country, powered by his strong muscles and full of energy. And now he was going to do something for Ada that she could not easily do for herself. She could be acid-tongued at times, old Adie, and so often over the years he had kicked back against her bossing. But he owed her, he knew that. Loved her even, if he was honest, like a big sister – almost a mom, even though she was only five years older.

But the walk had been a shock. The thick pall of smoke which loomed over Birmingham did not abate as he headed west. To the smoke was added a hellish red glow from the countless iron foundries across the region. Chimneys pumped smoke; the land was blackened so that even the remains of what had once been nature was dusted with coal and filth. Occasionally there came the hint of a fresh breeze, but soon it would be tainted by some ashy or chemical smell. It was a dark, despoiled land, scatterings of little towns and villages each carrying out their own manufacture. It felt broken, with no centre that he could identify, and it made him homesick for the familiarity of the tall buildings at Birmingham's solid core.

When he finally made his way, after several enquiries, to the Chance works, his confidence drained away further. Lord above, from what he could see it was a giant of a place – more like a small town! Wherever should he begin?

'Shh, hark at that – is that him?'

Ada held up her hand. It was late – well gone ten and Tom had still not come back. She and Elsie sat waiting. Elsie had got little Vicky down to sleep and come across to her old home to wait with Ada. They were both on pins, jumping at every sound which might signal Tom's arrival.

Finally they heard footsteps in the yard. Ada's heart rate took off and Elsie leapt up to open the door.

'Tom?' she called as they heard the weary tread of his boots on the stairs.

'Yeah,' came from below.

Ada got to her feet and the sisters stood side by side, clutching for each other's hands like children lost in a storm.

Tom appeared in the doorway and Ada's eyes hungrily scoured his face but he just looked tired, his expression not giving her any news of anything.

'Well, did you find him?' Elsie burst out.

'Yeah,' Tom said again, throwing himself into a chair.

'Don't just say "yeah" – *tell* us!' Elsie urged.

'I will but I'm starved,' Tom said irritably.

Ada scurried to the fire and set his dinner in front of him, mutton chops and potatoes. After downing a few mouthfuls – while the sisters, in desperate suspense, had no choice but to watch the powerful muscles in his cheeks working – the barometer of Tom's mood gradually steered itself to fairer weather.

'He's at Chance the glass-makers,' he said through the remains of a mouthful. 'I saw him. Queer cove he is – he was going to a lecture.'

'A lecture?' Ada repeated stupidly, trying to picture the young man that her tiny, fearful brother could have turned into. 'How d'you mean?'

'Seems they have them – at Chance and Co. And school and that. Anyway, took me a while to find him – it's a great spread of a place. But when they was all coming off shift, I asked around and another young feller said, "Oh ar, I know John Lunn – he's a taker-in for Enoch Smith. He'll be over at the school—"'

'So?' Elsie said. Ada could see her clenching her hands together as if to stop herself going and shaking Tom.

'So I went. He was there. Serious-looking feller, strong, like, light-coloured hair—'

'Well, what did he *say*?' Ada interrupted. God, it was like getting blood out of a stone.

Tom undertook a large mouthful of potato and had to complete at least half the task of chewing it before he could answer, by which time Ada was ready to throttle him.

'So I said, "Are you John Lunn?" And he said, "Yes, I am."'

Ada and Elsie gawped at this revelation.

'And I said, "I've been sent over by your sister, Ada – and her other sister, Elsie. They've been looking to find you, like—"'

'*And?*' Elsie half-shrieked.

'He dain't say much, to be honest. Just looked a bit sort of surprised and said he had to go because the lecture was starting. So I said, "Don't you want to hear from your sisters then? I work for your big sister, Ada – she wants to see you." So he said, "Tell her she can write to me." And he went into a room and wrote down where he stops and he come back and give it me.'

Tom reached in his pocket and handed Ada a scrap of paper: 'John Lunn', followed by an address written in a careful hand.

'It don't 'alf hum round there,' Tom remarked. 'The whole place is a dump – stinks of pigs.'

Ada's spirits were sinking almost as if someone had physically punched her. Did their brother not want to know them? Surely he would at least want to see Elsie who had been in the workhouse with him?

Elsie peered over her shoulder at the scrap of paper. She touched Ada's arm, sensing the desolation that was moving through her like frost.

'Let's write,' she said. 'He never was quick on the uptake, our John, and it's been a good while.'

Ada looked at her, grateful for this reassurance. Elsie was the one who had seen John at least until he was ten or eleven. Ada could only remember a sweet, timid four-year-old.

'Give him a chance for it to sink in,' Elsie said.

Ada nodded, although her throat was aching with unshed tears again. What was happening to her? She did not cry easily and this was twice in as many days!

'He did seem a bit bowled over,' Tom said. With a full belly now he became considerate. 'I don't s'pose he means anything by it, Adie. He just weren't expecting it.'

Ada finally sank into a chair again, suddenly exhausted. 'I s'pose so,' she said.

'And I s'pose he feels we left him – all of us,' Elsie said. Then she smiled suddenly and went and sat on the chair beside Ada. 'But you found him, Tom! Thanks – it was good of you to go.'

'Yes,' Ada said. 'Ta, Tom.'

'It was good – I liked it,' Tom said, picking his teeth with a splinter of kindling. 'See a bit of life outside. It's grim over there though, I can tell you.'

'So – we'd best write to him,' Ada said to Elsie. 'Tell 'im a bit about ourselves, what's happened.'

Elsie nodded, gently rubbing at the corner of her injured eye which often became dry as the day went by.

'Little John,' she said. And her eyes filled with sudden tears so that the rubbing became unnecessary. 'That's three of us in touch, anyway. We could go and see him, couldn't we?'

'If he wants to see us,' Ada said sadly.

'Course he does.' Elsie touched her hand. 'Don't fret, Ade – he'll come round.'

Nineteen

'Morning!'

Ada swept into the shop the next morning, raising her voice over the whirr and thump of the lathes and Tom's sawing.

'Right – we've got another order to supply to a firm called Nichols, as well as Beardsmore's and the others.'

She saw Gert and Margaret exchange looks. *We're going to have our work cut out*, the glance said.

'They don't want much – not to begin with. The company's not doing too well and they're trying to get back to strength. Tom, you can go round with a few boxes later, get them started and we'll see, all right?'

She looked round for a moment at the faces turned to her, suddenly full of gratitude. There was Gert, matronly mother of four now who Ada had known since she herself had started work as a child. Margaret, strong, hard-working and quiet except when she really had something to say, had also become someone Ada knew she could rely on.

There was Jess, round-faced, buck-toothed and a bit of a joker, still only just in her twenties. Jess had started in a button shop as a child, like Ada, and knew the work in her sleep. And there was little Biddy, now eleven, a pale, sweet-faced child who was already a dab hand at cutting blanks from the sawn sections of shell.

These women had seen Ada at her most distraught when she and Elsie had nursed their father in his last days.

And for once in her life Ada had shared her emotions – something she found it very hard to do. They had been kind, rallied round and she felt a deep trust in them all – even Biddy who was an old soul.

She smiled suddenly.

'All right – let's get on then, eh?'

But as she turned away she knew she could not share what lay heaviest on her heart today. Any tender concern that had been awoken in her for the heartbroken William Nichols had been pushed aside by the momentous event of yesterday. Tom had found her brother. She had a brother, John Lunn as he was known – at least they had not robbed him of his first name.

John Lunn, now sixteen years old and of her blood, existed in the world and now they knew where. And she was going to write to him. The thought made her both joyful and nervous. Where did she begin? And did John in fact want to know them?

'Dear John,' she wrote later. It was hard labour – she had done so little writing in her life and her big, looping copperplate from the distant days when she had gone to school had barely developed since.

'Dear John . . .' She ground to a halt and looked out of the upstairs window facing the yard, but seeing nothing.

'I'll write,' she had said to Elsie. 'You've got enough on your plate.'

But now, how to greet a young brother she could only just remember? A lad who had not seemed all that enthusiastic at the news of his long-lost family?

So many years have passed, John, and I don't know if you will even remember me, Ada, your big sister. They didn't take me to Dudley Road with the rest of you.

> *But I remember you, a little boy with fair hair, standing at our mother's knee . . .*

Overwhelmed she pushed the paper away, sank her head on the table and wept. The memories rushed in, their mother, her laughing eyes when Pa said something mischievous to her, herself and Elsie as playmates, the other three: copper-haired, dreamy Dora, John always wide-eyed and anxious-looking and baby Mabs with her huge brown eyes and black curls. Her greatest joy then had been making Mabs laugh, that gurgling chuckle and her face creasing up. But the last time she had seen Mabs she was barely a year old. And she had been adopted out of the workhouse not long after that.

The agony of it all, Pa disappearing, that day when they came home to find the house full of the blood and pain of a terrible childbirth and never saw their mother alive again – all of it swamped her and it was a long time before she could compose herself enough to get back to the letter:

> *It must be a shock you hearing from us out of the blue. I hope you have a good life and that we can all meet each other again and be a family. You are a Fletcher, like Elsie and me. Well, Elsie's married so she's a Drake – but Fletcher was our name, not Lunn. We've got our own company, Fletchers' Pearl Button Makers. We're doing all right.*
>
> *Please write back, John and tell us when we can meet. Elsie and me will be so happy to see you.*
> *From your sister,*
> *Ada*

*

Wrist still aching from clutching the pen, she went out to buy a stamped envelope, then slipped her letter into the pillar box along the street.

'Please,' she found herself whispering as she dropped it into the slot. '*Please.*'

Tom came back that evening after delivering the half-made buttons to Nichols's works for finishing as required.

'That's a rum business,' he said as he and Ada sat at the table. 'One of the women said half the workers've already left and they're only hanging on out of kindness – and because he seems to have got a move on a bit more lately and they've a wage coming in.'

'Did you see Nichols?' Ada asked, spooning out mutton stew. She found herself keen to have information.

Tom shook his head, shovelling down his tea at an alarming rate. 'One of the women came out when I was unloading,' he said once he could speak. 'Redhead . . .'

'Oh, that was the one I saw, I think,' Ada said. 'Bony woman?'

'Yeah. Any road, 'er told me that Nichols has been in a state for months. Kept forgetting to put in orders so there was no work. The first couple of times they put up with it and then they started leaving, one by one. Course, now even if they had supplies they've got no one to do the work so they're getting by on finishing.'

Ada nodded, sitting down. 'His wife's very ill, I believe.' For some reason she found she did not want to share with Tom that she had met William Nichols.

Tom nodded. 'So she said. But if 'e goes on like this 'e won't have a business.' He pushed his chair back. 'Going to see Dinah – ta-ra.'

Ada sat eating slowly long after the sound of Tom crashing down the stairs had died away. For a while her head was full of the usual calculations about the business and the things she wanted to do. With the extra bit of income from Nichols added to her savings they could get a drilling machine and next she'd look at another backing lathe so they could make buttons with a self-shank – the lathe would make a 'top hat' at the back that could be drilled through sideways and you would sew through there, not see holes on the top side of the button. Then there would be all sorts of extra styles they could produce.

But for once her mind wandered from all this and she found herself thinking about William Nichols again. About the sadness in those dark eyes, the anguish written all over his face, and once again she felt a pang. He was suffering so much, this man, and it had unsettled her. For a moment she imagined putting her arms around him, giving comfort . . .

'For heaven's *sake*.' She got up, shoving her chair back.

With brisk, almost angry movements, she filled the kettle to boil for the washing-up and put it over the fire with more of a slam than usual.

'Mooning over a man you don't even know,' she muttered. 'What the hell's got into you?'

Days passed. The business of having the lathe delivered and set up in the shop, settling in the new woman, Peggy, a few years older than Gert, who had heard that Fletchers' was a good place to work, occupied most of Ada's mind.

But as each day went by and there was no letter from John, her spirits sank. Would John not have been delighted, excited to hear from his long-lost family? Did their infancy, the tie of blood that they shared, mean nothing to him? Surely the lad could write a letter if he was going to school, let alone to such a grand thing as a 'lecture'! Or if not, get someone else to reply on his behalf?

She did not say anything to Elsie until a week had gone by. Elsie was tired, constantly fretting about Vicky. She's too hot! Is she warm enough? Was there enough fresh air coming into the bedchamber where Vicky slept with herself and George? Ada was not sure if she even remembered about John.

But eventually she went over to the Drakes late one afternoon, once again walking in to find Elsie ensconced with all the family, which made Ada feel like an outsider.

'Hello, Ade!' Elsie said, transferring her smile from Vicky, who she had been beaming down at, to her sister, so that even the greeting felt somehow second-hand.

Don't be such a fool, Ada ticked herself off inwardly. And she immediately felt better when Elsie said eagerly, 'Was there a letter from John?'

For a split second Ada clammed up, washed in her old shame about confiding family business in front of outsiders. But she knew they were long past that – after the disgraceful experience of her and Elsie's father reappearing after all those missing years, and the Drake family being so kind, she had nothing to worry about. After all, they *were* all family now.

She shook her head, raw emotions surfacing again.

'Not a word,' she said, sitting on the settle beside Elsie. Only now she realized how much she had been waiting every day for a letter. And how bitterly disappointing it was that John stayed silent.

Elsie looked at her, her face falling. 'He's had days,' she said.

'I'm going over there,' Ada announced, taking even herself by surprise. 'Now we know where he lives. I'll go Sunday. Early.'

Twenty

By the time Ada heard a church clock striking eight on Sunday morning, she was already making her way towards the little streets close to the great Chance & Co. works. She had been unable to sleep and in the end, left home before six.

The Birmingham streets had been still dark and shrouded in mist. As she walked towards the edge of town and further into the Black Country, the autumn glow of leaves which she could make out in the dawn's smoky light faded, the life in them extinguished by layers of smut and filth, or withered by whatever foul effluents poisoned the air. Everywhere she could see the digging for iron ore and delving for shallow yields of coal, or the gaunt shapes of winding mills where the digging reached for deeper seams.

These small, scattered towns of the Black Country were less hemmed in than the one giant, sprawling town of Birmingham, but somehow the more dismal for giving hints of a once green countryside, now scarred and choked by the black claws of extraction and industry.

She saw, as Tom had given hint of, the devastation of the countryside, the chimneys and winding mills, broken walls and wooden structures and the black, wasted land. But finally, she was in the town proper and standing in front of a row of cottages, behind the door of one of which, apparently, she might find her brother.

All the energy which had driven her two-hour stride to this row of little houses in a narrow, mucky street, seemed to desert her. Ada flagged, her legs feeling weak and trembly. For a moment she leaned against the soot-clogged bricks next to the door, trying to pull herself together.

Of all the things she had longed and wished for all these years, finding her brother and sisters had been the keenest. But now she was so afraid. Why had John not written to them? Didn't he want to know his family? Even before knocking, before setting eyes on him, she felt hurt, as if she needed to protect herself. She hesitated on the dreary step: at this moment what she most dearly wanted was to turn and hurry home. To forget the past, her once happy little family, and all the painful things that this visit drove into her mind again like a runaway flock of sheep.

From behind the door she caught sounds, a hum of family life. The household of Enoch Smith, whoever he was. Frightened someone would come out and catch her unawares, she made herself rap on the wood.

She heard a voice say something, coming nearer.

As the door opened, Ada became aware of a number of pairs of eyes behind the woman who opened up, all watching from the gloom of the narrow hall. A small, compact woman was looking at her, a frizz of dark brown hair on her forehead, the rest of it drawn back under a mob cap. Her face, though plain, wore an amiable expression.

'I'm Ada,' she announced, faintly. 'John . . . Lunn's sister.'

As the woman started speaking Ada panicked, already struggling to understand her. Tom had said it was like a foreign country over here. But she could make it out.

'Our John's sister?' the woman repeated. She stared, seeming dazed, then stood back as if asking questions was probably a waste of time. 'Come in – shut the door, will yer?'

The woman walked off, shooing her children away. Ada closed the door and followed along the narrow hall into the simple back room of the house. The first thing she took in was that she was surrounded by girls. Everywhere she looked, another one seemed to appear. Girls of all sizes.

And then she saw the males of the house. At the table sat a burly man with thick, dark eyebrows and a salt-and-pepper beard; beside him, a lad who was staring at her, seeming unable either to move or speak.

'It's your sister, John,' the woman said. 'Come to see yer.'

The room went absolutely silent. All those eyes fastened on Ada, who in her turn felt rooted to the spot as she and John took each other in. She saw straight away that it was him by the eyes, clear and grey, eyes so like their mother's and of the little boy she remembered, gazing at her now from this strong-looking lad's face. His hair was blonde, darkening to brown. He looked neither pleased nor displeased; just stunned. Neither of them knew what to do.

The older man got to his feet and to Ada's relief held out a hand.

'Enoch Smith,' he said in a deep, rumbling voice. 'This 'ere's John Lunn.'

'Yes,' Ada said. 'I'm Ada. Fletcher.' She looked at her brother. 'That's your name. It was the workhouse called you all Lunn.'

John licked his lips and at last said, 'Ada.' He looked as if his mind was whirling and he could find no more words.

''Arriet,' Enoch Smith said, nodding towards the fire.

In the shorthand of long married couples, his wife took his meaning and brought Ada a cup of stewed-looking tea, pulling out a chair for her.

'Yow'll've bin all round the Wrekin to get 'ere,' she said, after which her husband added something even more incomprehensible.

Suddenly, at the sight of his sister's bewildered expression, John's face creased and he started laughing. The crowd of girls which had been drawing gradually closer, all enjoying this novelty, set off laughing as well. The youngest, barely able to walk, pulled herself up on Ada's skirt and held herself steady, staring open-mouthed at her.

''Er's from Brummagem,' John translated. ''Er cosn't understond yow.' Then to Ada he added, 'I've been here a few years now – I couldn't make 'em out when I fust come neither.'

Mrs Smith fortunately seemed amused as well and Ada smiled back at her.

She urged Ada to drink up her tea, adding, apparently, a suggestion that when she had done so, she and John might like to go out for a bit of a walk together.

Soon after, once they had set off along the mean street lined with little cottages and frequently punctuated by pubs, John turned into a chatterbox so extreme that for the next hour Ada could barely get a word in edgeways.

'I'll show you Chance and Co. – that's where I work. Mr Smith took me in to work for him. I'm a taker-in – he's my chair. I fetch and carry for him. I'm gunna be a chair one day.' He announced all this with great pride. 'This is Spon Lane . . .' He waved an arm as they turned along a street with solid factory buildings extending all along one side as far as Ada could see.

'Tom told me it was very big,' she said.

'Tom? The one came to the school?' John said. 'Who's he?'

'He works for me,' she said quickly. Not adding, he's like a brother to me.

John turned into the works leading Ada in a tour. Building after building, chimneys sprouting from among them, and many tall, strange, cone-shaped things John told her were the glass furnaces, the railway and the cut running through – all accompanied by John's endless talking.

When they reached the school, solid brick buildings which Ada had to acknowledge were very fine, he stood back and gazed at them as if to do homage.

'I go to all the classes I can here,' he said. 'And lectures. There's Frenchmen working here and I pick up bits of French – and there's a reading room with newspapers. The children go to school . . . We work hard here – very,' he said with feeling. 'Some days I fall down to sleep as soon as I get home. But they treat you well—'

'So,' Ada attempted to interrupt. 'The Smiths seem very nice – how many daughters are there?'

'Oh – eight of 'em,' John said, off-handedly, before launching into another lecture about Chance & Co., about the glass . . . Ada gave little glances at her brother's face as he held forth. He was already taller than she was by an inch or two and watching his exalted expression it felt as if she was with someone who had experienced a religious conversion.

'It's our glass in all the windows of the Houses of Parliament, down London,' he boasted. 'And we made the glass for the clock face – called Opal Glass that is . . . We don't make just one type of glass, you know . . .'

As he talked and talked, Ada felt herself shrinking inside. His gabbling felt designed to shut her out, as if she was some stranger to be shown round, nothing more. It grieved her, was bringing her close to tears. Not one question had he asked her about herself, how she was, what her life had been. Nor the others – Elsie. Did he not want to know?

'. . . and the most marvellous thing of all,' he was saying. 'Every pane of glass in the Crystal Palace, for the Great Exhibition, that was made here by Chance! Imagine that!'

'But John,' Ada burst out at last, 'you don't have to imagine it. We were there, with our mother and father. Don't you remember? We all went – and Mabs was still a baby.'

The silence that fell then was almost worse than the babbling. He stopped, as if suddenly unable to move his feet, beside a long, brick, many-windowed building.

'Don't you remember?' she said, more gently now. 'We were all there together. Pa took us on a train. You were four, I think.'

A sharp memory came to her then: the sound of clapping as the young Queen processed along under the sea of glass above her head, how hot it was in there and she, Ada, straining on her tiptoes to catch a glimpse past all the hats and caps. Pa, beside her, had lifted Elsie and Dora, one hoicked up on each arm so they could see through the crowds. But down low, gripping his mother's skirts as he so often did, was little John. He never saw the Queen.

He was looking down now at the cindery ground, deflated, upset.

'I can remember . . .' He paused, struggling. 'A ceiling – everything very bright. And . . . and an elephant?' This was a question, as if he was not sure whether he had dreamt it.

'Yes!' Ada's spirits lifted. One thing they could both remember – at last.

He turned to her, and she could see that things were coming back. 'The train. I think I can remember that.'

'What about Mom – and Pa?'

Tell me everything you remember! she wanted to shout. *About how it was – our mother and father and all of us together. Tell me you remember! And what else? The workhouse – about the others . . . ?*

John looked away. 'Not much, no.'

'And me and Elsie and Dora?'

'Mary – and Annie?'

'Yes,' Ada admitted. This shadow family, the 'Lunns', was going to plague them for ever. Did he remember nothing about her at all? 'But they weren't their real names.'

'Yeah – now you mention it, Annie told me she was going by Dora when she wrote.'

Ada gasped. Her heart began to race. 'She wrote? You and she . . .? You know where she is then?'

John shook his head. 'She was working for some family. A doctor, I think. She come over to see me the once – couple of year ago, if that—'

'She came to see you!' Ada was almost jumping with excitement. She felt like grabbing John and shaking him like a rug to extract all the information she was so hungry to hear. 'Well, what was she like? Where is she?'

He shrugged and already her flash of hope was dying. 'That ginger hair – like she always was. She came over the once. Seemed a bit upset like, but 'er never said why. I've not heard from her since then – not even once.'

Twenty-One

'Tell us all about it then, our John.'

Margaret, the eldest of the Smith girls, was sixteen, only a few months older than John, but she already seemed mature and womanly and she bossed John about almost as if she was his mother.

'Tell us – no, you're not going out again!'

Clara, the next sister down, grabbed his arm and pulled him on to a chair. Clara, fourteen, blue-eyed with a heart-shaped face and thick strawberry blonde hair, was always the one who goaded him the most. She was full of energy, had a force to her.

'Let 'im catch 'is breath,' Harriet Smith instructed from the fire where she was stirring a pot.

'Leave the lad be,' Clara's father, Enoch, rumbled at her, but to no avail. He himself was often wearily defeated by the force of eight daughters, for he was no tyrant.

'No!' Clara brought her eyes down level with John's. He saw her pink lips purse up as she spoke and she was pretty as a rosebud. She smelt of rough soap, of girl. 'We want to know all about it!'

The Smith girls overpowered him like an army. Margaret and Clara led the charge, eleven-year-old twins Violet and Daisy not far behind and in the circle, Alice and Cissy, each steps down in age, little Susan and the baby Emma who was the only one not paying attention.

'That was my sister Ada,' John said.

'Well, what *about* her?' Margaret demanded. 'Where's 'er come from? What work does 'er do?'

It was only then that John realized he had asked nothing. Not a single detail about Ada's life, how it had been, who she was. Only about Tom. He felt foolish.

But why should he know or care? Ada was a stranger who he could scarcely remember. She had managed to avoid being thrown into the workhouse. And all those years she had sat on her hands and never bothered to come and get the rest of them out. Where had *she* been all this time while he could never forget he was a workhouse charity case? Who was Ada to him, really?

'How should I know?' he snapped, his voice harsh.

He got up, throwing off Clara's attempt to hold him down, and went stomping out of the house, to walk and walk, trying to burn off the hurt and tender emotions that were suddenly overpowering him.

'I don't want it,' he found himself cursing and ranting out loud as he strode away from town into soot-blasted countryside he had never seen before. He did not know or care where he was. The only thing he registered was the sound of a train rumbling past in the distance.

He could not have said quite what it was he did not want, but he felt it with a passion.

He had been twelve when first he was sent here four years ago, leaving the workhouse, the only world he could remember. He was to start on a seven-year apprenticeship and to live with the family of his gaffer, Enoch Smith.

At first he had been just as baffled as Ada by what the family and everyone else were on about whenever they opened their mouths. But over time he tuned into the language all around him and now was quite at ease.

'A boy!' Harriet Smith had cried when he arrived. That

much he had understood at least, in this foreign land. They all stared at him as if he was a performing bear. Little Emma the youngest now, was not born by then, but the Smiths already had seven girls and they all had to squeeze into the two bedrooms of the cottage. John would sleep downstairs by the fire. But they were kindly people and seemed happy to have him.

As John got to know the great firm of Messrs Chance & Co. and learn his work, Enoch Smith became like a god to him. This solid, bearded man was the 'chair' of his team, one of many in the huge glass factory with its numerous solid works buildings, hives of activity with furnaces and blowpipes, the men swinging back and forth with glowing orbs of molten glass at the end of the pipes. John found it beautiful – all of it. The roaring glow of the furnaces, the heat, the men's dance-like movements. It was a sight which still fascinated, even moved him, despite seeing it for all this time.

The place turned out crown and plate glass for windows and mirrors as well as flint glass for all the domestic items and scientific vessels you could ever need. He worked for Enoch in the flint glass section.

He learned that each team of glass-makers was called a 'chair', made up of four men. He, the taker-in, was the junior, the youngest by far. John's job in this boiling hot place, was to fetch and carry glass items between the furnace and the Lehr, or annealing oven, where it was cooled gradually so that it did not crack.

The other two men of this chair, apart from Enoch Smith, were the foot-maker who shaped the feet or stands of items such as glasses, and the servitor, or blower with his pipe, who blew the glass.

Enoch Smith was the workman, the principal who sat opposite the furnace. John loved to watch him, bent over with his tools to shape glasses and jugs, decanters or even glass lampshades, with what seemed miraculous deftness, skills acquired over a lifetime of work.

John would watch Enoch toiling in the glow of the furnace, sweat dripping from his forehead and the muscles straining in his hairy forearms. And he wanted to be Enoch Smith. This was his destiny. To work here, in this firm which seemed as big as a town, which had taken him in and was a place where he could belong. The work was punishingly hard – but here, he might become someone.

The hours were 'turns' of six on and six off, starting at seven on a Monday morning. For him, a turn consisted of endless toing and froing at high speed, carrying the molten glass on the long wooden paddle.

It was exhausting, hurrying with the long rod, supporting the weight of the glass on it, back and forth, back and forth. His back would twinge and ache. But when he first started, John had been so eager to please that his feet were blistered to shreds after a few shifts. And the six-hour shift patterns took their toll. At first he would collapse on the floor into sleep as soon as he got home, too tired even to eat, his body hurting all over. And soon he grew sick.

There was nowhere else for him in the house except to lie on his palliasse at the side of the room, mostly out of the way of the trampling feet of the other children when they were in the house. He lay tossing with a fever, a sick stomach. Harriet looked after him kindly, bringing him water, then broth and torn crusts to dip in it as he recovered.

Enoch drew up a chair and sat beside him one evening, so close that John could see the dark speckle of the pores in his skin. John felt awed as the man's fleshy, bearded face looked down into his, talking, only scraps of which John could follow, but it seemed to be reassuring.

'You'll get used to it,' was the thrust of what Enoch Smith told him. 'Take it easy – it's hard at first, but you're a good worker and you'll learn.'

It never stopped being exhausting, but he did adjust, week by week. John was commended for hard work, when some of the lads wanted to bunk off and play football on waste ground at the edge of town. He did not want that. Not at all. He felt he owed Enoch for taking him on, a workhouse boy. But he also wanted Chance & Co. and all it offered. And before long he realized it also offered some education. He started to attend the schoolroom, paying for it out of his wages, some of which also covered his rent to the Smiths. What else did he need money for? He was going to better himself.

The big firm of Chance & Co. became his world. His belonging. It was a world of heat and sweat and endless toil which dictated his days just as the workhouse had done. A world of men who he could look up to.

At home, it was a world of women – and that took him far longer to get used to.

'He's waking – he's opening his eyes!'

The first morning, John woke on his bed on the floor to a ring of faces all looking down at him. He only had to move his head, bewildered by what he could see of the white-washed cottage ceiling, the smallness of the room, to have a torrent of giggles pour over him as these girls watched his every move in fascination.

It went on like that for a while. They all yam-yammered on at him and he could hardly understand a thing. The twins, Violet and Daisy who were seven then, were so alike that even now he strained to tell them apart. Margaret bossed him, Clara would come up and poke him and run away giggling and little Susan, the babby as she then was, would sit gazing at him open-mouthed. He got used to them. After a time he sometimes allowed himself to be bossed and dragged into their games of tipcat or tag or hide-and-seek.

Then, about a year ago, by some mysterious process that he knew nothing of, he came back to the house to find Mrs Smith cradling another baby, feeding it from her chest – John would look away, blushing right up into his hair.

'I ay never doing that again,' she declared, to John's mystification.

Gradually he became one of them, could make out this strange way of talking. They all got used to each other.

'He's an odd lad,' John heard Enoch say to one of the others in their chair. 'Good worker though.'

Early on, he had a couple of brief letters from Dora, or Annie as he had become used to calling her, who had left the workhouse around the same time as himself. She knew he had gone to Chance & Co. and had written via the factory. She didn't say much, only that she was in service. And then the letters stopped.

John became a Chance & Co. lad. His world. A place where he could belong and forget everything else and everything he had been before.

Until a stranger called Tom turned up, claiming he was sent by John's sister. And a letter came from someone with a name that echoed through the years. Ada Fletcher. Fletcher.

He strained to remember her. A girl whose lap he sometimes sat on. Someone who he recalled as wiry, always rushing about. More like a boy than a girl, in his mind.

But that was all. For as long as he could remember he had been John Lunn. And John Lunn was who he wanted to remain. He did not want to think about anything else, or the terrible, swelling grief which heaved in him if he ever let his mind stray back there, as if he was about to barf up clots of the past.

He did not want to know about that. He was happy enough where he was.

And then one day, she turned up on the doorstep, this tall, gaunt, almost severe woman who said she was his eldest sister.

Twenty-Two

'You all right, Ade? You look worn out.'

Elsie looked up at Ada as she sat, suckling baby Vicky who was growing into a lovely bouncing babe.

'Feeding up, that's what she needs,' Matty Drake commented from over by the fire. 'Here, Ada –'ave a sit-down and a bit of this cake. It's not long out of the oven. Do you good.'

Ada, who had been feeling tense and in fact hungry, though she had not realized it, relented and sat down next to Elsie.

'Ta, Mrs Drake,' she said, accepting the wedge of cake which was dotted with bits of apple and smelt warm and delicious.

Since she hardly ever looked in the mirror, Ada was barely aware that she had begun to look gaunt lately. Almost severe. Elsie, on the other hand, had filled out, living with her lovely George who could not do enough for her while being fed up like a turkey cock by her mother-in-law. Elsie, who loved her food, was not complaining and as a nursing mother was ripe for being spoiled.

'We've got more than usual on at the moment,' Ada said. 'Another shop has asked us to help complete their orders. It's more money but we're hard at it keeping up.'

The extra boxes of half-completed blanks to send to William Nichols's shop had been even more of a challenge than they'd expected, but they were managing it along with all the work that went to Beardsmore's.

'I'll have to come back in, soon as I can,' Elsie said. 'Mom'll have Vicky, won't you?'

'Ooh yes,' Matty said eagerly. She was clearly looking forward to getting Vicky to herself.

The sisters chatted for a while and, as ever, Elsie's thoughts turned to their other siblings.

'When's our John going to come and see us?' she said sadly. 'You did tell him to come, didn't you, Ade? If it was me I'd've been over here like greased lightning.'

'I don't know,' Ada sighed. Her head was so full of other things that she did not dwell on all of it the way Elsie did. But she did feel sad. 'He seemed quite distant with me. As if he didn't really want to know.'

'Let the lad get used to the idea,' Matty put in. 'He ain't seen you in years.'

'I know,' Elsie was saying in frustration, 'but I want to see *him*.'

As she spoke, feet came running up the stairs and George hurried in.

'Ada! I never knew you was here – nice to see yer!' He dashed over and planted kisses on beloved cheeks – Elsie's and Vicky's. 'There's my girls. I'm just doing the deliveries 'cause Ern's still feeling bad.'

Ernie had been down with a stomach upset for a couple of days. Usually, plump, good-natured Ernie was the one to carry the soft bags of cut and polished gems from the Drakes' business round to other firms, mostly in the jewellery quarter.

'He's poorly all right,' Matty said. 'Wouldn't have cake.'

George shook his head regretfully. This was a sure sign. 'Back soon as I can.'

He kissed Elsie again, said, 'T'ra everyone,' and off he went.

Ada watched with a pang of envy. Her own home life

was solitary these days. Tom came and went, but she was often left alone, cooking up a bit of something to eat, exhausted by the long day.

Elsie, on the other hand, was now at the centre of a cosy family nest. Ada was happy for her – Elsie had come a long way since the frightened little workhouse child she had been. But with a pang, Ada felt her own difference. Her spikiness – the bony elder sister. The spinster. Even though she found it hard to imagine being anything else, at times she felt lonely and worn out by all her cares.

'Want to hold her?' Elsie said, as Vicky surfaced, pink-cheeked, a smear of milk across her plump cheek. Ada softened at the sight of her and laughed.

'Come on then, little niece. Come and see me.' And she held out her arms for the warm bundle who settled cosily in her lap.

Could she do this? she wondered, cradling Vicky's bun-like form. The warmth and love of it all. And yet, something in her rebelled at it. It made her feel stifled, and terrified that any trust she found would disappear and leave her bereft for ever.

Ada, telling herself she was far too busy at the time, had sent Tom to talk to William Nichols. Her workers had all knuckled down, Gert and Margaret, Jess and Biddy as well as Tom and herself, and worked like mad to create the extra boxes of blanks his firm needed.

'I'm grateful to all of you,' she said one evening when they were all there late, treadling away at their lathes, coated in dust and still turning out more and more work at gone eight o'clock. 'You've all collared hard and we're about there – get yourselves home now.'

Gert stopped abruptly and flexed her aching back.

'Thanks, Ada. I don't think we can go on like this.'

Ada saw Margaret, next to Gert, give a nod of agreement.

'We need someone else on it if we're going to carry on,' Jess said. 'I can't be out late like this – the babbies need me.' Jess had two little ones who her mother was having to take over on these late evenings and she was not best pleased.

'Couldn't we all just be one shop?' Biddy asked timidly. At eleven she was an old head on young shoulders and sometimes the one to point out the most obvious thing. 'And add on one more person?'

'That makes sense – if he's willing,' Margaret said. 'Doesn't sound as if that business is going anywhere.'

Ada nodded. The thought had crossed her mind but she had felt hesitant about approaching William Nichols. The poor man seemed in enough of a state as it was without effectively handing over the running of his business to her. Or so she told herself.

'I'll think about it,' she said to the staff. 'Go on – get off now.'

So the next morning she sent Tom over to William Nichols's works. She found herself waiting on pins for his return, wondering how things were going. This could be her opportunity to expand her business in the way she had always wanted. All the stages of button production under one roof, more staff, a growing, prosperous business. They could go from strength to strength. She need never actually see much of William Nichols because he was taken up with his sick wife . . .

She was down in the sorting room when Tom came back, and had to stop herself rushing out to meet him.

'Well – what did he say?'

Tom came inside and pulled his cap further back on his head to look at her. She was struck again by what a good-looking lad he was with his dark, curling hair and strong features. He had only got more handsome as he grew older.

'He didn't seem against it,' Tom said. 'Thought it might make sense – but it's a big step for him. He'd have to move all his machines over, give up the lease on the shop – and he might never get it back.'

How is he? Ada wanted to ask. *How is his wife – did he look as sad as before?* But she buttoned her lip. Tom would likely not have noticed anyway.

'He wants to see you,' Tom said. He was starting to move off. 'I'd best get to work . . . Go this afternoon, if you can, eh? That's what he said.'

Ada tried to quell the surge that went through her as Tom said these words. *He wants to see you.* A pulse of something – panic, excitement. For the love of God, woman, she scolded inwardly, pull yourself together!

'All right,' she said calmly.

Ada stepped into Nichols's works expecting to find the same half-deserted atmosphere she had seen the first time. But today, things felt busier. The women were hard at it, working through the boxes she had supplied, and William Nichols himself was there, bent over one of the lathes that was clearly giving bother. He didn't notice Ada at first and one of the women called his attention.

'Won't be long,' he said to the woman with the troublesome machine. As he came towards her in the shop's dim light, Ada was shaken to find that her first reaction to William Nichols – the way he had stirred her feelings somehow – grew stronger. This was not what she had expected. The way he walked, his slight figure, the thin, sensitive face and dark beard . . . She pulled her features into a severe and businesslike expression.

'Miss Fletcher?' He held out his hand and Ada had the presence of mind to take it. 'Let's talk outside.'

She found herself walking beside him into the yard and was flummoxed. Should she ask about his wife? She cursed herself for being so awkward over such things. But William Nichols himself was more straightforward.

'As you know, my wife is ailing and things have become very difficult here. Your lad's suggestion of putting the two shops together for the moment is one thing – but I've had to think hard about officially combining the two businesses altogether. I'm not even sure if that's what you're proposing, Miss Fletcher? Are you trying to take over my firm?'

His tone was calm, businesslike, but the man was no fool and she had to lower her gaze from the direct look he gave her. Yes, that was her dream, she had to admit – but in the circumstances it seemed high-handed and unkind.

'I . . .' Ada hesitated. 'I hadn't thought,' she fibbed, which seemed immediately a feeble reply. 'Or . . .' The words came out ahead of her thoughts. 'I can see you wouldn't want that. But as things are difficult, perhaps, in the meantime, we could join forces?'

She could hardly believe she had said it. Here she was, after these years of struggle building up her own independent business, suddenly offering to join forces with a man whom she had only met once before – what the hell was wrong with her!

William Nichols pondered this. He stroked his chin and paced the yard. As he did so, another faint cry came from inside the house and Ada could see that his thoughts were immediately shattered. It wrung her heart.

'Look,' she said, with a gentleness that surprised her as much as her offer in the first place. 'It doesn't have to be hard and fast. It might well benefit both of us. I've capacity in my shop. Bring your finishers over to me. I'll hire a couple more staff and we can work out our profits accordingly. If it goes badly, we'll have to separate out again.'

Ada realized as she spoke that she had no real idea of the proper way to do this. Papers to sign, agreements. But for some reason her instincts trusted this man and her soul reached out to assist. And in the end it might also be a way of growing her own business faster, in the way she had always dreamt.

After more chin stroking, William Nichols gave her another of his direct looks and this time she did not turn away. For a moment they held each other's look, her thin, rather intense face meeting his brown-eyed, anguished gaze. They were measuring each other's character and each saw in the other something they could trust.

'We'll keep the business as Fletchers' only,' Ada said, harsh suddenly because she was frightened of the feelings rising up in her. 'To begin with. But I'll be straight with you. So long as you are with me.'

A pang of some sorrowful emotion passed across William Nichols's face for a second. Then he gave a faint smile.

'I trust you will, Miss Fletcher,' he said.

He held out his hand and Ada took it, warm and slender in hers, as they shook on the new arrangement.

Twenty-Three

It did not take long to transfer William Nichols's shop into Ada's workshop in Galton Passage. His was a small firm but they had been making buttons from start to finish so he had all the necessary lathes. By the time everything was moved in it was a tight fit.

With the lathes came the three workers. Ada reckoned that even if Elsie was serious about coming back they would still need to employ three more. And it did not take long to find them in a city full of workshops engaged in the same trade.

'Our carding's still sent to outworkers,' William Nichols told her. 'I've not room for a sewing room and nor have you.'

Not yet, Ada thought, looking along the now crammed room with a swell of pride. One day they would have to move again to yet bigger premises and they would have an area for the buttons to be sewn on to cards for the shops. They would do everything from start to the very finish!

But for now, she had to deal with working out how the two of them were to split the proceeds and to manage the orders and all the staff new and old. And this included the redhead, Vi Spenser.

Vi complained from the moment she arrived. She had not wanted to move her place of work – least of all to somewhere run by another woman.

'I've further to go now,' Ada heard her moaning during the first dinner break. Then it was, 'My machine's broke – it's never been the same since the move. We should've stayed put where we were.' Fortunately William was good at fixing the machines and soon had it whirring round to Vi's satisfaction.

'Cut it out, will you, Vi?' Ada heard William Nichols say to the woman in a low voice. 'I've given you a lot of rope 'cause you're a good worker, but Miss Ada might not do the same.'

'She's not my boss – you are,' Vi protested, her thin face contorting as if she had just sucked a lemon.

Ada was surprised at the way he let this harridan talk to him. She kept quiet for a while, hoping Vi's resentment would die down, but it did not and soon she was causing a rift in the workshop.

Ada would walk in sometimes to find Vi having a go about something.

'There's no light in here,' she was complaining one day. 'How're we s'posed to see to work?'

'There's as much as in the other place, Vi,' one of the other workers said in a low voice. 'Just stop your carry-on or we'll be out.'

'I can't stand that one,' Margaret said when Ada and her own staff grouped together at the end of one day. ''Er never stops mithering about summat.'

'Can't you tell her to pipe down or find another job?' Gert said.

'She's a good worker in spite of it all,' Ada said. 'And she's not one of mine, is she? There's not much I can do. We'll just have to put up with her.'

Margaret rolled her eyes and Ada wondered if she had done the wrong thing rushing this situation through. Her workers had always been a happy lot together up until now.

Once everything was set up, Ada was left to deal with everything most of the time because William was at home watching over his wife. But she was getting sick of Vi's attitude, the way she was always resentful, always thought she knew better.

So when William came into the shop one afternoon, she said, 'I need to talk to you – out of here.' It came out sounding more curt than she really meant it and she was annoyed with herself as she led the way out into the yard.

'What's up with Vi Spenser?' she said, trying to speak more gently. 'She's not stopped complaining since she got here.'

'Vi? Yes, she can be difficult,' William sighed. He sounded bone tired.

'Well, why've you still got her working with you?' Ada asked, growing impatient. Often with him, because he was gentle and had a lot on his mind, she felt as if she was having to be the tough business-britches and she was not sure she liked it. 'She's not a bad worker but she stirs up everyone else and my lot are sick of her already.'

'I suppose I've always felt sorry for her,' he said. 'Vi was widowed young – left with four young children and her ailing mother. She's worked to keep them all ever since. There've been days when the little ones were younger I've seen her so faint she could barely stand. But she'd work on through it all. She's strong as an ox and determined with it. Complaining keeps the blood running in her veins, I think. I suppose we've all just put up with each other – she's worked hard for me.'

'I see.' Ada felt a grudging respect for Vi, with all her struggles – but he was the boss. Surely he should have the upper hand? 'So you're saying there's nothing we can do about it?'

William stroked his chin. Then suddenly a grin broke over his face, lighting it up in a way Ada had never seen before. She was shaken. His eyes were aglow with amusement, and he seemed suddenly younger, and so handsome. It was a lovely face which she had the strangest feeling she had already known for a long time.

'Well,' he said, mischievously, 'I don't want her sacked. But if you want to try and stop her keeping on, you have a go. Not that others haven't perished in the attempt, mind.'

The grin was so infectious that Ada found herself smiling back. It felt already like a joke they shared between them and there was a warm feeling to it, as if a barrier had been broken.

'All right,' she said, taking up the challenge. 'I'll see what I can do.'

Within days, William Nichols stopped coming to the works and everyone feared the worst. His employees seemed to get news from somewhere.

'Mrs Nichols is fading,' one of them told Ada. 'It can't be long now.'

'P'raps when it's all over we can get back to normal,' Vi moaned. 'Go back to our own shop and enough of having to traipse over here.'

The fact that Vi was off complaining again within earshot of her, riled Ada. She was tempted to go up and box the woman's ears as if she were a naughty child – or to let her go. There were plenty of others she could take on who wouldn't grouch like this all the time. But she controlled herself. It was no good lowering herself to getting in a row.

'Vi,' she said calmly, going up to her. 'A word.'

As Ada walked away she could feel the other women's eyes following her and knew that the Nichols's women would be making faces behind her back.

She led Vi Spenser down to the store room, aware at every step of the woman's hostile presence behind her.

Once they were alone she turned to face her. Vi's face was sour and aggressive, expecting trouble.

'I want to be straight with you,' Ada said. She found herself feeling shaky in the face of Vi's powerful personality, but she had to stand firm, show her who was in charge here. 'Up 'til now my shop's been a good place to work – and no one likes the way you're mithering and complaining all the time. And I'm not going to put up with it.'

Vi's mouth opened immediately to come back at her, her face almost a snarl.

'I ain't taking orders from you!' she started, despite Ada holding up a hand.

'You be quiet – let me finish!' Ada commanded, raising her voice. 'Now you listen to me. Mr Nichols tells me you've always been one of his best workers. So for the moment I'm choosing to believe him.'

Vi, expecting criticism, subsided, looked taken aback. 'Does he?' she said guardedly.

'And that you have been with him a long time and are very good and trustworthy.'

This also seemed to be news to the woman. She was not sure what to do with her face.

'I know it's hard for you all, having to move over here after what you've been used to,' Ada went on.

Vi's face soured again and she folded her arms tightly across her skinny chest. This was more like it – something she could get back to fighting with.

'And,' Ada said, 'it seems as if you're used to being the one in charge in your shop? You being the longest there?'

'I ain't in charge – Mr Nichols is,' Vi argued, raising her chin obstinately.

'No – but they look to you. I can see that,' Ada said. She had a strong feeling of having to pitch her will against this woman. She held on tight to her temper.

'We don't want to make trouble for Mr Nichols – not at a time like this, do we?' Ada said. 'So what I'm going to do is to put two of you in charge. You look to the women from your works and Margaret can take charge of ours. If they have any real complaints, they come to you and you come to me and we'll talk about what can be done.'

'So . . .' Vi stood a little straighter. 'Our lot – they've got to report to me?'

'That's what I said,' Ada said firmly. 'And you and Margaret may want to sort things out between you.' She knew she could rely on Margaret. She was full of good sense and wouldn't stand for any nonsense. 'It would be of help to both Mr Nichols and me – and I'm sure I can rely on you.'

Vi was taking all this in, on her dignity. 'All right,' she agreed slowly, as if looking for a catch in the situation.

'Well, that's settled,' Ada said. 'Don't be afraid to come and discuss anything. But Vi –' and now Ada's voice was full of authority – 'unless there's really something that needs saying, cut out all the moaning. All right? You've got responsibility here now – you need to set an example.'

A scowl had started to form on Vi's pale face again, but she managed to swallow any retort she might have been about to make. She nodded.

'Right – back to work then,' Ada said.

Vi gave another nod like a pecking hen and turned away, without ever uncrossing her arms. Ada watched her with grudging admiration. She was a fighter, that one – in some ways you did have to admire her, maddening as she was.

Twenty-Four

Dora was squatting in the yard rinsing a bundle of white clothing in the old tin baby bath. It was a warm, sultry day and she felt sticky and tired out.

'Asleep, is she?' her neighbour Mabel said, struggling out of the brewhouse with the maiding tub. She paused to scraunch her hair back with a rubber band. 'Wish my lot'd flaming stay asleep,' she added a moment later, nodding towards her three infants who were trailing about after her. 'Wish I could dose 'em up with summat.'

Dora smiled faintly.

'She getting you up at night a lot?' Mabel's next question coincided with hauling out the mangle, her forehead damp with perspiration before the wash had even begun.

'Oh yes – she's up and down,' Dora said. 'But I just tuck her in with me.'

Mable tutted. 'Make the most of it. It's when they start moving you really know about it. Where's Minnie then?'

'Out fetching in,' Dora said.

As she spoke, Dora heard a squeak from Rose inside and she got to her feet, steadying herself dizzily for a moment, and went inside.

Mrs Lacey was sitting at the table, as usual with all her carding work in front of her, but Dora saw that her head was slumped forward, hands resting on her belly, and fast asleep with her mouth half open.

Poor old soul, Dora thought. She had grown fond of old Mrs Lacey. She had been kind to her and Minnie in her rough way and since she didn't seem to have anyone either, she was glad to have them there. And she still worked so hard at her age just to make ends meet.

'Come on, gutsy,' she murmured to little Rose whose face was puckering up ready for a scream. 'I know what you want but there's no need to wake *her* up, is there?'

Cuddling the little girl to her she crept up the stairs.

Dora's young body was healing well from the wounds of childbirth. These first weeks of Rose's life had been a time of wonder, of feeling a kind of love she never knew she was capable of. But it had also been utterly exhausting. Now she and Minnie were having to learn to work with another little person to take care of as well.

Propping herself up on the bed she put Rose to her breast, who sucked with her usual efficiency and enthusiasm. Dora watched her for a moment, love washing through her. She knew now that all her hopes, all her strength would go into bringing up this beloved child – his, theirs. His child. Rose was so like Robert, his dark hair, the little smiles she had just started to give. Dora melted every time she looked at her. Imagine if he could see her – his little girl . . . But she stopped her thoughts abruptly in their tracks. They would lead to despair when there was nothing she could do about any of it.

After a few moments, she slid one hand under the mattress and pulled out her notebook.

Minnie had taken to sleeping downstairs for the moment, since Rose's birth.

'I like my sleep,' she said. She had gone out and bought a palliasse and a rough blanket and got her head down for the night. Which meant that now, when she was feeding Rose in the small hours, Dora sometimes lit the candle and carried on with her story.

Though she was always tired, since she'd had Rose it was

as if she had a new kind of energy: something had fired in her mind. Stories kept coming one after another and she would scribble away, saving up all the thoughts she had during the day when she was doing the labour that took so many waking hours. She would be bashing clothes with the dolly, mangling or ironing – the endless toil of it all – but suddenly she would think . . . I know – he's going to get in by climbing up that creeper at the back of the house, or she could have the dagger tucked right inside her corset . . . She would come back at any moment she could manage, day or night, and write away.

Minnie was her greatest supporter and audience. She worked like a Trojan – there was nothing idle about Minnie. She had begun to fill out over the past weeks and instead of a pale waif she was beginning to be quite sturdy, with muscular arms and colour in her cheeks. She hauled buckets of water, pounded and rinsed washing and took to the streets to fetch and deliver it.

'I'll get back to more of it soon,' Dora promised, feeling quite guilty.

'I know you will,' Minnie said. 'But you don't want to hurt your insides. As long as I get enough to eat I'm bars of iron!'

And Minnie could eat. Her favourite thing was pies. Give the girl a meat pie and she was ready for almost anything. Two were even better. Meat, then apple – that was bliss to Minnie. Dora had never seen anyone who could eat so fast – she watched pies disappear inside Minnie in pure astonishment. But she was more and more grateful for the girl's energy. Between them they could earn at least two shillings a day in a good week as long as they could get up enough work, so a tuppenny mutton pie from the pie man who patrolled the nearby street was cheap at the price to keep Minnie going.

Dora had begun to trust Minnie with her stories and sometimes she read one to her in the evening. This was complicated by the fact that Mrs Lacey kept intervening, 'Eh? Speak up, wench – I want to hear it as well!' Booming out the story at the top of her voice was not easy so mostly they saved it until Mrs Lacey had hauled herself upstairs to bed. She and Minnie sat together, as now in this warm summer, with the door still open a crack to let in some air, and Dora read.

Minnie was the greatest audience you could find.

'Ooooh!' she'd interrupt, hands clasped under her chin. 'No, he can't do that. Don't let him hurt her – you can't let him, Dora!'

Dora, smirking – oh yes, I can – would read on, making the worst possible things happen. The woman shoved on to the railway track or locked in a deep cellar where an evil spirit was known to be on the loose . . .

'I shan't sleep after that!' Minnie would protest at the end of all these horrors, her face stretched with emotion.

Except that she was soon flat out, sleeping the deep sleep of someone who had worked like a pie-fed dynamo all day.

Dora sat on her bed, writing the last lines of another story that had a romantic ending. She paused and lifted Rose to her other breast. This was not so easy. She was scrawling a few last words with her left hand when she heard Minnie's feet on the stairs.

'You up here, Dor?' Minnie appeared, her cheeks pink from her exertions and even a little tanned from her journeys to fetch washing. 'I got an extra one – one of them big houses down Easy Row – there's a lot of it. I'll need you to help.'

She came over to the bed and smiled, stroking Rose's round cheek with her finger. 'Hello, little sweetie-pie,' she said, leaning down to kiss the baby's cheek.

'I've finished it!' Dora said, closing the notebook on her scrawl.

'You've got to send it somewhere, Dor,' Minnie insisted. 'It's as good as the stories in the books they sell!'

They had taken to buying a cheap story paper to read now and then and Minnie was convinced that Dora could out-write any of them.

Dora got up, carefully moving Rose who was now well fed and fast asleep again.

'I'd have to write them all out again so they can read them,' she said, adding, 'and no one's going to want them.' But secretly she was excited. Minnie's adoration of her stories meant everything to her. 'In the meantime, let's get this wash on the go.'

She followed Minnie downstairs and placed Rose carefully in the drawer which was her little bed in the daytime, tucked in at the side of the room out of harm's way. On the floor near the range were three bundles of washing.

'You must've had a job pushing all lot that back!' Dora said.

'It nearly finished me off.' Minnie grinned. 'But I got a pie on the way home – damson. It was lovely.'

Dora rolled her eyes. 'You'll turn into a pie soon.' She looked cautiously at Minnie. 'No sign of him about?'

The only cloud on their horizon was the thought of Minnie's father turning up. She knew Minnie was all eyes whenever she was out, dreading him jumping out from somewhere.

'Nope,' she said, unknotting the top of one of the bundles. She seemed calm but Dora knew she lived on her nerves whenever she was out. Generally, she left off asking. There was no point in making a fuss about it if there was no sign of the bloke.

'This lot's mostly bedding,' Minnie said. 'No wonder

it was heavy.' Suddenly aware of the other presence in the room, she glanced at Mrs Lacey.

'Not getting much work done, is she? It's hot today though.'

Minnie went over to their landlady, frowning. 'Quiet though, ain't she? Normally snores like a trooper.'

She went up close and listened. Mrs Lacey's head remained on her chest and Minnie's expression sobered up abruptly.

'Mrs L?' Much more loudly she said, 'Mrs Lacey?' She looked at Dora, the awful realization beginning to dawn on them both. Minnie touched Mrs Lacey's shoulder. Then harder. One of her arms suddenly flopped down and hung straight, swinging heavily for a moment.

'Oh my Lord,' Dora said, as Minnie turned to her again. In astonishment she said, 'I think she's gone.'

'I've never seen anyone else come in or out,' Mabel told them when they asked if Mrs Lacey had any family. The older neighbours agreed. Everyone knew that Mrs Lacey had no children but it seemed as if she had not been exaggerating when she'd said she had no one in the world once Mr Lacey passed on.

'You're the nearest she's got to family,' Mabel said.

'I don't know what to do,' Dora said. She had so little experience of living in a family, of old relatives dying. 'What do I do?'

'You need to get Mrs Mills in,' Mabel told them.

'She's the one come to you with Rose,' Minnie said, as Dora looked bewildered. 'Remember?'

'And then you've got to get her buried,' Mabel said. 'She might've had a penny fund for that – have a search round the house.'

*

Dora and Minnie began looking through the house, going into Mrs Lacey's bedroom where they never usually went.

'Feels wrong coming in here, doesn't it,' Minnie said, wrinkling her nose at the powerful smell. Mrs Lacey's bed was a mess of yellowed bedding that had obviously not been changed in a very long time and there was a brim-full chamber pot under the bed. The room was full of a miasma of human smells, heavily overlaid with the stink of camphor.

'We'll have to burn that bedding,' Dora said, her stomach turning. 'She never asked for anything. I should have helped her,' she said guiltily, her mind only opening fully now to all Mrs Lacey's physical struggles. 'Why didn't she get us to sort her out? She helped me – there's many wouldn't have.'

'Well, it's too late now,' Minnie said, rummaging in the drawer of Mrs Lacey's dark wood chest of drawers. Other than that and a chair and, somehow surprisingly, a pretty cheval mirror, there was nothing else in the room.

'Didn't she say she came in from Redditch – years ago?' Dora said.

'Look.' Minnie sounded stricken. From the drawer she brought a little doll, only a few inches long, with a pale china face and a faded yellow frock. Dora went to look. Although its face was that of a baby, the doll had a great deal of hair piled on its head, some of it hanging loose.

'Oh,' she said. Something about the doll gave her the horrors. Even Minnie looked put off by the thing.

'D'you think she's had it since she was young?' she said.

They looked at each other, shaking their heads. It was awful to realize how little they knew about this old lady who had done them a kindness.

Minnie replaced the doll and pulled the drawer out further. Dora saw a few more yellowed items of clothing which made her feel sad. Minnie reached right to the back.

'Here – what's this?' Triumphant, she pulled out a bundle of papers and quickly searched through them. 'Look – here.'

Dora took the paper, soft from wear, and looked down it.

'She's paid in, every week – for years and years.' This felt unbearable, that Mrs Lacey's chief aim all these years seemed to have been ensuring a respectable death. Dora's eyes filled with tears.

Minnie watched her solemnly. 'Poor old thing,' she said.

Of Mr Lacey, apart from the brass wedding ring trapped on Mrs Lacey's swollen finger, there was no sign at all. Dora swallowed, her chest aching at the thought of Mrs Lacey's poor, struggling life.

'She was making sure she had a decent burial – and we've got to see she gets it.'

Twenty-Five

Dora was not sure whether to feel moved or heartbroken by Mrs Lacey's funeral. She had enough money in her fund for them to give her a good send-off – a carriage with black horses, the plumes fixed in their browbands riffling in the wind, a fine coffin lined with white satin, with brass handles and bunches of carnations and lilies.

But as the undertakers carried the coffin from the house to the waiting carriage, it was only followed by Dora and Minnie and a few other neighbours from the yard. No one knew anything about any other relatives, of hers or the Lacey family. In spite of the grandeur it felt so sad, so small a circle of acquaintance after a whole life.

'Well, I think we did her proud,' Minnie said, when they got back to the house at last, thankfully drinking a cup of tea. Dora sat suckling Rose.

'She did *herself* proud,' Dora corrected. She still ached with guilt and sorrow for Mrs Lacey. After all, this woman had been more of a mother to Dora than anyone else for a very long time. Sitting in her house, at the table where she had worked for such meagre pay, day in day out, booming at everyone and trying to hear anything past her increasing deafness, Dora missed her more than she had ever expected to.

But Minnie was thinking ahead.

'Once we've got her room sorted out, we've two rooms upstairs – a whole room for drying in!'

'Don't you want to sleep in there?' Dora asked. Mrs Lacey's old room was the bigger of the two.

'I'm all right down here,' Minnie said cheerfully. 'And it means we'll have more space down here. We can use the table for ironing, proper like – we can really make a go of it now.'

They took over Mrs Lacey's rent and the two of them got stuck in. The work was exhausting, day after day, up very early Mondays and out collecting bundles from their customers. Minnie still did most of this, wheeling the barrow along, but Dora tied Rose on to her with a shawl and managed to pick up a few of the closer ones. Once it was all collected, she marked up any items that needed it and they set to, checking them for stains. Sometimes she had to remove any candle wax stuck to them with a hot coal wrapped in a rag.

There followed days of lugging pails of water, soaking clothing, treating stains with lye or onion juice, lighting the fire under the copper, a tablespoon of salt thrown into the water to soften it and fasten the colour in clothes. Into the steaming water they pushed the load of washing, adding soap and Reckitt's Blue, then hauled it out into the maiding tub to be pounded with the dolly. After that, they had to pump up more water for rinsing, before the hauling out and wringing, mangling and finally pegging some items out or hanging them inside.

They bought a wooden clothes horse and strung up more lines in Mrs Lacey's old room (it was always called Mrs Lacey's room even after her presence faded over the weeks). They padded the table with Mrs Lacey's old woven bedcover – which after a thorough wash was the one thing worth keeping from that sad room – and were able to iron standing, or sitting at the table.

Minnie looked round the room when they had reorganized things and given it a good clean. The range was blackleaded and the pots gleaming, the small amount of furniture wiped down and little Rose asleep in her makeshift cot up against the wall. 'Well, look at that! We've got our own place and our own business. How's that, Dora? No more Miss Worst, the old witch, no one else telling us what to do . . .'

Dora smiled. Minnie seemed to have endless energy whereas she, feeding Rose and recovering from her birth, wearied a lot more quickly.

'Tell you what,' Minnie said. 'Once the rush part of the week's over, come Friday, I can deliver all the stuff back – and then there's the weekend. You can write!'

She beamed at Dora, hurrying to stoke the fire and stand the kettle on it.

'You can write and then you can send it in to a magazine. I know!' She whirled round. 'If you want I can copy it out for you. I can write all right. Well, a bit.'

'No!' Dora felt suddenly fiercely protective. These were her words, this was her dream! 'It's no good you doing that. You won't know if I want to change what I've put because they're my stories. I've got to do that.'

She softened, knowing she had snapped too harshly. Minnie meant well.

'But it's nice of you to say you'll take the bundles back. It's a job doing it carrying her.'

Minnie came and sat at the table while the kettle heated.

'This is nice,' she said, drawing in a deep, satisfied breath. 'I know this place ain't much but it's our little place. And it beats having to listen to all them women fussing over their hats. "Oh,"' she mimicked snooty voices, '"I think the brim is too narrow." "Oh, I don't like the colour of the feathers." "Oh, my head is so small and delicate I can't possibly wear this." I never want to see another flaming hat as long as I live – not to make one, any road.'

Dora laughed. 'And there was me thinking I might ask you to make me one.'

Minnie made a horrified face.

'I'm only joking,' Dora said. 'A cheap bonnet does me – I couldn't care less.'

The girls settled in together and worked, week after week, all through those months into the depths of winter.

Monday to Thursday was a heavy, hard-working time and by Thursday night each week, they were both salty with sweat, their hands rubbed raw and backs and shoulders screaming with aches and pains. Often on a Thursday night they would heat yet more water and fill the tin bath by the range, each groaning with pleasure as they soaked in the warmth. They were used to each other now, clothed or naked, like sisters.

'Here – pass her to me,' Dora said one evening as she lay back in the water, soaking her sore muscles. 'Might as well wash together, mightn't we?'

Minnie brought Rose, who was now six months old, and together they peeled off her little napkin and flannel shirt. Rose kicked her legs and gurgled. She loved having a bath.

'Come on, baba.' Dora held her arms out and when Rose felt the warm water on her skin she let out a little chirrup of excitement. Dora and Minnie laughed.

'You like that, don't you, little darlin'?' Minnie said.

Dora gently poured water over her soft skin and turned Rose to face her. She was a beautiful child. Dora gazed at her adoringly. Robert, Robert . . . But more and more, Rose also brought back another memory. The black curls, those wide brown eyes.

'She looks like my baby sister,' Dora murmured. 'Don't you?' She kissed Rose's damp cheek, 'You're like . . .' For an awful moment she struggled. What was her name? She could see her in her mind's eye, the brown eyes, the pink cheeks and dark hair. 'Mabs. You look like Mabs.'

'What happened – to Mabs?' Minnie asked carefully.

Dora looked up at her. She felt very naked suddenly, in every way, and she cuddled Rose to her, rocking her gently, as much to comfort herself as anything.

'They gave her away. In the workhouse. I don't know where she went.'

Minnie shook her head. 'That's so sad,' she said. She leaned in closer again and stroked Rose's pink back. 'I never had a sister. Nor a brother for that matter. Can I be your sister?'

Dora smiled, though she was still feeling raw and sad. So many people lost. Her brother and sisters. Robert. So many holes in her heart.

'Yes,' she said. 'Course you can.'

Minnie looked into her eyes for a moment. Then, in her extravagant way, she leaned down and put her now almost plump arms round Dora and Rose and kissed Dora's cheek.

All went well until the following spring. On an April day of sharp shadows, Minnie was out delivering some of the clean bundles of laundry. Dora was busy indoors ironing the last of the clothes to go out that week.

Rose, now ten months old, had to be restrained from crawling about the place by sitting her for some of the time in a little low chair with a bar across the front and she was not best pleased.

'Shoosh,' Dora said as the child began to squeak and whine, flailing her legs, which wanted to be off and away.

Dora's temper was already frayed. The drains had been blocked again, making everything more difficult, with filthy water spreading all over the yard. And she had reached a stage in the week where she was hot and tired. All she really wanted to do was to lull her little girl to sleep and sit down with her notebook – the book he had given her – and write. But the chores still left to do that day felt endless . . .

'Dor . . . Dora!' She heard the thump of Minnie dumping the rickety barrow outside before she came flying in as if her bloomers were on fire.

'What the hell's up with you?' Dora snapped, spitting on the second iron after replacing the first on the heat.

'He's out there. I saw him . . .'

Dora swung round to see the abject terror on Minnie's face. She looked almost like a different person – a scared little girl.

'You mean . . . ?'

'My father. He's out there – just standing there.'

'What – in the yard?' Dora's body tightened with dread.

'No – on the corner of Smallbrook and Tonks Street. I don't think he saw me and I turned round and came back down Inkleys instead.'

'You sure it was him?' Dora asked, stupidly.

'Course I'm sure – I know my own father. He's looking for me – I'm sure he is!'

Dora bent to pick up Rose who was still keeping on, and balanced her on her hip, trying to think clearly.

'But after all this time? You've been gone almost a year!'

'I know – and I thought it was all right. But I'm out and about such a lot and someone must've seen me.' She sank down at the table, shaking, and the face that looked up at Dora was white and desperate. 'He can't find us, Dor. I ain't going back there – never. But if he gets ahold of me I shan't be able to fight him. He's a brute.'

The horrible reality of this began to sink in. 'Are you sure he didn't see you?'

'I think . . . Yes, he didn't see me. But he was looking for me, asking after me – I know it!'

'And he wouldn't have been down here for some other reason?'

Minnie shook her head emphatically. 'He was just standing there. Oh Lor', Dora. He's a horror. He'll make me go back to him if he finds me.'

There came a crash from the yard as someone dropped some metal object on the ground and Minnie nearly took off from her chair.

'Lord above,' she panted, a hand on her chest. 'I thought my heart was going to stop. Oh, go and see, Dor. See if he's still there – he was just leaning up against the wall. Cap down over his eyes.'

'All right. Mind her for me.' She picked Rose up and put her in Minnie's arms, threw her shawl round her shoulders and went out.

It wasn't long before she reached the corner Minnie had indicated and from a short distance away she could see a man standing there. Her heart beat faster. He did seem to be looking for someone. Why stand there all this time otherwise? But after a moment she felt like laughing. She had imagined Minnie's father, Old Man Moon, to be a hulk with prizefighter features. Instead, she saw a pale runt of a bloke with legs skinny as an insect. For a moment she wanted to giggle. So this was the brute!

She hesitated, worried about going any closer. He was looking away, along the side street. But supposing he already knew what she looked like – had followed both of them? Then she thought, Damn it, I live here. Why shouldn't I walk the streets?

As she passed him she glanced at him. His eyes moved over her with no glint of recognition. She saw a hard, mean face.

'Oi!' She jumped as his voice followed her. Dora half-turned, dreading looking him in the eyes. 'You seen a wench – pushing a barrow like? Slip of a thing – brown hair?'

Dora pretended to think.

'No, never seen anyone like that round here.'

She walked home a very long way round, looking back, nerves a-jangle in case he was following. But there was no sign.

He was real all right, she thought. And he was after Minnie. What were they going to do? Supposing he followed her home? She got back to the house feeling very uneasy.

In the dark, small hours of the next morning, Dora was lying on her side giving Rose a feed. Rose was an accomplished feeder by now and Dora found she scarcely needed to wake; she could roll over, let Rose find her breast and doze off again.

Through her haze of sleep she was dimly aware of a noise outside, another metallic clink followed by other distant sounds from the yard. But she was too sleepy to take much notice, until Minnie suddenly erupted into her room.

'Dor? Dora!' she hissed.

Dora felt her shoulder being shaken like mad.

'What?' she groaned, exhausted. 'What's up with you?'

'There's someone in the yard, ferreting about – I can hear 'em.' She sounded terrified. 'It's him – I know it is.'

'What? Course it ain't. It's the middle of the flaming night! Go back to bed.'

'No,' Minnie said fiercely. 'Not 'til you come with me to look. I'll never settle – he might be out there.'

'Well, it's no good you going out there then, is it?' Dora said grumpily, though she was now full of unease as well.

'That's why you've got to go and look.'

'Oh, for goodness' sake. Here – take her.' Dora sat up and Minnie felt around in the darkness and took the sozzled Rose from her. Dora felt around for her boots. 'I can't see a blasted thing.'

'We mustn't light a candle – he'll see,' Minnie hissed.

Dora groped her way downstairs, her shawl flung round her, more irritated than frightened until she came to open the door. Suppose Minnie was right and this horrible and violent man was waiting for them out there? She could give him a piece of her mind, but was he going to take any notice of that?

As quietly as she possibly could she lifted the latch and peered out. It was so dark and cloudy she could see almost nothing. But there were odd sounds coming from down the end. They didn't sound like someone's angry father so she stepped outside and crept along the yard.

Closer to the end, where the refuse and ash were piled in stinking heaps, she tripped and something metal skittered away from her feet. Dora cursed quietly. Whatever that was, it explained the noise she had heard before – the thing clattering in the yard. Then she made out other sounds. Little snorts, a whimper, scraping and foraging noises. Closer, she could just make out the skinny back end of a stray dog rooting in the rubbish. Dora rolled her eyes and returned to the house. Minnie was waiting on pins.

'Who was it?'

'Not your father – unless he's turned into a dog.'

'Is that what it is? A dog?'

They got the giggles then and closed the door, tittering about in the downstairs room.

'Sorry, Dor,' Minnie said in the end. 'But we can't stay here – not now he knows I'm somewhere in this part of town. I'll never be able to rest easy. We're going to have to move!'

Twenty-Six

One morning, Vi came into the Fletchers' works, her face serious and woebegone. She bustled straight down to the other Nichols's workers and they stood in a huddle.

Ada made her way towards them, afraid something was amiss.

'What's going on?' she said, her voice sharp.

Vi turned, her shoulders set in a way which said, *This isn't your business.*

'It's Mrs Nichols,' she said. 'She's passed away.'

'Oh!' Ada felt a shock go through her that she certainly did not want Vi to notice. 'I see. How very sad. Thank you for telling me.'

Vi's face tightened. She cares about him, Ada thought, as she turned away. Cares *for* him even. A thrill of something passed through Ada – lemon sharp. Jealousy? Don't be so stupid, she ticked herself off. What of it, if the woman felt sorry for her employer? She was sad for him too – and relieved. The thought of that woman's long suffering – and his – had weighed on all of them.

'Poor man,' Margaret said soberly when Ada told the rest of them. 'It's been a long road.'

Everyone was sorry in a kind and natural way. But Ada, busy as she was checking a new delivery of shells, sending Tom up with the sorted ones to start cutting, checking on everyone's work, could not stop her mind straying to William Nichols. To that moment when he had stood down here in the yard and smiled. The lovely, mischievous face she had seen on him that twisted her inside. The way he brought out in her a tenderness that took her completely by surprise. It had felt as if they were close, in that moment, that they had an understanding. But now, knowing him to be lost in his grief for Jane his wife, she felt shut out and very distant from him.

Later, Ada needed company and she drifted across Galton Passage to see Elsie who was still not back at work. Baby Vicky had been worryingly feverish. But the little girl looked much brighter now and was feeding heartily when Ada arrived.

'She looks a lot better,' she smiled with a rush of relief. It would be unbearable if anything happened to that little child. She did not know if Elsie would be able to endure such a loss as had happened to Nancy, George's sister, when her little boy Billy died.

'Oh, she's doing well,' Elsie beamed. 'A proper guzzler.'

Matty Drake bustled over with a cup of tea.

'You look all in, Ada,' she said. 'Here you go – and here's a bit of sponge for you.'

'Ta – that looks nice.' Ada looked up gratefully. Matty Drake always wanted to feed anyone who came within fifty yards of her and Ada realized she was starving hungry. 'It's been a bit of a week,' she said. 'Mr Nichols hasn't been in for days and now – well, they say his wife's passed away, last night.'

'Oh, the poor man.' Matty sank down on the nearest chair, her generous backside and skirts spilling over the seat. 'She was no age, was she?'

'I don't know,' Ada said. 'I s'pose not.'

'Was it . . .' Matty leaned forward to whisper. 'You know – C?'

'I don't know.' Ada shied away from talking or even

thinking about it. She remembered those terrible cries of agony from inside the house.

'Well, I suppose you'll go over to give your condolences,' Matty said over the rim of her teacup.

Ada looked up, her pulse racing. This thought had not occurred to her. She had very little idea about things like this. 'D'you think I should?'

'I'd say so,' Matty said. 'After all, you're running a business together now. Partners, more or less.'

'Yes,' Elsie said. 'Of course you should pay a visit. Think if it was the other way round?'

Was this the right thing to do? Ada was still asking herself as she walked along the entry to Nichols's old works yard and the house. She felt a chill, even though the day was mild enough.

She braced herself to knock but as she raised her hand the door opened and a man in a bowler hat came out; startled briefly at her standing there, he gave her a perfunctory nod and disappeared, leaving the door ajar. Ada listened for voices but there was no sound. She knocked timidly.

William Nichols appeared from the back of the dark room seeming dazed.

'Oh – Miss Fletcher.'

'I came to pay my condolences,' Ada said. And then had no idea what to say next.

'Come in.' He stood back. 'It's good of you.'

Ada stepped into a simple cottage room with a fireplace and a plain table and chairs.

'She's in the back,' he said. 'Would you like to see her?'

'Oh . . .' Of course this would be the case – Jane Nichols in the house until the morning of her burial. She could hardly say no.

She followed him through to the back room. A candle

was burning on a stand beside the coffin which lay open on two supports. William Nichols went and stood looking down into it and she felt obliged to join him, in a room that also felt colder than the day.

Whatever agonies Jane Nichols had passed through in her final illness were now over. Lying shrouded in white was a pale but wholesome looking-face, long brown hair swept neatly back and braided so that a plait lay alongside her left shoulder. She was lovely, Ada thought. Not pretty exactly, but lovely. She could imagine that face lighting with joy, with love. A face that would gladden your heart as you walked in through the door. Tears pricked in her eyes.

'I'm sorry,' she said, still looking down at Jane's face. 'Ever so sorry.'

'Death's not the worst,' he said hoarsely. 'It's the way of getting there.' She felt him turn to look at her and slowly she too turned and met his eyes. 'It was a Calvary,' he said. 'You wouldn't put an animal through it.'

She shook her head. 'No.'

'But we're expected to go through it.' His voice was low and full of pain and rage. 'How is that the work of a loving God, that's what I want to know?'

'He let his own son be crucified,' Ada pointed out. In case he misunderstood her she added, 'I've always wondered about that – it just doesn't seem the thing to say.'

William looked at her and suddenly jerked out a laugh. 'No, it doesn't. Come and have a drink with me? I think the visitors are over for today.'

He led her back to the other room and poured from a jug of ale.

'This is all I've got – unless you want tea?'

'This'll do well.' Ada did not normally drink alcohol but she took the little pewter mug and sat down. 'It was Vi gave us the news,' she said. She found she must say this, bring Vi up again. 'She seemed upset.'

'Well, Jane was good to her.' He sat opposite her. 'Gave her odd things to help out. With us not having children we had a bit spare – Vi was desperate at times.'

I'm in his house, Ada found herself thinking. Where he has lived with her, all these years. *Their* house, she corrected herself.

'Did she work with you?' Ada asked. He wanted to talk about his wife, she could see.

He nodded. 'She was a good worker – finishing mostly. We met at another works, then I started up and she came to work for me.' He smiled sadly. 'We weren't blessed with children but we were happy enough, the two of us. Never separated even for a day. I don't know—'

His voice choked and Ada saw his shoulders shaking.

'I don't know how to manage without her.' Loud, male sobs came from him and he leaned forwards, head in his hands. Ada felt panic rise in her. What should she do? She could hardly put her arms round him.

'I'm so sorry,' she said. 'Truly sorry.'

After a moment she reached out and gently touched his shoulder. It brought him round and he straightened up, wiping his face on his sleeves, one arm, then the other. He didn't apologize and she was glad of that.

'It's a terrible thing, losing someone,' he said. 'I wake in the morning and I'm weeping – before I've even . . . But I'm not the first and I shan't be the last.' He shook his head. He was silent for a moment, then he said, 'Everything going all right with the business? I'll be back now, properly, like.'

Relieved, Ada assured him that all was well. That Vi was behaving herself for the moment, that they were doing well keeping up with the orders and had in fact got new ones from another firm.

'So it's working – the two of us merging?' he said. 'I'm in two minds, whether I should've stayed here, picked myself up now and built it up again.'

'Well, if that's what you want,' Ada said, trying desperately to decide what she wanted herself. She wanted to grow her own business, which was happening now. And, in all honesty, she wanted him near, wanted to work with William Nichols, be beside him . . .

'I think –' he stared at the door as if he could see through it into the yard – 'if you're content we'll carry on as we are for the moment. I don't know . . .' He drifted off again. 'I just . . .' Then he turned to look at her and Ada was caught in his sad gaze. 'I think it's going to be a while before I know what I want.'

She nodded and stood up. Because it was suddenly unbearable being there. 'Very well.' She held out her hand. This was business, that was all. That was how it was going to remain. 'I'm content to do that for the moment.'

And they shook hands.

Twenty-Seven

John had taken to going out for long walks on Sunday afternoons. He had to get out, away from all those girls and their teasing and pulling him about. Sometimes he thought he'd go mad.

The Smiths were Chapel if they were anything but Mrs Smith was the only one who attended services at the Congregationalist chapel in the High Street now and again, more as if she thought she ought to just in case there was a God, than because she actually believed there was one. Very occasionally John went with her as it seemed to him a good thing to do.

But those times were rare because, as Harriet Smith said, it interfered with her cooking. And once the Sunday meat was carved and eaten to the last sliver, John escaped and took to the roads.

That autumn afternoon had a mildness to it, a glow of completion. Stubble from newly harvested fields fanned out from farms which clung to some sort of living between the encroaching darkness of industry. Even the stubble was tarnished with soot. The hedges, the grass, the air, everything was tainted. Though farmers handled ploughs pulled by immense horses across their fields, poking up beyond were chimneys, winding gear of the coal mines and the dark bulk of factories, all cut through by the shining lines of canals with boats sliding along them. And there was the smoke, the endless smoke and poisons coating the air. Even in the daytime the sky had a sick glow to it from all the foundries scattered across the area, while at night it loured, blood red.

John's body was tired, always, but his mind was like a basket of kittens. He strode out, accompanied only by his shadow in the weak sun and the sound of his boots on the track. The Smith girls wouldn't leave him alone until he was vexed almost beyond bearing. Not Margaret, the eldest – he was of no interest to her, but all the others.

The worst was Clara. Teasing, coming up close and peering into his face with those eyes. They were a colour he could never make out because it kept shifting between blue and green. She was always trying to get a reaction from him, prodding his shoulder hard, making faces.

'John's gone deaf – are you deaf, John? Can't you hear me? Or is he asleep?' While John stared at the floor, rigid with awkwardness because he did not know what to do. 'Come on,' Clara would call to the others. 'We'd best wake him up.'

If John did not get up and run out, they would be on him in a pack, pulling his hair, fingers in his ears, down his collar, poking at his face.

'Wakey-wakey, sleepyhead!'

'Oh, leave the poor lad,' Mrs Smith protested sometimes. Or she'd urge, 'You want to fight back, lad.'

But John was not the fighting kind, not even with girls. Never had been.

Often when he strode along on his walks his feelings surged and steamed in him. Irritation laced with shame – here he was trying to make something of himself and all they ever did was treat him like a toy, a performing monkey who could not remember any tricks.

But mixed with all this were the feelings that came over him whenever Clara came near him. Those eyes, the little swelling parts on her chest which pushed at her muslin blouse and moved beneath it, soft and shuddery as milk pudding, the scent of her. And what it made him feel, stirrings in his body which he was ashamed of. It made him want to handle himself, to do dirty things. Sometimes at night, waking with a feeling of utter bliss, he found himself damp and sticky down there and he was washed with shame and confusion.

Today though, his mind was in turmoil for a different reason. In his pocket was a letter which had arrived the day before, addressed to 'John Fletcher' at the Smiths' house – because of course they knew where he lived now. The handwriting was small and childish.

Dear John,
   I know Ada came to see you. I coudn't come becous I was not long sinse having a babby, your nice her name is Victoria. But don't you remember us John? Were your family. Ime your sister Elsie but you'd know me as Mary Lunn. We all want to see you please come John.
   From your sister
   Elsie
   Drakes, Galton Passage, Birmingham

He remembered her all right. She and Annie – or Dora as she now seemed to be calling herself. He didn't recall their names from before but he remembered them in the workhouse and to him they were Mary and Annie. Mary small and sweet-faced, big shiny eyes and quiet, doing as she was told. Annie, pretty, that's what he thought. Dreamy-eyed and with that vivid, flame-coloured hair. He knew they had all been in there together until Mary was sent away. And then he and Annie had been sent their ways.

Why did his chest ache every time he thought about them, these girls? A quite different ache from the one he felt whenever Clara was anywhere near him. And now there was this other sister, Ada, who he barely remembered, coming and trying to winkle him out when he wanted to be left alone to live his life.

He strode on further and further, passing through small settlements which all showed signs of busyness and wreckage from some form of industry or other. Cramped brick forges and sheds and workshops everywhere you looked, and messes of cinders and metal spoil, rusting iron and rotting wood tossed about the place. Nothing looked clean or pure.

He was approaching the beginnings of another such place, near a rotting barn. In the distance, across a scrubby field, were a row of poor cottages and he could hear the chinking sounds of a forge, blacksmith or nail-maker, he thought. John stopped on the track, near the barn, his feelings boiling in him.

'But why dig it all up again?' he enquired violently, of a tangle of sooty brambles. 'Why not let things be?'

'Eh, eh!' He heard a voice from close by. 'What's this then? Got a right noddley-ead 'ere. Talking to that bush, are yow?'

John swung round to see a bunch of lads swaggering out from the barn, caps jauntily on heads, hands in pockets. One of them, he saw, had lost an eye: the socket was scarred shut.

Fear gripped him. Nothing about them was friendly. They were like dogs, circling for a fight for no reason, just a way to pass another long Sunday.

The leader, who had emerged first, had a face like a parsnip, long, pale and stippled with deep little scars. He wore his cap well back on his head to show thin, rat-brown hair and when he spoke he had two sharp incisors and only a light scattering of teeth between.

'Where've you come from then?'

He came right up close, in John's face. From his mouth came the stink of decay. John felt he needed to pee, badly, all of a sudden. He stepped backwards, but the lad, about his own age, followed.

'Smethwick,' he said. Then, as if this might give him some sort of status, 'I work at Messrs Chance.'

This was not the right thing to say. The five of them found it grimly hilarious and exaggerated falling about with laughter at this ridiculous incomer on their territory.

'Messrs Chance, eh!' they mocked. 'Oh, *Messrs* Chance! Look at 'im – what a sir we 'ave 'ere!'

'Ew – Smethwick! We don't like you lot coming round 'ere.'

Sparing him any more of their wit they started on him then. The first one punched John in the jaw and he reeled back, completely unable to defend himself as the rest of them piled in, kicking and raining blows down on him on this lonely stretch of track. All he could remember afterwards were the lightning bolts of pain each time one of them hit him and the feel of blood warm on his lips. And lastly and most humiliatingly as he lay hopeless on the ground, the warm seep of urine as he wet himself.

It was a long and terrible walk home. He had no idea just how far he had strayed when he strode out that morning and the return was a purgatory. His face was cut, his body hurting all over and his clothing wet and foul-smelling. The day was muggy, the air seeming to clag round him as he limped along. His right hip and groin were an agony. He almost wished it would rain. The few people he met stared or made comments and as well as his beaten-up face he was sure they could see, or worse still, smell, the shameful stains on his trousers.

He got lost and walked at least a mile in the wrong direction, until a lady put him right. By then it was dusk and a relief that nothing could be seen too clearly. By the time he staggered to the fringes of Smethwick and West Bromwich, it was long dark and even then he had a job orientating himself to the door of the house.

This was the moment he dreaded most of all. He paused on the step, knowing what was on the other side of the door. All those eyes. *Her* eyes, laughing, making fun. The mockery and carry-on that would go on for days. All he wanted was to sink on to his bed and sleep and wake to a day when none of this had happened.

It was just as he dreaded. The two littlest girls were already up in bed, but the rest of them all fixed their eyes on him the moment he walked in. But – and this was shockingly different – there were no squeals of 'John, where've you been? You've been out for *hours!*'

Instead there was a stunned silence. It was Harriet who got up first, her face full of concern.

'Oh Lor', John, what's happened to you?' She came over and peered closely at him. John wondered what he looked like. He could only see out of one eye, there was a taste of blood on his lips, and his cheek, mouth, eyebrow – not to mention the rest of him – stung and ached.

'Clara,' Harriet Smith commanded, 'heat up some pans of water. You lot – you'll have to make yourself scarce in a while. If ever I saw a lad who needs to be in a tub of hot water it's this one.'

Unbelieving, John allowed himself to be shepherded to a chair as Clara obeyed orders and went out the back to pump water. It was a relief to sit. He felt odd, as if his chest was going to burst. Clara came back and clattered pans and the kettle, setting them on the fire.

'I'll bring the bath in from the back,' Enoch Smith said,

getting up. The tin bath was suspended on the back wall of the house, from a long rusty nail. 'And you lot –' he gestured to the other five girls – 'go upstairs.' They melted away with no argument. John's sense of wonder grew.

'You can tell us all about it in the morning,' Enoch said, dumping the bath down by the range. 'Let's just get you cleaned up for now.'

When she had finished setting the water to boil, Clara drew up a chair beside him. John felt his innards tighten. Was she going to start on him now?

But he found her head tilted to look up into his face and her own wore an expression of perplexity at the sight of him, mixed with a girl's sweet sympathy. She laid a hand over his.

'Poor old thing,' she said sweetly. 'Who's gone and done that to you? Who'd want to hurt our Johnny, eh?'

And she reached up and he felt her lips plant a kiss on his cheek. That was when the floodgates opened. John felt his chest heave and he burst into shuddering sobs. He started weeping, his gruff boy voice jerking out cries of distress and he wept and wept and could not stop. And through it all, as it took him over, pouring out so such bottled-up sadness, he felt Clara put her arms around his shoulders to hold him close, her hand softly stroking his back.

III

Twenty-Eight

September 1864

'Look at this – if needs be we can hang up stuff down here!'

It was the first time Minnie had seen their new home. In the flickering candlelight, she whirled into a dance along the brick floor of their cellar below their rooms in Bread Street with a grin that showed all her gappy teeth. The three rooms on the lower floor and the cellar were theirs for three and six – sixpence more a week than they had been paying for Mrs Lacey's house.

Dora smiled, catching Minnie's infectious high spirits as she stowed one of their washtubs against the wall. It was long after dark and they had been on the go non-stop. But she felt a new burst of energy as well now they were here and she had finally got Rose to go to sleep. They had made it!

In the days before they moved, Minnie had been nervous as a kitten, terrified to go out in case her father was lurking round any corner. Dora had ventured out to find the new place, further north and a mile or so away – she just hoped that would be far enough.

Entering the main door, one stepped into a narrow hallway off which opened the main room, a long space which reached from front to back of the house. To the other side of the hall were two small rooms and at the back, the wide yard offered them not just two lavatories and a brewhouse but also a water pump. It was perfect.

'We shan't have to lug the water half as far,' Dora reported to Minnie when she got back. 'And no going up and down stairs!'

'I'll miss you two,' Mabel said when they confided that they were moving. 'You've been good neighbours, you have.'

'Well, come and see us,' Dora said. She told her the address, even though she doubted Mabel would really come.

'But if anyone comes asking,' Minnie said quickly, 'a man, especially, you don't know where we are, all right?'

Mabel nodded. She knew about Minnie's father. 'Course. I won't let on.'

They had hired a hand cart and waited until the light was dying – earlier now as the nights were drawing in – before they loaded it with their few belongings and the tools of their trade, the washtubs, maiding tub and dolly. Between them they managed to heft the iron mangle on as well.

The girls set off into the cool darkness. They soon warmed up, taking it in turns to carry Rose or push the heavy cart which had a wonky wheel and did everything in its power to make life difficult.

'Damn and blast this thing!' Minnie groaned, trying to wrench the cart into a straight line. 'I feel like pushing it in the cut after this!'

But now everything was safely inside and the cart could go back tomorrow.

'I'm starved,' Dora said. It was so cold, they could see their breath in the candlelight. 'Let's light the fire and get summat down us.'

They had brought a bucket of coal with them and the two of them got the range going, brewed tea and sat wrapped in their bedding as the fire caught, eating bread and a knuckle of ham. Dora felt her limbs relax as the warmth gradually seeped into them.

'He won't come over here looking for you, will he?'

Minnie shook her head. 'Doubt it. Not that lazy sod.' She looked over at Dora suddenly. 'You never knew your Dad, did you?'

'I can remember him, just about.' Dora said slowly. 'He was all right, I think. Full of beans, like. But then he . . . He just – vanished.' She struggled to remember that awful time of confusion. She could recall some things: her mother's distress and panic – how was she going to manage with five children and all alone?

'Wish mine'd flaming well disappeared,' Minnie said. 'Instead of Mom passing on.' She looked at Dora again. 'We're a right pair, aren't we?' She chewed thoughtfully on a mouthful, her mind racing ahead. 'We can get new business round here. There's some big houses – and some of the firms have overalls and that, save washing them themselves. We'll soon get going.'

Dora sipped her tea, hands round the cup for comfort. Sometimes she felt so exhausted. As long as they could keep up their energy and not fall ill, they'd be all right.

'Anyway,' Minnie went on. 'If you start selling your stories we'll be better off, won't we? Why don't you send one to one of those books? That one about the highwaywoman, that was my favourite!'

She grinned across at Dora, who despite sometimes resenting Minnie chivvying her, did love the girl's endless optimism.

'All right,' she agreed nervously. 'Soon as we get settled in.'

Although their work was punishingly hard, Dora and Minnie found life in Bread Street easier than it had been before. Having a pump in the yard made a lot of difference. The other occupants of the building these days were small shops and firms whose staff, apart from visits to the lavs, had no call to go out there.

The two floors above housed a variety of one-room shops making brushes, birdcages, one which made frames for spectacles, another which bound books. So in the daytime there was a good deal of thumping up and down the stairs. The men they bumped into said, 'Morning,' or 'How do?' and by the evening they were gone.

So there was no competition for washing in the brewhouse and they were able to do a lot more in there instead of in the house and risk hanging some of the washing in the yard. In addition, the cellar, though dank as any other, had a grille on the street side allowing air to flow in and help with drying the lines of washing and if necessary they could finish off the drying upstairs.

They kept some of the customers they'd had before and Minnie, happy to go out again, went round calling on the bigger firms to enquire whether they had any laundry they wanted doing.

'It won't cost you much,' she persuaded them. 'Just three shillings a week and then you'll know all the overalls are spick and span.'

Some grumbled they weren't paying for something their workers could do perfectly well for themselves.

'Ah – but is it perfectly?' Minnie asked cheekily. 'I bet we'd do it better.'

She won two of them over – a silversmith's and a toolmaker's said they'd pay for the staff's overalls to be washed every week, now that someone was asking.

The overalls from the toolmaker's were especially greasy and needed chalk and onion juice to get out as much as they could. Dora bashed and pounded them round in the maiding tub until her arms were shaking with the effort. Then she scrubbed the grease marks by hand. They weren't perfect, but the firm seemed happy enough.

'Get one lot of dirt off and we're only gunna put another lot on,' the man said who gave Minnie the work. He was kindly, giving them a chance. And when she delivered it back, no comment was made. They were happy enough to pay three shillings a week to get it all done.

Dora and Minnie cooked and ate and did all the washing in one room. The other two rooms on the ground floor were bedrooms and places for extra drying. They worked and worked, reaching the end of the day with back muscles twinging with exhaustion, hands raw and cracked from the harsh soaps and being constantly in water.

Minnie had started making a salve for their hands at home after asking the chemist what was in the one she had bought from him (and he, rather rashly, told her). Lard and eggs, honey and a drop of rosewater with oatmeal mixed in. Soon they had a bigger, cheaper supply of the soothing paste than they could ever buy ready-made. And their arrangements meant Dora could still always have Rose close to her, though at times it was a struggle to keep her occupied. She and Minnie barricaded off a corner of the room with chairs and a clothes horse to give her a place to move about and each of them would stop for a little while to feed Rose or play with her. She was a happy little thing, always in sight of them, and she would tinker for long periods with some pegs, a spoon, or little toys Dora had started to buy for her – a rag doll, a little mirror in which she would stare at herself and chuckle.

But now Rose was growing, starting to pull herself up on her feet.

'Heaven help us when she really gets moving,' Dora said, looking at her little girl's dark-eyed face and melting at the sight. Rose was the centre and meaning of her life and whenever she looked at her, really took the time to gaze upon the loveliness of her child, her heart would buckle, so assaulted by both joy and sadness that it did not know which way to turn.

In the midst of all this, at any quiet moment, Dora carefully wrote out her story. She bought some sheets of good-quality paper, a cheap fountain pen, some ink and a tuppenny envelope. Wincing as her cracked hands gripped the pen, she sat struggling to make her handwriting look as grown up and respectable as possible.

'Ooh, that looks nice,' Minnie kept saying excitedly, coming over to peer at it.

Dora tried not to be excited. The idea that she could be a writer, a proper writer, was a lifelong dream, buried so deep inside her that she hardly dared let it take hold. It took her hours to copy out her long story and by the end, everything about it seemed wrong. What was she thinking, sending it to someone to look at? How could she know if it was any good? Supposing no one wanted it? It would be terrible. Better just to keep dreaming because at least then she had the refuge of the dream.

But eventually she folded the papers carefully, glued down the envelope and wrote the address of the publication she had chosen – a family monthly called *Around the Hearth*.

She slipped out one afternoon taking Rose with her, balanced on one hip. Sliding the pre-paid envelope into the letter box, she held on to it for a second, unable to bear letting go. Her heart was thudding hard. Sending her little story out into the world made her feel scared, naked almost. Rose was wriggling on her other arm and she let the letter drop.

'Bye-bye, story,' she murmured to it. 'Good luck!'

And she walked home, full of excitement and fear.

Don't be silly, she told herself as she stepped back into the house. They won't want you.

She put Rose down with a few of her bits and pieces to keep her occupied, went back to the tubs of dark-coloured clothing she had left soaking and got to work, pounding the dirt out of them.

Within only three days, a letter arrived addressed to 'Miss Dora Lunn'.

Minnie brought it in for her, eyes wide with anticipation.

'Did you send it then? The story?' Her fingers searched the envelope and her face fell.

'It's quite thick. I think they must have sent it back.'

Dora snatched it off her, boiling with annoyance. Why did Minnie have to pick it up and start guessing what was inside? If she was to have a letter for the very first time in her life she wanted to be the one who found it and guessed at the contents!

Avoiding Minnie's eager eyes she quickly took it into the yard, hardly able to contain herself until she was inside the privy before she ripped the envelope open with trembling fingers. Her carefully written-out pages of story were inside, with a short note on a torn half-sheet.

Dear Miss Lunn,
I am returning your submission to our paper. Though it has moments of merit I'm afraid I find the tone of it a little mawkish and over-heated for our readers.
Wishing you better fortune in future,
James Sapphire,
Editor

*

So Minnie was right. Dora stood there feeling as if she had been punched. In those moments, she hated James Sapphire, and his ornate, looping signature, with a passion she had never before felt for anyone. Over-heated? What did that mean? Too exciting? Bad? Just *bad*? And mawkish? What did he mean?

Too upset even for tears she went slowly back into the house. 'Not this time, they say,' she told Minnie curtly.

And she tucked her skirt up and went back to the laundry, the sweat on her face mingled with the heartbroken tears of someone whose dreams were shrivelling and dying inside them.

Twenty-Nine

'Look who's here!' Gert cried as Elsie appeared in the shop at the start of the day. 'You starting again proper now?'

Ada's workers all turned happily to greet Elsie who was already pulling her hair under her cap and putting on her work apron.

'It's nice to be back,' she said, looking round with a grin. 'Even with you lot.'

Vi and the other workers from Nichols's smiled as well. Elsie had popped in sometimes with little Vicky and they liked her, even though at first there was a lot of whispering. '*Shame* about her face – what the hell happened? She must've been pretty . . .'

Elsie, who was sensitive to this, had turned to them the first time.

'If you want to know, I had acid thrown over me by a vicious, jealous cow. She's in prison now and I'm happily married to the best man you could find, so she's not done me much harm, has she?'

Ada, watching in surprise, saw Vi nod with respect on hearing this and a smile crept over her own face. Good for Elsie, she thought. She was learning how to deal with all the whispering and gossip around her, facing it head on.

Elsie was soon working away. She knew all the button-making skills now and there was a space for her on a backing lathe, the fast-turning tool shearing off the shell's gnarled surface from the back of the button and giving it a curved shape.

'Everything all right?' Ada asked, going up to her.

Elsie glanced at her. 'Yes – it's nice to come out for a bit. I think George's mom's over the moon to get rid of me and have Vicky to herself!'

The morning passed busily as usual and Elsie dashed off at dinner time to give Vicky a feed. She returned just in time to have a quick chat with the others before they were back at work.

'Where's Nichols?' she asked Ada as she walked back to her work station. 'Doesn't he ever show his face?'

'He's not long buried his wife,' Ada said tetchily, though in truth she had been wondering the same thing.

But shortly afterwards, William Nichols appeared. He nodded at her as he came in and headed along the shop to talk to his own workers. A moment later Vi was having a go about something. Ada rolled her eyes. Still, let her moan if that's what she wants. He can sort her out – because I'm not having it.

She felt tired and all of a sudden very irritable. She left the shop and went down to the sorting table. William Nichols had not said a word to her, he had gone straight to his workers. After all, she was the boss, wasn't she, Ada thought angrily as she started sorting through the latest batch of shells.

She could not admit to herself that her bad mood was about more than William Nichols's manners. She was wounded. Wanted him to notice her, to *want* to talk to her.

After a time, he came down again, seemingly in a hurry. He was preoccupied and nearly left without speaking to her, but then he suddenly noticed her in the gloom behind the table.

'Oh – Miss Fletcher.' He raised his hat. 'I've a few things to sort out today – I just came in to see if all is well.'

'Any complaints from Vi?' Ada asked, finding she wanted to keep him there.

'Nothing of any importance.' A shadow of a smile played round his lips. 'Anyway – I'll be in properly after today.'

And off he went.

In properly, Ada thought. They were going to be working together, day after day. Dragging her thoughts strictly towards business, she realized it was going to be a great relief to have someone else to run the place with – so long as it worked all right. And he seemed a reasonable man, or she would not have got into this partnership.

It was a practical advantage, she told herself stiffly. They were already doing well, getting more work. This company was going to progress, not stay as a tiny one-room shop like so many others.

What she found harder to explain was why the idea of working beside William Nichols every day filled her with such a sweet, pulsing excitement. The man had just lost his wife – he had no interest in her or anyone else. But despite all this, Ada could just not seem to help looking forward to it.

Days passed, weeks which took them into a new year. William Nichols came into the works every day as promised. To Tom's relief he was good at fixing any problems with the machines. He offered to take over the books which was also a relief to Ada.

'It's all right,' he said, seeing her doubtful look. 'I've no intention of diddling you.'

'Diddling?' Ada laughed suddenly, never having heard the word before.

'Swindling. Cheating. If you bring them down I'll take them and have a good look through – I don't mind that sort of work at all. And Miss Fletcher . . .'

He looked keenly into her eyes and something in her shifted. For heaven's sake, she scolded herself inwardly. She was like a mooning girl. She gave what she hoped was a cool and enquiring look.

'When all this first began I was not sure whether it would be on a very short-term basis. You've saved me in a crisis and for that I'm very grateful. But this arrangement does seem to be working well for both businesses, would you not agree?'

'I would,' she said. 'We're growing. Business is coming in – I'd say we're thriving.'

William Nichols nodded. 'We've had a chance to sound each other out, work together. I think we should establish the partnership on a legal basis. Combine our names?'

'Fletcher and Nichols?' Ada said.

'If you like.'

He did not sound all that concerned and she was surprised. She had jumped to get in and have her name in first place on their business.

William Nichols held out his hand. 'I can organize an attorney, if you are content.'

She shook his hand, meeting his eyes steadily. 'I am.'

Despite the business moving forwards – the partnership established, the new brass plate, 'Fletcher & Nichols', outside and work pouring in – William Nichols appeared like a ghost in his own life.

'Poor man, he's grieving,' the women said, when his sad presence was out of earshot.

'He'll never get over her,' Vi decreed, with the importance of someone who had known him longer than anyone else. 'She was the love of his life. Beautiful, she was, inside and out.'

They were on their dinner break, round the little table or, now there were more people, rowed up on a bench at the side of the shop.

Ada bristled on hearing Vi's words, irritated by her taking charge, being a know-it-all about her employer's feelings. But even more, Ada felt the sting of comparison. Beautiful inside and out. She could hardly compete with that, could she? And then she got cross with herself all over again for her growing realization that she had allowed herself to fall helplessly in love with a man who hardly knew she existed, except as a handy helper to rescue his business.

What a fool she was, she kept telling herself. Feeling herself flush whenever William appeared. Her pulse racing when she heard his voice. What in God's name was the matter with her? She who was never going to tangle with men!

All in all, Ada was in a very bad mood a lot of the time.

'What's up with you?' Elsie asked her one morning when she had just snapped at Biddy, the youngest by far in the shop. Elsie had taken Ada off out of the shop, to the small landing at the top of the stairs. 'She only asked you a question, the poor child.'

'Nothing,' Ada said, not sounding any less testy. 'I've just got a lot on my mind.'

Elsie moved closer, a mischievous smile on her lips. 'You wouldn't have a certain Mr Nichols on your mind, would you?'

Ada glared at her. 'What the hell're you on about?'

'Sis, anyone can see you've got a flame lit for him – the way you look at him.'

'What?' Ada was appalled – even more so by the fact that a blush was seeping up her cheeks. All her tender feelings – the ones she only allowed herself when she lay in bed at night, dreaming of being in William Nichols's arms, of his face, smiling, loving, close to hers – were apparently on show and she had no idea!

She swallowed and tried to calm her emotions.

'You're just being silly,' she said stiffly. 'You know I'm not interested in marriage and all that sort of thing.'

Elsie put her head on one side, serious now. 'Marriage is lovely, Ade. You're so set in your ways. D'you want to stay an old maid the rest of your life?'

'Yes,' Ada snapped. 'I do. And anything else you reckon you're seeing is just you thinking everyone should be the same as you!'

And she took off down the stairs, fuming and all a-jangle with emotion.

Ada tried to resign herself, to tell herself she was a fool. You could not hurry grief, she knew that. She and William Nichols worked side by side, discussed the business, orders and deliveries in a way that was never anything but calm and amicable. He was a reasonable man, she found. He was pleasant, polite. As the freezing days became milder and the spring arrived, her respect for him only increased.

She knew he had no interest in her. A cloak of sadness hung over him at all times. He tried to smile, even to joke with the workers and with her at times. But his face would sober immediately and if she came upon him when he was alone he often looked close to despair. How she longed to give comfort and how much she knew she was not the person he was longing for.

One evening the two of them were still in the shop after everyone else had gone. William had brought in the book where the accounts for orders were kept and he showed it to Ada.

'Seems Beardsmore's have upped their order from us?' he

said, coming to stand next to her. Ada peered over his arm at the figures.

'Yes,' she said. 'We're going to have to think about this soon – whether we can keep up.'

Now that they were producing finished buttons and only had to send them out for carding, they were also still supplying half-made blanks to Beardsmore's, as before. Everyone was working at full stretch.

'Yes, I see.' William stroked his chin and Ada heard the rasp of his dark bristles. 'We don't have room to take on any more workers, do we?'

'I think we can manage for now – that size of order anyhow.' She tried to fix her attention on the numbers, not the fact that as he turned to look at her she could feel, faintly, his breath on her cheek. 'But we'll have to watch it. I'd have thought it'd be better if we moved over to finished only – we can sell all of them straight into the market.'

There was a silence and Ada's cheeks blazed. She could feel William looking at her. She turned her head. His brown eyes were fixed thoughtfully on her and Ada could suddenly feel every stitch of her clothing on her skin. Her flesh, unloved, neglected – but not old. It was as if his gaze could see through to her.

He slammed the ledger shut then. 'Yes, you're right. As you usually are, Miss Fletcher.' She could hear a smile in his voice and she wanted to say, *Call me Ada, please.* But they were standing so close . . . And she still called him Mr Nichols. 'But I think we can manage these orders – at least for now.'

He stepped back and walked off, leaving the faint prints of his boots in the floor's white coating of dust. She watched his back, dark, slender. And then he turned.

'I wonder if . . .' He paused. 'Thing is, I need to get out. The four walls, you know. I thought, Saturday afternoon, I'd go somewhere. Change of scene. I wondered if you'd like to come?'

Thirty

Once the Saturday-morning cleaning was finished, the women all gone and the shop shut up, Ada went upstairs, relieved that Tom was out, as usual. All of a sudden she felt all a-flutter with nerves. No, who was she trying to fool? She had been all a-flutter the whole morning, but there had been enough to do with all the sweeping of the white pelt of dust and tidying up to keep her mind busy.

For a moment she sank down on the side of her bed and looked at her hands, feeling almost as if she had never seen them before. They were white, work-worn, the skin end-of-winter dry. Looking in the glass she saw her thin face, also dry and uncared for, her hair dragged up severely close to her head. Her heart sank. She looked such an old witch already. Six weeks away, in June, she would be twenty-four. An old maid, that was true – but was that really *so* old?

She tried smiling at herself. Her brown eyes softened and her cheeks lifted. That face she liked better, she realized. She must remember to do it more often.

Getting up, she picked through her few clothes in dismay. She was going out for an afternoon with a man. Was she? Was that what this arrangement was? Her heart said yes. Her head told her, Don't be so daft. This is a man who had not long lost his wife. He's grieving and he wants some company. You're just a work partner – convenient to ask.

Pushing her feelings away she took down what counted as her best dress from the back of the door. Sunday best – not that she was a churchgoer – in dark blue. She held it against herself and felt a wave of despair. She looked like a governess! Brighter clothes seemed to be coming into fashion and she had got severely left behind.

'I'm not some flibbertigibbet,' she murmured, laying the dress on the bed. 'I'm a businesswoman.'

But beside it, she added the one daring item of clothing she had, given to her by Elsie: a pair of navy-and-white stockings, the stripes circling her legs.

Before dressing, she stripped and gave herself a washdown all over. She always had a good wash at the weekend – still went across to the baths at Kent Street sometimes. Today it felt more like a ritual. A preparation.

She dressed in clean undergarments, chemise, her corset, pulling it as tight as she could stand (which was not very), bloomers and flannel petticoat. She rolled the new stockings on, feeling very daring, and thought about a crinoline. If there was one garment she loathed with a passion it was a crinoline, having to walk about with steel hoops swaying about under your clothes. She had resisted ever acquiring one. No, thank you!

Her more old-fashioned remedy, a corded petticoat and a stiff one at that, would still give her skirt a pleasing shape and she slipped that on.

She brushed and brushed her hair to shift as much of the white pearl dust as she could. Then she was struck by the dilemma of how to dress it.

'Oh, I don't know!' she raged, after trying this and that. She hurled the hairbrush down on the bed and to her own amazement felt like bursting into tears. 'What am I supposed to do?' She knew she should have asked Elsie who somehow always seemed to know about these things. But it was too late now, and shaming in any case.

What she did not want was to look hard. Careworn. After several attempts, she drew back the top half of her hair, smoothed it down and braided it, catching the plait up in a loop at the back and pinning it. She even found a length of white ribbon to tie in a bow at the top. The rest of her hair fell in dark honey tresses.

Finally, she slid into the dress and added a cheap little necklace she had of pearl and blue beads. She turned to smile into the glass. And had to admit she now looked quite nice. Like someone you might enjoy seeing at least.

She chose her summer hat – straw with a blue band – and keeping the smile on her lips, she went out to meet William Nichols on Livery Street, at one-thirty, as arranged. In Galton Passage she crossed with old Jonas Parry. He took one look at her and his face lit up in pleasure and surprise.

'Good day, missy – you're looking fine!'

'Thank you, Jonas.'

The blush that spread over her face was still there when she stepped into Livery Street, and deepened further when she saw that William Nichols was already waiting for her at the side of the road next to the open door of a cab! She was struck with surprise by all of it – not least that today he was wearing a black bowler hat when she had only ever seen him in a cap. It made him look handsome and rather noble. Her astonishment overcame her shyness at meeting him.

'Oh, my goodness – I thought we were going to walk!'

'That's no way to treat a lady,' William said with a little bow. He seemed strangely excited, full of a kind of energy she had not seen in him before. 'A cab there and back, that's what I thought – we can have a nicer walk while we're there. And keep your dress out of the mire as well.'

He stood back to let her climb in, carrying her warm black shawl over one arm. Thank heaven she did not wear a crinoline, she thought, settling on the narrow seat. Even getting in and out of here would have been mortifying.

William joined her, closing the door, and they were seated side by side, suddenly very close together, the little carriage jolting into movement. Slender as she was, Ada could feel her hip pressed against him, his thighs in his charcoal serge trousers, his black boots. She became intensely aware of the black weave of his jacket, the dusting of white on it, his hands, strong fingers – nice hands, she thought – resting on his thighs.

'It's very kind of you,' she said nervously, crossing her ankles. Would he notice her stripy stockings – and if so, what might he think? And whatever were they to talk about?

She need not have worried. As soon as they started to progress bumpily along the streets, William began to talk gently, naming the roads they were passing along – Snow Hill, Summer Lane – and landmarks – the General Hospital and north to Aston. She realized he was trying to put her at her ease and she was grateful. The journey seemed to pass quickly and the next thing Ada knew, they were climbing out and looking along the driveway to the imposing bulk of Aston Hall. She had barely had to say a word.

The day was cool but bright. Ada pulled her shawl around her, but there was no rain and the light was clear.

'The air feels fresher here, doesn't it?' William said as they moved towards the wide Jacobean mansion with its solid, elegant wings and clock tower at the centre. Ada gazed at it.

'I've never seen a house like it before,' she said, amazed by its grandeur.

'It's very old,' William said. He had quietened a little

now. 'They started building it in 1618, a Sir Thomas Holte. It's quite a place.'

Ada turned to him. 'Have you been here before?'

William looked down, suddenly intent on his feet. 'Once.'

He seemed reluctant to say any more. Of course, she thought, with a pang of something – jealousy? Something in her that she did not like, in any case – he would have come here with her. With Jane. She decided she did not want to think about it.

'Are we allowed to go inside?'

'Yes – it's open to the public,' he said. 'Come on – you'll like it.'

For the next couple of hours the two of them explored the house, the grand rooms of a size almost unimaginable to people who had lived always in the cramped dwellings which clung round the heart of Birmingham. The decorated ceilings, the marble fireplaces and wide, creaking floorboards; the grand staircase with treads so wide you could almost lie down on them – all of it was astonishing.

Walking into one room, Ada gave a loud gasp. Before her, a long gallery stretched ahead almost as far as she could see, the boards covered by a faded red carpet. Her eye was caught by the white ceiling decorated with ornate patterns like the most fancily decorated of cakes. And then there was almost too much to take in. The walls were lined with beautiful wood panelling, broken only, on one side, by another pale and immense marble mantlepiece reaching right up to the ceiling. All along the vast room were arranged marble plinths topped with white stone busts of men, and intricately carved chairs, and on the walls hung portraits of grand ladies and gentlemen in silken clothes and ruffs. Light beamed gently into the room through leaded windows as Ada gazed at the portraits.

'Who are all these people?' she murmured to William. 'It feels as if they're looking down their noses at us.'

'I don't know – the family probably.' He turned and smiled at her and again, that smile jolted feelings inside her. 'They can't do much to you – they're only paintings. And they're probably all dead by now anyway.'

Ada snorted and burst out laughing, which made him laugh as well as they walked along the gallery, admiring and trying to control themselves. And Ada thought she had never felt so happy.

Afterwards they wandered round the green of the gardens. It was breezy but they found a place out of the wind to sit.

'Look,' William said. 'I don't know if you're hungry? I brought these.' From his bag he took a packet in waxed paper and opened it to display hunks of fresh bread and ham. Ada's eyes lit up.

'I'm always hungry,' she admitted.

'Good. Well, tuck in.' He held it out and she took a doorstep of bread. It smelt delicious.

'I brought tea as well.' He produced a bottle, still faintly warm. She looked at him in wonder.

'I never even thought – I'm sorry . . .'

'That's all right. Now I'm on my own I have to look to my own stomach,' he said, staring across the grass back at the house. 'And it's always quite demanding.'

She laughed. It was a good feeling.

They sat side by side, eating. All that day, Ada felt herself opening, flowering. At home, working hard, always thinking of the business, she tried not to dwell on the couples around her. Elsie and George, Tom and Dinah, those kisses they were exchanging in her kitchen sometimes when she walked in. She closed her mind to it. To love. To the actions that took place mysteriously in bedrooms that resulted in a little baby like Vicky. It felt wrong to think of it in anyone else. Nosey and dirty. She pushed away even her own longing to experience such a thing. She did not bother with men – that was who she was. Ada, an old maid, and that was how she was going to stay, thank you very much. Build a business, make money for them all so that none of her family would have to live in poverty any more, or be servants to anyone else ever again.

But now, sitting here next to William, something new blossomed in her heart. She could not hide from herself that she was in love with him, this gentle, suffering man. For a moment, neither could she dismiss the thought of lying with him, his face looking down on hers, the smile, both of them unclothed . . .

To fight the blushes rising in her cheeks she said hurriedly, 'So – you said you had been here before?'

William chewed, swallowed his mouthful and took a good swig of tea, nodding as he did so.

'In '56 they had a big do here – called some grand name, the Fête Champêtre, I think it was.'

Ada thought back quickly. William was a good fifteen years older than she was. Where was she in '56? Her heart sank. Still living with the Connells. She would never have heard about any French-sounding do, here or anywhere else.

'It was raising funds for the General Hospital,' he said. 'Cost a bob to come in – there were crowds of the like I've never seen anywhere else. And they got the whole place up – decorations and flags and bunting. And there was dancing and entertainments, fairground rides.' His voice warmed as he spoke. 'We went on the merry-go-round several times because—' He stopped suddenly.

We. Ada cursed herself. Of course *we*. They were a married couple.

'I've never been on one,' she said, to fill the moment because William had caught himself in the middle of the memory. And how long would it be before this man was ready to give his heart to anyone but Jane? Her own feelings plummeted in her so suddenly they brought a lump to her throat.

'Well, it was quite a day,' he said. And gave her one of those amused looks that flared in him for a second before fading.

And from then on, from the almost over-excited man of the morning, who had raised his spirits to give her a nice day out, she could feel him sinking. They walked on a little more and she tried to interest him in talking about the business, their plans. She loved the idea of them scheming, building together.

But try as she might – and William tried too – she could feel that he was disappearing back into the sad and lonely person she knew from day to day. It wrung her heart.

They travelled back together in silence, each looking out at the passing houses and factories. Ada spent the journey giving herself common-sense talkings-to.

Of course he's still grieving. And I'm not the right person – I'm not her. But he did ask me to come – he must like me a little. I must be patient. Maybe he could feel something for me if I just give him time . . .

When he let her out, in the street where they had started off, she thanked him warmly.

'That was really nice,' she said, smiling at him.

She saw William force his features into a smile in return, but it was as if the pilot light had gone out in him.

'Glad you enjoyed it,' he said.

She could tell he was keen to get away now, to be alone, and she tried not to feel like a disappointment. Turning away, he tipped his hat and said, 'Well, see you Monday.'

Ada nodded. 'Yes,' she said. 'Of course.'

Of course. She was his business partner – nothing more. She tried to control her sinking feelings. This had been nothing – just an afternoon for William to distract himself.

He took two steps away, then turned. He was silent for a split second as if still trying to decide to speak. Then he said, 'Perhaps we could do it again, one weekend?'

Ada took a breath, despite her pounding blood. 'Yes,' she said. 'If you like. That'd be nice.'

Inside, their rooms were still empty. She flung her hat on the table, then went into her bedroom and did the same to herself, on to the bed. She lay staring at the ceiling for a moment. A spider crouched, legs all scrunched up, in one corner. She thought about the day spent with a man who she seemed helplessly to love, a man grieving for another woman.

The thoughts she could not seem to control forced themselves into her mind. Herself and William bedded together, their hands exploring each other's pale bodies, his eyes, fixed on her with loving attention . . . This longing overcame her every time she allowed herself the leisure to think.

Lovemaking – that act . . . And yet the very thought made her recoil. Because with that came marriage and living endlessly together and subservience to a man and endless childbearing – all the things which repelled her. Why couldn't anyone seem just to experience the Act – without all the rest of it . . .? But those women, bad women – she knew what *those* women were called.

Overcome by this storm of feelings which had been raging in her all day, Ada curled on her side and let out great gulping sobs, releasing the pressure in tears.

Thirty-One

John staggered out of the house into the chill morning, hurrying to join the early Monday 'move' or shift at Chance & Co., at seven. These three-hour 'moves' were usually worked in pairs of six hours, alternating with six hours of rest while another batch of workers took over, day and night from Monday to Wednesday. By then they had done a week's work – or eleven 'moves'. Any time worked on a Thursday or Friday counted as overtime and each of those moves worked would add threepence to John's wage of four shillings a week. It was almost unheard of to work on Friday and Saturday.

But setting off now, shivering in the dawn, John was facing the relentless three days and nights ahead of him and for the first time he almost felt he could not face it at all. His slowness that morning had made Enoch Smith impatient and he had set off without him.

'Don't be hard on the lad,' Harriet chided him. 'He's not been well.'

But Enoch strode out of the door and that morning John would not be walking into the furnace room proudly alongside his chair. Harriet had thrust a chunk of hard beef and a lump of bread at him as he left and he chewed on it going along.

Approaching the works, he looked up at the leaden sky with great plumes of charcoal-coloured smoke leaning across it and felt like weeping.

His wounds had healed over from the beating those

thugs had given him a few weeks back but his mind and soul were far from strong. He felt shaken and fragile. And full of inner turmoil.

In his time apprenticed at Chance, he had had no trouble with other lads. He did not have many friends either – he knew he was seen as a bit odd. A quiet, studious lad, quaint but harmless. And he had found his place of comfort outside work in the schoolroom where he – also quietly – thrived.

So being set upon by those strangers for no reason, the viciousness of the beating, had left him shaken. The venom of it had reached into his mind as well as his body. It had released a pent-up store of hurt and sadness in him that he had not known was there. He had broken down and cried – in front of Clara and the others!

And now, on top of everything else, there was Clara. The fact that he could not stop thinking about her, his eyes following her whenever they were in a room together, however much he did not want them to. She had been nice to him. Sweet and sympathetic – not like the girl who was always teasing and poking at him. That was what had made him cry. Her being so kind. He had wanted to lean on her, lean into her and let himself be comforted like a little child.

And now he was embarrassed and did not know what to do with his thoughts and the way his body let him down when those thoughts came to him.

He turned into the works, the great city-like business of it, the tall, smoking cones of the furnaces dotted all around it. All weekend, the glass was being prepared for the week, the clay pots set on Friday nights, filled with a mixture of clay and sand and other materials and smelted down overnight so that the contents were only about a third the size. The pots would be filled once more, and then a third time, over the weekend, sealed again each time and left in the furnace. By now, Monday, the material inside was ready for working into glass.

Across the room he saw Enoch already seated, bent over, and he went to him, ashamed. But Enoch looked up at him with his usual benevolence.

'Ah, finally rolled out of bed, did you?' And he winked.

And John knew that things with Enoch were all right and that work must now begin.

It happened later that morning. He was soaked in sweat, he and the other takers-in scurrying back and forth between the chair and the annealing ovens. They scarcely ever moved slower than a trot and the work was exhausting. Every day, after working for only twenty minutes he would be drenched in sweat. He was well used to the work by now, but today it was as if the long handle and flat wooden paddle at the end on which the heated items rested were made of lead. His mind was racing – Clara, her cheeky face, the rosebud lips, her hands on his back stroking him and those round bulges on her chest . . . His mind boiled and the muscles in his back and shoulders were painful almost beyond bearing. Then his arms started to shake. He felt panic rise in him. What was the matter with him? He did not feel as if he had a fever, but he felt strange, weak, and as if shaken inside and out.

Enoch had just fashioned a jug, a curved and beautiful molten shape, glowing as he pulled it out of the flames. It was a generous-sized thing and John felt the heft of it as he raised it parallel to the ground and set off, trying to keep up his usual speed as the next item would be ready very soon. He got halfway along to where the annealing ovens were and felt his arms lose all power. There was a terrible moment of shaking as he tried to keep the thing raised off the ground, but it came crashing down, the jug lurching off and sinking into a molten mess at his feet.

John groaned with horror.

'You'll be for it,' one of the other lads called out, hurrying past in the opposite direction.

'Scoop that up.' One of the servitors saw what had happened, saw John's utter dismay. He hurried over. With a couple of bits of wood they scraped up the unmendable slumped remains of the jug. 'Mr Smith'll dock it off your wages. Go on – get yourself back for the next.'

Enoch Smith turned from his lean into the furnace, his face a-shine with sweat, and gave John a look such as he never wanted to see on the man's face again, this man whom he worshipped.

'What's ailing you today, boy?' was all he said.

And John had expressions of sorrow and shame sprouting like weeds on his lips. But he could not find a shape or sound for them and he never said a word. He braced every bit of strength he could find and carried on working.

'I want to come with you.'

Clara stood over him, hands on hips as he was pulling his boots on, about to set off for his afternoon out. He wouldn't go as far as usual, he was thinking. He'd stick to places he knew, closer to home. He was nervous after being set upon when he was just minding his own business.

Since his shameful outburst afterwards, and her being sweet to him, John could hardly look the girl in the eye. His face flushed red and not just from bending over.

'No,' he murmured. 'You'd best stop here.'

Clara bent over and gave him a painful poke in the ribs.

'I wanna come. Mom,' she broadcast across the room, to John's extreme irritation, 'you don't need me, do you? I can go for a walk with John?'

Harriet had all but finished clearing up after the dinner.

'If you want,' she said. With a mischievous smile she added, 'You can make sure nothing goes amiss with him.'

'*No*,' John said, getting up in a rush after this humiliation. 'I'm going on my own!'

'Oh, *you*,' Clara said huffily. She gave him such a shove that he nearly bashed into the door frame. 'You're mean, you are.'

John threw her off and strode out, slamming the door.

'Flaming girls,' he muttered to himself, charging along. 'They don't know nothing, they don't. Always keeping on . . .'

He was walking at a great rate, taking no notice of where he was going. Even so, within a couple of minutes he heard footsteps trotting along behind him and she soon caught up with him.

She was different now. She had thrown her checked green-and-red shawl on and was all sweet and wheedling.

'Go on, John. Let me come. I want to be with you.'

For a moment he could not speak, was paralysed by not knowing how to react. When he cranked his head round eventually, Clara was looking up at him – she was a head smaller – her big blue eyes fixed on him, those rosebud lips in an appealing pout. And she was lovely – so lovely.

'Please?' She smiled winningly and all he could do was melt. Despite himself a smile twitched at his lips. His heart was singing – she was here! She wanted to be with him.

'All right,' he said grumpily. 'If you must.'

'Where're we going?' she said.

John shrugged. He desperately wanted, and did not want, Clara there beside him and he could not work out which of these emotions he felt more strongly.

'That way,' she pointed, taking charge. And John could only follow her lead, helpless to her.

Thirty-Two

They walked in silence for a while, heading west into a mellow afternoon, winter's harshness gone and the warm flowering of May now making itself felt. John relaxed in the sunshine and in air that was, if not clean – because it was forever tainted with smoke and acrid stinks of industry – at least moving with a slight breeze.

Around them as they walked, there was little to surprise them. A huddle of cottages here, a mine shaft or forge there. And soon their attention was more on each other than their surroundings. Clara soon got fed up with his silence and started – that was how it felt at first – on at him.

'You never tell us anything about yourself, John Lunn,' she said archly. 'Not about the past nor the present neither.'

This was true, but then no one had ever really asked. They were children when he arrived, but now they were almost grown up – he eighteen to her sixteen.

'Go on – tell me about summat. You've got a sister – I saw her. More than one sister. So tell me.'

'What?' he said. He sounded stubborn but at that moment genuinely did not know what she might want with this question.

'Well, where was you born?'

He had to think about that. He had been living with the Smiths for more than six years now, since he started his apprenticeship at Chance & Co. The place that had become his haven, his reality. Anything before that had faded like a dream. He rooted around in his memory.

'Birmingham,' he managed.

Clara laughed. 'Well, I know that. But where? In the workhouse?'

'Not the workhouse,' he corrected her sharply. No, that was not his shame! 'In a house, I s'pose. Yes, a house.'

Clara waited. And the wait made John long to fill this well of silence. So much of himself that had remained hidden and mostly unconsidered since he arrived rushed to his mind and he was filled with a great longing to pour it out, but as usual the words were locked inside him, like something he had swallowed and which needed to be let out.

As they walked along, Clara gently put her hand on his back. She didn't say anything, but she kept it there. John didn't look at her. His feelings swelled inside him and this kind touch, this promise of understanding, set him off.

'I s'pose I don't remember much – but a few things I do. I remember my mom. Dark hair, she had, and lovely eyes, big, blue, like. Or grey – sort of both. And she looked at you nice – kindly, like. My father was – I dunno, he frightened me a bit. And then after a bit he never came home . . .'

The hand moved, slowly down his back. And with great daring, with a feeling, he reached round for her. He took the cool little hand in his and gripped it. And he talked and talked.

'What's this place?'

Clara looked round with a kind of awe. They had walked some way, were still holding hands and John was in a state of bliss, of release.

Before them a hill rose, seemingly higher than any other in this rolling landscape. But its sides had been gouged like a great beast on which some other creature had feasted, leaving ridges, like spine or rib, at the top.

'Them's quarries,' he said. He had been past here on

his walks. 'I dunno where we are exactly, but I've seen it before.'

Just ahead of them was the beginning of a village. In a field to their right, muscular, hard-working horses were grazing.

'I s'pose they're the quarry horses,' John said.

Tumbledown brick cottages shouldered each other along the edge of the road and as they walked closer, they could hear the clash of hammers on iron. In one doorway stood an old man, bent, gristly-looking as if he was all sinew without an ounce of fat on his bones. He wore a leather apron tied at his waist, and his beard spread like a great smoke-grey bib across his front. He was leaning, puffing on a clay pipe and clearly having a rest. Someone else was still hammering inside the dilapidated workshop.

John and Clara let go of each other's hands. The man stared. His face was deeply lined, his gaze piercing enough to be intimidating. But he gave a slow nod, straightened a little and tipped his cap back.

'Afternoon,' John called to him.

The man tipped his cap again and they drew in closer.

'Where is this place?' Clara asked and John could see that her girl's prettiness softened the man.

'This? This 'ere's Heaven,' he announced.

John and Clara exchanged doubtful looks. The place didn't seem any more marvellous than where they lived themselves.

Just then another face appeared at the door, a young man not much older than themselves, curious to see who was outside.

'This here's Perry Lake,' he said cheerfully. 'Round 'ere we call it 'Eaven.'

John and Clara laughed.

'What're you doing out 'ere?'

'Just out for a walk,' John said.

'What're you making?' Clara asked.

'Nails,' the lad replied.

With that, the old man took his pipe out of his mouth again and disappeared inside as if there was something he realized he must be doing. A moment later the metallic clinking started again.

'Eighty-one he is,' the lad said. 'Still at it.' Cheerfully he added, 'It's that or starve, ay it?'

He asked a few more questions. Where had they come from? Smethwick, about two miles distant, seemed to affect him as if they had come from somewhere halfway across the world, Timbuktu perhaps.

'Can we go up there?' Clara asked, pointing towards the ridge.

The lad shrugged. 'You can. Just don't fall.'

They said goodbye and set off, finding a path where they could head up the hill. The grass was jaded with layers of dust and through it, the ground showed black. The quarry fell away to one side and as they climbed up what was left of a scrubby heathland, they saw a long pool of water in the bottom of the clawed-out layers of the basin. The breeze grew stronger and John saw Clara pull her shawl more tightly round her, even though they were warming from the climb.

In one place the path was so narrow that John walked on ahead. As they climbed higher it began to feel a little dizzying looking down. He was not used to heights at all and it felt strange to see the fall of the land and the great spread of everything beyond.

He was lost in his thoughts when he heard her screams.

'John – John! Help me . . .'

He whirled round and thought, to his horror, that Clara had vanished completely. He tore back and looked over to see her lying on a narrow ledge below, clinging on to the rough stones and weeds beside her, her face looking up at him in terror.

'I'm coming!'

The first drop from the top was steep, the reason Clara had not been able to save herself. But John did not stop to think that he might overshoot the place where Clara's fall had been halted and go hurtling down the rest of the way to the bottom of the quarry. All he could think of was her. That she was, he realized, the most precious thing in the world. The most precious thing he had ever known . . .

Twisting round in a flash, he fed his legs down first, fingers and nails tearing against the stones and earth as he slowed himself, sliding down to where she was, to reach her, *her* . . .

Clara was taking up most of the ledge. She tried to bunch her legs up, give him room to land. He came down the last couple of feet at such a rate that he landed with a jolt, one leg going right down over the edge, the rest of him scrabbling desperately to hold on to anything that would save him. He grasped Clara's leg: they both began to move over the edge to the depths of the quarry below.

'No . . . No . . .' he heard her whimper.

There was a second as they hung in the balance. A second when he saw a root, three fingers thick, sticking out of the crumbling stones, above her, almost beyond his reach. With what felt like more than human ability he swung for it and managed to grab it with his left hand, pulling and pulling and adding his other hand until he was close up to the quarry face again, his body half shielding hers from falling now. He clung for a moment, panting loudly.

'Oh, John.' Clara's voice was small in a way he had never heard it before. 'Oh, John, thank God.'

He got his feet on to the ledge, strong in her need of him.

'Get up.' He reached for her hand. 'I'll help you up first – there's places to put your feet.'

He helped her climb, supporting her from behind. The distance did not seem so great, seen from this angle, but it was rough and steep. Clara scrambled up, her face appearing immediately she reached the top, anxious to see him to safety.

John found his footholds easily now, pulling himself up and swelling with relief. At the top, he flung himself down beside Clara. They sat side by side, feet sticking out over the edge, panting, even laughing now.

'I thought I'd had it,' she said. 'I tripped and . . .' She shuddered. She was still trembling with the shock of it. Her laughter faded and John saw tears well in her blue eyes. The sight of her melted him, filled him with feelings of protectiveness such as he had never felt before.

He moved closer and dared to put his arm round her.

'It's all right now, eh? You're all right, aren't you?'

She leaned her head against him, quieter than he had ever known her, and wiped her eyes.

'I thought I was going to die.'

Her face turned up to him, those sweet lips, her eyes seeking his, so soft and vulnerable suddenly, and John knew then, admitted to himself, that he was helplessly in love with her.

'John?' she said timidly. 'Will you kiss me?'

He barely knew what a kiss was. And yet he did. They both did. Keeping his gaze fixed on hers, he said, 'You're lovely, d'you know that?'

And then he did as she had asked, sliding his other arm round her and holding this girl, his girl, the most precious thing in his world.

Thirty-Three

'Dor!'

Dora heard Minnie's excitement and her hurrying feet as she charged in through the front door. Frantic, she pushed the paper she was writing on under the starch bowl, slid the pencil into her pocket and had her hands in the bowl starching collars and cuffs as Minnie came tearing in.

'Dor!' Minnie's face was pink and beaming. Dora guessed that a pie might have been consumed on the way home, she was so bursting with energy. 'I've got more business, lots, just along the street!'

'Oh – what's that?' Dora looked up, hands still working.

'The Red Lion.' This pub was on the corner of Bread Street. 'They've got rooms – we can do their sheets and pillercases. They were looking for someone when I went in 'cause the woman who does it's got the pox – they *told* me that!' Minnie fanned her blushing cheeks. 'You know, *that* kind of pox – and now she's run off to Portsmouth.'

'What – why?' Dora said, trying to keep up with the extraneous twists and turns of the situation.

'I *dunno* – but the long and short is they need laundry done and there was me, walking in and asking, and they said if the price was right . . . I'm going back to collect it – all right?'

'Course it's all right,' Dora smiled. ''Specially as we don't have far to go to take it back.'

Minnie skipped out and Dora heard the sound of the barrow rumbling off along the street. She dried her hands and took her paper out again – the last thing she needed was it getting wet – and quickly took it in the other room to hide it away. Then she went back to her starching.

She didn't know really why she was being so secretive about this writing. After all, Minnie was her best friend and her biggest supporter. But it felt like something she wanted to keep just as hers for now. She could not stand the thought of anyone at all seeing it because it was tender and personal.

At the same time she was excited. After that letter came from James Sapphire, editor at *Around the Hearth*, rejecting her story, she had felt for days as if someone had punched her. She went about aching inside. What had she been thinking? She was a washerwoman. A nobody from the workhouse. How could she have dreamt of such a thing as being a real writer? That was only something gentlemen and ladies did – people like Harriet Martineau and Mrs Gordon if she had put her mind to it. Even so it was mostly gentle*men*. She was a fool to have these dreams.

Since then she had submitted two more of her stories to other magazines. Both came back, but neither of the rejections stung quite like that of Mr Sapphire, a man whom she couldn't help loathing to the depths of her soul even though she had never met him.

But in the meantime she had discovered two things. One, thanks to Minnie, that something called a Free Library had opened, only a short walk away on Constitution Hill.

'You can read books there and you don't have to pay anything!' Minnie announced. 'I just went past it on my way back – anyone can go in there!'

One Friday afternoon when they had finished delivering the last of the week's bundles of laundry back to their owners, Dora left Rose with Minnie, who loved playing with her and thought of her as a little sister.

Dora tidied herself up, put her hat on and walked up Snow Hill to Constitution Hill. She had not heard about this library before – a place where anyone could just read books the way she had been able to at the Gordons' house! A pang of grief went through her thinking of this. Sitting beside Mrs Gordon, reading, being taught things. And Robert. Robert. It was only then she thought, Robert and Rose begin with the same two letters. She had not planned that but the thought made her happy.

The building was solid and grand with high, arched windows. It took her all her courage to walk inside. I'm not nobody, she thought as she pushed open the heavy door. I can read. I've read books.

Inside made her gasp. There was a high ceiling, tables and chairs, a man seated at one, his cap resting respectfully on the table beside him. Reassured, she saw that he looked like a humble working man. She drank in the hushed, musty atmosphere of paper and bindings. And all along one side of the room, shelves and shelves of books reaching high up the walls.

But the books were guarded. In front of them was a long desk at which stood three men, all of whom had already noticed her coming in through the door. And were staring at her. Dora felt herself shrink.

'Yes?' one of them said as she approached. 'Can I help you?'

'What do I . . .' Her voice sounded much too loud in the hush and she quickly lowered it. 'How do I . . . read a book?'

The man curled his lip. 'You mean, how do you choose a book to borrow?'

He had a little beard and moustache and a tight expression. I bet he's constipated, Dora thought.

'Yes,' she agreed humbly.

'Jeavons, let me . . .'

One of the other men, who had a gingery beard, a kindly expression and an air of authority, came and took over and to Dora's relief, 'Jeavons' faded into the background.

'So – what can I get you to read? A novel, perhaps? I know you ladies are partial to a novel.'

'Yes, please,' Dora said, trying to sound as genteel and as much like Mrs Gordon as she could. 'I'd like *The Tenant of Wildfell Hall.*'

'Ah.' The librarian looked mildly surprised. 'Miss Anne Brontë. It's a sizeable book . . .'

'Yes,' Dora said. 'I know. I've already read *Agnes Grey* and *Jane Eyre.*'

The man smiled. 'Do you wish to borrow the book?'

Dora could see Jeavons listening in with an expression that suggested that any book would leave the library over his dead body.

'Yes, please.' She liked this librarian. He had a twinkle in his eye.

'I'll need to issue you with a card. Just one moment. Name?'

He wrote the name 'Dora Lunn' carefully on the ticket and Dora took the thing like a piece of treasure. He went to the shelves, found the book and, to the apparent alarm of Jeavons, handed it over.

'You'll know, I suppose, that the three Brontë sisters published their books under men's names to begin with? Currer—'

'Ellis and Action Bell. Yes,' Dora said. The man looked a bit disappointed that she already knew. Mrs Gordon had told her about all this. *Absurd*, her mistress had murmured. *Absurd that we should have to hide our sex.*

And off she went, with the book under her arm and that whole wall of books in her mind like a challenge.

The second thing was that one day she woke up feeling different. Recovered, like a weathervane that has changed course.

But I *am* a writer, she thought, sitting up in bed, cuddling Rose to her. She lifted her right hand and stared at it. The painful cracks and chaps were healing again now summer was coming, but her hands were always reddened and a mess. One day, she was going to stop spending her time scrubbing other people's frowsty clothes. She would sit at a desk with a proper pen, like the one Robert had offered her, and make up stories all day long.

'I am a writer,' she said to the little girl, who looked up with her shining brown eyes and laughed at her mother's smile. 'I am. And that's what I'm going to do. So sod James Sapphire.'

Because she knew with deep certainty what she was going to write next.

That night, once Rose was asleep and she and Minnie had eaten the remains of a mutton shoulder and bread, Dora sat on her bed, laid the copy of *The Tenant of Wildfell Hall* beside her for company and started writing.

Her hand flew over the page. The story of a family; a mother and father with five children, all sisters except for one, the disappearance of the father, the tragic and bloody death of the mother – the forcing of the children into the workhouse . . .

Dora wrote and wrote. She wept, having to stop because it felt as if something was trying to climb out of her chest, something huge and full of pain. She curled on the bed and cried in a way she could not remember crying in all her life, even in those first bewildering nights in the workhouse, sleeping with other children who twitched or rocked or cried out in their sleep.

By morning the first part of the story was complete – the

story of a girl whose head is filled with golden dreams, whose mind teems with stories, but whose family are scattered. She ends up in the workhouse.

She slept for an hour or two and woke when Rose started squeaking for food. Even after so little rest she felt full of electric energy.

I'm not going to copy it out again, she thought as she sat cuddling Rose, the little girl's fingers coiling into her own autumn leaf curls. Dora smiled down at her, melting with love.

'Look at you, you little chubby chops,' she murmured, leaning down to kiss her warm cheek. 'You're the most beautiful thing in the world.'

I'll send it, she thought. Today – before I change my mind.

Once Rose was satisfied, Dora sat her on the bed with her little rag doll and picked up her sheets of paper, closely covered in her hurried handwriting. In some certain way she had never known before, she knew that it was good. And, by a strange instinct, she felt that the man she was going to send it to would understand.

As Rose gurgled beside her, she pondered. She would find time later – she would buy an envelope and go back to the library to write the address, to prepare her writing at a proper table. That seemed the right and only place to do it.

All she needed now was a title for it. Hearing Minnie starting to move about in the other room, she wrote, carefully, 'Tragedy and Triumph by . . .'

By whom? Dora Lunn? She was filled with a sinking feeling. How could she believe in that name? It sounded so meek and womanly.

Why should we hide our sex? Mrs Gordon had said.

But that was Mrs Gordon, Dora thought, folding the precious sheets of paper, and she was a genteel lady, not a washerwoman. If Anne Brontë and her sisters had to pretend to be men to get their stories published, then she felt it wise to do the same.

The name – yes, this was the perfect name! – presented itself to her straight away. It jumped into her mind as if somehow she had always known it.

Leaning over her papers again, she finished, 'by . . . Richard Fletcher'.

Thirty-Four

'I'm going out for a few things,' Ada called into the workshop. The girls were finishing their Saturday clean-up, the air swirling with dust as Tom swept the floor and Gert, Margaret, Jess and Biddy – as well as William's workers – cleaned up round their lathes and workstations before knocking off.

Leave them to it, Ada thought. William had been in and gone again and she needed to get out, her nerves jangling all morning. He had asked her if she'd like a 'bit of a walk' again that afternoon as it was a warm, breezy summer day. And ever since, she had been in a state. She'd go and get some food in for the weekend and stretch her legs, she thought, as butterflies danced inside her. It would be good to get away from the stench of the boneyard behind, which was truly rank on days like this.

A walk. He's asked to see me again, was all she could think as she turned out of the gloom of Galton Passage into the sunlight and clamour of Livery Street. So he must like me a bit . . . She ticked herself off for being so juvenile. He just wants a bit of company and I'm all there is on offer – stop being so . . .

This thought was interrupted. As she passed Snow Hill station a young woman, her face concealed by the brim of a black straw hat, came hurrying along towards her. Her arms were clenched across her chest as if she was holding tight to something under her shawl.

Ada instinctively moved out of her way but just as the

girl drew close, her hat lifted off, revealing a head of autumn red hair, simply and carelessly dressed. The hat whisked past Ada, grazing her cheek, then went wheeling and dipping along the front of the station. As the girl made a sound of dismay, Ada's immediate impulse was to chase after it, and in a moment she had pinned the brim down with her toe and picked it up.

'Here,' Ada said to the girl, who had run after her. She was clutching some sheets of paper tightly to her chest. With her other hand she took the hat.

'Thanks ever so much.' She fixed it firmly back on her head and went hurrying off again.

There was something intense about her and Ada turned to watch her compact little figure weave through the milling groups outside the station, with great intent, as if she was on a mission. In that brief moment, Ada had seen a round, grey-eyed face with slender brows and that bright hair fastened back low in her neck. Though she was polite, her mind was obviously miles away as she dashed off.

As Ada walked on down Livery Street, past the warren of workshops and businesses – a furrier, a beer seller, a gunmaker, a jeweller, a gilder – the image in her mind sent vibrations of recognition through her. For almost the first time that day, it even drove out all thoughts of William and their walk that afternoon.

Because something in that face, in the way the girl moved, that hair . . . Somewhere in this town, Dora was living and working. The feeling grew stronger. The last time she had seen her little sister, she had been ten and Dora, she reckoned, must have been six. Ada almost walked straight past the baker's round the corner, she was so caught up in her thoughts.

Dora. She must be what – nineteen now?

That girl could have been anyone, Ada told herself as she

paid for her loaf of bread. So, she had Dora's colouring, but she could have been anyone . . .

As she walked on though, she became more certain. Something in the girl's face stirred her deep memory. That was Dora – surely it was, she thought, her heart pounding as she tucked the loaf of bread under her arm. And now she had lost her again. How was she ever going to track her down?

'I've to be over at Elsie's by half-past four,' she told William. She was burning to see Elsie now and tell her – and was also trying not to expect anything of her walk with him.

'Let's just go for a stroll then, eh?' he said. 'Shall we go down to St Phillip's? The garden there is nice.' It was also the only place to enjoy green space for miles around.

'Feel the sun on our faces,' Ada said, keeping her tone light. She certainly wasn't in need of a route march – she was tired after the week's work. She had come prepared this time, with a bottle of tea and some oat biscuits wrapped in wax paper to make it more of an occasion.

It wasn't far. As they wandered down to Colmore Row, Ada stole her hand into her pocket and for a second, gripped the brown-and-cream trochus shell that she had carried with her for years. It was her comfort and good-luck charm and at moments of nerves or worry, she would cradle it in her hand. Over the years her palm had smoothed the surface to a shine.

Crossing over into St Philip's churchyard they found that many others in the city had had the same idea. The burial ground was scattered with groups and couples, chatting, eating and lying back in the warmth.

They found a place in the sun on the scuffed grass and sat side by side facing the church, looking around at all the others relaxing and laughing. Ada was suddenly filled with panic. They had already talked about practical things that concerned them both: the drilling lathe that was playing up, the increased orders coming in . . .

But now things had gone quiet. William stared ahead of him, his expression nothing in particular, neither amused nor sad. Ada, insecure as ever, thought, he's thinking about *her*. Wishing his Jane was here instead of me. It made her long to catch his attention, and the only thing she could think of to say was what was filling her mind.

'I think . . .' She stopped, swallowed, finding her throat had closed. 'I think I saw my sister this morning.' William turned to look at her. 'Not Elsie. I mean, one of my sisters who I haven't seen – not since they were taken away.'

'Good heavens.' He seemed affected by this and the concern and emotion on his face warmed her. 'Where?'

'By the station – but it was all over in a flash.' She explained what had happened, about the hat, the fleeting moment in which they had looked into each other's faces. 'It was her.' She looked up at William and he was listening closely. 'Some things about a person don't change, do they? I'm sure it was her – only I've gone and lost her again.'

'Perhaps she lives close by?' he suggested kindly. 'And you'll run into her again.'

'I just hope so,' Ada said. Tears were tingling in her eyes and she felt embarrassed. She turned her head to wipe them away. 'I haven't seen her since she was just a little one.'

William hesitated, as if wondering whether or not to ask. Then, quietly, he said, 'What happened? To your family?'

For a moment she wanted to shut down, not to share her family's sadness and shame. But she made herself look up at him. He had to know her for who she was, or there would never be anything real between them. And she told him.

She had promised to be at the Drakes' for her tea that day. By the time she got to Elsie's she felt better – relieved of a burden. She had poured out her family's story to William and he had listened attentively and treated her with care. She was warmed by his reaction – his sympathy.

'I lost two of my sisters when we were children,' he said. 'One older, one younger – we all of us fell sick but I recovered. Life's never felt right without them since, which is why Jane . . .' He tailed off as if he could not bear to say any more. 'But losing them while knowing they're likely still out there somewhere – that's a different thing.'

'It is,' Ada said. 'And I feel badly about it, always – that I'm never doing enough to find them and I don't know how to begin.'

She was sitting forward now, hugging her bent knees, and William was close to her so that sometimes their legs brushed against each other's.

They had shared the tea and the biscuits and it turned into a relaxed, friendly afternoon. They lingered until Ada said she should be getting over to the Drakes'.

'I hope you have a restful Sunday,' she said, as they parted.

William inclined his head in a sad way that seemed to say, *I am alone, so my leisure time is bittersweet.* But he parted with her cheerfully.

'Don't worry,' he said. 'Have faith that you and your sister will be brought together again. Fate has already played a hand.'

Smiling, Ada agreed that it had.

The Drakes' upper room was, as was usual at the weekend, chaotic. Matty Drake presided over the cookpots steaming on the fire, the table was half laden with bread and cakes and the place was stuffed full of people. George was chatting to Nancy's husband, Walt, with Ernie listening in. Elsie's father-in-law, Edwin, was attempting the feat of remaining fast asleep in the chair, despite everything. Nancy and Elsie were trying to contain Charlie who was now three and attempting to flatten two-year-old Vicky. Lizzie, now nearly fifteen, was playing with a kitten that nobody seemed to have ever seen before and which was at risk of losing its life in the general hubbub.

'Get that creature out from under my feet!' Matty protested, heaving a large plate of freshly baked buns over to the table. 'It'll have me over!'

Ada looked round with amusement – she was going to have to be patient to get a word in anywhere here.

As they all finally settled with heaped plates and cups of tea, she was about to speak to Elsie when Matty leaned over towards her.

'Elsie's got summat to tell you, Ada – ain't you, Else?'

Elsie blushed and Ada saw George eyeing her, even though Walt was talking to him about something on the other side.

'Not here, Mother!' Elsie whispered, her face a mass of blushes.

'Oh, pardon me,' Matty subsided, half offended.

'What?' Ada was opposite Elsie.

Elsie mouthed at her, *I've caught for another one.*

'Another . . .? Oh!' Ada grasped her meaning, and saw the satisfied smile on Matty's face.

Now George was blushing. And looking in their direction.

'Oh, I'm happy for you, Else,' Ada smiled at her, searching for something to say. It was all so foreign to her. 'They'll be company for each other,' she offered.

Elsie smiled and Ada could see she was happy – if a little queasy.

'I've got summat to tell *you*,' Ada said, as the chat started again round the table. And she watched the amazed emotions gather in Elsie's face as she said, 'I think . . . I mean, I'm pretty sure . . . I saw Dora this morning.'

Thirty-Five

It was a filthy day. Summer rains had poured down for two days now, and the yard was awash with water and filth. Every corner of Dora and Minnie's rooms was filled with washing, hung on wooden clothes horses or strung on lines from the ceiling, so that getting across a room was a dance of weaving between damp sheets and chemises.

Dora stoked the fire; the things hung close to it gave off steam into the air.

'I'm going to get rheumatism,' Minnie moaned, holding her hands up to the fire. 'It feels like the middle of winter already.'

There was a silence as Dora went round the room feeling the washing to see what was driest. The only other sound was the spatter and gurgle of rain from the street. Then suddenly they heard running feet. Minnie went over and peered out of the window.

'It's the letter carrier!'

Dora's stomach turned over. She was always waiting these days. Waiting for news of rejection – or, one day, God willing, something better . . .

Minnie stayed peering through the window.

'Oh – he's coming over here!'

A moment later there came a click and the sound of paper hitting the floor in the hall. Dora rushed out before Minnie could get her hands on the post.

There were four letters – three of them for the businesses upstairs. But the fourth was addressed, in a sloping, hurried hand, to 'Mr Richard Fletcher'. Seeing it sent a bolt of panic through Dora and she pressed the envelope to her chest, hurriedly leaving the other letters on the first step of the stairs.

'Just going out to the privy!'

'Why're you doing that?' Minnie shouted after her. 'It'll be a cesspool – use the po' in here!'

But Dora was out at the back, sloshing across the yard with the letter tucked in under her shawl. She couldn't care less that her feet were soaked through – she had to read that letter in complete privacy without Minnie barging in!

She slammed shut the badly fitting door and leaned against it in the gloom. With the wind whispering in through the cracks, she gazed at the letter. Because she knew from the feel of it that it was just a letter – they had not sent her pages back.

At last she unfastened it and saw a brief note in the same rushed hand:

Dear Sir,

It has afforded me much pleasure reading your affecting story of the Jackson family and I have to confess to being struck by it. More than by many offerings which make their appearance on my desk. So much so in fact that I cannot help but wonder whether Richard Fletcher can truly be the fellow he purports to be, or whether his words flow from the mind and heart of a softer being. Whatever the case, I am always delighted when I find promise in a new aspirant. Your story, by sheer merit, has skipped its way over the heads of our more sober contributors. Especially coming as it does from Birmingham, a city I hold high in esteem and affection.

Since you have assured me that further episodes will be forthcoming, I will be happy to retain this first for the

Christmas edition of All the Year Round, *if you will give me permission to condense it just a little. I am sure it will hold our audience in thrall.*

Such permission being granted, and with your assurance of a continuing story, I would entreat you to send me a second instalment in short order. As a serial extending over several months, I am able to offer you £7 per page.

Faithfully yours,
Charles Dickens

Dora stared and stared, oblivious to the damp, the swoosh of rain and stenches from effluent from the privy being washed across the yard. In this wet, stinking little shack she might have been in heaven.

It has afforded me much pleasure . . .

She clutched the letter to her like a lover. She had given pleasure to Mr Charles Dickens – author of *Oliver Twist*, of *David Copperfield!* – and *seven pounds per page!!*

It was an unheard-of amount of money! Even the first episode must cover three or four pages. Was any of this real? Dora stood there stunned, pinned to the splintery door until she realized her whole body was trembling with both cold and excitement. She pushed the door open and went shrieking across the yard.

'Minnie! Minnie – you'll never guess!!'

'We're gunna celebrate,' Minnie said later, when this extraordinary news was even now only beginning to sink in. 'You'll be rich, Dor. I always knew you were special.'

Minnie's delight was genuine and wholehearted. It was only after a good while, the two of them crouched by the fire amid the slowly drying week's wash, that Dora began to take in that this was really happening.

'Mr Charles Dickens likes my story,' she said in ecstasy

as she tried to poke more life into the fire. 'He likes it and he's going to pay me.'

She looked across at Minnie, seeing the joy in her own face mirrored in that of her friend.

'I'm so happy, Minnie. I don't think I've ever been this happy, ever!'

'You're a writer now, Dor,' Minnie said. 'A proper one. Soon you won't need to be washing everyone's dirty smalls.' A cloud passed over her face for a moment. 'You won't forget me though, will you?'

'Never!' Dora said, shocked. 'We're a team, you and me. You're . . . Well, you're like a sister, Min. We'll stick together, you and me, won't we?'

Minnie nodded happily. 'I'm going to go now – get some grub.' She leapt up and pulled her coat and hat from the back of the door. A celebration for Minnie naturally meant food.

'I'll try and iron some of this lot dry.' Dora looked up at the wall of laundry. 'Doesn't matter if Mr Dickens thinks I'm all right – this lot want their sheets.'

'Can we afford buns as well?' Minnie said pleadingly, at the door.

Dora got to her feet. Affectionately and full of joy she went and hugged Minnie's skinny form. 'Course we can,' she said. 'Two each!'

Thirty-Six

'Here we are – quick, it's sizzling hot!'

It was Christmas Day and Minnie came racing in carrying a roasting pan with a crispy, bronzed chicken, hands padded with a thick cloth as she hurried across to the table and plonked it in the middle, laughing with excitement. The fat was still sizzling and packed round the bird were crispy, golden roast potatoes.

'Tip a bit of the fat in here so I can make the gravy and we can set to!' Dora said.

They had really gone to town. This was not just Christmas – it was a celebration of everything, which so far as Minnie was concerned meant eating as much as humanly possible. Soon the two of them were tucking into the chicken with potatoes and carrots and Brussels sprouts, all washed in Dora's chicken gravy. They had brought in a jug of ale from the outdoor at the Red Lion, who had also let them use the oven that morning to cook their chicken.

Bobbing in a pan of simmering water on the fire was a muslin-topped pudding, keeping warm for later.

'Oh . . .' Minnie sat back halfway through her meal and stared first at her plate and then at Dora with a contented sigh. 'I can hardly believe this. It's like a dream. This is the best meal I've ever had!'

'Me too,' Dora said. 'It's like heaven.'

'And all because of you,' Minnie said. The ale was loosening both tongue and emotions. 'You've been ever so good to me, Dor – and I'm so happy for you. I'm proud to know you, that I am.'

'I'm proud of *you*,' Dora said. 'Getting away from your old man and starting afresh. I don't know what I'd've done without you. Sisters, eh?'

She held out her pewter mug and Minnie did the same. They clicked them together.

'Cheers! Merry Christmas!'

Dora was all smiles, fizzing with joy inside. She had already sent Mr Dickens her second instalment of the story and was well into writing her third, buoyed up in confidence.

'How're you going to finish it?' Minnie had asked her one day, frowning. 'If it's about your family and that, you don't know how it's going to end.'

'Oh, I'll think of something,' Dora had said airily. Because she would. She knew she would. It would end however she wanted it to end.

A few days ago, the two of them had gone into one of the stationery shops in town which sold papers, including *All the Year Round*, the Christmas edition. Hurriedly they searched the racks in the dark shop until Dora heard Minnie gasp.

'Oh! Here it is!'

Dora's heart started to pound. It had not taken long for her disguise as 'Richard Fletcher' to be blown because she was to be paid by cheque. And neither she nor 'Richard Fletcher' had a bank account. She wrote to Mr Dickens, explaining the situation, and had received a jovial reply.

> *A number of members of the female sex grace our pages these days, though continue with your preferred nom de plume if you will. However, I shall address a cheque*

to Miss Dora Lunn and suggest that she open a bank account forthwith.

Promptly, she received the cheque in the post, for more money than she had ever seen before – £24 10s 6d. It was still hard to believe that this could ever happen. That she, a little workhouse girl, had such an unheard-of thing as an account at Taylors & Lloyds bank!

And now, here was her story, printed in a magazine and on the shelf in front of her – and on other shelves in shops all over the place! Awed, she reached out and picked up a copy, leafing through quickly until the right page opened and Minnie let out a squeal.

'Oh! There it is. There's your name!'

Dora gazed and gazed. There was her title, 'Tragedy and Triumph' by Richard Fletcher.

'You buying that, or what?' the man behind the counter grumbled.

'Yes, we are, if you want to know,' Minnie said snippily.

Dora could see she was about to announce that one of the very writers whose story was in the paper was standing right beside her and Dora grabbed her arm.

'Don't say anything!'

'Why not?' The conversation took place in a hissing whisper.

'Well, for a start he's not going to believe I'm called Richard Fletcher, is he, silly? And any road, he's a mardy old sod so why bother?'

Minnie subsided.

They paid for the paper and Dora carried it out like a sacred relic. Once on the pavement they stopped and jumped up and down, squeaking like small children, not caring that people in New Street were staring.

'We're going to celebrate,' Dora said. It was only a few

days before Christmas and the sky was a grey lid over the town, threatening snow. 'We'll have a proper blowout, eh?'

In the middle of their Grand Meal, the partly dismembered hen still on the table in front of them and Rose down for her nap, Minnie suddenly said, 'What're we gunna do, Dora? Just carry on the way we are? After all, you've got money now if he keeps paying you the same.'

Dora immediately felt cautious. Her bubble might burst at any moment. She had never felt much security anywhere and it was too soon to feel safe now.

'But I might never get any more stories published,' she said. 'At least we've got work. We could take on someone else if we need to – expand?'

'We could, couldn't we?' Minnie was excited. 'Everything takes so long, with all the marking up and deliveries on top of all the rest. If we had some help . . .'

They sat and dreamt together about how things might be, their little business a growing concern, more money coming in . . .

'But let's see how it goes, eh?' Dora said. 'This might be a flash in the pan – the only time I have any luck.'

She finished up her delicious plateful and sat back, groaning, her cheeks flushed from the food and from drinking more ale than she was used to.

'I think I'm gunna burst. Not sure I can fit in any pudding.'

'What?' Minnie said, bewildered. Minnie always had room to fit in anything, though it was a mystery where she put it all. 'Course you can. It's Christmas Day – you *can't* not eat pudding!'

John sat squashed in with all the Smith girls round the table, presided over by Enoch Smith. He had visibly aged over the years since John arrived. He was a barrel-chested, sinewy man, his beard now even longer and bushier than before, and his face which spent so much time close to the raging heat of the glass furnace was leathery as a saddle, his eyes a piercing blue. Enoch's appearance was quite frightening, but he was in fact the fair-minded, gentle man who John had always known. And deeply respected.

The family tucked into their joint of Christmas beef. 'Come on, lad,' Enoch had instructed. 'You'd best learn how to carve.' The girls were all larking about and chatting as ever, but John sat quiet. Though now, unlike before, he did not feel left out or lost in all the friendly chat and banter. Because beside him, stealing a glance at him every so often (even now, no one else knew), was Clara, his girl.

John was in love, head over heels and hanging upside down. He loved as he had never before had the chance to love anyone since his infancy. Clara, with her dancing eyes and challenging nature, was for him. She was the miracle who was on his side, who listened to him. Who was as pretty as it was possible for a girl to be. And most amazing of all, she loved him back.

So John sat, that Christmas dinner time, in a haze of joy, beside the girl he loved and surrounded by this chattering, female family who had taken him in.

In Galton Passage, only a few streets away from Dora and Minnie, everyone was crammed into the Drakes' upper room. And a tight fit it was, with the Drake parents and Ernie and Lizzie; Elsie and George and Nancy and Wally with their children and Ada, as well as Jonas Parry, who was always invited to any major celebration.

Everyone squeezed in, finding somewhere to sit even though they could not all fit round the table. The small children, who had been fed beforehand, played on the floor.

The windows were steamed up, the room full of cooking smells and the atmosphere one of great jollity.

'You're looking well, sis,' Ada whispered to Elsie.

'Yes, I don't feel too bad this time,' she said, beaming. 'P'r'aps it's a boy. They say girls make you sicker!'

'Old wives' tales,' Matty said, dividing up an enormous pudding.

Matty, as ever, was at the centre of her household, pink from the fire, presiding over all the food – beef and all the trimmings had come before the pudding. But, Ada thought, watching her pass round the plates, Matty did not seem quite herself. She suddenly felt concerned. Matty seemed tetchier than Ada had ever seen her. And once or twice – Ada watched her carefully, though hiding the fact in quick glances – she was sure she saw Matty wince with pain.

'Is she all right?' she whispered to Elsie. 'She looks a bit – I don't know – not quite right. And she's not eaten much.'

Elsie's face clouded. 'I don't know. She's been a bit off colour – but she won't say.'

'What're you two twittering about down there?' Matty called sharply along the table.

'Just talking baby names, that's all, Mother,' Elsie replied with a smile.

Ada was surprised at this lie. She realized, when she saw Ernie leap up to help at the end of the meal, that the family were more aware and more worried than they were letting on.

As she pondered this, Ada realized Elsie was staring closely at her, her eyes full of mischief.

'Can't say the same about you,' she said quietly. 'You're looking very fine – glowing I'd say. Anything you're not telling me, sis? There wouldn't be a certain Somebody . . .?'

'Don't be daft,' Ada almost snapped back, feeling unwanted blushes seep into her cheeks. Good Lord, she thought, was it that obvious? 'You know me – when have I ever been that sort?'

'Oh,' Elsie said, suddenly serious. 'Anyone can be that sort if they find the right feller. Don't you want to love someone and be loved back?'

Ada thought about this as she ate Matty's delicious fruit pudding. Was that true? She was still not yet quite convinced it could be true of her – could it? She had spent all these years hardening herself, not needing anyone else and putting all her energy into the business. Now she felt like a rusty machine that had forgotten how to love or give of herself – if she had ever known in the first place. But now . . . But she was not letting on about how she felt now!

Afterwards, they all sat round, replete and dozy. Jonas and Edwin, in the more comfortable seats, put their heads back and were soon emitting snores which made Lizzie giggle as she played with the little ones.

Ada tucked in beside Elsie and Nancy on the settle as they often did.

'Here,' Elsie said, holding out a paper with a coloured Christmas design on the cover. 'George got me this as a Christmas present, said it'd make me sit down and rest. Fat chance with Vicky round my feet all day, but it was a nice thought.'

Ada took the paper and leafed through it, though without much interest. It contained a lot of stories in close print.

'It'd take me too long to get through any of these,' she said, handing it back. She was not much of a reader even if she had time. She had never had the leisure to improve at it.

'That was the idea,' George put in, still in his chair by the table. 'I'm trying to get her to sit still!'

'It's nice, George,' Elsie said lovingly. 'And it's helping my reading along. Here . . .' She took it from Ada and turned one of the pages. 'This amused me.'

Ada read, 'Tragedy and Triumph'. Above what seemed to Ada a great thicket of words, appeared the name of their author, Richard Fletcher. 'Oh,' she smiled. 'Feels funny seeing that.'

'D'you think we dreamt him coming back and he's really still alive and started writing stories for a living?' Elsie joked.

'I wouldn't put anything past him,' Ada said.

But the laughter faded, leaving a bitter taste. They remembered their father's end all too clearly, all the broken promises and dreams. Ada had taken it especially badly. For her, her father had been like a god and his comedown had shattered her feelings about him – about trusting anyone.

'Well –' Elsie put the paper away, still smiling – 'it's not as if he was the only Richard Fletcher in the world, is it?'

Thirty-Seven

Over the months since the summer, Ada had managed to keep her feelings for William Nichols pushed into the background. They had to work together almost every day and for the sake of her business, she could not spend her time with her head in the clouds. If the other women noticed she would really be in trouble, she thought grimly. They would never give her a minute's peace – especially Elsie, and Gert who had known her since she was a child. And she felt she would lose her authority.

The business was thriving like a dream. William's workers had settled in and got used to the new arrangement. Vi enjoyed her status as representative and lorded it over the others to begin with, but under Margaret's steady influence and everyone else ignoring her if she started, even she had settled down.

And new orders were coming in, the work expanding, and Fletcher & Nichols was gaining a good reputation in the business for quality and for producing work on time. This was all Ada had dreamt of when she and Elsie set to with a few tools in that one room of theirs.

But sometimes her authority weighed heavily. Each morning she drew herself up and marched into the shop. She had to be the one in charge, sorting out the business itself, any issues between the women. It all took its toll and sometimes she felt it would be so much easier to hand the whole lot over and just be one of the workers again, without all this on her plate. Even though she and William had joined forces, it still felt as if the real running of the place fell to her.

Some days, William seemed sunk in grief. He was a hard-working, sober man usually of few words. Other days he managed to be smiling and amiable. And it was his smile which was Ada's undoing, that sudden lighting up of his features into someone happy and lovely to look at, so that she instantly forgave him for not seeming present at other times. It only took him to smile at her in that warm way, and her body would pulse harder – something which drove her mad with irritation at herself, but which she could not seem to help.

The weeks passed in hard work. Autumn had come and the days drew in. Things were going well. And then one evening, in December, everything changed.

There had been days of ice, when the boneyard at the back was frozen, so that although the air across Birmingham was acrid and sulphurous from legions of coal fires, at least for a while it was not polluted by the putrefying stench of bone marrow and carcass. But a piercing wind had got up, whistling and buzzing through cracks and window frames.

Ada had been on her feet all day. They had all been working at full tilt since the morning to complete the orders before Christmas, and Tom and William Nichols himself had pushed basket-carriages full of buttons to their out-workers to get them carded and delivered to various firms.

It was late in the day and William was still not back. Everyone else had left and Ada was clearing up in the store room, when she heard the rumble of the basket-carriage in the yard. A moment later he walked in, rubbing his gloved hands together, his face raw with cold.

'God, it's a bitter night,' he said through clenched jaws. 'I was bent over pushing against the wind.'

'I know.' Ada tried to laugh but it came out more as a cough, her chest was so tight. 'I'm perished standing in here.'

There was a pause, then she offered, 'I'll make tea – warm us up?'

'That'd be nice,' William said. 'See me home.'

She ran upstairs to put the water on to boil and came down again to find William in the shop, bending over, adjusting one of the machines.

'Your Tom,' he said, hearing her footsteps but not looking up. 'How old is he now?'

'He's . . . Nineteen.'

'I've only ever seen him on cutting. Doesn't he work a lathe?'

'No,' Ada said. 'Come to think of it. He's seen it all done endless times, but – he was young when he started, and strong, so that's what he's been doing . . .'

''Bout time he learned then, isn't it? Give him more chances?'

Ada nodded, embarrassed that she had not thought of this – and Tom had never asked. It felt suddenly as if she had been holding him back all this time – that she had taken for granted he would just keep on working for her, doing the same job.

'You're right. I'll talk to him.'

William straightened up. 'He might want to branch out on his own one day, I suppose.'

He hesitated. 'He's not your brother, is he?'

Ada shook her head. The shameful feelings washed through her, about her past and her family, even on behalf of the Connells who partly felt like her family. Though she had told William about her own family's tragedy, she had not gone into any detail about the Connells. She explained, briefly.

'Oh, my word,' William said. He seemed to be looking at her with new eyes.

'So Tom and I sort of grew up together. I'd best go and brew the tea.' She moved away before he could ask her any more. As she ran up the stairs she wondered if she should invite him up, but that didn't feel right somehow.

They thawed out just a little, drinking tea and standing together in the dim gaslight of the shop. William looked round with apparent satisfaction.

'It's going all right, isn't it?'

Ada nodded over the top of her cup. 'I think so. I still wish we could have our own carders. Save all this outwork and traipsing about.'

'There's just not the room,' William sighed. 'Tell you what, though – we've got a good range now but I think we should start the New Year with some more lines.'

Ada nodded. The same thought had occurred to her. They had a well-skilled staff now.

William picked up a few sample buttons and peered at them. 'The flowers are always popular . . .'

All the buttons were decorated with a combination of designs such as 'canoe' shape, a little, rounded, diamond-shaped declivity in which the holes were drilled for sewing; flat dish shapes, scored buttons with tiny lines cut into them; and turned ones with concentric rings, either just round the edge or several of them, decreasing in size towards the middle.

'We've got a good, solid stock – all the usual. But perhaps we could do smaller runs of specials now – the abalone flower design's nice and people like it . . .'

Ada was nodding. 'Squares and ovals?'

William put his head on one side. 'Squares are a devil to do up in my opinion but some people like them – you'll always find folk who'll suffer to be different!'

Ada laughed, aware that she was not one of those people. The more serviceable her clothing, the more she liked it.

'You know, I was wondering,' she said slowly. 'Button makers are ten a penny, and we're doing all right, but – what if we were to branch out, do handles as well?'

It was as if they both had the same thought at once. 'We could—' Ada began.

'Get Tom trained up?' William said. 'If we could spare him? Beardsmore'd take him, wouldn't he?'

Ada made a face. 'If we was to grovel, yes, probably.'

William laughed then, a full-hearted guffaw, his face lighting up and seeming suddenly to shed years. Ada saw the glint of his teeth in the dim light, his dancing eyes.

'I don't think we're likely to see you doing that.'

'I will if I have to,' Ada said, pretending to be on her dignity.

She turned away slightly, the feelings she had been pushing away all these weeks rising in a rush. The longing, the desire of a moment, shouldering aside all her fears about what those feelings might lead to.

'It's a good idea,' she said, as matter-of-factly as she could manage. 'I'll speak to him about it.'

There was a silence. The wind buffeted the building. Ada felt suddenly as if the two of them were alone on a ship, surrounded by a wide, dark ocean.

She noticed a shift in the air, in the light, as William stepped closer to her. His shadow fell over her. Ada's breathing had gone shallow. She entered a state in which she had to surrender to whatever was coming. She could only let go and see where it took her.

'Ada?'

When she dared to look up, William had tilted his head to look into her face. She felt a light tickling sensation on the back of her hand which was resting on the top of a lathe and looked down to see his fingers, gently caressing her skin. Her eyes met his, which were full of questioning uncertainty, of longing.

Neither of them spoke another word. William stepped closer and she was taken into his arms. In astonished wonder, she wrapped hers round his slender body, smelling the cold and smoke of outside on his coat, the tickle of his beard against her cheek. And, alone here, with the wind shrieking outside, she surrendered to kissing and being kissed, and to whatever might follow to change her life.

Those few days later, as she sat eating her Christmas dinner with Elsie and the Drakes, however much Elsie might have noticed the new glow on her and be asking questions, Ada was certainly not ready to talk about it. It was far too new and terrifying – and joyful. And she could not decide which of those feelings she felt the most.

Thirty-Eight

January 1866

Dora was hurrying out into the hall clutching a thick envelope with her ink-stained fingers just as the new young man, working for one of the firms upstairs, came hurtling down and nearly flattened her.

'Sorry!' He went dashing out of the front door, a fleshy-cheeked, blonde-headed lad. The door slammed. Dora tutted.

'Where's the flaming fire?'

She was about to dash out to the post box when the back door opened and Cissy, the girl she and Minnie had taken on to help them, struggled in lugging two brimming pails of water.

'Here – give me one.'

Dora, knowing full well the weight of those pails, took one of them off the staggering thirteen-year-old and they carried them into the main room where one copper was already steaming on the fire. Minnie was sorting through a pile of white cotton stuff.

'Ta,' Cissy said shyly. 'I've filled the one in the brew'us already.'

She was a pale girl with curly, mouse-brown hair, a face spattered with freckles and was thin as a twig. Her numerous family lived round the corner. Cissy seemed to be one of the older children and so far as Dora could gather, her mother suffered with her health. Cissy was in awe of Dora and when she found out she wrote stories she almost curtseyed every time she saw her.

'You finished then?' Minnie looked up.

'Yes – just going to the post.' Dora grinned. 'I think he'll like it.'

'Good, 'cause I could do with a hand. Cissy – tip those in that one and get it going and when you've done that . . .'

'Shall I take her?' Dora nodded at Rose, who was two and a half now and into everything. The little girl grabbed the rim of the bucket that Cissy had just emptied. In the process she overbalanced and plonked down on to her backside with a shocked expression.

Cissy chuckled. 'You can leave her, Miss Lunn. She's all right. You're all right, ain't you, chickie?'

She righted the bucket and ruffled Rose's dark hair. Cissy was lovely with little Rose, treating her like one of her many younger sisters.

Dora slipped out to the sound of Minnie dispensing orders. She seemed to like bossing Cissy about. It was the first time she had ever had the chance, Dora thought, smiling as she walked along Bread Street. And Cissy was almost like a little dog, waiting eagerly to be given commands.

It was a great help having her there. She was willing enough and Dora liked her. They didn't give her the more skilled jobs – starching or dealing with stains or ironing. But for washing and rinsing, dollying and mangling clothes as well as collecting some of the bundles, she was proving a great help.

It gave Dora more time to write and she had just completed the fourth part of her story. On the table in her room were the first two editions of *All the Year Round* with her stories in them. She could still hardly believe it. She, a lowly person, had written something that was thought good enough to be published – and to get paid more money than she could ever have dreamt!

One day, when she said as much to Minnie, her friend frowned at her.

'You're a funny one, you are. You're ever so humble, but you always know you can do it, don't you? Write it, I mean?'

Dora thought about this. It was true. She might be humble, a child of the workhouse and a washerwoman. But she'd had a family once. A good family. And she knew she was meant to write and that she was going to do it no matter what anyone said.

She was walking along, not minding the clouds threatening rain because she had the full, clean, satisfied feeling of having produced something, when someone seemed to be talking to her. It made her jump.

'Sorry – what d'you say?'

She looked round to find the blonde lad from upstairs, smiling jovially at her.

'I never meant to knock you down earlier,' he said. 'Only the gaffer sent me out to fetch these . . .' He held up a cloth bag, the sides pushed out in an angular sort of way, without saying quite what 'these' were. 'I've only been 'ere a couple of weeks. My name's Jonny.'

'Oh,' Dora said.

Jonny burst out laughing.

'That all you can say? What about telling me your name?'

Dora realized she was not experienced with this sort of thing.

'My name's Dora. Dora Lunn.'

'Well, hello, Dora Lunn.' Jonny held his hand out and all she could do was take it and return the greeting.

'You're ever so pretty,' Jonny announced. 'D'you fancy walking out one afternoon? Sat'd'y?'

'No,' Dora said. 'I've got to be somewhere else.'

They were almost home again and they paused outside the front door.

'Have you now? Where's that then?'

'The library,' she said, going to the front door.

It was his turn to say, 'Oh.' With a baffled expression.

Dora went about her work, thinking of the next instalment of her story while ironing piles of clothes, pressing the flat iron on to shirts and collars, chemises and petticoats and hearing the damp hissing out of them.

And she had plenty else to distract her with Rose toddling about. There were no other children on the yard behind, surrounded as it was by businesses and factory walls, so the three of them kept an eye on her, steering her away from the fire and keeping her occupied.

But the next day, when Dora was passing through the hall, Jonny appeared on the stairs again.

'What about Sunday?'

'What about it?' Dora said.

Jonny looked patiently at her.

'You do know I have a baby daughter?'

'Do you?' He must have seen Rose, Dora thought impatiently. 'But ain't you got a husband?'

'He died,' Dora explained untruthfully. 'Of consumption.'

'Well,' he offered. 'I suppose she could come too.'

Dora watched him go back up the stairs. She had not an ounce of interest in him. Now he knows, he won't pester me again, she thought.

Images of Robert surfaced in her mind again, so painful that she paused in the hall to lean her head against the wall, washed in longing. How could she ever love anyone but him? And Rose was so like him that she was a constant reminder. She tried to drag her thoughts away from memories of that time. Dwelling on it would make her bitter.

'What did he want?' Minnie asked when she went back into the downstairs room.

'He wants me to walk out with him.'

She had Minnie's full attention. 'His fizzog's all right. And he looks a strong feller . . .'

'Well, you walk out with him then,' Dora snapped.

'Hey, what's up with you?' Minnie said. 'You're ungrateful, you are. I shouldn't mind being asked out by a nice-looking lad.'

'Oh, I expect you will be,' Dora said more kindly. 'I just don't . . .' She hesitated. 'I've just got enough to do.'

And, she thought, picking up a pile of clothes to sort them, I want the man I love – not just any old man. Once again, a pain went through her, so sharp that she found tears in her eyes.

The letter arrived a day later from Mr Charles Dickens. Dora always opened the return letters with her heart pounding hard. Supposing he did not like her story and sent it back? Supposing she couldn't do it anymore? But the envelope was reassuringly thin. The letter, as usual, was addressed from Gad's Hill Place, in Kent.

'*Another riveting instalment!*' Mr Dickens had written. He added a few editorial queries. Then at the bottom, added:

> *Perhaps one day we might coincide in London? Could I entreat you to conjure a reason for such an occasion? I am frequently in town so please let me know if you are able to travel from the Midlands. Our readers are much in approval and I should like to encounter the*

hand and mind behind the creations of Mr Richard Fletcher!'

Yours most sincerely,
Charles Dickens

'Is it all right?' asked Minnie. She and Cissy both looked eagerly at Dora.

'Yes. He's quite happy.' Relief was still flooding through her. 'And – well, he's asked me to go and meet him.'

'What, Mr Dickens?' Minnie gawped. 'Down *London*?'

Cissy looked even more bewildered, never having heard of Mr Dickens, and London being a place that might just as well have been on the moon.

'Yes,' Dora said. 'Where else?'

'Are you gunna go? You could leave Rosie with us – we'll mind her, won't we, Ciss?'

It occurred to Dora, with a giddy feeling, that she could easily afford a ticket to London and back now. She was so cautious about spending money that she just let it accumulate in her bank account. But she would go – of course she would. In fact, she wanted to set off straight away – a personal invitation from the famous writer Charles Dickens!

'I have been to London before,' she said airily, trying to seem calmer than she felt. She felt like jumping up and down. 'To the Great Exhibition.'

The others goggled at her even more.

'P'raps I'll take the next instalment in myself – it's nearly finished.' She turned away with a grin. 'Save the price of a letter.'

Thirty-Nine

As soon as Ada saw Elsie come rushing into the shop carrying Vicky on her hip, she knew something was seriously wrong. Elsie's baby was due to be born any day, but up until now she had insisted on coming into work.

'I'll only sit stewing at home, else,' she told Ada. 'I'll go home when I can't cope.'

But today she hurried straight up to Ada.

'I'll have to stop at home. It's Mother – she's ever so poorly.'

Up until now, Matty Drake had insisted there was nothing wrong, but it had reached a point when she could no longer hide it.

'She's lying down and she's in such a lot of pain,' Elsie said, unable to hold back her tears any longer. 'She's not up to minding her –' she nodded at the little girl '– and nothing else is getting done neither.'

Margaret came up to them, smiled at Vicky and stroked her cheek.

'Summat amiss?'

'It's Matty,' Ada said. 'She's taken bad – Elsie's stopping at home.'

'Not Mrs Drake?' Margaret said, shocked. Everyone knew Matty as a coach and horses that never stopped moving.

'Go on, Else, off you go,' Ada said. 'I'll pop over later, all right?'

Elsie nodded, wiping her eyes.

*

Elsie crept up the stairs, past the lower room where the rest of the family were working, to their home above. She slipped inside and carefully put Vicky down.

'You need to be quiet,' she said, a finger to her lips. 'I think Nana's asleep and we don't want to disturb her, all right?'

Vicky nodded, solemnly. This was all very strange for both of them. Matty was usually the absolute heart of the household, bustling about, in charge of everything.

Elsie looked round in dismay. The main room was chaotic. Unwashed crockery and pans, a pile of washing that Matty had been sorting to take down to the yard at the back before she was taken bad and took the unheard-of step of retreating to her bed.

'You'd best get on with it,' Elsie murmured to herself. She had a dragging feeling in her body and it was awkward to move, but she knew the others had a lot of work on. 'No one else is going to do it.'

First, she crept over and put her head round the bedroom door where Edwin and Matty Drake slept. Matty was asleep, but her face wore a look of deep unease, as if she could feel her pain even while sleeping. There was a yellowness to her, Elsie realized, seeing Matty's face in the morning light through the window. She had not seen that before.

Standing looking down at her beloved mother-in-law, Elsie was filled with an icy sense of foreboding. The look of Matty's face, the way she had been over the past few weeks, had deeply changed her. There was something terribly wrong, no matter how much they all tried to wish it away.

'Oh, Mom,' Elsie whispered. Matty was like a big, comforting bird under whose feathery wings she had found shelter. 'Don't leave us – please.'

She felt like kneeling by the bed and sobbing, but she pulled herself together and went back to boil water for washing-up.

Ada had the same feeling of dread, seeing the state Elsie was in and hearing about Matty Drake. It was on her mind all morning.

They were busy and at full stretch. First of all, Tom had gone to Beardsmore's to learn new skills for a few weeks. Before he went, he had handed over the cutting to Vi. She was keen to pick up new things, so William and Ada had decided she should be given the task. Vi was a strong, gristly woman and set about learning fast. She listened carefully to Tom's instructions about the angle of the cutter.

'See this block of fat?' he told her. 'Mutton fat that is. Grease the cutter with that and you'll get the best cut.'

Ada had seen Vi flexing her tired arms, on and off during the day, but she was determined and she just kept going. She couldn't help a sneaking admiration for the woman even though she had never grown to like her.

Old man Beardsmore had agreed that Tom could come and learn off some of his expert workers – Ada was surprised how readily he had agreed. It was because Tom was a man, she thought, and that Beardsmore felt he should be trained up to take over her company. Old Alf Beardsmore had always had a job putting up with a woman running the business.

Tom was like a man reborn and Ada was grateful to William for the suggestion.

'I done etching today, with acid,' he had said last night at the tea table. He was lit up with excitement. '*We* could do that. We can get the acid from Cannings and you use it to burn off the bits you don't want and you use a resister like, on the parts you want to keep where they are. There's some right pretty stuff you can make – flowers and that.'

Ada smiled. 'That sounds a bit of all right. When we've got these new lines settled in and you're back, maybe we could do some specialist lines – you know, a bit superior.'

Tom looked thoughtful. 'Thing I don't like about Beardsmore's,' he said, 'part from the old man, of course, miserable old bugger . . .' The two of them laughed. 'It's so big. Swarms of 'em in and out. But old Percy Rogers who's showing me this stuff – he's one of the few who's got time. Everyone else is too busy turning out big orders.'

This had given Ada food for thought. All this time, she had thought about nothing but growing her company. Of course big orders meant more money – they needed to rely on bulk. But she could see what Tom meant. A vast room full of workers whose names she did not even know did seem less attractive. She decided it was something she and William needed to discuss – their joint aims in running the firm.

But as she went about her work that morning, William busy up at the other end of the shop, she was grateful that Elsie and Matty's problems were close to the front of her mind. Because having a conversation with William these days was getting more and more difficult.

Since that night, here in the shop, where they had walked into each other's arms and kissed, William had withdrawn. At first she thought it was shyness. When she came into the shop and he was there, he avoided her eyes. He was always polite and they discussed their work in a civil way. But there was no warmth – let alone the special warmth that might have followed such a hungry kiss.

He doesn't want anyone to know, Ada thought at first. She was happy with this. Keep work and play separate. But now that a few weeks had passed, she knew for certain he was avoiding her. He left in the evenings just before seven when everyone else knocked off, so there was never any opportunity to be alone with her.

Ada had gone from feeling confused to hurt, and now anger was building out of that hurt. Her feelings were like cut nerve endings, with nothing to staunch the pain.

What have I done? she kept thinking. Should I say something?

But her own pride and William's obvious avoidance of talking about anything other than mother-of-pearl and lathes and deliveries, kept her from saying anything. It hurt too much. She was frightened that if she started she would just burst into tears and that would never do.

She looked along the shop. Everyone was busy working. With Vi on a new job and Elsie not here they were having to work extra hard. William was watching Vi, making sure things were being done right. For a moment Ada watched his face, thought of the smiling look of love that she had seen on it. She had to turn away quickly, so as not to show her emotions to him or anyone else.

Elsie, having done the washing-up, and tidied and dusted the room while also having to keep Vicky occupied, sank on to a chair facing the heap of washing.

'I can't,' she said out loud.

The thought of lugging it all, and Vicky, down to the brewhouse, of carrying pails of water, the dollying and mangling . . . No – it was just all too much. She sat for a moment, breathing in deep breaths. What she really wanted was to lie back and fall asleep.

'This won't do.' She stood up, having to struggle to get her balance. 'Come on, lovey – we're going to go and see Grandpa and your pa.'

Taking Vicky's hand she helped her slowly down the

stairs and went into the workroom. George looked up from his bench and smiled at the two of them. Edwin and Ernie and Lizzie all looked glad of the interruption as well.

'You all right, love?' George said.

'Can you take her – just for a few minutes? Your mom's not well and I'm taking the laundry to get it done. I can't manage. There's some woman in Bread Street – I'll take it round there.'

'Come 'ere, little'un,' Lizzie said. 'You can come and play with your auntie for a bit, can't you?'

'Thanks, Lizzie,' Elsie said as Vicky happily raised her arms to be picked up.

'D'you want me to take it?' George offered. He looked concerned.

'No, I'll be all right,' Elsie said. 'A little walk might get things going, you never know!'

George looked bashful at this and kissed her goodbye.

Elsie carried the bundle out from Galton Passage and along to Bread Street, feeling she was waddling like a duck. Uncertain, she stopped outside a row of houses. A moment later, a blonde lad came striding along the street and went to the door of one of them.

'D'you know where the women who do the washing live?' she called to him.

He held the door open and nodded towards the inside. 'Here.'

As soon as Elsie stepped in to the room she could feel the steamy atmosphere through the open door and she saw two workers toiling away. One was a strong-looking brown-haired girl who was tipping soap powder into a steaming copper. The other curly-haired and very young looking, was busy pounding clothes in a maiding tub that was almost as big as she was. The child looked unwell, Elsie thought, or at least, terribly underfed like so many young children in the town.

'What d'you want?' the older girl asked. She did not sound uncivil, just busy.

'I've got washing needs doing,' she said. 'I know I'm not a regular, but . . .' Unable to stand any longer, she sank down on one of the chairs. 'I'm due, any minute.'

'Ooh, well, you'd best get home then,' the girl said. 'If you want to sign up regular, like . . .?'

'I don't know,' Elsie said, gradually getting her breath back. She was feeling a bit odd. 'I can't say.' Looking round, she said, 'Is it just the two of you?'

'Oh no,' the elder girl said. 'There's three of us.' She picked up a pad of rough paper and a pencil. 'Give us your name?' Laboriously, she wrote, Elsie Drake, 3 Galton Passage. 'All right, that's not far. We'll bring it back Thursday.' She eyed the bundle. 'That'll be three bob.'

Elsie gladly agreed and thanked the girls. But walking home, she felt a sudden, powerful tightening across the front of her body. She leaned against the nearest wall for a moment, gasping. The sensation, tightening her muscles until her belly was hard like a drum, gathered to a peak, then passed off. She knew these pains all right.

'Oh, Lord,' Elsie thought, gasping as the pain eased off. 'I'd best get home – sharp like.'

Forty

Dora walked out through the grand frontage of Euston station, clutching the map she had bought at the stationer's inside. This day felt like an astonishing adventure, as if she had already travelled to a different country.

The forecourt was busy with passengers arriving and departing, porters carrying luggage, shrieking women holding hats on in the breeze and panicking about something or other, omnibuses coming and going and a row of hansom cabs, the horses dozing with lowered heads.

Dora stood bewildered. Where did she begin? Looking at the map, the safest thing seemed to be to head for the river. You could be sure of a river – it went only this way or that. But how to get there?

It still never occurred to her that she was comfortably off, had more money in the bank than she could even understand. But she had barely spent any of it, afraid that the source of income would dry up. She had, however, bought new clothes for herself and Minnie. Today she wore her new dress, a soft crimson and faun plaid, new black leather boots and a long black coat and hat with a brim. She felt quite queenly walking along and as if she was an imposter. This took some getting used to.

And even now, the thought of having a cab all to herself seemed a crazed extravagance.

She approached the nearest among the swirl of horse-drawn omnibuses. It was filling up fast, people sprouting like stalks from its roof, the voice outside shouting,

'WOOLWICH ARSENAL!' She had no idea where that was and people were jostling her out of the way. She was used to the energy of her home town, the hurrying and getting on with things. Londoners seemed to be energetic in a different way and she felt like a foreigner.

'You getting on or not?'

'Where d'you wanna go?' someone else asked, more helpfully.

'The river,' she said, feeling desperate.

'The river!' Everyone laughed. 'Not gunna do yerself in, are yer?'

'That one's going to Embankment,' a quieter lady told her. 'That'll do you.'

She climbed aboard the other omnibus and sat inside in the very last space at the end. Everyone seemed to prefer to sit close to the door. She found herself squeezed between a dark-eyed, exotic lady with hair piled high under her hat, who gave her a slight smile, and a thin little lady in black who kept her elbows tucked in tightly as if she was afraid of contagion.

Soon they set off, rocking and swaying to the sound of the horses' hooves. It seemed a long way, especially as a boy up near the door was sick all over his feet.

Until the bus finally lurched to a halt and there came a yell of 'EMBANKMENT!' Dora was still too caught up in the journey to think about her arrival. Her heart started thudding like a drum. She was here to meet Mr Dickens, for goodness' sakes! The most loved and popular writer in the country – if not the world. And he had invited her to come and greet him in a café near Wellington Street. From the map she saw that if she walked east along the river and then turned in, she was not far off. And she was early.

It was a cold, bright day and she walked alongside the

busy Thames, entranced by the broad stretch of water, so wide as it travelled towards the sea, compared with the sections of the narrow cut which was all the water thoroughfare that Birmingham could offer. The sights made her feel ecstatic, on top of the happiness already bubbling inside her: the broken glint of sunlight on the ripples, the water busy with craft, some tall and majestic with umber-coloured sails and towering over the gaggle of small, busy, sail-less boats.

She turned along a side street, turned again and found herself walking the great curve of the Strand. Strand, she thought. It must have been right beside the river once. Grand buildings rose each side of her, the sky a cloud-patched strip between, and all around, a hubbub of omnibuses and carriages and crowds of people.

After a moment, amid the noise she heard something else: a loud, commanding holler from somewhere along the street. Gradually the noise grew, a rhythmic sound accompanied by more shouts, until other people started to crane their necks to look, the traffic slewed away on each side and the sound became clearer: men marching.

Soon she could see them, neat lines of them in the red uniforms of the infantry. Brass buckles and buttons glinted, the colours shone in the bright sunlight and each of them held a rifle a-slant against his shoulder. Dora stepped nearer to the edge of the road, fascinated as they marched closer, what seemed like hundreds of them, led by three men on sleek chestnut horses. Was the Queen there? she wondered. Was this what happened when Her Majesty went out anywhere?

The rhythm of marching feet was loud as they passed, and kept passing, their faces determinedly watching the head of the man in front. People cheered and clapped. A woman threw a posy of flowers. Dora watched as it bounced off one of the men's shoulders and fell, the petals trampled underfoot. The last men were coming through.

And, almost beside her, among the last of the troops, there he was. Thinner in the face, a little taller perhaps, but him. Unmistakably him.

'Robert!' It burst out of her: she could not stop herself.

His head flicked, startled, and their eyes met for a second. He could not do anything except keep marching and Dora started to move along with them, all other thoughts emptied from her mind. She hurried along, almost trotting to keep up, always keeping Robert in sight, not caring who she jostled or who cursed at her. It was him – it was! And if it was the last thing she ever did she was going to see him, speak to him – it was as if she was possessed.

She kept up her scurrying, desperate mission for the best part of half an hour, not knowing now where she was or where they were going. Nothing mattered except that he was there, her love, just ahead of her.

Eventually a huge building came into view that could only have been a barracks. It was enormous and imposing. And then she was gripped by fear. The building was swallowing up the column of men who were disappearing in through the gates, and it would swallow him in turn – but there was no way she could get in.

Perhaps she was mistaken and he had not heard her. Or he had heard – she was sure he had! – but had forgotten all about her. Had no care to see her again. She had just been the toy of a privileged young man who had moved on to a new life, leaving her with his child. He would have met other women since then. Women from a background more like his own, with money and education. What on earth did she think she was doing, rushing after him like this? This was where he belonged now – one of this strong band of men. He would have no time for her!

More of the front end of the parade had disappeared, like the head of a snake vanishing into a hole, between the two rounded towers at the barrack entrance. She only had moments – she had to find out once and for all. At least see if he would look at her, remember who she was, what they had shared.

She dashed along until she was almost level with him. About three-quarters of the men had marched in through the gates now. The brick building loured over her, like a prison with its blind windows and tall iron railings. He was heading for the gate – but now she did not dare to call his name. It was quieter here and she felt afraid and foolish.

Just as she drew level with the gates herself and the last lines of men were heading inside, a flash of red peeled away from the body of men like a single petal from a giant flower. Before she even knew what was happening, he had seized her hand and pulled her further along the street. There was nowhere to go or to conceal themselves – only more of the railings fronting the building.

'Oi – Gordon!' one of the others shouted as the last men turned in.

But he ignored them and the two of them were suddenly there, face to face in the street, panting with exertion and disbelief. And there was no time.

'I've got to get in there—' He glanced anxiously along the street. Then back at her. Him, his face just the same, his hair cropped short, his lovely eyes.

'I knew it was you,' she gasped.

'Couldn't turn to look,' he said. 'I saw you – but I couldn't believe . . . Look at you – you look astonishing.' He gazed at her in wonder and suddenly she felt beautiful. Robert had only ever seen her before either dressed as a maid or in her one faded frock. 'What on earth are you doing here? No – don't explain.'

'Do you love me?' she burst out – because he would be gone, she could see, and she had to know.

Emotions wrangled in his face.

'There's no one like you, Dora. Always.'

'Always!' Her heart soared. He was true. She knew he would be true. Now, she could tell him.

'You – we – have a daughter,' she gabbled. 'Her name's Rose – she's two. Three in June. She's lovely – she looks just like you . . . '.'

The shock vibrated through his face. 'No! Oh, Dor – how've you—?'

'I'm all right – we're all right . . .'

There was no time to finish anything – even a sentence.

'They're sending us abroad. To India – very soon.'

'Oh.' It was a cry of pain. India. He was to be gone – again. And so very far away.

'I'll have to stick it out – I've no choice. Look, I've got to go.'

She scrabbled in her bag for pencil, paper. Scrawled her address.

'Write to me?' She thrust it at him.

Robert took it, nodding, tucked it into his pocket.

'I'll wait for you,' she said.

'Oh, Dora. One day . . .'

For a brief moment their lips touched. She could see in his eyes that he was true. And then he was gone – tearing along the street to disappear before they closed the barrack gates.

Dora's legs were trembling so much that she had to cling to the railings. She loved those railings because they were where he was, they held him, inside this place. Her Robert, her love. She rested her head against the bars and let the tears of joy and pain run down her cheeks, her chest feeling as though it was about to break open.

Because however long he was gone for, however long she had to wait, Robert still loved her. He loved her – she could see it. And suddenly everything else in her life which was dear was added to this great joy, this gift of love and life.

It only occurred to her when she had righted herself and dried her eyes, that she had very little idea where she was and that she had completely missed her opportunity to meet Charles Dickens.

Forty-One

Walking along Bread Street towards home that evening, Dora could hardly remember how she had got there. The day had been so extraordinary. All she could do on the train was relive those moments. Walking along the Strand, the glint of brass and red uniforms, the blood-stilling moment when she recognized his face. And those snatched, precious moments with him. Robert. The love she had never expected to see again, there in front of her, the brief brush of his lips against hers which told her everything she needed to know . . .

'Dora, isn't it?'

She was jolted out of her passionate thoughts so suddenly that her temper flared. It was him again, the blonde lad from upstairs. Jonny, he'd said. She stared at him.

'No need to look at me like that!' he joked. 'Anyone'd think I'd never spoken to you before. So – when're you going to come out for a walk with me, eh?'

'For the love of God, just leave me alone!' Dora almost shouted. Here she was, having found the love of her life after all this time – and here was this booby on at her again. She stormed away to their front door. 'Just leave off, all right?'

She didn't bother looking back to see what his reaction was.

When she walked into the house, the main room was draped with damp washing, the two empty washtubs stacked one on another by the hearth. Rose ran straight to her in excitement.

'Mama, Mama!'

'Hello, my sweet!' Dora swung the little girl into her arms and Rose wrapped her arms tightly round Dora's neck, planting wet kisses on her cheek.

'Hey, you're throttling me!' Dora laughed.

It was only after these loving greetings that she began to take in the scene that confronted her. Minnie's face. And Cissy, sitting curled up on a stool, her elbows sticking out because her arms were wrapped over her head as if she was expecting to fend off blows.

'Dora . . .' Minnie pointed at Cissy as if she just didn't have words to go any further.

'What's up? What's happened? Let me put you down, chubby-cheeks,' Dora said to Rose. She lowered the little girl to the floor, took off her hat to lay it on the table and unbuttoned her coat. She had been expecting to be showered with questions – though it was a relief not to be.

'Show her, Cissy,' Minnie insisted. 'We're not angry . . .' She looked at Dora, seeming bewildered. 'She's acting as if I'm gunna lamp her – and I'm not. Ciss,' she added again loudly, as if Cissy had been struck with deafness. 'We're *not angry*.'

It was Dora's turn to be bewildered. 'What's going on? Why would we be angry?'

'We wouldn't,' Minnie insisted. 'That's what I keep saying. Oh, stand *up*, won't you?'

'Cissy?' Dora went over and carefully prised the girl's arms from over her head, then drew her to her feet. Cissy kept her head down, eyes fixed on the floor. 'What's happened, dear?'

Slowly, Cissy raised her head and looked at Dora. The girl's blue eyes were full of an anguish that Dora found almost unbearable.

'Turn her round – sideways,' Minnie instructed. 'Hold your frock against you.'

Cissy moved without needing further explanation and stood sideways on. After a second of wondering what she was supposed to be looking for, it became obvious. Cissy smoothed her clothing down at the front and it was quite clear: her little body, stick thin, suddenly bulbed out at the front like the profile of an onion.

'Oh!' Dora cried.

'See?' Minnie came over and put her arm round the girl's shoulders. 'No one's cross with you, Ciss, we keep telling you.'

Cissy didn't cry or say anything. She just stood looking flayed.

'D'you understand what we're saying to you?' Dora said, realizing they hadn't said anything very much.

Cissy shook her head.

'That you're expecting a baby?'

Cissy's eyes sought Dora's, in desperation. 'That's what she said. But I ain't, am I? I dunno about anything like that.'

Dora drew back, feeling suddenly completely exhausted and starving hungry.

'Stick the kettle on, Min,' she said. 'It's been a bit of a day. And we need to have a little talk, Cissy.'

They sat drinking tea and eating bread and jam, Rose planting herself firmly on Dora's lap. Cissy seemed gradually to take in that no one was angry or about to punish her. She had had no idea that she was expecting a child except for having some 'funny feelings inside'.

Dora reckoned, looking at her, that she must be six months gone. How had they not noticed before? But Cissy had only just turned fourteen. And seemed innocent as a babe herself.

'Who put the baby in your tummy?' Minnie asked her.

Dora frowned at her. It felt too harsh a thing to ask straight out like that.

'I don't know,' Cissy said. She looked so bewildered. 'How do babies happen?'

'I bet you didn't know when you were her age,' Dora said to Minnie. 'I didn't, I know that.'

'Well, you weren't much older,' Minnie argued.

'I was – I was sixteen. Well, fifteen. But even then I never knew – not really.'

Carefully, they explained this particular fact of life to Cissy, whose face brightened like someone stumbling on the right answer.

'Oh, that'll be me father then. But he done it to me sisters and none of them's got babbies in their tummies.' She frowned. 'Don't think so anyhow.'

Dora rubbed her hand over her face for a second to hide her horror. She couldn't bear to ask how old Cissy's sisters were. Even Minnie was silenced by this.

'Cissy,' Dora said after a moment's thought. 'You eat up your bread and jam and get yourself off home, all right? Don't say anything to anyone, not about the baby or anything. And when you come in tomorrow, we'll have another little talk, all right?'

'Yes, Miss Lunn,' Cissy said. She stuffed the crust of bread into her mouth and stood up. 'And you're not cross with me?' she added indistinctly.

'No, dear,' Dora assured her, feeling suddenly very old beside this child. 'We're not cross.'

They both watched Cissy take herself off.

'Poor child,' Dora said. Only then, tears rushed into her eyes. The only physical relations she had known were with Robert. They had discovered each other together, with all the awkward new love of two young people who trusted each other. And seeing Robert today had brought it all back.

But Cissy must trust her father as well, she thought. She had never heard her complain about him. He worked on the roads, had a sick wife and apparently had incestuous relations with his daughters. Her stomach turned at the thought.

'She's got to come and live here,' Minnie announced, jerking Dora out of her thoughts. 'I mean it. You took me in when I needed somewhere to go. My father was a brute and a bully but he never did that,' she added hastily. 'Not dirty things. We've got to help her.'

'But they only live round the corner,' Dora said. 'They'll come and get her back.'

'Not if we promise to keep her and look after her,' Minnie said. 'I'm not talking about kidnapping her. The two of us can bunk up – like you did with me – leave you in peace to get on with your writing.'

Dora cuddled Rose close, feeding her a little cup of milk as she struggled to take all this in.

'If we're gunna build up this business, she can be part of it,' Minnie said. 'Us girls together.'

'But she's going to have a baby,' Dora pointed out.

'So what? You had a baby an' all.'

'What about those other little girls?' Dora found herself whispering.

'We can't do much about them,' Minnie said. 'But we can help Cissy. Take some of the heavier jobs off her for a start.'

'All right,' Dora agreed. 'I can pick up some of that.'

However well off she felt for the moment through her writing, she was always afraid that it would not last. She wanted their laundry business to keep going and to grow – not just for Minnie's sake, but for her own. And now, it seemed, also for young Cissy.

'I'll go and see them tomorrow,' Minnie said. 'She can still pay them some of her wages – but they won't have to keep her. I should think they'll be glad to have one less mouth to feed.'

She cut another hunk of bread, smeared jam all over it while saying eagerly, 'So, what about Mr Dickens – what's he like?'

'I'm afraid I don't know,' Dora admitted.

Forty-Two

'Ada?'

Ada had been with the others in the shop earlier that day, when she heard Elsie's frantic voice up the stairs. The others all looked over as Ada rushed to see what was wrong.

'Get someone to fetch Mrs Mills,' Elsie gasped up at her. They could all hear. 'The baby's coming and Mom can't help.'

'I'll go – I know where 'er lives!' Before Ada could say anything, little Biddy downed tools and sped past her down the stairs on her skinny legs.

Ada helped Elsie home. Elsie had to stop twice as they climbed the two flights of stairs to the attic, doubled over, moaning with the pains.

'Where's Matty?' Ada asked softly.

'In bed, asleep I think,' Elsie said, sinking on to the bed. 'Oh, Ada, she looks so poorly.'

It was not long before Mrs Mills appeared. She took one look at Ada's white face and said, 'Go back to work if you want, Miss Fletcher. We'll be all right for a bit. Could you put some water on to boil as you go down?'

'I'll tell George as well,' Ada said, hurrying away to do as she was asked. She carried water up and set it on the fire. On her way down she went into the Drakes' shop. Edwin, George, Ernie and Lizzie all looked up as the door opened.

'The midwife's here,' Ada said gruffly. 'She's having it.'

'Oh!' Lizzie cried.

George's expression twisted into a contest between panic and excitement.

'Oh, my word,' he said.

'I need to get back – I'll come over a bit later, all right?'

Ada crossed the Passage, fighting feelings of shame. She should stay with Elsie, shouldn't she, since Matty Drake was out of action? But the feelings of horror and fear that overcame her when anything to do with childbirth came too close to her held sway. She just couldn't bring herself to be there.

Climbing the stairs, more painful thoughts assailed her. William and his first wife, Jane, had not had children. She wondered if he longed for them, had wanted a family. What if William still longed for children? How could she ever give that to someone, the way she felt? Even to William?

Climbing this set of stairs, she realized her legs had turned weak and trembly. Anything to do with the birthing of children made her fearful and queasy.

Eager faces turned to her as soon as she walked in.

'How is she?' Margaret asked.

'Oh, it'll be a while yet, I'd say,' Vi put in, as if the authority on the subject. 'She wasn't all that far on.'

'I have had four children myself,' Margaret pointed out.

'I think it's a boy,' Biddy said, her eyes shining.

'Oooh, I doubt it,' Vi said. 'Not the way she was carrying.'

Margaret looked at Ada and rolled her eyes.

'Right,' Ada said abruptly. 'Let's get on.'

It turned out to be a long business and the little one did not show her face to the world until the small hours of the next morning.

Just before six, when Ada was already dressed, she heard knocking downstairs.

'Who's that?' Tom said, busy stoking the range.

'I bet it's George.' Ada ran down the stairs, begging, *Please, please, let everything be all right . . .*

A pale, exhausted but beaming George was on the doorstep.

'She's had another girl,' he announced, all lit up. 'We're calling her Olive. Olive Susan.'

'Oh, George – that's . . . What marvellous news,' Ada said, feeling as though her legs might give way. She clutched the door. She had not slept well at all, afraid that the long delay meant Elsie was in trouble. 'Is she . . .?'

'She's all right,' George said. 'Getting some sleep.'

'I'll be over later,' Ada promised.

As George was walking back home, a spring in his step, William arrived.

'Morning,' he smiled. Ada was about to reply when he nodded towards George. 'Everything all right?'

'My sister's just had another daughter,' Ada said. Her relief and happiness for them surfaced then, her face breaking into a tender smile.

'That's a blessing,' William replied, smiling back and looking at her in a way he had not done for weeks. 'A great blessing.'

Their eyes met. And in that moment Ada felt something in her give way. That look, the joyful way he greeted the news. Imagine seeing his face if it was she who had given him a child! And he seemed lighter somehow, happier. Love lit her within. She could do it. She would – for the love of this man! She would learn to do the things a woman needed to do.

He had been about to go past and up into the shop, but he lingered outside.

'I was wondering –' he looked past her, through into the building, his face more serious again suddenly – 'if you'd like a walk at the weekend? There's something I need to discuss with you.'

Ada went across the Passage and up to the Drakes' place to find the family all buzzing about in a state of excitement. Elsie sat enthroned in bed with the new baby in her arms, George beside her. Matty was seated on the chair by the bed, Edwin and Ernie both standing nearby with a bashful expression, and Lizzie kept moving back and forth with cups and plates. The room smelt of ale and hot toast: Elsie was devouring a large helping of it as Ada came in.

'Come and meet our little lady!' George cried.

Ada, glowing with happiness for Elsie and George and for herself after William's invitation, felt a wide smile light up her face. She went over and kissed Elsie, gazing at the face of her new, sleeping niece.

'George told you, did he?' Elsie laughed. 'Olive Susan – we liked the names.'

Ada made a fuss of them both, happy that Elsie was well and happy. She sat on the bed and it was only then she was fully able to take in the sight of Matty Drake. Ada tried not to show her feeling of shock. Matty looked so ill – much thinner, yellow round the eyes and clearly not feeling well at all.

'Another granddaughter then?' Ada said carefully. 'That's lovely, isn't it?'

Matty smiled, but when she spoke her voice was weak and small. The Matty they all knew was shrinking away horrifyingly fast. 'She's a beauty. If they go on like this, though, they'll have to find somewhere else to live.'

Everyone laughed at this and talked and then Nancy arrived with her boys and there was more tea made.

Ada stayed a while and drank a cup of tea as everyone rejoiced and tried hard to act as if nothing at all was wrong.

As she left, Ada said quietly to Elsie, 'Tell me if there's anything I can do, Sis.'

'Oh, don't worry, I will,' Elsie smiled sleepily.

Ada criss-crossed Galton Passage as often as she could during those days, knowing how poorly Matty Drake was and wanting to help Elsie. Elsie, young, well-fed and healthy, recovered quickly, but she still needed a few days in bed and Ada was glad to keep her company when she could. Lizzie Drake, who had just turned sixteen, was now a young woman herself and a dab hand in the house.

On the Friday afternoon Ada went to see them. Olive was feeding well, her little cheeks bulging in and out as she suckled and the sight made Ada laugh.

'She knows what she's about, doesn't she?' she said.

'She does,' Elsie said, gazing adoringly at her. 'She's a little poppet.'

Vicky sometimes came and gazed in wonder at her little sister, but otherwise barely seemed to notice that anything had changed.

'She's not going to remember a time when Olive wasn't here, is she?' Elsie said. 'She's so little.'

Ada got up, folding the little knitted blanket under which she had been warming her knees.

'Just as well,' she laughed. 'I'd better get back now. George'll be in soon, won't he?'

She kissed Elsie and the girls and went down. Just as she was about to let herself out into the street there was a knock at the door. Ada opened it to find two women waiting outside.

'Mrs Drake?' A plump, pink-cheeked young woman stood beside a wooden barrow loaded with bundles. She was holding out one of the bundles, a ticket attached to the top of it. When she spoke, Ada saw square, widely spaced teeth which gave her an appealing look.

'Oh,' Ada said. 'Yes, that'll be my sister – she's upstairs. I'll take it. She's paid, has she?'

'Yes,' the girl said, as Ada took the bundle.

Ada was just about to thank her when she straightened up and caught sight of the person who was standing behind the laundry girl. A young woman with an unusually – for a washerwoman at least – smart black hat with a wide brim. For a moment Ada wondered if she in fact had anything to do with the laundry – but then why would she be standing there? She also had a powerful feeling of having seen her before. She took in more details: the bright ginger hair visible under her hat, those intense eyes . . .

The other woman seemed equally fascinated by her and was staring straight at her. So much so that the first girl noticed and looked back and forth between the two of them, in puzzlement. They seemed about to move on and Ada knew she could not let them go.

'Are you . . . ?' She started speaking even before she knew what she wanted to say. 'I mean – do you run the laundry? I think my sister might need to come to you again.'

'We do,' the plump one said. 'Round in Bread Street if you want to be put on our books, regular like.'

'I'll have to ask them,' Ada said. The other woman was still staring at her. Not sure how to get any further with this, she thought to say, 'Can I ask what your names are?'

The first girl looked a bit surprised, but friendly enough, and she said, 'I'm Minnie. Minnie Moon.'

Ada looked at her companion. Even as she opened her mouth, Ada knew, somehow, that this was how it was. She could sense it.

'I'm Dora Lunn.'

Ada nearly sank down on the step. For a moment she

was speechless. Clutching the door jamb with her free hand she managed to say, faintly, 'Sorry to ask, but – were you ever in the workhouse?'

The young woman's face told her everything.

'Dora Lunn,' Ada said in wonder. She let go of the door, put the bundle down on the step and reached for the young woman's hand. 'Come over here . . .'

Dora did not resist, as if she already sensed what was afoot. Ada led her across Galton Passage.

'Look –' She pointed to the modest brass plate screwed on to the wall near a window facing the Passage: 'Fletcher & Nichols, Pearl Buttons'.

'Dora, your real name's Dora Fletcher. I'm Ada Fletcher. Your sister.'

Dora stared at the plate. Traced the letters lightly with her fingers almost like a blind person.

'And over there – where we just were, that's Elsie's house. Our sister. She's upstairs.'

Dora gazed deep into Ada's eyes. 'Ada,' she said wonderingly. Then at last, 'Oh! Yes. *Yes.*'

The sisters wrapped their arms around each other and Ada felt the sobs begin to shake Dora's slender body. And then Ada heard her say something she didn't understand.

'All in one week,' she sobbed. 'All this – in one week.'

Forty-Three

'Come on. Come and see Elsie.'

Dora heard Ada's voice as if through water, she was so dazed.

Ada drew back and held her by the shoulders. Her own eyes were full of tears, her voice choked with gladness.

'She's just had a baby – she's got two little daughters.'

'You go, Dor,' Minnie said. 'I'll take the rest round.'

Dora stared at Minnie for a moment, trying to recall who she was and what they were doing there. Minnie, her closest friend. The laundry. She could not read Minnie's face. It was solemn, almost sad. Why was she sad? Dora could not make sense of any of it.

'Thanks, Min,' she managed, and the girl went off, pushing vigorously, the barrow rumbling away along the street with its bundles.

Ada – her sister! – picked up the bundle of laundry, balancing it awkwardly as she put her other, bony arm through Dora's.

'You lead the way,' Dora said, reaching for the bundle. 'I'll take that.'

'It's heavy,' Ada warned.

'I'm used to it,' Dora said and Ada gave a little laugh.

'Course. You would be.'

Inside, she followed Ada up two flights of stairs, gradually overcome by a creeping sense of familiarity. When she had first set eyes on this gaunt, almost forbidding-looking woman, it had taken seconds to trace anything familiar in the face that she had not seen for fourteen years. It was now, following her . . .

Does the way a person moves ever really change? she thought. It had been the same with Robert, even as he went marching along the Strand in that forced, military movement. Even so she had known it was him – had recognized him partly by the way he moved. And now Ada, the neat swing of her hips, elbows hugged in tight, the brisk mounting of the stairs. Yes, that was what she had been like, her Tomboy eldest sister. Deep in her memory was that movement . . . Ada running, climbing . . . *Pa's*— She gave such a loud 'Oh!' that Ada turned round.

'What's the matter?'

'*Pa's lad*,' Dora said. 'That's what he called you, wasn't it? His lad?'

Ada gave a faint smile. But there was a bitter edge to it and Dora was not sure what it meant. 'He did. Back then.'

Ada was about to go on up when she turned back again, speaking in a low voice.

'I need to tell you. About Elsie. She's married now – and happy – but a while back, a terrible thing happened. We don't need all the ins and outs but there was a girl Elsie got on the wrong side of. She came at her one night and threw vitriol over her. Burnt all down one side of her face.'

Dora gasped.

'It's healed as much as it's ever going to. But – just so's you're ready for it.'

Dora nodded, still trying to take in the awfulness of this as they went on up.

At the top, Ada quietly pushed the door open.

'Oh, you're still awake,' Dora heard her say. 'Thought you might've dozed off by now.'

There was a soft reply from inside.

'They brought the wash back,' Ada said. She hesitated, seeming unsure how to begin. 'Came with – a bit of a surprise.'

Ada stepped back and ushered Dora into the room. Dora saw a rounded little figure sitting reclined in bed, a tiny infant tucked in beside her. At first glance Dora could recognize nothing from the scarred face that looked at her. But then Elsie turned her head and she saw the sweet, pretty other side of it, a tiny mole beside that big blue eye. Elsie. Yes – little Elsie. It was her all right. Her sister.

Of course, she looked bewildered at a stranger walking into her bedroom. But Dora saw her frown as if trying to work something out. Dora took her hat off to show her flame-coloured hair which was plaited each side and looped neatly back in the nape of her neck.

'Hello, Elsie,' she said, her voice choking. 'I'm Dora.'

In a moment they were in each other's arms and the tears were flowing.

'I can't believe it,' Dora kept saying. And she and Elsie were laughing and crying at the same time and kept repeating that they couldn't believe it and Dora said, 'All in one day – both sisters at once!'

She looked down into the crook of Elsie's arm and saw a tiny face looking blearily up at her.

'Who's this?' she laughed tearfully.

'Olive,' Elsie said. 'She was born this morning. And I've another little one – Vicky. Her auntie's looking after her. So you've got two nieces as well.'

Dora straightened up and looked from one to the other of her tear-stained sisters. Once again she shook her head in disbelief.

'This is the best week of my life,' she said.

*

Ada brought chairs and made tea. Dora sat in a glow of joy. She, here, with two sisters, about to share a cup of tea, to talk. What could be more of a miracle?

As Ada came to sit down, she said softly to Elsie, 'How's Matty?'

'My mother-in-law,' Elsie explained softly to Dora. 'She's very poorly – in such a lot of pain.' Her face showed just how worried they all were. 'George keeps popping in to check on her. She's asleep for now, though.'

Dora could see that Elsie was at the heart of a happy family, despite their problems, and she nodded sympathetically.

And then they began on their questions, sometimes all talking at once.

'We came back for you, Ada and me,' Elsie told her. 'To the workhouse, to try and get you and John out. We'd never want you to think we didn't. But the pair of you had already gone and Mrs Hodges wouldn't tell us where you were.'

Ada was nodding along.

'I went into service – a doctor's family, near Five Ways.' Dora told them a little bit about it – but not Robert. Not yet. 'They were good to me really. Mrs Gordon helped me read and write and taught me things. Let me use the library.'

'That's where I saw you before!' Ada exclaimed, almost leaping out of her seat. 'I knew I'd seen you somewhere! We bumped into each other in the street, near that library – d'you remember?'

Dora looked vague. 'Sorry, I don't. Anyway, it was the library in their house I meant.'

Together, Ada and Elsie filled her in on what had happened to them. How they had found each other when they had also been in service.

'Any road,' Ada said, skating over the more painful details. 'We'd had enough – decided to start up on our own. So we came out – set up the business.'

'It's Ada's business really,' Elsie said. With a look at Ada that Dora could not quite read, she added, 'And William Nichols's now as well.'

'You started it every bit as much as I did,' Ada said. She looked down and seemed pinker about the face, Dora thought. She could not make sense of this.

'Ada's doing well,' Elsie said. 'She's got a good head on her.'

'I'll show you when you've got time,' Ada said. 'But I see you've got a business?'

There was too much to say, so that they kept jumping from subject to subject, leaping over time periods and only managing to cover the most basic information.

I can't tell them everything now, Dora thought, her shocked mind floundering in a sea of memories. She told them about Minnie and how they had started up. But she could not go into Robert, or Rose, or her writing – or a whole range of other things. It was all too big to begin on. And she could see that Ada and Elsie didn't want to go into certain things either, by the looks they exchanged when they talked about their time in service in Highgate. Or when she herself asked, 'I wonder what happened to our father?'

All she could remember about him was that he had been there and then was there no longer. The memories were all broken up and overlaid by so many others.

'Did he ever come back, d'you think – to the area?'

And again her sisters – sisters, here with her now! – brushed the subject away, this time avoiding each other's eyes. And little Olive began to wail and Elsie's attention was taken up with her.

Dora and Ada sat watching, quiet for a moment, until the little one was pacified at the breast. And then Ada turned to her and said:

'We don't know anything about where Mabs is – and I don't know where to start. But I did go and see John.' Her face was sad. 'I went over there – he works at Chance, the glassworks, lives with a family.'

'He doesn't want to know,' Elsie said bitterly. 'I've written to him asking him to come and see us, but he never even answers.'

Dora was struggling to take all this in. Mabs? She could just remember her little sister, the shining brown eyes, her chuckle. But she and John had stayed together in the workhouse until they were split up and sent away.

'Maybe it all hurts too much,' she said. 'He doesn't want to think back on those times.'

Ada and Elsie looked at her in silence. And she could see that this point of view was one they could understand.

Forty-Four

'You going up the school tonight, John?' Harriet Smith asked, handing him a piece for his dinner. He could feel the faint warmth of the bread through the paper as he pocketed it.

'Yes, I'm helping out with the little'uns tonight,' he said happily.

'I'll walk with you,' Clara said, pulling her shawl round her.

There was an immediate outburst of oooohing and laughter from her sisters.

'Shut up, you lot.' Clara made a face at them. 'Ready, John?'

'He's ready all right,' Daisy, one of the twins who were now nearly fifteen, said with a smirk.

'Ready to come and wring your neck,' John retorted, making threatening gestures with his hands.

The girls all laughed and pretended to be scared of this new John – who was suddenly much surer of himself.

'Go on you two, out you go,' Harriet said, smiling. 'I'll keep some tea for you, John.'

As he and Clara headed out of the door there were gales of giggles from inside. Clara looked up at him and rolled her eyes. John melted at the sight. Her head was swathed in her warmest, brown shawl and strands of her hair peeped out round her face. A face he loved so much he wanted to seize hold of her and cover it in kisses every time he looked at her. But there was no time for that this morning and Clara would have given him short shrift anyway.

'Come on.' Clara tugged his arm. 'Or I'll have Mrs Greatbatch after me.'

They parted on the corner, John to go to Chance & Co. and Clara to Mrs Greatbatch's baker's shop. John leaned in just to snatch the briefest of kisses and Clara laughed.

'Cheeky. See you later.'

He watched her set off, with her long black skirt and the brown shawl, her bouncing, energetic walk. And felt the sense of joy and wonder that went through him every time he saw this pretty, loving girl.

For John, these last months had been the happiest of his life.

Chance & Co. was already like a home to him, this tough, exhausting and all-embracing place. He worked hard and, tired or not, continued to try and get an education. Each time he walked into the handsome buildings which Chance had built to house its schools, he felt a thrill of pride and expectation.

As well as his own schooling he had started assisting with the children one evening a week, helping them with reading and writing. The classes were held after work, each child paying threepence a week for at least some chance of education, despite the lateness of the hour.

Looking along the rows of pale young faces, John could see eyes glazed with weariness and often there would be a number who fell asleep. Some were sent by their parents. Quite a few regularly disappeared for weeks, preferring to earn money working overtime. But a handful of the boys were very determined, wanted more from life. And John loved them for it. He saw himself in them.

They looked up to him, he could see. And at the grand

age of nineteen, John sometimes felt like an old man in comparison.

He did truly feel like a man these days: strong and capable in himself. Now, when the Smith girls teased him, he could come back at them with some witty or withering reply. Harriet treated him like the son she never had and he knew he had Enoch's regard. They had not made a mistake in taking in the workhouse boy.

And there was Clara. Clara who, by some miracle, loved him. He knew it was true. Her eyes, her lips spoke truth. Her hands, when they were alone, caressing him. Her laughter, her scolding him, even their rare quarrels and makings-up – all told him that she loved him, heaven only knew why. He could not have put into words what he felt for her.

'D'you really love me?'

He had asked her this only a few days ago when they had gone out for another walk – one of the only ways they could ever be alone.

It was a windy Sunday afternoon and they were in a muddy lane. Clara had been laughing about something but suddenly she turned to him, her face solemn in a way that made him lurch inside.

'I do, John. I'm not messing with you.'

He flung his arms round her, round this beautiful, mysterious body of hers that he had never yet seen. Sometimes he thought he would explode if he could not make love to her. That's what he felt in his body – his mind was less sure of the practical details. No one had ever talked to him about . . . that. About what was supposed to happen. He was just sure of his burning desire to unpeel her clothing. To see her revealed. The thought made him unbearably excited.

'Oh,' he breathed into her hair. 'And I love you. I do!' He wished he could think of more things to say. Poetry and all that – but the words didn't come. Instead he drew back and looked down into her face.

'Will you marry me?'

Clara hesitated. She didn't seem surprised. Just calm and sensible as was her way.

'I love you, John, and I want to be your wife. But I don't want us to get married – not yet.'

She looked up at him, frowning slightly.

'It doesn't feel right, the way things are – you living with my family and wanting to marry me when you won't see your own family. Your sister Ada came all the way over here to find you. And you've got more sisters – maybe more of your own people somewhere – and you don't do anything for them.'

'Well, they've never done anything for me,' he snapped. He hated to argue with her, but an argument was brewing whether he liked it or not.

'It's not their fault your mother and father died, is it? Or that they took you to the workhouse? They were children as well.'

'Ada was never in the workhouse. And she never lifted a finger to come and get us out or look after us. She was the eldest and she never bothered . . .'

Words spewed out of him, rage and hurt he'd barely even known he felt.

'I don't see why I need them.' He started walking, striding along so Clara had to trot to keep up. 'I've got you – and your mom and dad have been family to me. More than they ever have. I don't want . . .'

He trailed off.

'What?' Clara said sharply.

He could see plain as anything that she disapproved of the way he was over this and it hurt his feelings. But still.

'I don't want to have to bother with it all. They're nothing to me.'

'Well.' Clara stopped then and there and seemed on the point of turning back. 'That's not nice and I don't think much of you for it, John Lunn – or Fletcher, or whatever your real name is. Don't expect me to marry you if I don't even know who you are. It's a family you marry, not just a person, and if you can cut them off like that, how do I know you won't just cut all of us off if it took your fancy?'

John was stunned. He had never seen her like that before. Clara was already charging off along the path away from him and this time it was he who had to run to catch up.

'Don't be like that,' he pleaded. 'I'd never do that! Just . . .' He was panting and suddenly close to tears. 'I don't know what to do.'

Clara remained mute. She stuck her chin out and kept moving with fast, angry steps. They walked all the way home in silence, which to John felt like being on the other side of a wide river from her and it was terrible. But he could not give in. His feelings of betrayal were too strong. Betrayal and . . . Something else he could not understand.

They made it up later, sitting upstairs on the side of a bed when no one else was there. But all John could say was, 'Sorry, but I can't. I just can't do it. It's my family and I think I should be the one to decide.'

Clara leaned her head on his shoulder. She didn't say anything. The anger passed and since then they had been friends again, though John felt sore every time he thought about it. He didn't know when he would dare find the courage to mention getting married again. All he knew was that he did not want to think about his family. The Fletchers, whoever they all were now. He wanted to stick his head in the sand and pretend that none of his past life had ever happened.

But his spirit had other ideas. One morning soon after that, he had a dream at dawn, so vivid that he would never completely forget it for the rest of his life.

He was in a room which felt familiar – like many other rooms with a fireplace and brass fire tools – but with little metal flowers hanging at the end of the curtain rail fastened over a wide window. He was sitting on the hearthrug beside a brass fender, polished to a shine. With him was a woman with long black hair and loving grey eyes. In the dream he was staring into the fire, the glow licking round dusty scraps of coal. But he knew she was there and that with her were the rest of them, the girls. He recited their names to himself: Ada and Elsie, Dora and Mabs. He was quite sure of them, these names surfacing like bubbles. He could see their faces as they were when he was a young child: Ada, honey-haired and energetic; pretty little Elsie with her big eyes; Dora with her bright red hair and eyes like their Mom's, strong in her dreaminess; and Mabs, with black curls and huge brown eyes. His sisters. Their faces. And he was filled with warmth, with a sure sense of belonging: his home, his family. As it faded, the vision receding from him as if down a tunnel, the feelings were replaced by an anguish so deep that it made him curl in on himself in an agony of new-found emotion.

He opened his eyes at last, thankful that no one else was in the room to quiz him about his tears, the way he was sobbing like a small child. He lay feeling peeled and shredded. Like a naked baby. It was the most terrible feeling. Hard as he tried to forget about the dream and banish it from his mind, it stayed, stubbornly troubling him.

*

Shortly afterwards, something else happened which came on suddenly and for a time, blotted out thoughts of everything else.

He was at work that freezing winter day. At least it was freezing outside, the warm glow of molten glass a contrast to the grey outside. The heat of the furnaces was intense and their bodies had to get used to the shock of moving from one extreme temperature to the other. John had been there long enough to be more than used to that.

But that day, while on his usual high-speed route between Enoch's chair and the annealing ovens, it was as if all strength suddenly left him. He only just managed to get the jar he was carrying set down without dropping it. He paused, wiping the sweat from his face – but even inside he now felt cold.

In seconds, his innards seized urgently and it was all he could do to get himself to the lavatory in time. After that, he could not remember anything much. A vague recall of being carried, cold air on his face and a pain in his arm where someone's fingers were gripping it.

After that, the days were lost in a haze of fever and sickness. John lay on his palliasse at the side of the main room as there was nowhere else for him to go. There was no privacy, except that the girls would leave in a panicking crowd at crucial moments when he needed to relieve himself. His head pounded, his guts cramped and griped within him and for a long time he slept and tossed and turned, hardly aware of anything.

Harriet looked after him, with Clara. Later he found out that the twins, Vi and Daisy, had also been taken ill and were lying upstairs. The rest of the girls had bedded down, squeezed in on the floor of their parents' room.

John was too sick to realize the crisis the family were

living through, such severe fever in the house and the fear that they might all be carried off.

He lay, burning up one moment, shaking with cold the next, in a weird, fevered world of his own. The temperature changes made him imagine he was at work, his legs attempting to run back and forth as he did there, for hour after hour. Now and then he heard Enoch's deep, rumbling voice in the house and he tried to answer him, in what he thought was a command at the works.

'What's he saying?' he heard, one day. One of the girls was leaning over him. 'I can't make it out.'

He had no idea how many days passed before the worst of the crisis was over, but one morning, as he surfaced from a more tranquil sleep, he realized he was coming back to himself. He lay very still, thankful to be alive. Thankful for everything and somehow softer in himself. He was awake.

He opened his eyes and looked around the room: the table, the chairs, the range, how beautiful were these familiar, homely things! And when the others came down they saw it immediately. Clara dashed over to him, still in her shift, a shawl thrown on.

'John! Oh, Mom – he's opened his eyes! John, are you feeling better?'

He managed a weak smile. As they came to him, one by one, he saw the toll that these days – weeks? How long was it? – had taken on them. Harriet and Clara both looked thin and haggard about the cheeks.

'How long?' he whispered to Clara.

'You've been lying there more than two weeks,' she said, kneeling beside him, stroking his forehead.

John felt so weak he could not even summon the strength to raise his arm and touch her hand.

'Time for some beef tea,' Harriet announced. 'You might keep it down you this time.'

They sat him up, propped him against the wall like a rag doll, and Harriet brought a cup of her weak, meaty brew. John sipped, as Clara cuddled up beside him. Her face was the most beautiful thing he had ever seen. But what he said was, 'This is the best beef tea I've ever had.' And it was. It tasted like the food of the gods.

Harriet and Clara laughed. Clara put her head on his shoulder.

'You been all right?' he asked, afraid he might have made her sick as well.

'I'm all right. Vi and Daisy are past the worst,' she said. She looked up at him, eyes full of pain. 'I thought we was going to lose you.'

He took her hand then.

'No. Tough as old boots, me.'

And then, his chest contracting again with the need to weep, he said, to his own surprise, 'I've decided – I want to see my sisters.'

Forty-Five

Ada did something that week she had never deliberately done in her life before. Not just for the sake of it. She went into town one afternoon – leaving the works to fend for itself! – and bought herself a new frock.

It felt so strange, wandering around the shops in New Street and High Street, doing this trivial yet vital thing of dressing herself. She was full of new, tremulous feelings. This Saturday afternoon, once they had closed up the shop for the weekend, she was to go for a walk with William, this man with whom she had had to accept that she was in love. Who filled her with feelings of desire, of longing for a home and family that no man had ever aroused in her before.

And just for once, she wanted to attend to herself. Dress nicely, arrange her hair – be a woman who is meeting with a man she cares for.

All the same, shopping did not come easily to her and she was stiff and a little severe with the shop assistant. But she emerged having ordered a soft sage-green dress with lace at the neck which set off her hair and was to be delivered to Galton Passage the next day, after a few small alterations.

In her room, she practised arranging her hair in front of the glass. For a moment she sat staring at her thin but lively face, her mind drifting from the task. What a momentous week! Just days ago she had sat in the same room as two of her sisters – Elsie with her new little one, and now Dora.

Ada frowned slightly thinking of Dora. She was filled with happiness. Despite their different colouring, Dora looked so like their mother that it had made it even more emotional seeing her. But what was puzzling to her was that Dora was apparently running a laundry business. She had explained briefly that she and Minnie had set it up together because of not wanting to be in service – just as she and Elsie had set up their own business. But Dora was not like any washerwoman Ada had ever seen before. True, she had been wearing gloves, for her hands must be rough and workworn. But she looked well fed and prosperous, her clothes in good condition, her hair beautifully arranged. It was a puzzle.

They had all promised to meet again on Sunday, so there would be more time to get to know her sister again, to find out everything that had happened.

But before Sunday was her Saturday walk with William. Once the dress arrived Ada hung it on its hanger from a hook on the back of her bedroom door, looking at it, excited, every time she went in there, stroking her hand down the soft elegance of its skirts. She had liked the way Dora wore her hair. She brushed out her own long locks, divided them into four and started to weave it, before drawing the four plaits back and pinning them back low in her neck. Yes, that looked very nice.

Carefully, she took the dress down and slid into it, fastening the little green buttons at the front – beautifully made cloth-covered buttons – and teasing the lace so that it lay flat and perfect.

Once attired to her satisfaction, she smiled into the mirror and saw the face of a woman filled with happy expectation.

William was waiting for her, as promised, just inside the Passage at the Livery Street end. He was sideways on to her and as she left the entry and walked towards him she was able to observe him for a moment, standing squarely, not leaning against the wall. He looked deep in thought – nervous? she wondered.

He seemed to sense her and turned towards her. As he did so, she thought she saw something in his face, a tremor of some emotion, and wondered if her own features had shown him the same.

'Where shall we go?' Ada asked, blunt with nerves. 'I've brought this, in case.' She pointed to the rolled umbrella she was carrying.

William's face fell. 'I should have given it more thought,' he said.

The middle of town did not offer many places to walk.

They ended up walking north, up Constitution Hill, and when the clashing noises of traffic and the busy pavements allowed, they talked about work. It was not the place to talk about anything else.

'Let's turn off here,' William said, after they had skirted the busy streets of the Jewellery Quarter. 'Look – it's more peaceful in there.'

The one green space on offer was the newly opened cemetery and they started walking round there. The clouds came and went, leaving patches of sunlight, and there was no need for the umbrella.

Ada felt more and more nervous. If William had something to say to her, was this where he was going to get around to saying it?

'It's a bit lonely being buried in here,' she said, looking round at the sparse number of graves so far allotted.

William gave a small laugh. 'It does feel as if graves keep each other company, doesn't it?'

'Like a crowd, sort of watching you – when there's a lot of them,' she said.

As they walked on, the atmosphere between them

became more and more charged. She wondered if he would take her arm, or pull her into an embrace. Would they kiss here in this quiet place? Why didn't he say something?

'Ada,' he said eventually. 'Will you stop a moment?'

She stopped and turned, determined to look him boldly in the eye, even though she was starting to tremble all over and did not want him to notice. What she saw in his face was not what she was expecting. She thought he would look as he had before – warmly towards her, but shy. Bashful, even, if he was going to ask the question she thought – and hoped – was coming. What she saw instead was pain and something else – something like shame.

'Ada.' He stopped, almost as if frightened to go on. 'I've come to a decision.'

She nodded, frightened now and not trusting herself to speak.

William looked down, gathering himself before he could face her again.

'What I've wanted, all these weeks. This time. With you.' It all came out in jerks, like a faulty engine. 'Has been – what I had before. I wanted to love . . . What I mean is, I do . . .' He corrected himself.

The warmth stole through her but it was mixed with foreboding. He held up a hand as if afraid she might reply too hastily.

'If I could love anyone else it would be you,' he said hastily. 'But I can't . . . be here. Can't settle.' In a rush, his confession came out. 'I've got to leave Birmingham. I've booked a passage to America. I know I can get work there – the same sort of work.' As he spoke he became more distressed. 'I just need to get away – from all of it. The past. The business. I don't think I can ever start again here. I just can't.'

She was frozen, staring at him. Foolish woman in a new

dress. Foolish, hopeful woman, who had allowed herself to think . . .

'You must take the business – run it all as your own,' he seemed to be saying. 'You're a fine businesswoman, Ada – I know it'll do well. I'll make it over to you, and—'

'But what if you come back?' she managed to argue.

He looked fully at her then, his eyes full of sorrow.

'I don't expect I shall.' He reached out to touch her hand but Ada withdrew, as if from a snake. She found herself backing away, already in so much pain as to reject more. Another man leaving, betraying. She could not speak, not to say anything agreeable or sympathetic.

'Go then,' was all she could manage. 'That's it. Go. Like all the rest of them.'

And she stormed away across the bare cemetery, their only witnesses to her pain the quiet dead. He did not follow.

Shaking, all the hurt and humiliation and sense of betrayal jerking out of her in sobs as she climbed up to her empty rooms, Ada closed her bedroom door and flung herself on the bed. The new dress she had handled with such care could be crumpled, destroyed now, for all she cared. Destroyed with her hopes, her sense of herself as a woman who could love and be loved. She had contained herself as she strode back down Constitution Hill, arms folded, holding everything in tightly. She could already feel herself shutting off again, closing down any avenues which might make her vulnerable to such terrible feelings. Tight, determined Ada. Ada who was to be alone.

But the emotions would out and she only just made it along the entry and inside before they forced themselves from her. She lay on her bed, clutching at the quilt, her mouth against it to howl her anguish.

'You made me think you loved me,' she sobbed. 'Why did you have to? Why couldn't you just have left me alone?'

She knew he wasn't a bad man. But he was a man who had torn her open, allowed her to feel tenderness, to feel desired – and to allow joy. And then he had snatched it away.

In those moments she vowed, twice bitten, first by Pa and then by William, that she would never, ever open her heart to a man again. She would be Ada Fletcher her whole life long – and let no one come near.

Later, when the storm of crying had passed, she heard the crash of Tom's boots on the stairs and he came breezing in.

'All right, Ada? What's to eat?'

'There's some cold ham,' she said dully. She was sitting in the one comfortable chair by the fire. Eating was the last thing she wanted.

Tom went and energetically sliced ham and bread and sat chewing at the table. He would not ask about her day, her walk, because he had not known she was going in the first place. No one knew – though Elsie suspected her relationship with William.

Tom chattered on about Dinah and how they had decided to 'get wed' the following year and Ada listened, quite glad of his young, animal spirits and the distraction from her own thoughts.

Eventually, well fed and watered, Tom looked across at her.

'You all right?' he asked.

'Yes,' Ada said calmly, looking down at her lap. 'I'm all right, ta.'

Forty-Six

Minnie had been all agog when Dora got back that evening. Cissy had gone home and Minnie was sitting with Rose on her lap as she ate her tea. Rose wriggled with excitement at the sight of Dora.

'Careful – you nearly knocked it out of my hand!' Minnie scolded the little girl, but she was laughing. 'Come on,' she urged as Dora took off her hat and coat. 'There's a drop of tea in the pot. Tell me all about it.'

Dora smiled but she could sense an edge in Minnie's voice. Dora finding she had a family nearby might change everything and she understood that Minnie was on edge. She topped up the stewing tea and took the strainer – because God knew what might be mixed in with the tea, iron filings, the lot! – and poured them each a cup.

'Don't fret,' she said, sitting down. 'It has been quite a day though.'

'So that woman's your sister? And you've got another?'

Dora nodded, dazed. 'I can hardly believe it. There were five of us and we were the three eldest.' She saw Minnie's face, the girl trying to be glad for her but looking sad and worried. Dora reached out her hand and touched Minnie's.

'Don't you worry. You and me are going to stick together, no matter who else comes along – eh?'

Minnie grinned. 'All right. Go on – tell me then.'

The next afternoon, Dora walked round to Galton Passage, this time carrying Rose. She had said she would go and see

Ada and look around her works premises. But first, there was something else she wanted to do.

With Rose wrapped in a shawl, she lifted her on to her hip. She played 'peep-bo' with it for a moment, popping the corner of her shawl lightly over Rose's head, then flicking it off again, laughing at Rose's chuckles and seeing her dark, laughing eyes appear out from under the shawl.

'Monkey,' she said fondly. 'You're getting too big to be carried. Come on then – we're going to go and see your aunties.'

As it was Saturday, she and Minnie had done their laundry for the week and Ada's works would be shut up by now. Earlier in the day, Dora had asked Minnie if she wanted to come too.

'Not this time,' Minnie said, sounding suddenly shy. 'You go and get to know them a bit on your own. I'd just be in the way.'

Dora felt tears rise in her eyes and she stepped over suddenly and kissed Minnie's rounded cheek.

'Thanks, Min – you're every bit as much of a sister to me, you know that, don't you?'

Minnie smiled, emotional as well. 'Go on with you,' she said, bending over to hide her own tears.

Now, setting out with Rose, there was a lightening in the air, spring peeping round the corner. The sunlight was pale, strained, but she could feel a faint warmth on her face.

Dora's spirits soared. All this, life has given me! Happy thoughts came from every direction. Robert, Robert . . . His face that afternoon, there, in front of her and still loving her. She had seen it plainly in his eyes that he was true. Even if he was going to the other side of the world, to know that he was there, to have heard him say those words . . .

'One day, you'll meet your pa,' she whispered to Rose. 'Your lovely pa.'

The little girl stared at her and gurgled. She loved being carried about, being able to look around. Dora laughed with her.

All this, and her writing, and now her sisters . . . She felt as though she might burst with joy.

Turning into Galton Passage she went first to the Drakes' and climbed the stairs, hearing sounds coming from the floor above. The door was ajar and when she knocked, it was opened further by a friendly-looking man. Before she could say anything, Elsie called out, 'Dora! Come in. George, look, this is my sister, Dora!'

Dora liked George Drake immediately. His serious, kindly face and clipped brown hair, his manner of greeting her, shaking hands with a tiny bow as he did so, and his smile, all spoke of a genuine and pleasant person.

'This is a great day,' he said. 'Elsie's told me all about it – she's so excited and happy.'

'I know, 'Dora said. 'I can still hardly take it in – two sisters in one day!'

Amid the welcome she became quickly aware of two other presences in the room. One was an old man with a long white beard looking like Methuselah who was getting out of his chair, the other a little girl, sitting staring at them from the floor.

The old man held out a gnarled hand. 'Jonas Parry,' he said creakily.

Dora smiled. She liked him straight away as well. He looked like a gnarled sailor from a storybook.

'Jonas is our neighbour,' Elsie said. 'But he's an extra grandpa as well.' She sat down again with Olive and her eyes fixed, startled, on Rose. 'Oh, who's this?'

'This is my daughter, Rose,' Dora said.

Her cheeks flushed so hot that she felt as if everyone

must be able to see, but she was not explaining anything – not now in front of them all.

'Come and sit her next to Vicky,' Elsie said, also obviously deciding not to ask. As Dora put Rose down, Elsie exclaimed, 'Oh, isn't she beautiful – she's like Mabs was!'

The two little girls were staring at each other.

'Your Vicky's like her father,' Dora observed, reaching down to tickle the little girl's soft arm. Her fine hair was the same brown as George's. *My girl is like her father as well*, she wanted to add.

'She is,' Elsie smiled. Dora tried to focus on the undamaged side of her face and Elsie could sense her difficulty. She touched her scarred cheek. 'Did Ada tell you what happened?'

Dora nodded, meeting her gaze. 'She did. What a terrible thing.'

Elsie was staring at the two little girls. 'When was she born – Rose?'

'June,' Dora said. 'The nineteenth.'

'Oh!' Elsie gasped. 'Vicky was born on the fourteenth – they're almost the same age! And cousins! And George's sister Nancy's got two little lads and they're not that far apart in age either – so Rose'll have lots of children to play with.'

The two of them laughed in delight, gazing down at their little ones.

A faint, anguished sound came from another room and George jumped up and hurried out. Elsie's face clouded.

'His mom. The doctor says they should take her to the hospital, she's that poorly. It's terrible to see her.'

'I'll take myself off – leave you two wenches to it,' said Jonas Parry, creaking to his feet and going to the door. He raised one of his hands in parting.

'See you soon,' Elsie said. 'Oh, Jonas, when you go out, d'you mind popping in and telling Ada that Dora's here?'

She smiled at Dora as he left. 'So, we can have a proper natter. Hey, what's up?'

Now that Jonas Parry had departed, Dora's view of the edge of the room which had been blocked by his legs was clear. On the floor by the settle she saw a little pile of magazines. and the top one, she could swear . . . She got up and went to pick it up.

'Elsie,' she said, feeling suddenly bashful. 'I need to tell you something. Well, several things . . .' She opened the page of the Christmas edition of *All the Year Round* and laid it on Elsie's lap.

'"Tragedy and Triumph",' Elsie recited. 'Oh yes, I read that – it was ever so good. I got George to get me the next one because it reminded me of us – I couldn't stop reading it.'

'Thing is,' Dora said, realizing how ridiculous this was going to sound, 'it *is* us. I'm Richard Fletcher.'

Elsie stared at her in mild amusement at this daft idea.

Dora decided to dive in and get it all over at once.

'I chose the name Richard Fletcher because it just jumped into my head and I wasn't sure Mr Dickens would take anything and publish it if it was by a woman . . .'

'Dickens?' Elsie was gaping at her. None of this was making any sense. 'What – *Charles* Dickens?'

Dora nodded. 'So I've been writing as Richard Fletcher ever since even though it probably doesn't matter and I could have used my own name – although it turns out Dora Lunn isn't my real name anyway . . . But you see, I'm not just a washerwoman. I'm a writer as well . . .'

She could tell Elsie was struggling to keep up with all this.

'And the other thing is – about Rose. I'm not married even though I go about saying I'm a widow because you know what people are like. Rose was born out of wedlock and I hadn't seen the father in all that time even though he didn't desert me – he had to go away even though he didn't want to – and then I went to London last week and he was marching along the road because he's a soldier and he still loves me, he told me but they're sending him far away – to India, I think, so I don't know when he'll be back but as long as I know he's somewhere . . . And we'll write to each other . . .'

As she spoke there were footsteps coming up the stairs and they both looked round to see Ada in the doorway.

'Ade,' Elsie said, now looking even more as if someone had just hit her over the head, 'I think you'd best come and sit down.'

Forty-Seven

'Leave Rose here while Ada takes you for a look round,' Elsie said. 'She won't mind, will she?'

Dora looked down at Rose and Vicky who, after their initial wariness, were now busy with some little wooden toys and chattering away to one another.

'She'll be all right,' Dora said. 'I leave her with Minnie – and Cissy – quite a lot. Cissy's a girl who works for me,' she said, thinking, oh dear, Cissy was now another whole thing she was going to have to explain.

Rose didn't even notice her leaving and Dora turned back at the door and smiled at Elsie.

She had immediately warmed to her next sister up in age. It was terrible what had happened to her face, but she could see that Elsie and George were devoted to one another and none of it had held Elsie back. She was at the heart of a loving family and she looked happy.

Following the ramrod-like back of her eldest sister down the stairs though, she felt less at ease. Ada had not seemed particularly impressed with Dora's writing success. She barely knew who Charles Dickens was for a start. Dora didn't mind this – she could see that Ada's life had been one of struggle and her mind taken up by the business all the time. She was strong and practical. But she was also forbidding. And today, it felt as if Ada had hardened from the person she had first met when she came to the laundry. Though it was only a few days ago, she had seemed softer and kinder then.

Before they had even stepped outside, they heard a voice ringing along Galton Passage:

'*Blessed is the man that walketh not in the counsel of the ungodly...*'

'That's Jonas,' Ada said, seeing Dora's startled face. 'He does that.'

Jonas was now leaning against the next building along, his face tilted upwards, full of dignity and sincerity. '*Nor standeth in the way of sinners, nor sitteth in the seat of the scornful...*'

'Round the back,' Ada said as his words followed them up the entry into a yard behind. The rank stink which lingered in Galton Passage only grew stronger and Ada saw Dora cover her nose.

'It's the boneyard.' She nodded towards the wall at the end. 'We're used to it, I suppose. What with that and the smuts off the railway it's no place to hang about – or hang laundry for that matter.'

Dora smiled, making herself uncover her nose.

'We can hang out some days,' she said. 'Depends which way the wind's blowing.'

'Down here's our store room,' Ada said, opening the door into a gloomy, brick-lined room. Dora saw a long table and a row of bulging sacks behind. 'And sorting room.'

She went over, dipped her hand into a couple of sacks. In her sister's bony hands Dora saw a collection of shells, brown and white swirls, a flat shell with a gleaming inner belly. It was too gloomy to make out the colours but she could see the beauty of them. Ada's face softened for a second and Dora could see her pride in the materials she worked with.

'Beats working with people's dirty undies,' she said, smiling to draw Ada out. But her sister's face remained severe. 'They're ever so lovely,' she added quickly and again she saw the softness tease at Ada's lips. This had been the right thing to say.

Ada led her upstairs and showed her the long workshop, all quiet now and brushed clean, though Dora could see the haze of white dust thickly coating the windows. She looked over the rows of lathes, the cutting tools, and the wooden boxes in some of which gleamed countless little mother-of-pearl buttons.

'It's all women working here,' Ada said as they stood by the cutting table, 'except for Tom. He's out at the moment but you'll meet him.' She turned and Dora saw a more vulnerable look in her eyes. 'D'you remember the Connells, in the yard when Mom was alive? Nellie, and all the boys?'

Nellie. The name awoke something in Dora's mind, a thin girl, barefoot. Something about her that . . .

'She always stank of vinegar.'

Ada looked surprised she could remember. 'She did. Her mother – Mrs Connell – took me in when you were all gone. Tom, well, he was the closest thing I had to a brother back then.'

Dora felt dizzy, flooded with scraps of unsure memory. 'Their father . . .?'

'Seamus Connell.' A complicated expression passed over Ada's features. 'Rough diamond. He wasn't all bad though.'

'What happened to them all – Nellie and Sarah?'

Ada sighed. 'Oh God, that's a long story. Look, come up and I'll . . .'

Dora raised a hand. 'I need to get back to Rose. But show me around – we'll talk another day.'

As Ada took her upstairs Dora asked, 'So the plaque says Fletcher and Nichols. D'you run the business with someone else?'

There was a pause before Ada said, 'At present, yes.' And moving on quickly, 'Here, come in.' As they stood in the main room she added, 'That's my bedchamber – Tom's is the other side.' Dora saw the range, a table and chairs and a larder cupboard.

'Does it pay well?' Dora asked, thinking it seemed a simple, bare place for a woman who must gradually be becoming quite prosperous. Maybe Ada shared her own fear of not wanting to push out, spend too much money in case everything was suddenly taken away.

Ada looked at her. 'My workers do all right. They're paid well, for women. Anyway, I don't see why men think they should always earn so much more.'

Dora nodded, surprised. 'Yes, I suppose so.'

She wanted to ask her sister so many questions, but as well as feeling the pressure to go back to Rose, she barely knew where to begin. And Ada, this Ada of today, was more severe, sadder than the glowing woman she had met only days ago. Her face was pale and pinched, as if she had not slept well, and the light had gone out of her eyes.

Are you all right? she wanted to ask, but there was something so tight and forbidding about Ada that she didn't dare. She was turning to go when Ada said, 'You do know, I always wanted to get you out. I thought about all of you – all the time. But . . .' She shrugged helplessly. 'There was nothing I could do.'

'I know,' Dora said, feeling for her. 'It can't have been easy being the one left behind.'

Ada gave her a startled look, as if it was the first time anyone had tried to understand her, what had happened to *her*.

'No.' She looked down. 'I never forgot about you, though.'

Dora reached out and took her sister's hand.

'I'm sure, Ada. And you should know that going into service where I did – it gave me a lot. Mrs Gordon wanted the best for people and she taught me things I would never have learned anywhere else.'

And I wouldn't have had Robert, she thought. But she could not begin on him now.

Dora saw a softer, almost bashful look on Ada's face now. She could see how much guilt her sister had carried over all of them.

'Thanks, Dor,' she said. Suddenly she smiled, shaking her head. 'So you're Richard Fletcher. Well, you've done better for yourself than the real one, I can tell you that.'

'Our father?'

Ada nodded. There was a bitter edge to her now, but Dora could sense that it was not directed at her. 'When you've got time, come back and we can tell each other all about it – those years.'

Dora dared to move closer and plant a kiss on her sister's cheek. It was then that she saw the tears rise in Ada's eyes.

'Go on,' she said almost roughly. 'Off with you now.'

She wanted to ask Elsie about Ada, about whether something had happened, but when she crossed over to the Drakes' place, there was a rumpus going on which wiped it all from her mind.

Even from outside, she could hear terrible moans of pain from upstairs which made her stomach clench. She guessed immediately that it must be Elsie's poor mother-in-law. Just as she set foot inside, George came tearing down the stairs, his face stretched with distress.

'Is it here yet?' he cried, pushing past her. He vanished out towards the main street.

Dora hurried up to Elsie and the children. She found Elsie with a lovely-looking blonde woman who Elsie told her was Nancy, her sister-in-law. Both women were crying.

'They're taking Matty to the hospital,' Elsie explained

through her tears. 'She's that bad. Nancy – this is Dora, my sister.'

To Dora's surprise, given her grief, Nancy came over and gave her a warm embrace.

'We're so happy for all of you, finding each other,' she said. 'Sorry, this is a bad time – our mom . . .' And she sank on the chair and cried helpless tears.

'Their dad – Edwin – he's in with her,' Elsie explained. 'He and George're going to get her out into a carriage. None of us knows what to do for the best any more.'

'Is there anything I can do?' Dora asked helplessly.

'I don't know,' Elsie said. 'I don't think so . . .'

Dora felt it would be better if she got out of the way. She gathered up Rose, kissed Vicky and then Elsie.

'See you soon, sis.'

Elsie seized her and held her tight.

'I'm so glad,' she said. 'So glad you're here. I wish you could have seen Matty – before. She was so kind, so good to me . . . But now . . . We must go and say goodbye to her . . . We'll see you soon, all right?'

But as Dora left the room, she saw George Drake struggle out of a neighbouring room with a man who must have been his father. Between them they were supporting the moaning figure of a woman, wasted and yellow-skinned, who must have been Matty Drake.

Dora turned back into the room. 'They're leaving. You go now,' she urged Elsie and Nancy. 'I'll stay with the children.'

As Elsie and her sister-in-law rushed from the room and Dora was left with three little girls and two young boys, she realized that family life was wrapping itself round her more quickly than she had ever expected.

Forty-Eight

Matty Drake died in the General Hospital two days later and Elsie found herself suddenly the female in charge of the Drake household.

Ada visited to find the house sunk in grief. They had all been able to see how ill Matty was, how reduced from her plump, bustling self, but she had still been there, wife and mother – and now she was gone.

'Oh, Ada,' Elsie sobbed. 'She was so good to me – I loved her as if she was my own.'

'I know,' Ada said, in tears herself. 'She was a great lady.'

She had been very fond of Matty and could see what wonders George and all his family had worked in Elsie. They had given her a home and love and safety, and now one of the main pillars of that had gone. Elsie was going to have to be not just a mother to her own little ones, but a stand-in for Ernie and especially Lizzie as well.

The day of the funeral was the first time the three sisters had appeared together in public. Ada had thought to tell Dora and she was so glad to have Dora there as the two of them walked behind the family, Elsie and Nancy side by side in their mourning weeds, George walking with his father.

As they lowered Matty's pitifully small coffin into the ground, Ada found herself dwelling sadly on life's fragility. We'll all be dead soon, she thought. Dead and gone. And just for a moment, William's departure for America did not seem so bad set against the great revolving wheel of life and death in the world.

Ada kept her own heartbreak to herself. It was not hard, as the others were all distracted by Matty's death. It wasn't just that she had the habit of hiding her more tender feelings, but because she also felt so humiliated and let down. She had broken open a tender, vulnerable part of herself, her own longing to love and be loved, only to be rejected. This was the most painful thing of all and she vowed that no one, not even Elsie, would ever know the extent of her agony.

From the day of their walk in the cemetery up until now, William Nichols had stayed away from the works. Whether he was preparing for his journey or sparing her feelings, Ada did not know. But she was sure she could not have stood him being there in the works, day after day.

Late in the afternoon a few days after Matty's funeral, when the workers had all gone, Ada was down in the store room, working by the light of an oil lamp. She sensed someone at the door and looked up. Seeing him, she froze, shrinking into herself, like one of the creatures who had once lived inside the shells.

'Evening,' he said, lifting his hat. His whole demeanour was apologetic and much as she wanted to hate him, she just couldn't. 'I wanted to catch you, Ada.'

Still 'Ada', not 'Miss Fletcher'.

'I was sorry to hear about Mrs Drake,' he said. Ada nodded. She was not in actual mourning clothes but her dress was a sombre grey in honour of Matty.

'I've decided to sign the business over to you,' William went on. 'Legally, I mean—'

She went to interrupt and he raised a hand to stop her.

'It will be for the best, I think, once I'm gone . . .' He didn't finish but she could hear the finality in this. Once across an ocean he was not turning back. 'I want you to have it. You helped me out when my business was at rock bottom. You kept my people in work – I owe it to you, Ada. And I know you'll thrive.'

Hardly needing to say a word, she agreed to meet him at the solicitor's the next morning.

It was a stiff, formal meeting in a dark office on Bennetts Hill and it did not take long. There were no objections and all they had to do was sign the papers that put Ada in full possession of the business. None of this was a pleasure or a triumph for her, but a thing of bitter sadness. But she kept her back ramrod straight, her face much the same, and did what was requested of her. The solicitor, a thin, rather frightened-looking young man, appeared mystified by the situation. But, Ada thought, it's none of his damn business.

Now the sole proprietor of a larger pearl button business than ever before, Ada went down the narrow little staircase with William following. They stopped outside the offices on the sloping street. This was unbearable. All she wanted was to get away from him, from the pain he had brought to her.

'Thank you, Ada,' William said. He looked into her face, smiled almost.

'Well, thank *you*,' she said, looking down. Awkward. Cold. 'I'll do my best.'

There was a silence.

'I must get back,' she said.

He could tell she did not want him to walk with her.

'My passage is booked from Liverpool – on Friday,' he said. 'I'll come and say goodbye before I go?'

'It will do just as well to say it here,' she said, starting to move away. 'Goodbye, William.'

She did not turn round, as she walked back up Bennetts Hill, to see him watching, though she could sense that's what he was doing. The whole encounter made her feel as if her skin was being scoured all over and she could not bear to be in his company a second longer. She turned up towards St Philip's church, knowing he could not see her any more, that now she would never have to see him again. In three days' time he would be gone from England, gone from her life for ever. And she could firmly bar up the doors of her heart.

'Mrs Smith, could I ask you something?'

John managed to find one of the few moments when he could be alone with Harriet Smith.

'Course you can, John.' She smiled at him. 'You know I think of you as a son, don't you?'

This had warmed his heart. He had only the sketchiest memories of his own mother and Harriet Smith had been so good to him, he almost thought of her as a mother by now.

He had only just gone back to work at Chance & Co. after the several weeks of sickness, which they concluded had been enteric fever. He had been as sick and weak as a puppy and he owed Harriet and the others another debt for nursing him. It had taken John much longer than the twins to get back to strength. No one could be sure how any of them had contracted it.

'What is it?' Harriet turned from trying to inject life into the fire under her cookpot.

'Here – let me do that.' John took the bellows off her. 'You sit down.'

Harriet sank gratefully on to a chair and pulled a dish of muddy potatoes towards her to start on them. She was never idle for a moment.

'I think I ought to go and see my sisters,' John blurted out, glad of the distraction of pumping away at the fire.

He heard a chuckle from behind him. 'Our Clara been

on at you, has she? Right, though, she is. You ought to set things straight with them.'

'She's gunna come with me,' John said. 'But – ought I to write to her first? To Ada, I mean, my big sister? Or should we just go?'

Harriet sat still for a second, thinking.

'If it was me . . .' she said, 'I'd send a message. If you two are going to go traipsing all the way to Birmingham, you don't want to get there and find she's not there, do you?'

'That's what Clara said.' John straightened up and looked at her. 'So that's what I'd best do.'

Harriet put her head on one side.

'What's ailing you, John? I'd have thought finding your family'd be a happy thing. And it's no offence to us, if that's what's worrying you.'

John felt his face bloom with a painful blush. It was not a question he really knew how to answer, even to himself – why he found the idea of his sisters so difficult. Even though now he hungered for them as well. It was the hunger that was the problem. He even found himself suddenly close to tears thinking of it and that was mortifying.

'I s'pose it's just been a long time,' was all he managed, in a choked voice. 'We never grew up together, like. I don't even know them, not really.'

'Well,' Harriet said kindly. 'They must want you, or Miss Ada wouldn't have come all the way over here looking for you, would she?'

John stood straighter, swallowing down his emotion.

'Right then,' he said. 'I'll write to her.'

Forty-Nine

'I'll go and collect, shall I?' Dora said to Minnie the next Monday morning.

Monday was always a frantically busy day and Dora wanted to show she was pulling her weight whenever she could and not just leaving it to the others.

'Nah – me and Cissy'll go,' Minnie said. 'You finish getting the water on.'

Dora knew she was not imagining the sniffy tone of Minnie's voice. Ever since Dora had found a remnant of her family, Minnie had been in a mood, however much she tried to reassure her.

'But Cissy's getting so big,' Dora protested. 'It's not good for her.'

'I don't mind.' Cissy's freckly little face smiled heroically. She worshipped Minnie and would do anything to please her. It had been Minnie who went to Cissy's family to propose that she and Dora take Cissy in.

'All right then,' Dora said, scooping Rose into her arms. 'And you, missy, need to keep out from under my feet.'

She stood at the door holding Rose, watching uneasily as Minnie and Cissy set out with the barrow. This whole business with Cissy was a worry. The child was thin as a twig, but luckily her frock hung so loose on her that her rounded belly was not obvious to anyone. She was not big in any case. From what Cissy said, Dora realized she might be further on than she had guessed. It was not going to be a big baby at this rate, and just as well, poor little mite.

Cissy's family had seemed all too keen to wash their hands of her.

'I dunno if her mother even knows what's been going on,' Minnie said when the two of them came back from the family with Cissy's pitifully few belongings. 'Cissy's never said – didn't know how. But her mother couldn't see the back of her fast enough.'

Minnie was completely disgusted. But Dora could sense that this was not just about Cissy. Minnie's father had come looking for her once or twice, it seemed, before they moved on. And although the last thing she wanted was to be found and dragged back to live with him, it felt as if he had soon given up and not bothered. He had been the only family she had.

Minnie and Cissy shared the bed in the next room and Minnie was like a little mother to Cissy. She seemed to relish both this closeness – and leaving Dora out. When she stopped to think about it, Dora felt hurt – jealous even. They had been a team up until now, hadn't they?

Don't be daft, she told herself, putting Rose down so that she could get to work. Why shouldn't Minnie care for someone? She had so many good things in her own life, her success, her newly found family. Of course Minnie was going to need something for herself.

'You stay put, little'un.' Trying to work with a lively little child around was a constant headache and she was never at ease leaving her on her own. But Rose was learning. Dora put the chairs near the range to block her from reaching it. She kissed Rose and gave her some bits and pieces to mess with. 'You stay there, all right? I won't be long.'

Taking the two pails, she started hurriedly hauling in water from the pump outside, her mind drifting to her own concerns and all the amazing, joyful things happening to her. She had written to Mr Dickens, apologizing for missing him in London. She had been 'unavoidably detained', she told him. So far there had been no reply – but he was such a busy man. He was even known to travel abroad. Abroad! she thought, loving the word. It spoke of a much bigger life than the one she had known up until now. An adventurous, exotic life, that perhaps one day she might even taste herself? And Mr Dickens would understand, she knew he would – she trusted him.

Then there was the astonishing miracle of her sisters, living only a couple of streets away all this time. She was not sure of Ada yet. Searching her memory, she realized she had never been quite sure of Ada even back then. Ada, the bossy eldest and always their father's favourite child.

But Elsie's reaction to meeting her had been so warm, so happy. And they had drawn her into the family, even to Matty Drake's funeral, straight away. She had family and now Rose had cousins, Vicky almost like a twin sister. It was more than she could ever have dreamt of.

She emptied the buckets into the copper, peeped indoors and smiled to see Rose still sitting where she had left her, chatting to herself. Full of energy, she took the buckets out again and pumped away, filling them almost to the brim and thinking about whether they could stretch to investing in a horse and cart. It would speed up the collection and delivery no end. Where might they stable it and who would look after it? None of them were experienced with horses. But they were getting more and more business. The Red Lion along the street had recommended them to two other public houses with rented rooms. Their commercial washing was starting to overwhelm them, added to their private domestic customers.

I've got the money, Dora thought. We could move, expand. Secure a living for Minnie – and Cissy too . . .

As she left the water in the brewhouse to heat and went

back inside the house, the letterbox clattered and an envelope fell to the floor. She heard feet clumping down the stairs as she bent to pick it up. Turning it over, her heart gave a jolt and she gasped as she stood up.

'Ooh – good news, is it?'

The voice came to her as if from another world. She looked up and found herself face to face with Jonny from upstairs, who was grinning suggestively at her.

'Oh, go away and leave me *alone*,' she snapped. Clenching the letter between her teeth, she picked up the buckets. 'Go on – out the way.'

'Huh, mardy bitch,' she heard, as if from a great distance away as he slammed out of the door. Because after that, she was lost.

Robert ... It was from Robert. A London postmark and his messy, boyish writing. Taking a knife she sliced open the envelope. The next moments of reading were among the happiest of her life.

Chelsea Barracks,
London
March 16th, 1866

Dear Dora,
I am not the one with the words, not like you – I hardly know where to begin. Military life has been hard. I can manage it. Put up with it. But I will always resent my father forcing me into it and I have not been much at home. However, every time I have been back to Birmingham I find the memory of you in every room of that house, every corner of the garden. I know we were young, but that does not discount what we had. And I was foolish – younger than you in many ways. But now, your telling me we have a child and what you must have

suffered made the thoughts of these past years almost unbearable on your behalf.

 I did not know if you would still remember me, feel anything for me. And perhaps you felt abandoned. That I must be a man of my class who would use and discard you. I have to face that that, in reality, is what I have done. But it is not how I feel.

 I've never written a letter like this before, but there are things I need to say. Dora – there is something about you that makes you my completion. With you things feel right – always did. You may have been a servant in our house but I always knew you were as clever as – cleverer than – me. You would become someone of substance, not remain a servant for ever. My mother could see it too, I believe. And I can say the complete truth: no one I have met, no woman, has ever matched you. It's as if you are part of my soul – and now we are to be torn apart again.

 In three days we sail for Calcutta. It will take many weeks and then what service we – 107th Regiment of Foot (Bengal Light Infantry) – will then face remains to be seen. But what I do know is that my sentence has a long way yet to run. I shall not know my child. I shall not be able to see you and I do not have the gall to expect you to wait for me. I will let you know an address if and when I can. If you would care to write it may reach me and I would do all I could to reply.

 I want to tell you that you have my heart. God alone knows whether there will be a future for me – disease or battle may carry me off. I do not know what faces us in this far and strange land. But if I am spared, perhaps in our more temperate land one day . . .? I hardly dare to hope.

 My darling Dora, love of my heart, pray for me. And let us both pray that one day we might meet again.

> *Yours truly,*
> *Robert Gordon*
> PS *I wonder how you support yourself and I feel utterly unequal to all that you have had to manage. I am asking myself constantly how I can help support you. As a last resort, if need arises, I advise you not to let pride prevent you from turning to my mother. As you know, she is a woman of generous soul.*

Dora sank on to a chair by the table, her body shaking and tears flowing.

'Oh, Robert, my Robert . . .'

She clutched the letter to her, his words more heartfelt than anything she could have dreamt of him writing. Robert's fear, his longing not to go, to be living another life that he had chosen, all came to her. But he had no choice.

And he loved her. Still loved her.

'I'll wait for you,' she sobbed. 'Of course I'll wait for you, my love. Just knowing you are there, in the world, and that you love me . . .'

She was so lost in mixed emotions – love, longing, above all joy – that it was some moments before she looked up and realized that Rose had stopped what she was doing, startled by the sounds of her mother crying, and was sitting staring fixedly at her.

'Oh, my sweet.' Dora got up, laughing, and went to her, wiping away her own tears. She put her arms round her little girl in the chair and kissed and kissed her cheeks.

'That was a letter from your daddy. Your lovely daddy.' And again she was weeping with joy. 'His name is Robert, and one day, he's going to come home and be with us.'

She pulled back, held Rose's face gently in her hands and smiled at her. The little girl smiled in return, despite not knowing the reason for all this.

'Right,' Dora said, getting up. 'I must pull myself together.'

By the time Minnie and Cissy came back Dora had tucked the letter away in one of her notebooks in the bedroom and the water was hot and ready for the wash to begin. The day passed in the usual flurry of busyness, Dora pounding loads of clothes in the maiding tub all morning, with a new, ecstatic energy. Despite her aching muscles, she could hardly stop a smile spreading over her face throughout the day, but she did not want any questions from Minnie, of a 'What's got into you?' variety.

The day was calm, quite warm for March, so they hung the sheets out in the yard. Soon the room was draped with pillowslips and clothes.

Late in the afternoon, Dora was pouring tea for them all to go with a plate of bread and jam when she heard a knock at the front. Since knocks on the door were never for them she ignored it, until she heard voices outside and a knock on their inner door.

Minnie opened up and standing in the hall was Ada.

'Oh!' Minnie said. 'Hello?'

'Ada!' Dora went to greet her. Her sister had not been here before, to see the place. Of all times to come, thought Dora, embarrassed by the state of the room. 'Come in – we were just brewing up.' As Ada stepped inside, she added, 'Sorry about all this.'

'It's your business,' Ada said matter-of-factly. 'Can't be helped, can it?'

'Well – Mondays,' Dora added, pouring a fourth cup of tea and quietly giving thanks that they had just enough cups. She lifted Rose on to her lap and nodded to Ada to sit opposite her. Minnie and Cissy kept back, staring, intimidated.

'I won't stop long,' Ada said. 'But this came.'
She opened out a letter and pushed it towards Dora.

Dear Ada,
I'd like to come over and visit you and Elsie. I'll be coming on Sunday afternoon with Clara Smith.
  Yours sincerely,
  John Lunn

Ada tutted as Dora finished reading.
'Lunn,' she said contemptuously.
'We thought that was our name,' Dora said. 'That's what they called us.'
'He knows it's not his name now though, doesn't he?'
'Habit, I s'pose.'
Ada seemed very cross about this and Dora realized that the Lunn name – the four of them being called something else through some administrative bungle – really pained Ada. It separated them from her even more.
'He's written, and he wants to come – that's good, isn't it?'
Ada agreed, seemingly with a grudge, that it was.
'Who's Clara Smith though?' Dora said.
'One of that family he lives with, I think,' Ada said. 'There's I don't know how many girls. Turn round and another one appears.'
Dora laughed and Ada softened a little.
'Best if you all come to me,' Ada said. She downed the rest of her tea and got up. 'The Drakes are in mourning and it'll be quieter at my place. Three o'clock?' She glanced at Minnie and Cissy who were still standing in the background. 'Just you?'
'I'll bring her.' She stroked Rose's hair and Ada nodded. 'We'll see you then, Ada.'

And with no goodbye kiss or anything of that nature, Ada was gone. The three of them all breathed out.

'She's a bit of a tartar, that one,' Minnie said, looking relieved.

Dora was tempted to tick her off for that comment about her sister – but it was hard to disagree.

Fifty

As soon as Dora drew close to Galton Passage, she spotted her brother. Even among the bustling people on Livery Street, something about the young man caught her eye. He was walking slowly away from her, arm in arm with a girl, a twist of strawberry-blonde hair emerging down her back from under her bonnet.

In the years since she had last seen John, he had of course grown into a man. But any worries that she might not be able to recognize him instantly vanished.

She followed the two of them, seeing that they must have arrived early and were waiting for the clocks to strike three. Catching up, she passed, glimpsed the profile of young Clara Smith – pretty, lively, she thought – and John. Yes, the face of her brother.

'John?'

Both of them stopped and John's face lit up.

'Annie!'

They stood gazing at each other for a moment, taking in what was familiar, what had changed. John's face had fined down from his boyhood. His jaw was now firm and when he raised his hat, his hair had darkened a few shades from the blondeness of boyhood. But there was something about his face, even as a man, that sent a thrill of recognition through her. Something of their mother.

'Clara, this is my sister—'

'Dora,' she interrupted. 'That's my real name. Dora Fletcher.'

'Dora,' John said. 'Yes. Course.'

They moved into an awkward half-embrace, eased by John looking at Rose, perched on Dora's hip. 'Who's this then?'

'This is Rose, my daughter,' Dora said as John stepped back. She saw his mind fill with questions which she certainly did not want to go into now. She quickly nodded at Clara, who smiled happily back. Dora felt an immediate liking for her. She looked sensible, Dora thought, and kind.

'She's a pretty little thing,' Clara said, eyes on Rose. 'Pretty name as well.'

The two of them smiled, their liking for each other growing.

'We was just waiting,' John said. ''Til three. She might get cross if we came early.'

Their eyes met and they all started laughing. Ada had already made an impression as the stickler oldest sister.

'Come on,' Dora said. 'It must be nigh on three.'

They turned into Galton Passage and Dora pointed out the brass plate on the wall – mainly to Clara.

'Here, look. This is the business . . . Oh.' She peered more closely. The wording which before had read 'Fletcher & Nichols' had gone and a new, shinier one read 'Fletcher's Pearl Button Manufacturers'. Dora frowned, but said nothing. She was about to direct them along the entry when they heard the nearest clock strike three.

'There,' Clara said. 'We're on time.'

Ada was at the door to greet them, smiling, looking more relaxed and happier than Dora had seen her lately – to her relief.

'Elsie'll be over any minute,' Ada said. 'She's got a lot on her plate over there, with her mother-in-law gone . . . Go on up and sit down, all of you.'

There was already a large kettle whispering on the fire

and a moment later they heard more steps on the stairs. Elsie same in carrying Vicky and looking flustered.

'I've just got Olive to sleep,' she panted, 'so I've left her.' She placed Vicky down beside her and emptied a cloth bag of little toys she had brought on to the floor. 'Here, Rosie – you can come and play as well!'

The two little ones settled, they all took each other in. Elsie went and gladly embraced John as Clara and Dora watched, getting the feeling that in fact it was Elsie, as much as Ada, who was to be the centre of the family. There was something strong and sure about her.

'Tom!' Ada called through to the next room. 'Come and say hello. I don't know if you remember Tom Connell,' Ada said. 'Nellie's brother?'

Dora saw a young man come in, dark-haired, very handsome, looking shyly at this gathering in front of him.

'Tom's your age, Dora,' Ada said. 'I lived with his family, for a bit.'

Dora saw Ada and Tom exchange a look which seemed to speak volumes, but she had no idea what it meant. And Tom was shyly saying hello.

'I dunno if I remember you all,' he said. 'Ada's talked about you so often, I don't know if that's what I remember.'

Dora was straining her own memory. She had a notion of the Connells, of boys running round the yard, a lot of them, but she could not pick Tom out especially.

'I'll leave you to it,' Tom said after a few minutes, and he took off down the stairs.

'Gone to see Dinah,' Ada said. 'They're getting wed soon. He's a good lad.'

There was an awkward silence.

'Let's have some tea,' Ada said, and Elsie helped her. The handing round of cups and slicing of a cake broke the ice.

Soon they were all talking, dredging up memories of their mother and father, comparing who looked like who.

'Ada, you always looked like Pa,' Elsie said. 'His colouring – everything.'

'And Dora's like Mom,' Ada said. 'Your face, I mean – not the hair! You got that from Nanny Fletcher – she was a redhead.' Dora felt a flush of pleasure, of belonging. Here they were again, together. That was a miracle – and she looking like their mother and grandmother! She had never known that. It warmed her right through.

'John looks even more like her, don't you think?' Dora said. 'From what I remember.'

'I wish I could remember more,' John said sadly.

'You were very small,' Ada pointed out.

'Not as small as Mabs,' Elsie said.

There was a silence suddenly. Their baby sister. Dora looked across at Rose. Mabs had been even younger than her own daughter was now.

'She wouldn't remember us at all, would she?'

'She was lovely,' Ada said and Dora was startled to see her almost in tears. 'Great big brown eyes, d'you remember?'

Dora did, just about.

'I wonder where she is,' Elsie said. 'They sent her to a family somewhere.' She turned to Dora and John suddenly. 'Mrs Hodges wouldn't tell us where you two were.'

'Mrs Hodges,' Dora said. 'Oh yes! Her and her husband . . .'

'Hodge the Lodge,' John added. They all laughed, including Clara. Dora saw her take John's hand and give it a loving squeeze. He's got a good one there, Dora thought, wistfully. One day she was going to have to explain about Rose – and Robert.

But for today, their talk was all about the past, those

happier times which bound them together, even if now that all felt like another life entirely.

'D'you remember the puppy Pa brought home?' Ada said. She had come alive, Dora saw. Her whole demeanour was more youthful, laughter in her eyes.

'Oh yes!' Elsie said. Dora could not remember.

'We called him Piggly,' Ada said, almost childlike again. 'He used to sleep in our bed – d'you remember, Else?'

'But he ran off,' Elsie said. 'You were upset for ages after. And Pa's friend Jem – remember him?'

Ada seemed to ignore this and Dora was puzzled, as if suddenly Elsie had trodden on ground that Ada did not want to visit. Dora's mind seethed with questions. What had happened to their father? Did anyone know? But just as she did not want to go into her past today, she understood that the others had things they did not want to talk about. This was an afternoon for just celebrating being together.

John told them all about Chance & Co., and she could hear all the pride in his voice. And Clara talked a little about the family and her sisters – told them John had just been seriously ill.

'They looked after me good and proper though,' John said.

He told them about the school and his book learning and after giving him a suitable time to talk, Elsie picked up her bag and drew out something else. Dora started, realizing it was the Christmas *All the Year Round*.

'Well, look at this,' Elsie said, with genuine pride. 'Our Dora is a writer – with stories published by Mr Charles Dickens himself!'

'No!' John exclaimed. He and Clara pored over the magazine with such astonishment that Dora started to laugh. 'Is this you?' He pointed at the Richard Fletcher pages.

'It is,' Dora said.

'Richard Fletcher?' John looked round, as if his brain was cranking into action. 'Wasn't that . . . ?'

'Our father?' Elsie said. 'Yes, it was.'

'The name just came to me,' Dora said. 'I didn't know why at the time, 'cause I didn't remember it. It must have been somewhere in my head. So I chose it as my writing name.'

John and Clara stared at her as if she had suddenly grown an extra head.

'But you're a woman,' Clara exclaimed. 'And a washerwoman! You're just – well, normal!'

'Yes,' Dora agreed. 'I am.'

'Well,' Clara said, quite overcome. 'I'll be blowed.'

And all the newly united Fletchers laughed.

John and Clara had to set off to make the long walk home. After taking their leave with promises to come again, they had barely walked any distance along the street when John, bubbling with excitement, turned to Clara.

'Stop a tick, will you?'

Bemused, Clara halted in the street and John flung himself down in front of her, on one knee, grasping her right hand in both of his.

'John!' Clara started laughing.

'Marry me now – will you?' he cried. 'You've met my family!'

Two jokers passing joined in with, 'Go on, marry 'im, wench – put him out of his misery!'

Clara, seeing that John was not going to get off the ground until he had an answer, leaned down close and whispered, 'Yes, John. I will.'

John leapt up, took her in his arms and spun her round, his precious, precious Clara.

*

A while later, George Drake appeared, bringing with him a very cross-sounding baby.

'She's had a good stretch,' he said, smiling round at them. 'But she wants you.'

'Thanks, love,' Elsie said, taking little Olive to suckle her. 'I'll be back over in a while, all right?'

'Shall I put the kettle on again?' Ada said.

After a little while, Elsie got up and stepped over to Dora, Olive cradled in one arm. She hooked her other arm through her sister's, beaming at her.

'What a little poppet,' Dora said. Olive, with a milky chin and sated expression, was looking around her.

'Rose is a little poppet too.' Very quietly, Elsie added, 'You'll have to tell us all about it, one day.'

She looked into Dora's face and squeezed her arm.

Ada was handing round more tea when there was a great hammering at the downstairs door.

'Is that John back?' Ada frowned and hurried to the stairs.

Dora and Elsie heard a to-do downstairs and Ada came running back up, followed by Minnie.

'Dora,' Minnie gasped. 'It's Cissy – she's having it. Can you come home, quick?'

Fifty-One

The next half-hour was all hurry. Minnie immediately rushed back to Bread Street. Elsie hurried home to leave the children with George, then dashed round the corner to fetch Mrs Mills. Dora, as she picked up Rose and followed Minnie, realized that Ada was showing every sign of coming with her.

'There's no need,' Dora said, laying a hand on Ada's arm. Seeing her sister's face she quickly backtracked. 'I mean, not unless you want.'

'We're all family now,' Ada said, so kindly that Dora found tears in her eyes. 'Your troubles are my troubles.'

As they hurried along Livery Street, Ada panted, 'It's not that little girl she was talking about – the one who was there the other day?'

'It is,' Dora said grimly.

'But she's only a child – what, ten, eleven years old?'

'She's fourteen,' Dora told her. 'But I'm surprised she's even started with her monthly, she's so small.'

'God in heaven,' was all Ada replied.

They rushed into the house and to the room which Minnie and Cissy shared. Minnie was kneeling by the bed where Cissy lay under a thin quilt, her belly like an obscene mound on her tiny frame, her face deathly pale.

'Is she coming – the lady?' Minnie asked desperately.

'Elsie's bringing her,' Dora said. 'Here, take her, will you?'

She thrust Rose into a startled Ada's arms and leaned over the bed.

'Cissy, can you hear me?'

Cissy nodded and opened her eyes.

'It hurts, bad,' she moaned, and she started to cry like a little child.

'D'you want me to fetch your mother?' Dora asked.

Cissy shook her head, hard.

'I'm going to put water on,' Dora said, indicating to Ada that she should follow her into the bigger room.

Dora brought in two pails of water and stoked the fire. Ada had put Rose down and was – with obvious effort at this strange pastime – playing with her, when Elsie came dashing in, Mrs Mills with her.

'In here . . .'

Cissy was writhing and moaning on the bed and Dora filled with dread. Especially when she saw Mrs Mills's face. The woman was a calm, unemotional sort who had seen many things in her time. But at the sight of Cissy, she turned pale.

'Help her – please, just do summat for her,' Minnie begged, sobbing.

Mrs Mills took Dora's arm and pulled her out of the room amid Cissy's howls of pain.

'How old's that girl?'

When Dora told her she shook her head in horror.

'I'd've put her at younger. She won't be able to birth it – she's too small,' she said. 'Get the doctor. Go to Dr Williams, he's a good one.'

Her eyes met Dora's and the full seriousness of the situation sank in. We're going to lose her, Dora thought. Lose both of them.

She hurried into the other room. Ada and Elsie instantly looked up.

'I'm going for the doctor,' she said.

*

Dr Williams lived only two streets away. He was a man in his forties, well educated and showing what seemed a genuine human concern. He followed Dora immediately with his medical bag, quizzing her all the way as to the details of the situation.

'Fourteen?' She could hear his anger. 'No woman is ready to give birth so young. I shudder to think how—'

'Her father.' Despite the sheer indecency of this conversation, above all with a man, Dora found herself wanting to tell the truth. 'She told us.'

'Dear God,' Dr Williams murmured. Dora appreciated that his anger and indignation were genuine.

They hurried straight to Cissy, who was gripped by agony. It was pitiful to watch. How could this tiny, bird-like body stand this? How long would Cissy be able to tolerate it?

'Out of the way,' Dr Williams said abruptly. The women scattered to the edges of the room.

Dora knew that normally Cissy would have been frightened to death and mortified by all these eyes watching her, and this big man touching her so intimately. But she was barely conscious, unaware that anything else was happening apart from the world of pain that had taken her over. She moaned, a thin, continuous sound of distress which every so often grew and peaked into a cry of agony. But Dora could hear that the cries were getting weaker. The only other sound was Minnie's quiet weeping in one corner of the room.

Dr Williams started to get up, straightening his legs, but he rested his knuckles on the bed, head bowed, obviously trying to think. After a moment he straightened up and beckoned to both Dora and Mrs Mills who left the room with him.

'I fear her pelvis is too small – she can't birth this child.'

It was like a knell of doom. Dora felt it like a cold hand round her heart.

'But . . .' she began.

'What about the knife?' Mrs Mills said brutally.

'I am not a surgeon,' Dr Williams said. 'I might only butcher her. I fear she is too weak and too far gone to take to a hospital.'

'Could it be done here?' Dora asked. 'Not in hospital. Sure it's better to try . . .?'

'Only a surgeon could do this. I am not authorized . . . And I am not sure I could find anyone at this short notice.'

Dora cut across him with a sudden cry as her mind fixed on the solution.

'Stay with her. Please, doctor, look after her – keep her alive. I'll bring someone.'

'Miss . . .?'

'Fletcher.'

'I've no idea who you've got in mind, but . . .'

'Dr Gordon – Sidney Gordon. From the General Hospital. I'll bring him – at least I'll try . . .'

And grabbing her hat, she was out of the house and tearing along the street.

In the carriage she managed to hail in Great Charles Street, she was already questioning her own sanity. It was at least two miles to Frederick Street. She had to get there and back and what were the chances of Dr Gordon being in – let alone agreeing to come with her? But she had to try.

'Fast as you can – we need a doctor,' she said to the driver, so urgently that she saw him turn pale. She could tell he was doing his best but her fists were clenched, the knuckles white as they trotted briskly along, cursing under her breath every time there was an obstacle that slowed their progress.

Turning finally into Frederick Street made her heart swell – memories of her life there, of Robert, of love, so sweet and joyful . . . And at last they were here!

'Stop. Wait here.'

She dashed to the front door, an entrance she had never before passed in or out of. She lifted the knocker and hammered commandingly. In a moment the door was opened by a maid she did not know.

'Get Dr Gordon for me – straight away, please,' she ordered.

The maid was not having it.

'Dr Gordon is resting,' she said importantly.

'Just get him!' Dora was raising her voice now and after a moment a half-familiar figure appeared out of the library. Alicia – Robert's elder sister.

'Miss Gordon!' Dora called, relieved. 'Please, we need Dr Gordon desperately – to save the life of a young girl who is in childbed. Please, please, ask him to come!'

Alicia, who Dora appreciated now had always been a person of good sense, hurried to the library.

'Mother,' Dora heard. 'There is someone in need. At the door.'

In seconds, Mrs Gordon hurried from the library and peered at her through spectacles – that was new. Her face filled with astonishment.

'Dora?'

'Yes, it's me. Please, Mrs Gordon, call your husband. A girl will die, else.'

The woman didn't hesitate. Dora saw her stride over to Dr Gordon's study and a moment later he appeared with a bag. Dora was impressed – moved almost. She had always found Dr Gordon terrifying, but now, when it came to it, he was devoted to his calling.

'Oh, thank you – thank you!' She managed to hold back her sobs.

'Come and see us, Dora . . .' Mrs Gordon called after them.

And Dora suddenly found herself seated in the close quarters of a Hackney carriage with the distinguished surgeon who was Robert's father. He turned to her, his sharp features serious and stern.

'Tell me,' he ordered, in his clipped Scots way.

'She's fourteen. Looks younger. The doctor says she's too small and she'll die.'

'*Fourteen?*' Dr Gordon swallowed this information quietly, but his face took on a grimmer look. He was silent for a few moments. 'I'll do what is called a Caesarean section. It's risky, but it has been done successfully on a number of occasions now. If she's too small to birth the child, it will have to be cut out.'

'Like Macduff,' Dora said.

Dr Gordon's head swivelled, his face registering astonishment.

'Who "was from his mother's womb untimely ripped". I used to work in your house, Dr Gordon. Mrs Gordon was very good to me – she helped me to read and allowed me to use your library.'

For the first time, Dr Gordon smiled and suddenly – it made her ache – he reminded her powerfully of Robert.

'Well, well,' he said.

After a few moments of silence, he added, 'I hope there's water on the boil.'

Her opinion of Dr Gordon rose with each passing moment of that day. On arrival in Bread Street he rushed out of the carriage. Dora paid the cab man and followed, finding him already with Cissy, examining her. She looked much the same as when Dora had left – weak, hardly aware of her surroundings, and in agony.

Dr Williams had stayed and, once he had got over his amazement at the actual appearance of Dr Gordon, the two of them prepared for the one action that might save Cissy.

'Everyone out,' Dr Gordon ordered in his clipped way. 'I need these in a bowl of boiling water – scald the bowl first. I need another clean cover for the bed – and a table. Bring me a table . . .'

Dora, Minnie and Elsie scurried about, obeying orders, Elsie scalding the instruments, Minnie and Dora carrying in Dora's work table for the doctor to lay his things on. 'Bring a pail for waste . . . And boil more water.'

Ada sat looking after Rose, asking repeatedly if there was anything she could do. Dora could sense her helplessness.

'You're doing the best thing being with her. Here,' she added, rushing to fetch Rose a heel of bread. 'Give her this.'

And then the hurrying was over. All of them – Dora, Ada, Elsie, Minnie and Mrs Mills – waited, brewing tea for themselves and the doctors, as Cissy, unconscious from the drops of ether Dr Gordon had dropped on a gauze over her nostrils, hung between life and death.

Dora sat cuddling Rose. Minnie could not keep still and kept pacing up and down the room.

'Come on, Min, sit down and rest a bit,' Dora said.

'I can't stand it,' Minnie said. 'It's horrible – and seeing her like that.'

'You won't help her wearing yourself out,' Ada remarked, and Minnie, who was rather in awe of Dora's elder sister, obeyed and finally sat down.

There were no sounds from the room across the hall. Minnie crept out once and came back to say that all she could hear were the men talking in low voices.

The best part of an hour passed. Finally they heard the

door open and Dr Gordon call out, 'Bring more hot water, and soap, if you please.'

Minnie ran to obey, carrying in a deep enamel dish.

'What's going on?' Elsie asked, on tenterhooks as much as anyone else.

'I don't know. He took it off me at the door. But I think they're washing. His hands were all . . .' She made a face, which then crumpled. 'It's so quiet. I think she's passed on . . . And the baby – there's no sound of a baby. Why won't they tell us?'

Minnie was about to give way to her sorrow when they heard footsteps and both doctors came into the room, their faces solemn.

'Well,' Dr Gordon said, buttoning his sleeves. 'There was no hope for the child. The mother is still with us – for now. I have sutured – that means sewn – the wound. The stitches will need removing.' He looked at Dr Williams who nodded respectfully. He would be able to do that. 'Try to keep the wound clean – bathe it with boiled water? As for whether she will pull through – that, I'm afraid, is in the hands of the Almighty now.'

'You've been very fortunate,' Dr Williams said to them reverentially. He turned and bowed to Dr Gordon. 'And it has been a privilege to work alongside you, sir.'

Dr Gordon nodded his thanks, gathered his things and stowed them in the bag. Dora got up, hoisting Rose on to her hip.

'I must away . . .' He raised his hat and moved off so fast that Dora had to hurry to catch him in the hall.

'I have means,' she said. 'We can pay you. We are so grateful to you.'

Dr Gordon looked down at her. 'No need.' He smiled then, and Dora could see what Mrs Gordon must have seen in him – something that had always puzzled her. A warmth she had never quite glimpsed before. 'Williams will keep an eye. We shall have to hope for the best for the poor girl.'

He reached out a hand and gently touched Rose's cheek. 'What a pretty child. Good day.'

And he was gone. Dora stood, taking in the fact that Dr Gordon had, for the first, and perhaps only, time caressed the cheek of his own granddaughter.

Fifty-Two

Ada dragged herself wearily out of bed the next morning. After tea and a hunk of bread and cheese she went down to the shop. Usually, she reckoned to be there first but today, the others were already coming in.

The others – but not William. He had sailed by now, must be already somewhere on the high seas. Pausing on the stairs, she felt her emotions swell. There was deep sorrow and regret – but also, a sudden uprush of joyous relief. She gripped the wooden banister rail feeling as if even that was a precious part of her life. Ahead of her lay a day of familiar faces, of things being back to normal, almost, and this felt like a wonderful and safe thing. Her world – the life she had created.

'Morning, Ada!' Gert peered up the stairs, having caught sight of her in the gloom. Gert, who had known her since she was a child, was the only one of her employees who did not call her Miss Fletcher.

'Morning, Miss Fletcher.' That was little Biddy Ryan. Ada reached the bottom of the staircase and smiled at the child. She was fond of Biddy, an eager little thing, who loved the beauty of the shells as she had always done.

'Morning, Biddy. Family all right – your mother?'

'Yes, thanks, Miss Fletcher. She's all right now.'

Ada even found herself pleased to see Vi. The day's work began, the sound of the treadles, the sawing, grinding, drilling. For a moment she stood at the far end of the shop, watching them all work in the white dust haze. Her business. All hers now – just her name on the brass plate. She felt a powerful sense of satisfaction as she turned to go downstairs to the sorting table.

Alone, examining the shells, she tried to keep her thoughts away from yesterday.

She had slept badly and even when she did manage to sleep, her dreams were full of menace, of blood. She woke a number of times, pulsing with horrible feelings and wishing the morning would come.

It was obvious why. Of all the things which most frightened and disturbed her, childbirth was the worst. Yesterday she had been so close to that poor child as she laboured and struggled in an undeveloped body, nowhere near ready for this task. It would be a miracle now if Cissy survived.

And afterwards, Ada had seen the instruments, the bloodied rags brought out of that room and the shock of the tiny corpse wrapped in muslin, cradled in one arm by Mrs Mills.

'Old Joe Wright's lying in a few doors down from me,' the woman said. 'The family will take her.' For it seemed the little one had been a 'her'. She would be wrapped and placed in this Mr Wright's coffin before the lid was closed.

'Here.' Dora slipped some coins into Mrs Mills's hand. 'For you – and give the Wrights this, will you?'

Such it was, with young and old. With life and death. Ada knew all this perfectly well, but still, her dreams were a curse to her that night. They were parts of life she would soonest avoid. All of it brought out a horror in her.

'I saw Elsie,' Gert said quietly to her as they stopped for the dinner break. 'She told me what happened.'

The others were all listening as they sat round, perched on benches and stools. Ada felt bound to explain.

'Oh, my word, how terrible,' Margaret said. 'A child – and small at that, by the sound of it.'

Biddy had gone pale hearing even a watered-down version of what had happened.

'Your sister went and got a surgeon?' Vi said. 'What – one of them doctors that . . .?'

'Cut open the body – yes,' Ada said drily.

'How did she know where to find one of them?' Gert asked, astonished.

'Used to work for him, she said.' Ada had been as surprised as the others at the time. 'I don't know why she thought he'd come out like that, but he did.'

Gert stared at her. 'It's one thing after another with you lot, isn't it?'

'But how's she getting *on*?' Biddy asked, her little face creased with tension. 'The girl – Cissy?'

That whole Sunday, Minnie stayed with Cissy almost all the time. Since the operation Cissy had not once opened her eyes and Minnie was desperately worried. Dora, in between bouts of writing her next episode for *All the Year Round*, kept coming in to see how the child was.

She lay pale and still, so still that without leaning close to her it was hard to be sure there was still life in her. They both prayed that she was simply sleeping.

'Look at her,' Minnie wept. 'She's like a little waxwork. I'm saying my prayers all day – God's got to let her live!' She sank her head against Dora's shoulder. 'I don't know what I'll do if she goes – she's like my little sister!'

'I know.' Dora put her arm round Minnie's plump shoulders. 'And you're like mine.'

Minnie turned brimming eyes up to her. 'Am I – really? Even though you've got your real sisters back now?'

'Course you are.' Dora kissed her. 'Never doubt it.'

And Minnie happily snuggled up close. Dora squeezed her arm, remembering, with a faint smile, the waif she had been when they first met.

The doctors had told them to keep an eye on Cissy's wound. Very carefully they stripped back the layer of wadding that Dr Gordon had laid over her stitches. It was a raw, pitiful sight, the little belly cut from top to bottom, the sides sewn back together like a sack. There was no flesh on her bones and the stitches looked dark and alien against her skin. But so far it looked clean, not red or angry. Minnie gently wrapped it again and covered Cissy up.

Dora lured Minnie out to eat and drink something but otherwise she sat or lay beside Cissy day and night.

Dora cleaned up Rose and played with her, then put the little girl down for a nap on her bed. She sat at her table, which the day before had held the bloodied instruments and rags, and tried to keep her mind on what she was doing. Her story had now almost reached the present day. Should she write about Cissy – about what had happened to her? Even couched in the most delicate language, Cissy's condition and how that had come about, followed by the gory events of the day before, might be too much for the stomachs of Mr Dickens and his readers.

She picked up her pen and stared ahead of her. But that was the story and one way or another she would find a way of telling it.

By two in the afternoon, she had finished her writing for the moment. She felt she had found ways to describe the actions of an incestuous father, of the child she called Kitty in the story, without using any graphic or undue language. The father 'lay with her'. Was that not all that was needed to tell them a great deal more?

She sat back in her chair and took out the letter Robert had written to her from London.

'My Dora . . .' Her whole being leapt with joy just at those words. She was starting to read the rest when she heard a cry.

'Dora! Come quick!'

Dora leapt up, heart pounding, and rushed into the other room to find Minnie kneeling on the bed, her face close to Cissy's. She looked round, all lit up.

'She's awake! No, Ciss, don't move. You've got to keep still.'

Dora went over and saw the girl's pale blue eyes looking around her in complete bewilderment.

'Cissy?' Cissy's eyes focused on her, her delicate brows frowning slightly. 'It's Dora. D'you know where you are?'

Cissy gave the ghost of a nod.

'I've been dreaming . . . Funny dreams . . .'

'Cissy.' Dora knelt by the bed, looking at Minnie, as if asking permission. 'D'you remember, before you went to sleep? You were having a lot of pain because of the baby? So a doctor came and put you to sleep, and then he took the baby out.'

'No!' Minnie cried as Cissy started to try and feel her belly. 'Don't touch – not yet. You're very sore there and you've got to keep still. It's a big cut – it's got to knit back together, see?'

Cissy did not see. She started trying to get up and then sank back with a mewl of pain.

'Please, Cissy – just keep still,' Dora said. 'We'll bring you some milk and something to eat as soon as you feel like it. But you've got to keep still for a day or two at least.'

'Can I have slops?' Cissy said, brightening. 'With sugar?'

'Course you can!' Minnie was laughing with relief. She went off to heat up the milk.

When she had gone, Cissy looked at Dora. 'Where's the baby?'

'Oh, Cissy.' Dora took her hand and stroked it. 'I'm sorry. It's very sad, but she didn't live.'

Cissy nodded, not seeming to be able to take in any of this, as if it was all a crazed dream. And Minnie carrying in a bowl of bread sopped in sweet milk was the moment when Cissy's face brightened up no end.

Days passed. Dr Williams came in every afternoon as Dora had asked him to.

'You're looking after her well,' he said. And after a few days, 'The danger is passed. She's healing nicely and she should get up and move about – gently, of course, to begin with.' He smiled. 'You have done the work of the Almighty – you have loved her back into life.'

Dora was still digesting this analysis when Dr Williams added, 'You were exceedingly fortunate in Dr Gordon. He is one of our most advanced surgeons – up to date with all the new ideas about germs and sterilizing instruments and so on. Had you had a more old-fashioned surgeon, things might have gone very differently.'

'I see,' Dora said, though in truth she didn't really know what he was talking about. 'Well, it's lucky I knew who to ask.'

Having written late into that Sunday night and posted her pages to London the next morning, Dora had joined Minnie in all the laundry work and they were hard at it for the early part of the week.

'Just like the old days,' Minnie said happily as Dora staggered in with buckets of water.

Cissy was doing well and even offered to sit and sew the identification marks into some of the clothes.

When Ada popped in on Tuesday to ask after her she

was amazed to see Cissy on a chair, busy with a needle in her hand.

'Well, you're looking better, miss,' she said.

Cissy looked up at her, rather fearfully, and nodded.

'I've come to tell you John wrote to me – he and Clara have set a date,' Ada went on. 'April the twenty-first – it's a Saturday afternoon.' Dora saw her sister's face soften and look almost excited. 'I thought we'd hire a carriage – go over together.'

Dora laughed. The prospect was delicious. 'That would be very nice.'

'Oh, and here, this is for you, I believe, "Richard Fletcher",' she said wryly, holding out an envelope. 'It was on the floor in the hall.'

Dora hurried to dry her hands and fetch a knife to slit open the envelope. As her eyes moved down the letter, such a surge of excitement went through her that she squeaked, one hand over her mouth. They were all looking at her.

'It's from Mr Dickens,' she gasped. 'Oh – oh! I can hardly believe it.' Every line of the letter filled her with joy. Firstly, Mr Dickens wrote that she must not dream of apologizing for their missed encounter – life was full of such exigencies of fate and there must, there would, be another opportunity! And secondly, her latest instalment had brought tears to his eyes.

'I do not think that I have ever once before witnessed this particular tragic situation recorded in literature,' he wrote, 'and in such an affecting way that I marvel at what you are able to conjure from the comfort of a desk . . .'

And everything after that was a cause for celebration. Even before she shared the news with the others, she thought, They won't understand that this is everything I have always wanted – that this was always my dream.

'What?' Minnie demanded. 'Come on – spit it out.'

'Well, he says he likes the pages I've just sent to him. And then, he says he wants me to send in another story when this one is finished – which it nearly is, I think . . .'

They were all waiting.

'*And* he says he wants to publish all of my story that's been in the magazine in one book. I'm going to publish a book – a whole book, with covers and everything!'

She was almost dancing round the room.

Ada and Minnie looked at each other.

'How much will he pay you?' Minnie said.

Dora shrugged, bewildered. This thought had not yet even crossed her mind.

'Well,' Ada added. 'That's very good, isn't it?'

And Dora knew they did not understand what this meant, this dream of hers, how it was everything she had longed for. But this did not take away the sheer, bubbling joy of it.

She rushed up to her startled sister and planted a kiss on her cheek.

'Yes, it is! It's very, very good.'

Fifty-Three

April 1866

'Oh,' Minnie said glumly, peering out of the window. 'It's raining.'

'I know, I can hear it.' Dora was pushing Rose's wriggling arms into a little white cardigan. Rose was not an enthusiast for getting dressed. 'Let's hope it clears up – I've hired a closed carriage for us, at least! – Hold still, you little monkey – you've got to look your best for your Uncle John's wedding!'

Cissy came over and helped her fasten a white ribbon into Rose's dark curls.

'She looks ever so pretty,' Cissy said.

'Thanks, Ciss.' Dora smiled at her.

Just as Minnie had taken Cissy under her wing as a young sister, Cissy was now doing the same with Rose. She never mentioned her own blood family and not once had anyone called to show any interest in whether she was alive or dead. Both Dora and Minnie felt very protective towards her.

With their care for her – especially Minnie's devoted nursing – Cissy had recovered marvellously. Dora's generous income from her writing meant they could all afford to eat well and Cissy had filled out a little and today was quite rosy-cheeked under her scattering of freckles.

Minnie and Cissy were to stay behind today. And by the time the carriage arrived in Bread Street and Dora, holding

Rose, climbed inside before they set off for Galton Passage, the rain was easing off. As the horses' hooves clopped along the street, Dora, Rose on her lap, sat looking out with a dazed sense of joy. She was going to collect her sisters, and they were going to John's wedding – her little brother. It was almost too much to take in.

And when the others all piled in, Ada, followed by Elsie, with Olive in her arms and then George holding Vicky's hand, it all seemed so right and inevitable, while so miraculous. These two women, these sisters who she knew in her bones, who were so familiar from her youngest years – but who now she was having to learn about all over again.

George squeezed in beside Dora so that Vicky and Rose could be close together, and Ada and Elsie sat opposite.

'How's little'un?' Ada asked as they lurched into movement.

Despite Ada's gruff ways, Dora could hear a tenderness in the question, which touched her. Ada could see Cissy was already family, in the way that all of them had made new patchwork family because their own had been lost to them.

'She's doing ever so well,' Dora said. 'Minnie's feeding her up like a turkey cock and Dr Williams said she's been lucky not to get an infection.'

'She must be stronger than she looks,' Elsie said, cuddling Olive close to her. She looked round at all of them, taking in her husband and two sisters, and a smile spread across her face.

'Well,' she said. 'This is something, isn't it?'

For a time they chattered about this and that. Elsie was taking on the role of the mother of the household, but as far as Dora could see, was thriving – although the pain in her eyes was obvious when she talked about Matty Drake.

'We miss her so much,' she said. 'Poor Lizzie – she keeps crying and we hardly know what to do for her.'

'You're doing your best, love,' George said. He reached across and stroked her hand and Dora felt an inner lurch of longing, seeing all the love in that touch.

'I know – I just feel so sad for her,' Elsie said. She looked at Dora and Ada. 'We know what it's like to lose our mother, don't we?'

After a time, even the children were lulled by the motion of the carriage and everyone fell silent, Rose and Vicky, each on a parental lap, their eyelids growing heavy. Dora's eyes met Elsie's and they smiled. *Peace at last*, their look said. And they had room for their own thoughts.

Dora, still marked by the pain of seeing George's loving touch, looked out of the window, wondering about Robert. He must be in India by now. It was a long voyage – how long? She was not sure. It hardly seemed real.

I love you . . . She sent the words from her heart, imagining the lands and seas they must cross to reach him. Could he feel her, when she thought of him?

She thought of Dr Gordon's light caress of Rose's cheek, Mrs Gordon's plea, 'Come and see us . . .' She could not face that, she knew. Just could not go and sit with this good woman knowing that she was the mother of her grandchild – a child she perhaps longed for – and not tell her the truth. Of course she could not tell her! And the shame of all that had happened . . . No, she could not go back there. But she regretted it. Mrs Gordon was someone she would have liked to see again, to tell her all she had achieved and to thank her.

Her thoughts moved happily on to her writing. A book!

They were going to publish a book – and pay her for it! And she would write more and more . . . In that moment she knew, with sudden clarity, what she was going to do. How life was going to change . . . She was a woman of means now. A smile curved her lips upwards. Yes, that was what she would do.

Ada had also had a stab in the heart at seeing George's love, such a demonstration of kind devotion. Love, she thought, she had at least had a taste of – before it was snatched away. In her cool moments, she could see that William was a confused man, full of grief and need. And in his need he had tried to reproduce the love he had had – and to do it with her instead of the woman he really wanted. In those moments she could forgive, but every time she let herself think about it, the ache of it spread through her. And the coolness heated to a sad bitterness. Just for a short time she had thought she might be a different sort of person. A woman in the full sense. But no – she was Ada Fletcher, the businesswoman, the tough, no-nonsense one with no time for love or emotions.

She stopped herself on this road to endless self-pity and looked at her sisters. Elsie with her love, her daughters. Dora, beautiful, mysterious Dora, staring out of the window as if her thoughts were miles away. One day she would surely explain who Rose's father was?

Whatever had happened to Dora, she was a strong one, Ada could see. Free to make her own decisions, earn her own money. And now, husbands or no, they all had each other. Was that so bad a life, after all? She had a growing business herself, was becoming successful . . .

Ada straightened her spine, a smile on her lips. And now she had her sisters, and they were going to their young brother's wedding. Today, this day, was good and they were blessed.

The wedding was in the chapel at Chance & Co. amid this giant industrial complex covering several acres. As they piled out of the carriage into weak sunlight, they could see John at the door, looking as if he was about to explode with pride and excitement.

'Look at him,' Dora said to Ada. 'This place has been the making of him.'

Ada nodded, smiling. 'He's done well.'

It was to be a small wedding – family only. And soon after they had gone inside the elegant brick chapel, Dora heard a sound behind them, a mass rustling and giggling, and turned to see the Smith girls arriving with their mother and father. She nudged her own sisters, feeling a moment of excited togetherness. *Sisters!* We're sharing this together!

They watched as eight females, Harriet Smith and Clara's seven sisters, all shuffled into seats the other side of the aisle, the younger ones peering curiously across at John's other family on the opposite side.

A moment later John hurried to the front and the organ struck up. A shadow darkened the doorway and they turned to see Clara on her father's arm.

'She's so pretty,' Elsie murmured appreciatively, gazing at her soon to be sister-in-law.

Dora was moved. Elsie had been so lovely-looking herself before her face was viciously scarred for ever. But she could hear no envy in her sister's voice, just admiration.

Clara did look pretty. The loveliest thing about her was her smile – open and heartfelt. Dora immediately knew that there were no sides to Clara – that they could trust her with their brother. She wore a simple white dress, her hair taken back under a veil with a band of anemones. She carried a little bouquet of white blossoms.

The burly, forbidding-looking man with an impressive white beard who was supporting her on his arm was just as eye-catching. He turned his leathery face towards them as he processed past with his daughter and gave a serious nod which they returned.

Enoch Smith looked every bit the patriarch, Dora thought. But everything John had ever said about him expressed respect and gratitude for a man who was both skilled and kindly.

As they moved to the front, Dora caught a glimpse of John's face – the love and awe as Clara moved to meet him and her eyes filled with tears.

Afterwards, they ate sandwiches and drank ale in a nearby pub.

The landlord and lady did them proud and they took up two long tables. John was fizzy with excitement and there was much laughter and giggling from the younger Smith girls. Ada saw Elsie laughing along with them. After a time she realized one of them had plucked up the courage to ask what had happened to her face. There was a sudden quiet, all of them riveted, and gasps of horror. Ada watched, moved by the dignity Elsie showed in telling the story.

Then Ada watched John and his sweet Clara, both obviously brimming with happiness.

'I fell in love with this girl the first time I saw her!' John announced when the drink was in, and everyone laughed and cheered.

Ada was grateful to find herself sitting beside Harriet Smith. As soon as she had first met Harriet, Ada had felt a trust in her, that she was a solid, honest person. Harriet turned warmly to look at Ada.

'I'm glad he came back to his own family,' she said. 'Took him a while. I suppose he's not the best at saying what he means.'

Ada smiled. The two of them had a job understanding everything each other were saying, but the main thing was wanting to understand and the rest would follow.

'He was very young,' Ada said. 'I don't know how much he could remember about us.'

Harriet's face was full of sympathy. 'Such a sad thing. Terrible for any family. You've all come through well, I'll say that for you.'

'I wanted to say to you . . .' Ada said hurriedly, as things were beginning to get a little rowdy. 'Well, to thank you, I mean. You and your husband, for looking after our brother. You've given him so much . . .'

'He's been my son.' Harriet looked wryly round the table. 'What with all these girls, I could do with one.'

Ada laughed. 'Well, you've both been very kind. And you've given him a mother after we all lost ours.'

Harriet gently touched Ada's hand. 'He's a good lad. You should be proud of him. You're all back together now?'

'We are,' Ada said. 'But – we had another sister. The youngest, Mabs. Mabel she was christened. We don't know where she is.'

Harriet shook her head. 'Life can be very cruel.'

They were interrupted by Enoch Smith pushing his chair back and standing, like a great ocean god at the end of the table.

'Right. A toast. My daughter, Clara – and John, our son-in-law.'

'On the right side of the law now, are yer, John?' one of the twins called out – they both looked the same to Ada. Everyone laughed and raised their glasses.

'John and Clara!' they all chorused.

Ada saw her two sisters exchange looks, then both of them sought her out as well. For a moment the three of them, all cheering on their little brother and his sweet bride, held between them a moment of pride, of love – and of a sense of miracle.

Fletchers. Together again.

Fifty-Four

February 1867

Dora paid for the stamps and handed over the precious package, then walked out along the street. That morning she had wrapped the book in brown paper, so carefully, and tied and knotted the string, all the time feeling as if she was preparing more than a parcel – it was an offering.

Her book had been released as a whole work to the public two weeks previously. When the first parcel, containing four books, had arrived at the house, she had opened the wrappings with the same reverence. Copies of her book. A whole book.

The binding was dark red with gold lettering and there, on cover and spine, the name she had chosen to represent her from now on: 'Dora Fletcher'. This after Dickens had written:

> *If you are going to change to your real name, I would advise you do it now. After all, there is less need these days for a woman to conceal herself behind the mask of a man.*

They had also decided to change the title. The book was now called *The Family Lunn*. It was a good, solid title, Dora thought as she held the precious thing in her hands, opening the cover, turning the creamy pages to see her words, first laid down in secret, now open to anyone who chose to read them.

She had still not met Mr Dickens, life being the busy thing it was. But she would – one day, she was determined. It was another thing to look forward to. She would travel to London to meet this great man, to whom she owed so much. And now she would meet him under her own name. Dora Fletcher. The name of someone who could call herself a writer.

Minnie and Cissy had been awed and astonished. Ada and Elsie were full of pride. Dora gave each of them a copy. But there was something else she needed to say to Minnie and Cissy.

One Saturday, when the great rush and toil of the week's wash had stilled, she had gone out to buy three Chelsea buns, brewed tea for them all and said, 'I want to talk to you both.'

She saw them look at each other. This was serious.

Once they were all settled she sat opposite them.

'I want to set you both up,' she said, jumping straight to the point. 'I'm making a good living, as you know, and what I want is to write – and write. But you two are like sisters and I want to make sure you have a good living.'

She saw Minnie's face tighten. 'Are you going away, Dor?'

'No! Oh no, I'm not. But I want you both to have the business. What I think we should do is this. We find premises where we can work better – not live in the midst of it all the time. Ground floor, with a pump nearby and more space. There's plenty of work and you can take more people on if you both want. Make a real good business out of it. I'll set you up and you can run it, the pair of you. So you never need to worry . . .' (Or marry, if you don't want to, she thought, but did not say.)

'Oh, Dora,' Cissy exclaimed. 'Would you really do that? Oh, Min, what d'you think? We could do that, couldn't we?'

'And you'd live near?' Minnie said doubtfully.

'I'd live near – course I would,' Dora said. 'I'd help out to start if you need it. But what with Rose and all the writing I need to do . . .'

They were both nodding, their excitement mounting.

'We could get more business – get more help,' Minnie was saying, her canny mind immediately going into action. 'We could be quite something! Oh, shall we do it, Ciss?'

Cissy got up and jumped about in excitement. 'Yes, let's – let's do it!' She suddenly flung her arms round Dora's neck and kissed her cheek over and over. 'Oh, thank you – thank you, Dora!'

'Is it all right if we eat the buns now?' Minnie said.

Walking back from sending off the book, Dora's feelings, her longing, were close to the surface. Despite all her success, all the good things that had happened, the only cloud hanging over her life was that she was separated, for who knew how long, from Robert.

He had written from India – three times now. He was alive. He wrote loving words and she wrote back. Her first letter was very long, explaining all that had happened to her since they parted. She wrote words of love, of devotion to him, also reassuring him that she was well able to support herself by her writing. His letters were loving too and full of admiration, though the distance from him in time and place when they actually arrived, made him seem so very remote. But they were all she had to cling to.

Writing the address on the parcel, and the letter in which she explained to Mrs Gordon that she was now a published writer and this was a copy of her book, tore open the wound even further. In the letter, she thanked her former employer for all her kindness and teaching during those years in Frederick Street.

Mrs Gordon. Rose's grandmother. That was a part of the story that was not in the book.

She found she could not go straight home. Her body was restless to walk and so she headed towards the middle of town. So many places held memories of him – the Bull Ring, the streets they had wandered when barely more than children.

She paused for a moment in the chill winter air to look up at the statue of Nelson, keeping watch over the Bull Ring, its restless crowds moving about their everyday business, each one carrying in their heart dreams of their own.

The two of them had sat there together, she and Robert, talking, laughing, in their forbidden love. Nelson stood stonily above her, his eyes seeming to gaze out to the surge and spray of the seas, the vast oceans dividing her from him.

Look after him, she pleaded silently to the statue. *Look after my love and keep him safe until we meet again.*

Acknowledgements

Research for this story came from a good many different sources, but I have to thank especially:

The Morning Chronicle's Labour and the Poor: Birmingham, Volume IX by Charles Mackay

A Popular Encyclopaedia of Victorian Women Writers by Russell James

New Media and the Rise of the Popular Woman Writer, 1832–1860 by Alexis Easley

The Birmingham Pearlies from George Hook & Co

Recollections of Victorian Birmingham by Stephen Roberts

English Laundresses: A Social History, 1850–1930 by Patricia E. Malcolmson

Do keep in touch – it's always lovely to hear from you.

My website is at: anniemurray.co.uk

My Facebook page is at: facebook.com/Annie.Murray.Author.

On Instagram you can find me at: instagram.com/anniemurraywriter/

Hope to see you there!

Publishing spring 2027 . . .

Nobody's Daughter

Available to order now!